VEIL OF SHADOWS

SHILOH WALKER

BERKLEY SENSATION, NEW YORK

THE BERKLEY PUBLISHING GROUP
Published by the Penguin Group
Penguin Group (USA) Inc.
375 Hudson Street, New York, New York 10014, USA
Penguin Group (Canada), 90 Eglinton Avenue East, Suite 700, Toronto, Ontario M4P 2Y3, Canada
(a division of Pearson Penguin Canada Inc.)
Penguin Books Ltd., 80 Strand, London WC2R 0RL, England
Penguin Group Ireland, 25 St. Stephen's Green, Dublin 2, Ireland (a division of Penguin Books Ltd.)
Penguin Group (Australia), 250 Camberwell Road, Camberwell, Victoria 3124, Australia
(a division of Pearson Australia Group Pty. Ltd.)
Penguin Books India Pvt. Ltd., 11 Community Centre, Panchsheel Park, New Delhi—110 017, India
Penguin Group (NZ), 67 Apollo Drive, Rosedale, North Shore 0632, New Zealand
(a division of Pearson New Zealand Ltd.)
Penguin Books (South Africa) (Pty.) Ltd., 24 Sturdee Avenue, Rosebank, Johannesburg 2196,
South Africa

Penguin Books Ltd., Registered Offices: 80 Strand, London WC2R 0RL, England

This is a work of fiction. Names, characters, places, and incidents either are the product of the author's
imagination or are used fictitiously, and any resemblance to actual persons, living or dead, business
establishments, events, or locales is entirely coincidental. The publisher does not have any control
over and does not assume any responsibility for author or third-party websites or their content.

VEIL OF SHADOWS

A Berkley Sensation Book / published by arrangement with the author

PRINTING HISTORY
Berkley Sensation mass-market edition / September 2010

ISBN: 978-0-425-23635-2

BERKLEY® SENSATION
Berkley Sensation Books are published by The Berkley Publishing Group,
a division of Penguin Group (USA) Inc.,
375 Hudson Street, New York, New York 10014.
BERKLEY® SENSATION and the "B" design are trademarks of Penguin Group (USA) Inc.

PRINTED IN THE UNITED STATES OF AMERICA

10   9   8   7   6   5   4   3   2   1

continued . . .

"A page-turner from the very start. Intense and fast-paced, the action is gritty, the emotion heart-wrenching and the characters lively. Sexy and romantic, this tale has plenty of action—of the erotic kind—and is loaded with suspense. No wonder Ms. Walker is loved by fans everywhere. This is a winner."

—*Fresh Fiction*

CHAINS

"This book is a double page-turner. The story is thrilling, and the sex just makes it better—two great reasons not to put it down until the end!"

—*Romantic Times*

"Breathtakingly wonderful . . . Smoothly erotic . . . Utterly amazing . . . Will definitely keep your pulse racing!"

—*Errant Dreams Reviews*

"Exciting erotic romantic suspense."

—*Midwest Book Review*

FRAGILE

"[A] flawlessly sexy suspense novel . . . Exhilarating."

—*Romantic Times*

"An excellently crafted mystery and romance!"

—*Errant Dreams Reviews*

"Suspense, romance and an ending that I can't say anything about—because that would be a spoiler . . . I recommend reading this one."

—*The Best Reviews*

"Intense, sexy . . . Ms. Walker has created another unforgettable . . . fast-paced, edgy tale."

—*Fallen Angel Reviews*

HUNTER'S SALVATION

"One of the best tales in a series that always achieves high marks . . . An excellent thriller."

—*Midwest Book Review*

Hunters: Heart and Soul

"Some of the best erotic romantic fantasies on the market. Walker's world is vibrantly alive with this pair."
—*The Best Reviews*

Hunting the Hunter

"Action, sex, savvy writing, and characters with larger-than-life personalities that you will not soon forget are where Ms. Walker's talents lie, and she delivered all that and more . . . This is a flawless five-rose paranormal novel and one that every lover of things that go bump in the night will be howling about after they read it . . . Do not walk! Run to get your copy today!"   —*A Romance Review*

"An exhilarating romantic fantasy filled with suspense and . . . star-crossed love . . . Action packed."
—*Midwest Book Review*

"Fast paced and very readable . . . Titillating."
—*The Romance Reader*

"Action packed, with intriguing characters and a very erotic punch, *Hunting the Hunter* had me from page one. Thoroughly enjoyable with a great hero and a story line you can sink your teeth into, this book is a winner. A very good read!"   —*Fresh Fiction*

"Another promising voice is joining the paranormal genre by bringing her own take on the ever-evolving vampire myth. Walker has set up the bones of an interesting world and populated it with some intriguing characters. Hopefully, there will be a sequel that ties together more threads and divulges more details."   —*Romantic Times*

For Ann W. and Angie W.,
who believed in this new world from the start.

And for my family,
always for my family.
I love you.

ONE

The first time she saw the man, Laisyn Caar knew he was going to be trouble.

Syn really, really didn't have the time nor the inclination to deal with it. Obviously, fate didn't give a damn.

Like a lot of the refugees they'd taken in over the years, he wore threadbare clothes and he carried little in the way of material goods. Many refugees arrived on the base camp on solar-powered gliders or riding a baern. The big pack beasts could carry two people easy, and because they were somewhat protective of their owners, they proved to be very handy guard animals.

This man was on foot. He had a pack strapped to his back and enough weaponry to have her eyebrows going up.

All those weapons were the first thing that set him apart.

Even though he was surrounded by other refugees, he looked to be traveling alone—that was the second thing that set him apart.

It wasn't wise to go anywhere alone. Not here. Not even now that the Gate was out of commission. They no longer had to worry about raids from Anqar but it was far from safe in their devastated pocket of the world. Demons ran amok in the heavy forests covering the valleys at the base of the Roinan Mountains. There were still Warlords as well, those who had been in Ishtan when the Gate collapsed. Syn suspected those Warlords weren't too damn happy about being trapped in a primitive, inferior world, good only for the slaves it provided for them.

Going anywhere alone was a bad, bad idea.

But there he was—a lone, rather wild-looking wolf amid a bunch of scared and nervous sheep.

His hair was black, as black as her own, but it didn't have the same blue-black hue to it. It was dense and dark, no hints of red or brown. He wore it pulled back in a stubby tail that left his rough features unframed. He had high cheekbones, a broad forehead, and his mouth looked as if he never smiled. Broad shoulders stretched the worn cloth of his tunic. If it had ever had sleeves, he'd long since ripped or cut them off. His arms were long, tanned and roped with muscles. He had thick wrists, and she had suspected part of the reason for those rather impressive arms was the blade she saw sticking over his shoulder.

It wasn't a sword. She didn't need to see it to know that— long swords weren't exactly the weapon of choice. Pulsars were—handheld weapons that delivered a pulsating blast that could either disable or kill. But all of her soldiers carried blades and they could use them if they had to.

Somehow, Syn suspected this man would prefer the blade over the pulsar he had strapped to his thigh.

The most arresting feature about this man wasn't his weapons, or his face, or the way he seemed to take in everything with one quick, trained glance. It wasn't even the patch he wore over his left eye, although her gaze did linger there a minute. She imagined his lack of vision on that side didn't slow him down one bit.

No, the most arresting thing about him was the way he carried himself.

He kept to the back of the group, and if she didn't

know better, she might have mistaken him for one of her own. Except for the threadbare clothes and noted lack of cavinir, the flexible body armor most of the rebels wore, he blended in perfectly with her troops. Ready and aware, fully prepared for danger even this close to the camp.

It made her wonder how rough the journey from Sacril had been. It also reminded her that she had a job to do, and she forced herself to look away. It may be great fun to briefly ogle one of the more interesting men to enter through their gates. But doing so didn't get the job done.

Right now, she needed to get ready to speak with the commander, she needed to speak with the men who'd accompanied the refugees and then she had to speak with the refugees themselves. And that was going to be such fun.

Sighing, she flicked a hand through her short, dark hair. "At least this is the last time."

She hoped.

The Roinan territory was just too dangerous now. The refugee camps had been decimated over the past few weeks. Most of the refugees entering through the main gate didn't realize it, but in a couple of days, they were going to be on an eastbound convoy. Kalen was evacuating the territory. Civilians wouldn't be forced to leave, but they couldn't remain in the camp, and the only people getting an escort were those on the convoy.

If they didn't join the convoy, they were on their own.

Once these refugees were out of here, the rebel army would focus on the demon infestation and *only* on the demon infestation. Splitting their time and energy between helping the refugees and culling the demons had proven too dangerous. They were losing lives, they were losing ground and they were losing both too fast.

It had to stop. Considering their limited resources, they had to focus on the threat presented by the demons. It was the only logical choice.

But somehow, Syn suspected these men and women weren't going to be pleased with logic.

***

It was organized chaos.

There was no other way to describe it. Xan stood on the sidelines, watching as the soldiers herded every last refugee into a long, low-ceilinged building.

Two men stood at the door, questioning each person that entered.

"Any combat experience? No? Sit on the right. Yes? Sit on the left. That's all you need to do for now."

Any and all questions were ignored. But that didn't keep the refugees from asking. The line moved interminably slowly. Xan kept a light hand on one of the straps that held his pack in place, the other on the shorter blade at his waist. He had dealt with enough thieves over the past few months to know that none of them was above robbing people blind right under the noses of the only law this part of the world had.

From all reports, this forsaken territory had been cut adrift, left to falter or thrive on its own as the rest of the world recovered.

Well, perhaps the Roinan territory was not completely on its own. The outside still took in refugees. Xan had heard they even had "programs" designed to help the refugees integrate into life outside a war zone. Motivated by guilt, perhaps. It might be the only way they could allay the guilt they carried for allowing these people to fight a war that should have been fought by all.

At *one* time, that war had been fought by all.

The Gates—bridges that connected an alien world to this one—were controlled by Anqar and had allowed slavers to raid this world. And the magic needed to control them was one wielded by Anqarians—by their Warlords and Sirvani.

For centuries untold, Anqar had preyed on this world, kidnapping women and using it as their breeding ground, The Anqarian Warlords needed women with strong, talented blood—preferably witches—to keep their race strong, and fewer and fewer women were being born to their people. When the time came for them to seek a bride, they looked across the Gates to this world . . . and took one by force.

But then, over time, for reasons none truly understood, the Gates started to falter. And as the Gates fell, the raids across the world became more infrequent, until finally, only one strong Gate remained.

The Roinan Gate.

When that happened, the world outside of the Roinan territory seemed content to pretend that everything was just as fine as could be.

For some time, only Kalen Brenner and his army of rebels stood between the one remaining Gate and the rest of Ishtan. The rest of Ishtan seemed quite content to let it remain so.

But they took in the refugees who couldn't fight.

Sometimes, they even sent back supplies.

When they remembered.

Xan finally reached the door and met the gaze of the soldier closest to him. The man looked Xan over from head to toe and then a smile of camaraderie lit his face. "I don't think I need to ask if you have combat experience, do I?"

Xan just shrugged.

"You do have combat experience, right?"

He gave a curt nod and was waved inside. He didn't sit. He took up a position with his back against the wall. He wasn't the only one. A handful of others were doing the same, guarding their backs, even now, when they were in the one safehold this territory had. One by one, each of them met his gaze. A quick glance, a nod, and then they all resumed their survey of the crowd.

Xan settled in beside them and started his own survey. It was a sorry lot of people, that was for certain.

As more and more people packed in, he gripped his blade tighter.

What in the hell had he gotten himself into?

***

It was standing-room only. Close to three hundred, she figured. Fortunately, a fifth of them were soldiers who'd made the decision to return east. They'd served at Sacril, one of the rebel outposts, and when Kalen made the decision to call them back, most of them had decided they'd just as soon join the convoy. It would be added protection.

Syn would be glad when this was over. She would be glad when she could give her troops a clear, direct focus—the demons. She would be glad when she no longer had to balance and juggle numbers to figure out how to provide the safety the refugees needed without compromising the safety of the camp and without cutting back on the efforts to secure more of their land.

In short, she would be glad when this day was over.

It was hard enough maintaining order in the postwar chaos, but dealing with a bunch of lost and scared civilians had her wishing for a dark, quiet room, a hot bath and a big, bottomless glass of frostwine.

Later, she could get the dark, quiet room and probably even the hot bath. She needed that hot bath, too. If nothing else, it might ease the raw ache of cold settled inside her. She was always cold these days, always chilled. Nothing helped for long.

The frostwine could do a decent job of warding the cold off for a while, especially if she could have it with the bath. But that particular luxury was one she didn't have. One she probably wouldn't have again for years to come. Frostwine, like so many other luxuries, was something that was lost to them. Just like the world she'd almost forgotten—a world that wasn't dominated solely by war.

For now, she told herself. *For now . . . Someday, you'll be able to start rebuilding that world. After you make it safe again.*

She followed along behind Bron and Kenner, letting them clear the way while she took in the last group of refugees. The last . . . It was hard to even consider that idea.

For as long as she'd been here, there had been refugees arriving at the camp. Most had come seeking to serve in the army, but over the past year or so, that number had slowed to a trickle. Too often now, those arriving at the camp had requests for "security" while the refugees tried to rebuild. Or food. Shelter for a few nights. Aid in rebuilding their homes.

The rebel army's resources were stretched thin as it was, and these people wanted Kalen to give them yet more.

Those with half a brain had abandoned this area years earlier. It seemed as though the only ones who remained were those in the base camp—the rebel army. Except that was far from the truth. Every week brought in more refugees, many of them so gaunt and thin, it hurt to even look upon them.

She didn't need to ask their stories.

She already knew.

They fled to the mountains, fled to the north, to the south. They couldn't go east—this was their home. Going east, to them, seemed too permanent, some kind of unspoken acknowledgment they had given up. They had to stay. They wanted to rebuild. They just needed some help . . .

That was the story.

In actuality, they needed their heads examined.

It would be years before these mountains were completely safe again. Maybe longer.

And the typical soul just wasn't equipped to fight the demons that crept out in the night. So they ended up at the different outposts, or right here at the base camp, begging and pleading for help that the army couldn't keep giving.

Something had to change.

She knew Kalen had made a wise decision, but that knowledge didn't make her job any easier.

With her men at her back, Syn forged her way to the front of the hall. Bron and Kenner took their respective places on either side of the dais as she strode up the steps, the soles of her boots making deliberate thuds on the wooden floor.

With every step, she felt more and more eyes cut her way. Slowly, the dull roar of voices faded down to a muted murmur as one by one, row by row, the refugees took note of her.

She was here to make an impact. She stood a good head shorter than most of the people in the room and although she was strong, she knew she didn't look it.

But Syn knew that attitude made all the difference.

And attitude, she had in spades.

She stopped in the middle of the dais and linked her hands behind her back. It was loud, people whispering to one another, looking all around, staring at Bron and Kenner with wide eyes, and then up at her with confusion.

"My name is Laisyn Caar. Around the camp, I'm known as Captain. My superiors call me Syn." She lifted her voice, knowing it would carry through the door and even out into the common area in front of the west hall. Most of the talkers fell silent.

"Let me make a few things clear right up front." Now just a few were whispering.

One of them was a woman sitting next to the man who'd caught her eye. She was leaning over him, all but climbing into his arms trying to get his attention. Syn dropped off the dais, talking as she went.

"This is a military base. It may not be recognized as such to those out in the rest of the world. But that is how we see it. That is how we run it." She took her time, making her way up the aisle, occasionally looking at some of those sitting down and watching. As she passed, those still whispering fell silent.

All save one.

She drew her culn from her belt and twisted it. Immediately, the metal baton expanded to three times its size. It was now nearly as long as she was tall, and solid.

She used it to tap the shoulder of the only person still talking.

"And that means, when I am talking, every last one of you will shut up."

The brunette turned around and stared at Syn with irritated eyes. "Excuse me—"

Syn lifted a brow and repeated herself. "When I am talking, every last one of you will shut up."

The woman went red. Then white. "Who in the hell—"

Somebody next to her jabbed an elbow into the woman's side. Syn pretended not to see it. "What's your name?"

"Vena Saurell." She glared at Syn, a disdainful look on her face. "And who are you? The commander's personal assistant?"

Syn smiled. "No. I'm one of his captains. I'm third in command, and I have the authority to have you hauled out of this camp, this very second, kicking and screaming, should I so choose."

"Like hell."

Syn glanced toward the door. The two soldiers standing at ready stepped inside and flanked Vena. "I'm going to start from the beginning. My name is Laisyn Caar. Around the camp, I'm known as Captain. My superiors call me Syn. Let me make a few things clear right up front. This is a military base. It may not be recognized as such to those out in the rest of the world. But that is how we see it. That is how we run it. And that means, when I am talking, every last one of you will shut up."

Still smiling her nice, pleasant smile, she cocked her head and said, "Now, Vena Saurell. Are you going to shut your mouth or should I have my men escort you out of the camp?"

"You can't make me go out there alone. It's not safe."

"No. It's not safe. And yes, I can." She wouldn't. She'd just have the woman tucked away inside a dormer, with the door locked, until she could be placed on tomorrow's convoy. She'd done it before and she had no problem doing it now. "Now, am I clear?"

Vena glanced at the two soldiers flanking her. They didn't look at her. They stared straight ahead, just like a good soldier should. Then she looked at Syn and nodded, slowly. Something ugly flashed in her eyes but she fell silent.

"Good." Syn twisted her culn and it folded back in on itself. Tucking it back into the loop on her belt, she returned to the dais.

There always had to be one person. Always one person who had to challenge her. After all these years, Syn was almost used to it. But it still annoyed the hell out of her. She focused on those sitting on the right side of the room. "Are there any among you that have any sort of real combat experience?"

A few lifted their hands. She nodded and then focused on the other side of the room. "Every one of you told the men at the door you have combat training—is that correct?" Some nods, a few muffled affirmatives. Back in the back, her newest, dearest friend Vena just glared at Syn. Smiling at her, Syn asked, "Vena, I take it that means you have real combat experience?"

"I—" She opened her mouth to say something, then snapped it shut. Either somebody had gouged her with an elbow again, or she was growing something more than just a brain stem. Instead of saying anything else, she just nodded.

Damn. Syn would much rather just get that woman off of her base.

Looking back at the nonfighters, she asked, "Are any of you healers, witches, psychics or medics?" There wasn't a witch among them—Syn had already looked. It didn't surprise her, but it was disappointing. They needed more witches. Unfortunately, though, witches, as a whole, had the common sense to get out of a bad place when it was clear the bad was only getting worse.

There were two medics and one psychic. She made mental note of their faces and then selected out the others who'd claimed some combat experience. She gestured all of them to the front and then looked at the remaining civilians.

"This is a military camp," she said, her voice soft, but firm. "We're still fighting a war here, even though the Gate is gone."

Something about the gravity of her voice had them stirring uncomfortably in their seats. Syn could see it.

Her gut twisted as she went on. "As of today, a new policy is going into effect. The army is making the demon threat its new focus—until that threat is contained, it will be our only focus."

People started to whisper among themselves, and some of them were watching her with outright hostility.

"We've called our men in from the outposts. Sacril and the other outposts are being abandoned for the time being. We will no longer maintain them."

"But—"

Syn lifted a hand. "Please, let me continue. When I'm done, if there are questions, I will answer them. In the past month, attacks on the outposts have increased. Attacks on the eastbound convoys have increased. Attacks on our hunting groups, our scouts, have increased. The demons are becoming more aggressive, more violent. The army's focus must be containing that threat."

"But we're safe here." This came from a middle-aged woman, her voice soft, her eyes censuring.

"We don't have the resources here to feed, protect and see to an additional three hundred souls," Syn said quietly. "And if we allow nonfighters now, then in a few weeks, we have more coming seeking refuge. As of today, the only civilians allowed in the camp are those who can provide us with certain useful skills—namely, witches, healers, medics and psychics. Since none of those apply to you, you're being sent east tomorrow on the outbound convoy."

Voices rose.

She lifted a hand and cut them off. "This isn't up for discussion. I'm sorry. But we're not here to play bodyguard; we're not here to provide security for you while you rebuild your homes. For the next few months, probably the next few years, the mountains will be too dangerous for civilians, and we don't have the manpower to offer you any kind of protection, not if we want to concentrate on eliminating the current threat."

"What threat?" one of the men demanded. He stood up, glaring at Syn. "The Gate is gone—we don't have to worry about raids anymore. We just need some help . . ."

Syn shook her head. "You need more than *some* help. Every last one of you. Otherwise, you wouldn't have abandoned your homes and gone to Sacril. You come to us seeking shelter, or food, or hoping we can provide you with some sort of bodyguard detail while you rebuild your homes. One of the last confrontations with Anqar decimated nearly half of our forces. We have roughly fifteen hundred able-bodied soldiers and we're already stretched thin—we can't possibly provide the security needed to every last soul that asks. It can't be done."

"But this is our home," he gritted out.

"I know that. And I am sorry. But this isn't up for discussion."

"I want to talk to the commander." He glared at her.

Syn angled her head to the back. Kalen Brenner had quietly slipped in just a few minutes ago. His timing, as always, was impeccable. "Feel free. There he is."

The man turned around. Kalen strode forward and stopped in front of him. "This is your home," he said, his voice flat. His silver-gray eyes were not unkind, but there was nothing soft in that gaze, nothing yielding. "I'm aware of that. It's mine as well. I can fight to protect it. I can fight to protect your land. I can fight to clear it of the demon infestation— then we can truly call it *home* again. And it will be *safe*. But I can't do that if my men and I are playing bodyguard for all the civilians who want their homes rebuilt."

"But . . ."

Kalen shook his head. "There are no buts. If you want your home rebuilt that badly, then do it. I can't force you onto the convoy tomorrow—I won't force anybody. But I can force you out of my camp. If you want safety, go east. Find a life there. This isn't the time to rebuild here."

He scanned the faces of the civilians. Syn did the same, seeing the disappointment, the grief, the denial in their eyes. They'd come here with hopes, dreams of rebuilding their lives, and in under five minutes, Syn had been forced to smash every one of those hopes and dreams.

Sometimes she hated her job. The cold knot inside her chest grew, expanded until it seemed to encompass everything—all of her. She suppressed the need to shiver, kept her teeth from chattering. But still, she was so cold.

The job. Focus on the job.

Kalen joined her on the dais, off to the side. Syn didn't waste any more time. She gestured to the civilian medics and the lone psychic. "You three remain here. The rest of you, you're dismissed. Outside, there are some of my men who'll get your information and explain about the convoy."

They departed, an air of defeat clinging to them. Syn was sorry for it. But they'd be alive. Alive . . . and maybe in a few years, they could return to the mountains. She had to take comfort in that. If they allowed them to stay here, they'd likely be dead within a year. Hell, a month.

Her men and women couldn't protect everybody—there just weren't enough of them.

After the door closed behind the last one, she focused on the remaining civilians. "Medics and psychics are always needed here. You have the choice to stay, or you can join the convoy tomorrow. It is your call, completely. But if you stay, be prepared to work. Be prepared to work hard. And be prepared to die."

Horror flashed through the eyes of the youngest medic. Syn focused her gaze on the young woman's face and said, "We're still fighting a war. We can't go a week without a demon attack and they are getting more desperate and more aggressive with every passing day. Those are the ugly facts of life here. If you can't handle them, then you need to leave. Any of you three want to leave? Do it now."

Not one of them moved.

"You're going to be trained to fight. You'll be expected to take part in daily training. You'll be placed on job rotation. You'll have one rest day a week. Other than that . . . you work. You eat. You train. You are ready to fight, should the need arise. This is our life—if you don't want that fight, then leave."

Still, none of them moved.

Damn. She wasn't as good at scaring people off as she used to be.

With a curt nod, she gestured to one of her men waiting by the door at the back. "This is Lothen, one of my men. He'll get you a permanent dormer and get you added to the job rotation. If none of you have any questions, you may go now."

Now it was just the fighters she had to deal with.

* * *

"Man, she's a serious bitch."

Xan didn't bother looking at her. Vena Saurell wasn't letting that slow her down. She seemed determined to glue herself to his side, staying with him even as he waded through the crush of people gathered in the common area outside the west hall.

"Don't you think? I mean, hell, I came here to fight and all, but she doesn't have any right to tell these people they aren't worthy of protection."

Ignoring her wasn't going to make her disappear, he decided. So he stopped in his tracks and crossed his arms over his chest.

"I don't recall hearing her saying that. What I heard was a woman willing to fight to secure these lands—she can't do that if she's too busy taking care of refugees."

The woman's lip curled. "Seems to me that the purpose of this whole damn army is to protect the refugees."

"The best way to do that is to eliminate those who are preying on them," Xan replied with a shrug. "Once the demons are gone, the refugees will no longer need the protection of the army. It is not an easy choice to make, but it seems a wise one."

"Maybe." Vena made a face. "I'm not too impressed. But she doesn't need to be such a bitch, does she?"

"If it keeps people alive, she can be the queen bitch," somebody said from behind Vena.

She went red and then white. Xan barely managed to restrain his grin as she turned to face the commander of the Roinan rebel army.

Kalen Brenner was a name known pretty much throughout the world. One would have to have lived under a rock to not know this man. Vena obviously hadn't lived under a rock.

Syn stood at his side, her slender arms crossed over her chest. With a faint smile on her lips, she glanced up at the commander and said, "Captain Bitch, Commander. We don't have kings and queens here." Then she dismissed Vena and focused on Xan.

Xan had spent much of his life learning to school his emotions, his reactions, everything. In that moment, he was very glad.

He would hate for his reactions to show in just that moment.

He looked at Captain Laisyn Caar and thought only one thing:

Want.

It was a powerful, all-consuming urge that damn near obliterated every other thought in his mind.

Feeling more than a little dazed, he stared at her, committing her features to memory. He'd felt a stir of interest when she'd addressed the whole of the group earlier, but now, standing this close to her, *interest* didn't begin to touch it.

She had cat eyes. Green-gold, with a hint of amusement and disdain in them that was ridiculously arousing.

She was slender, almost delicate, with narrow arms, narrow hips and only the slightest of curves. Her mouth was bow-shaped and full—very soft, very kissable.

Her eyes weren't the only catlike feature, either. The smile on that very kissable mouth, her softly pointed chin, even the way she held herself.

She studied him, her gaze lingering on the hilt of the

long knife she could see over his shoulder. Xan held silent as she finished her survey and then looked at him. "Interesting blade you have there—it's a bit larger than the standard-issue ones we have on hand. Pulsars and blasters are more widely used here than knives."

"I can use either," he said, absently touching a hand to the pulsar strapped to his left thigh.

She lifted a brow and nodded toward his knife. "And how good are you at the blade?"

He just smiled. The knife fit in his hand like it had been made for him. And it had—he'd made it himself. He'd been crafting his own blades for years.

Syn's smile widened and then she looked away from both Vena and Xan, dismissing them. "Commander, we're scheduled to meet with Elina and Lee in the next few minutes."

The commander nodded. Neither of them spared Vena or Xan a second look.

Xan only lingered long enough to admire the view as she walked away. Then he let the crowd swallow him, leaving Vena standing there, still blushing furiously.

* * *

"It's not going to happen," Kalen said shortly.

He didn't even bother glancing at the report disc Elina had put together for him.

Lee, Elina and Syn stood in front of his desk. Elina didn't look surprised, but Syn could tell the woman was pissed.

Lee glared at her husband. "You didn't even read the damn report."

"I don't need to," he said flatly. "I'm considering the safety of all in making this decision, and the answer is no. No amount of reports will change that."

"Well, of course not," Lee replied. "Not if you don't bother to read them."

Kalen flicked a glance up at her. The silver of his eyes flashed, but Syn couldn't tell what he was thinking. He was too good at hiding his emotions. "Is there any solid, concrete information in there about whether or not the Warlords will feel Lee's magic? Or whether or not you know for a fact the energy is safe and isn't going to suck a weaker witch inside, drain her dry?"

"No." Elina spoke for them all.

"Then there is nothing in those reports that will change my mind." He shoved the disc off to the side and focused once more on the reports the weapons master had provided. "Now, since that is settled, we need to start preparing for our next supply run. Unless somebody from back east finally decides to respond to my last dozen requests, we'll have to make a run within the month."

He focused on Syn's face.

From the corner of her eye, Syn could see Lee and Elina's expressions. Elina's face was impassive.

But Lee looked mad enough to spit nails.

Syn suspected she was going to make Kalen's life hell for the next few nights.

Good.

Why couldn't they convince him?

Why wouldn't he give them a chance?

That cold, empty ache inside her spread, took up a little more ground.

He had to give in. Had to listen . . .

Shifting her gaze to Elina, she just barely managed to keep her thoughts shielded. *He's killing us and he doesn't even seem to understand it.*

Elina's face was impassive. But she knew.

Kalen didn't understand. He didn't have the magic inside him. He wasn't a witch. He *couldn't* know. When he didn't let them use their magic, he was cutting off a part of them, and sooner or later, it was going to have consequences—for the three witches left in camp, they could be devastating.

"Your report, Syn," Kalen said, jerking her to attention.

Syn had a hard time maintaining her composure as she delivered the supply report to the commander. She was so

furious, she could hardly see. So cold, she felt sick with it.
"We can hold out a few more weeks, then?" Kalen asked
after she'd given him a quick rundown.

"Safely, yes. Possibly longer," Syn replied. "Will that be
all, Commander?"

He gave her a narrow look. For the most part, when
they were discussing things among themselves, Syn rarely
called him Commander. She called him by his name—
they were friends, friends who'd bled together, sweated
together, come close to dying together on more than one
occasion. *Commander* was saved for times when they were
out among the troops, rarely for discussions such as these.

Unless she was pissed. And she was. Kalen leaned back
in the seat and studied her face, then glanced at Lee and
Elina. "I'm sorry. I know this is hard."

Syn said nothing. Lee glared at him.

Elina tucked a lock of hair behind her ear. In a polite,
amicable voice, she said, "You don't fucking know what
hard is . . . Commander. You think you know. But you
don't." She reached up and tapped her brow as she continued. "Imagine if that psychic gift of yours just suddenly
went away. Poof—gone, just like that. It's part of you. You
rely on it. Magic is even more intrinsic to the soul than
psychic skill—but you know how hard this is. You know
what it's like to have part of your soul taken away."

She shifted in her chair, drumming her fingers idly on
the arm of it. "No, Commander. You don't know. So let's
just drop it."

"Fine." A muscle jerked in Kalen's jaw. "Lee, Elina,
you're dismissed. Captain, update me on how the search
for Dais is going."

* * *

Dais Bogler rammed his knife into the belly of the buck
and cut upward. It had been a while since he'd been forced
to hunt, kill and clean his own dinner, but he hadn't forgotten how. That kind of skill wasn't easily lost.

Blood, hot and slick, coated his hands.

For a moment, he imagined it wasn't the blood of a corcer, one of the herd beasts that lived in the Roinan Mountains.

In his mind, it was Kalen's blood.

In his mind, it was Lee's blood.

In his mind, it was Morne's blood.

Morne—damn the man. Why hadn't he seen it?

Morne—a fucking Warlord. Sirvani. Whatever in the hell he called himself. The bastard had hailed from Anqar and not a one of them had realized it.

It was a vile twist of fate that the people from Anqar didn't truly look any different from those in Ishtan. Human-oid. As a whole, Warlords and the Sirvani were tall and lean, strong—they were a conquering race, so naturally they were strong. But they looked human. Nothing save their language, their dress, their customs, set them apart from the peoples of Ishtan.

Morne had hidden himself with the rebels, and he'd done it all too well, too easily. He spoke their tongue, and he did it without an accent. He did not wear the garb of a Warlord, and he most certainly hadn't adhered to Warlord customs. He'd made himself seem as one of the rebels.

A wolf among sheep.

And because of this particular wolf, more than any other, Dais was well and truly screwed.

There were nights when he lay awake and wondered if he shouldn't just end it, put a blade to his wrists and be done with it. Sooner or later, the rebels would track him down. As long as he was in Ishtan, he was a man marked for death, and unless he was very lucky, it wouldn't be a pleasant death.

But Dais wasn't about to give up quite so easily. Not when he'd worked so long, so hard. There had to be a way. There still had to be a way.

He even had a glimmer of a plan. But until he found the right people, he couldn't very well put it into motion.

Tomorrow, damn it.

He'd find them tomorrow—

But that was something he'd been telling himself for weeks. The Roinan mountain range was huge, heavily forested, and the Warlords knew they couldn't risk being found by Kalen's men, so they stayed on the move. Far too quietly.

A noise, far off, muted, caught his attention. Instincts kicking into high gear, he gathered his gear and abandoned what would have been his first decent *hot* meal in weeks. The game was slowly starting to drift back in the mountains, but it was still scarce. He'd been existing off scrawny rabbits and cokrels and what precious little vegetation he could harvest without being noticed.

Except he *had* been noticed. He kept his growl behind his teeth and took off into the undergrowth of the woods, moving in an uneven line that would eventually take him to the river. The water level was lower than normal and the current was moving slowly. If he had to, he could take to the water and let the river carry him farther away.

"The river," he muttered, tugging at his lower lip, forgetting the buck's blood that still stained his hands. "Just take to the river for a while, maybe."

Might be best, actually.

Safer.

Away from the people who'd kill him without blinking an eye. For now. Perhaps if he lay low for a time, they might stop continually combing the forest for him.

Damn them all.

Damn them straight to hell.

***

With a feral smile curling his lips, Morne emerged from the brush and eyed the dead buck at his feet.

Faintly, very faintly, he could smell something other than the forest, something other than the dead corcer's blood.

Man.

A man had been here, and not long ago.

He could think of only one man it could be.

Morne already knew that Kalen had the camp under heavy lockdown. One single soul wouldn't come out this far on a hunting excursion, and even if one was that stupid, one buck wouldn't do much to feed the camp.

But it wasn't one from the army. The commander wouldn't allow anybody to leave the camp alone, and Morne could only sense the presence of one.

So either it was one of the foolish few who hadn't yet abandoned this forsaken land or it was a traitor.

Dais.

Morne had heard the whisper of sound, the soft sigh of man's presence, as he searched for Dais. He'd been searching fruitlessly for weeks, but this time, he'd been close and when the earth sensed the presence of a man, it had whispered to Morne. Through his healing gift, he had a connection to the earth. It spoke to him, called to him almost the same way it would call to a witch.

Closer. He was getting closer.

He followed the track to the river, and there, he found more to guide him. Again, his gift roused and whispered to him. It was a different aspect of his power this time, though—his empathy. He'd missed Dais only by moments. Mere moments, not enough time for the residual emotion to clear.

Anger. Fear. Desperation. It was strong enough that he could even pick up on some of the remnant thoughts connected to those emotions. *The river—take to the river for a while. Damn them. Damn them straight to hell . . .*

"If I go to hell, I take you with me," Morne said quietly.

A breeze kicked up, blowing his hair back from his face as he stared at the river. If he reached, if he focused, he could almost pick up on Dais's emotional trail. The man could only ride the river for so long.

"You're a dead man."

TWO

It wasn't quite dawn.

Xan was already up, sitting in silence on the bedroll in the dormer he'd been assigned to. There were nineteen others sharing the same area. Seven women and twelve men. He had the pleasure of listening to loud snoring, soft moans, the occasional grunt, and one man had even talked in his sleep.

He hadn't slept much, but he had stopped needing more than a few hours of sleep years earlier. Now he just waited.

Often, it seemed as though he'd spent most of his life waiting. For the next fight. For death. For a second chance. For hope.

Now he waited for the sunrise.

Come dawn, he'd start on this new phase of his life.

Serving in the rebel army.

What the bloody hell had he been thinking?

But it hadn't had much to do with thinking. It had come down to a lack of options. Xan had to wonder if this lack of options would be the death of him.

From behind him, there was another snore—sounding like something between a wild animal's growl and a person struggling for breath. It was that snore that was responsible for waking him.

He hadn't expected his lack of options would land him in a squat, narrow building with nineteen others. If he had known this was what awaited him . . . Halfway through the thought, he cut it off.

He was here, like so many others, because he had no choice.

He'd learn to deal with it.

With that thought in mind, he rose from his bunk and slid his blades into place, strapped his pulsar to his thigh. It wasn't easy leaving his personal belongings—what precious little he had—secured in the small footlocker, but he did it.

On his way out, he strode by the bed of the snorer and delivered it a solid kick. The man came awake with a start, and as Xan disappeared outside, he heard somebody behind him call out, "Thank you!"

* * *

"You bastard—"

That was all Lothen managed to get out before he ended up flat on his back with all of the breath knocked out of him. He lay there choking and sputtering for air. His opponent stood there expressionless. Lo came to his feet and shoved sweaty hair back from his face. "That was a dirty fucking trick," he wheezed.

"Sometimes it takes dirty fucking tricks to stay alive," Xan replied.

Syn stood off to the side, with her arms crossed over her chest. The man had some serious moves on him. She called out to Lo and gestured for him to leave the sparring circle. Catching Bron's eye, she nodded toward their newest. Bron cocked a brow—she saw the question in his eyes. She answered with a smile, and as Bron entered the circle, she stripped away her weapons.

Bron kept him moving. A fellow captain, a lifelong soldier, Bron fought with speed and stealth. He'd started out as a scout, but now he was in charge of one of the combat units. He was good. He was fast. But he wasn't as fast or as good as their new guy. Syn could only think of one other guy who fought so naturally—like it was as natural to him as breathing.

"He's good," Kalen murmured from just behind her shoulder.

She grinned. "Now, why am I not surprised to see you here, Commander?"

"Just passing by and caught sight of our new boys. Decided to take a look."

Calling Xan a *boy* didn't fit, Syn thought to herself.

"You playing today?" he asked.

Syn lifted a shoulder. "Unless you plan to."

Bron went flying past them—literally. He landed with an "oomph" and lay there for a few seconds, a dazed look in his eyes. His lean face went red as he tried to breathe.

Syn and Kalen grinned at each other. Then Kalen said, "I'll pass. Lee and I are doing some hand-to-hand tonight. I'd rather not start off injured. I'll let you have the fun today."

"Coward." Syn clucked her tongue. She watched, gauging the distance, as Xan started toward Bron. As he offered a hand to the other man, Syn moved.

She went for his feet and as he went down, she slid away.

It was like hitting a brick wall, she decided. A heated brick wall. She was so used to being cold, but the moment she touched him, even though her touch was an attack and not a caress, his heat chased away the chill and left her entire body suffused with warmth.

He outweighed her, outreached her, and stood nearly a head taller than she did. Which pretty much described every sparring partner she'd ever had.

That unreadable gaze of his didn't change, but she sensed some surprise coming off him as he came to his feet. Bron was up, too, and he moved so that he stood just a little behind Syn and off to the side. It was a choreographed move—they'd done this a thousand times and they'd do it a thousand more.

"So now it is two on one," Xan said, his voice emotionless.

"It can be a lot of fun." Syn flashed him a cheeky smile, keeping her weight on the balls of her feet. Her heart was racing. Her skin felt warm, edging close to hot as she waited.

Xan didn't make a move toward her, even though she stood the closest. He circled around, trying to make for Bron. Even after he had Bron back down, he didn't engage with her. Syn lifted a brow and asked, "You do have a second opponent you have to take down."

"I'm not putting a woman on the ground."

"Okay." It wasn't the first time she'd been told that, and she'd handle it the same way she handled it every other time. The cold knot tried to settle back inside her, but it faded when she attacked him—when she touched him.

He deflected her next attack. And the next. Bron was back on his feet at that point, though, and as he moved toward Bron, Syn went for another takedown. Xan went down and as he did, he tried to catch her feet.

She was prepared for him, though, springing away at just the last second. Xan got back on his feet, and this time, the look he shot her seemed a little bit perturbed.

"You can either spar me straight on, or I'll keep coming at your back."

"I'm not fighting with a woman."

"Then get out," she told him. She wasn't touching him now, and as she crossed her arms over her chest, the cold knot returned. "The gate's that way. You can walk out now. If you move quickly enough, you can probably catch up to the convoy. But you don't get to pick and choose your poison here, my friend. You do it my way, or you hit the road."

His eye narrowed on her face. "You sound very certain of that fact."

"With good reason."

With the exception of Xan and Syn, everybody turned to look at Kalen as he entered the circle. He stood a few inches taller than Xan. He wore cavinir—a light, form-fitting armor that clung to a hard, leanly muscled body.

Kalen had been born a warrior, forced to become a leader. At a time when he should have been dreaming about girls and dreading his impending adulthood, he'd been on the front line of their war.

He circled to stand in front of Xan, pinning the other man with a cool, silvery gaze. "Nobody stays in my camp without proving they can hold their own. Nobody stays in my camp without showing they know how to handle them-selves, without showing they know how to take orders. That includes training—you either spar with Captain Caar, as ordered, or you get the hell out."

"I don't believe in harming women," Xan growled.

"It's not about harming women." Syn moved between them and gave Kalen a narrow look. He inclined his head and fell back, letting her handle it. There was one thing she could rely on to chase away the chill, and that was anger. Right now, it flooded her, and she welcomed it—welcomed it and channeled it.

Giving Xan a pointed stare, she said, "I'm not calling you on the floor to get hurt, Xan. Trust me, I don't like pain, although I am used to it. But this isn't about hurting me, hurting women. It's called training—we all do it."

"Then train women against women. Females are natu-rally weaker than males—the risk for injury to the woman is too high, even in training."

"So this is about having a level playing field?" Syn snorted. "Sure, because we're fighting a war where there's always an excess of fairness."

Xan stared at her, his black gaze unflinching. "I do not raise my hand to women."

Syn smirked. "That's a way of thinking that could end up with you getting hurt—in a serious way." She glanced past him and her smile took on a decidedly devilish twist. "Bron, you're out. Elina. Coryan."

Elina Corsairs, long and lean, came at him from his right, a blur of movement. She was all speed and grace, and as he moved to deflect her attack, the other woman came up behind him.

Coryan Holder stood at six feet and her body was nearly as broad as Xan's. As he backed away from Elina, Coryan caught him in a wrestler's hold and wrenched him off his feet. He went down, and as one, the three women in the circle moved on him.

Elina ended up on her ass first. She would have moved back in but Syn caught her eye and shook her head.

Now facing Coryan and Syn, Xan grimaced. He looked between the two women, his gaze measuring.

Finally. Syn knew what sort of picture they presented. Coryan had the muscle mass to rival a man's and her face was scarred, hardened from battle and years of a harsh life. Syn had faced that same hard life, and many of the same battles, but she was slender, not particularly tall and she looked . . . well, soft.

He'd go for Coryan next, she figured. Eliminate what he perceived as the biggest threat.

This wasn't a new scenario for her. Too many of the men who wanted to join the rebellion showed up with preconceived notions—they were fighting a war against those that preyed on their females, and having those females involved directly in the fight went against their baser instincts.

He feinted toward Coryan but at the last minute, he changed direction. Moving too damn fast, he came for Syn. Only one thing saved her—he wasn't used to fighting somebody half his size. She darted away, relying on her flexibility and years of experience to evade him. It was close, though. She felt the disturbance in the air ripple against her flesh. He didn't waste any time and came at her again, harder. Faster.

Syn took his legs out from under him, but he was prepared this time, and when he went down, so did she. Trapped under his bigger body, she sucked air into her lungs.

Heat.

Once more, touching him flooded her with heat, heat that suffused every fiber of her being, chasing away the chill. For the briefest moment, they were close, close as lovers, and she let herself revel in that heat, let herself feel his strength, feel all of him. But not enough . . . nowhere near enough.

Through their clothes, she could feel the heavy thud of his heart, beating so close to hers.

Then he spoke, and the spell shattered.

"This isn't a fair fight," he said in a monotone.

Working her hands in between them, she jabbed at his neck. He went red and gasped for air. As he went to shove away from her, she caught him between his legs with her knee.

It was utterly silent, save for the strange, choked sound he made deep in his throat as he rolled to the side. Syn came to her feet and stood over him.

"You're damn right it's not a fair fight," she told him. "But then again, you can't win a war, you can't survive, if you're busy complaining about a fair fight."

She moved to the edge of the circle, watching Xan from under her lashes. He recovered quick, rolling to his feet and watching her with a mix of disbelief and anger. The anger melted away, replaced by that same measuring gaze he'd focused on every other fighter he'd met in the circle.

About damn time.

"When I was ten, my mother was taken from me—she'd hidden me with my older brother, told him to keep me quiet, no matter what. I couldn't do a damn thing to help her. All I could do was listen, helpless, as five Sirvani dragged her away from me. I never saw her again." A knot tried to form in her throat, but she ignored it. "My father had died the year before in a raid. My brother died two years later on a scouting mission. I was just a child and I was alone. There's nothing fair in that. But complaining about it didn't bring them back."

"Fighting an unfair fight will not bring them back," he said.

"No. But it might help another girl—it *has* helped other girls, other boys. Innocent children. The women of this world can't sit by the wayside, letting the men fight. If we want safety, we have to fight for it. It's about survival, not fairness. I didn't learn how to survive by only fighting the battles I *could* win. I learned how to survive by fighting the battles I *couldn't* win."

He inclined his head. "Point taken."

Kalen stood at her back. Bron was at her right. Elina and Coryan waited patiently at her left.

But she didn't look at any of them. She took three steps, placing her body once more inside the circle.

"Let's try this again," she said, staring at Xan and nothing else. "We do this my way, or you leave. The next time I tell you to step into the circle and fight a woman, what are you going to do?"

A faint smile curled his lips just before he attacked.

He won, but that was little surprise. Just getting him to square off with her in the ring was enough of a victory for her. Nobody needed to know she got a little added bonus— for the few brief moments they sparred, she stopped feeling so damned cold.

* * *

"She's a ballbuster."

As he looked up, two men settled down across from him. One was Bron, but Xan couldn't remember the other warrior's name. He'd fought him briefly in the circle before Bron had stepped in.

"I beg your pardon?" he said, cocking a brow and look-ing from one to the other.

"The captain. She's a ballbuster." Bron grinned at him.

Xan now knew that from experience—he was damn near certain he had bruises in a very sensitive part of his anatomy.

"You're smarter than some of us." Bron picked up his fork and took a quick bite before continuing. "The first time I left the circle after she really came after me, I prac-tically crawled out."

A reluctant smile curled Xan's mouth. "I must admit, I'm relieved to know I'm not the only man she's put on the ground before."

"Far from it. You did better than some of us, too. You didn't just give her a run for her money. Hell, you beat her. Not too many people I can say that about." The other man popped a forkful of food into his mouth and washed it down with a gulp of water. "She's got a habit of putting men on their asses two or three times a day, minimum. It's kind of her hobby."

"Her hobby?"

"Yep. I'm Lothen, by the way. Just in case she scram-bled your brains as well as smashing your balls. Friends usually call me Lo."

"Actually, it's what everybody calls him. His friends don't call him much of anything—he doesn't have any." Bron smirked at the other man. "She's one of his favorites. Puts him on the ground about once a week."

"It's the only way she can put her hands on me without Janis getting pissy," Lo said around a mouth full of food.

"You wish." Bron braced his elbows on the table and stared at Xan with curious eyes.

Actually, he was looking at his covered eye—what remained of it. "Mind if I ask what happened?"

Xan ran his finger over the patch and murmured, "My misbegotten youth."

"You did that when you were a kid?"

"I was technically a child, yes." Ten—to be exact. He'd been ten years old when it happened. The same age Syn had been when she lost her mother. He frowned and rubbed the heel of his hand over his heart. She'd been just a young thing, and left all alone . . .

"Technically. Misbegotten. You talk like some sort of university professor. What exactly do you do, other than kick ass and piss off the captain?" Lo took another swig of water and grinned at Xan.

"Did I piss her off?" Xan asked, forcing himself to concentrate on the conversation instead of her. It was hard, though. In those brief moments before she'd all but unmanned him, he had been painfully aware of how perfect her body felt under his. Soft . . . delicate . . . but still so strong.

"Nah, probably not. I bet she loves it when a new recruit makes her reiterate herself in the circle," Bron drawled.

"You know, at this point, she's probably used to it," Lo said with a shrug.

"Used to having her authority questioned? Yeah, I bet that goes over swimmingly."

While the two of them nattered on at each other, Xan found himself staring at his plate and scowling. No leader liked being questioned—they gave orders and orders were to be followed. Living in a war zone made it even more crucial for orders to be followed. When they weren't, when they were routinely questioned, it made the leader seem weak.

Syn was anything but weak.

And yet . . .

***

She wasn't an easy woman to find.

Xan had spent much of his free time learning the layout of the camp. But he might as well be chasing his own shadow, in circles, for all the good it did him. He'd had absolutely no luck finding Syn. He'd spent his morning in weapons training and he hadn't seen her once. The afternoon was spent in the work detail orientation. After it was discovered he had a skill for weapons, he was placed on that detail, which seemed to involve everything from repair to designing new weapons.

Of course, he could expect to be repairing weapons for a good long while, since he was the newest one in. He'd have to work his way up to actually helping design them, even if he could wrap his mind around the complicated technology.

Every spare moment he had, he had been looking for Syn. With no luck.

When he heard a voice behind him, he was hard-pressed not to swear. He pretended obliviousness, but that did no good, either. Vena fell in step next to him, walking so close that her hand brushed against his, walking so close that if he wished, he could see clear down the veed front of her black cavinir tunic. The clothes she wore clung to her curves like a lover.

"Hey . . . you must be off in your own little world," she said, trailing one fingertip down his arm. "I called you two or three times and you didn't even hear me."

"My mind is elsewhere."

"I can tell." She shot him what he assumed was meant to be a coy look, glancing at him from under her lashes as she trailed her tongue along her lower lip. "Are you feeling well? I saw what happened in the circle. I couldn't believe what that woman did. She doesn't exactly have what I'd call *leader* qualities."

Guilt pricked at him and he grimaced inwardly. He really did need to find Syn and offer an apology.

"Actually, she handled it exactly as I would have," he said, not bothering to glance at Vena. "She is in charge of training the new recruits, evaluating their skill with combat. I came to join an army, and I know how the chain of command works. I was given an order, and I didn't adhere to it. Had it been somebody under my command, I would have done the same thing she did—showed the fool the error of their ways."

Vena rolled her eyes. "It's not like you abandoned your post or something, Xan. You just didn't want to get rough with a woman . . . It's admirable."

"There is nothing admirable about disrespecting a comrade in arms." Never mind the fact that he was having a difficult time thinking of that particular woman as a comrade in arms . . . He kept thinking of her in *his* arms. Kept remembering how soft, how strong, she felt under him—right before she rammed his balls somewhere in the vicinity of his throat.

Just in front of them, he caught sight of a familiar dark head. He glanced at Vena and said, "If you'd excuse me, there's something I need to take care of."

He left the other woman standing behind him, her eyes drilling holes in his back. He could sense the heat in that gaze but brushed it off. The woman behind him didn't matter.

It was the woman in front of him that held his attention. He caught up with Syn just before she would have disappeared into one of the low, squat buildings that made up the bulk of their camp.

"Captain, may I have a word with you?"

"Not a good time—I'm supposed to be clear on the other side of camp, twenty minutes ago." She glanced at him and shook her head. She ducked into the building, using her foot to hold the door open as she grabbed a battered leather pouch from a table near the door. She slipped her head through the strap and adjusted it so it lay crosswise between her small breasts.

Xan fought the urge to stare at that strap of leather with a bit of wistful envy. He won—barely. But he couldn't stop himself from thinking about laying his head there, resting it just there, in the shallow valley between those slight curves.

You are not helping matters, he told himself.

Syn closed the door behind him and started back down the hard-packed, earthen pathway. Considering how small she was, she walked awfully damn fast.

"It will not take long. I just want to apologize." He fell into step next to her, only to stop when she did.

Syn turned and studied his face with narrowed eyes. Her gaze lingered on his patch and he was appalled to realize he was close to fidgeting—this close to reaching up and adjusting the black material that hid the scarred ruin of his eye.

"Apologize for what?" she asked bluntly.

"For earlier." She knew damn well what he was apologizing for—he could see it in her green-gold eyes. "As uncomfortable as I am sparring with a female, you are in charge and I should have shown more respect for that fact."

Syn pursed her lips and continued to study him. He had utterly no idea what she was thinking about—that catlike gaze revealed nothing. Then abruptly, she gave a single nod of her head and said, "Fine. Apology accepted. Now . . . if you'll excuse me, I'm needed elsewhere."

Without waiting for a response, she turned around and strode away.

* * *

Actually, Syn wasn't needed elsewhere. She had told a friend she might come by for a drink. She desperately needed to unwind, to relax. To forget for even five minutes that she was a captain in an army where half her friends had died, where more yet would die before things were finished.

She wanted to share some laughs with a friend and forget that she was Captain Laisyn Caar. More, she wanted to forget she was basically a powerless witch. It was too much like being a toothless, clawless predator.

She wanted to forget she was the highest-ranking female in the rebel army, a female who regularly had to prove her authority over those under her.

She wanted to forget all of that and just be Syn. Even if it was just for a while.

But it wasn't like she had orders to be somewhere. Still,

she strode away from him as quickly as she could. Standing this close to him did some seriously weird things to her body.

From the time he'd said her name, she'd felt warm. As he'd walked beside her, she'd felt a silken, liquid heat settle low in her belly.

As much as she enjoyed how he managed to melt the ice inside her chest, she had come to realize it wasn't wise to enjoy it. It wasn't wise to enjoy anything about him. Not the way he made her heart race, not the way her skin flushed when he was near. Not the way she found herself thinking about him, far too often.

Simply standing close to him was a lesson in arousal, and it was a lesson she really didn't have the time or the inclination to learn.

Somebody who could affect her like that was best kept off-limits. On the rare occasion when she needed some sort of physical release from the tension, she preferred to do it with somebody who knew her, somebody she knew and trusted . . . somebody she could keep at a safe distance even as they . . . released tension.

Reaching the bend in the path, she glanced back.

He was still standing there.

Watching her.

Her heartbeat sped up even more, and her knees went a little weak. Damn it.

"I don't need this," she muttered under her breath. "I really, really don't need this."

Deep inside, there was a voice whispering, *Maybe it's exactly what you do need. He could make you forget all about being Captain Laisyn Caar.*

Yes. He could.

One hundred percent, completely and fully.

That was why she needed to keep him at a distance.

But even as she insisted on that, she was having a hard time entirely believing it, and her body longed for his warmth.

THREE

Hunger gnawed at him.

Dais had left most of his meager belongings stashed while he took down the buck. He'd been forced to abandon his gear in his haste to get away from whoever had been searching for him. All he carried now were his weapons, his empty canteen and a sodden pouch with rations that hadn't held up well after his trek down the river.

"Will nothing go my way?" he muttered.

The question had no sooner left his mouth than he heard it.

Voices.

Far off, moving closer.

A smile curved his lips. Perhaps fate was finally going to shine on him.

About bloody time.

* * *

And then again, perhaps fate was more in the mood to taunt him.

Hours later, Dais stood on weary feet before a Warlord as he repeated his story for the third time. His clothes were stiff with river water and his belly was a tight, cold knot. His throat was parched.

He needed food. He needed water. He needed a damn bath.

But the men before him weren't in a congenial mood—basic courtesies were either beyond them or they simply didn't care to extend them.

It was intolerable. Before, when he had served as a spy to Raichar Taise, he had been respected. Honored. Granted, only Char and his Sirvani, a few select others, had known of Dais's existence, but he had never been left hungry, never been left thirsty.

Nor had he been mocked.

But the Warlord in front of him watched him with a sly smile on his mouth. "That is the most absurd tale I've heard in quite some time. Do you expect us to believe you?"

"I have no reason to lie, my lord." *Tale?* Dais clenched his jaw shut to keep from sputtering as he fought not to flinch under the Warlord's unyielding stare. He'd spent weeks searching for Anqarians. Now that he had finally found them—or rather had *been found* by them—this bastard mocked him.

It was utterly humiliating.

There had been a time when he could have faced down a bastard like this without blinking an eye. But that had been before . . . back when he wasn't being hunted by his own people like a fucking animal.

Turning traitor didn't come without its risks, and Dais was fully aware of those risks. Getting caught had always been a possibility, and he wasn't fool enough or arrogant enough to believe otherwise. But being aware of the *possibility* and dealing with the *reality* were two very, very different things.

He couldn't continue to run. Not with winter edging ever closer. Plus, the forest was proving to be more and more dangerous for a man alone. Even if he managed to evade the demons, he couldn't evade nature. He couldn't evade basic facts.

He needed food.

He needed shelter.

Winter was coming and Dais had to either secure himself a place here or head south.

But he didn't want to head south. He wanted to be *here*, because if ever another Gate was raised, it would be here. Though the Roinan Gate had collapsed, there was still power in the air, and when the Warlords acted, it would be here.

Dais would be here when it happened, because come hell, high water or demon hordes, he was going through the damn Gate. He wasn't going to spend the rest of his life like this.

If he stayed here, he was a dead man. At least in Anqar, he might have half a chance.

But first he had to get them on his side.

"I assure you, Warlord, there is nothing absurd about this." Refusing to let any of his desperation show on his face, he met the Warlord's penetrating gaze. "It's not a child's tale; it's not some campfire story that's been bandied about—it's simply fact. She was Warlord Raichar's child. Her mother was a rather powerful witch."

"And you say this woman has *Gate* magic? Women do not have *Gate* magic. The Gates do not recognize women."

"I beg to disagree, sire. They will recognize this woman." He lifted his hands and fought to look humble—it wasn't terribly hard just then. He had precious little pride, precious little arrogance left after the past few weeks, a fact that incensed him to no end. What he did have was rage—he had that in spades, but that didn't serve him right now. If he showed the rage, then he'd be lucky if he only ended up dead.

He'd bide his time.

Sooner or later, he would be able to indulge in the anger. But until then . . .

He forced himself to give a pathetic smile. "Please understand, I cannot claim any deep knowledge of the Gates, and I do know that before meeting this woman, I'd never heard of a woman who could raise a Gate. But she can."

"To my knowledge, Char's daughter has been dead for many years." It came from the depths of the tent. Dais couldn't tell who had said it.

The small shelter was crowded. There were five Warlords of varying ages and varying strengths, and numerous Sirvani. The Sirvani, with their shaven hands and bare chests, stood on guard, between Dais and the Warlords.

As though Dais was fool enough to try to go for one of them.

So far, the youngest Warlord had done all of the talking. The rest of them looked on, watching Dais as though he was some bug they'd discovered—like they couldn't decide whether to squash him or just leave him be.

"I'm aware of the rumor," Dais said, lying without blinking an eye. He knew next to nothing about Raichar. More's the fucking pity, too. If he had been aware of this little twist, perhaps he could have made better plans.

"Rumor." The youngest Warlord watched Dais with a smirk on his lips. The bastard hadn't so much as offered a name. Dais knew enough of Anqarian customs—withholding a name was an insult among their kind.

Shit.

The Warlord was young, but there was a great deal of power in him. The others looked to him in deference. Dais could understand why—just looking at him was enough to dry the spit in Dais's mouth.

Like the others, he wore a thick chain around his neck. Light fell across the stone set in the metal—it was Warlord blue. That particular stone was worn only by Warlords and Sirvani—Sirvani, their little Warlords in training. The closer to black the stone got, the more powerful the Warlord.

This man's stone was the same shade of the night sky.

It was dull, though. Before the collapse of the Gates, the stones had always had some inner glow.

"Let's say Char's daughter did not die—let's say this woman is indeed who you claim."

Dais inclined his head.

"How do you know this?"

"I know a great many things, sire. I deal in . . . information. It's my specialty."

"You make it sound so grand, offworlder. So elegant, so noble. But you're just a spy," the Warlord said, that small, amused smile curling his lips.

Shame and humiliation curled inside him but he didn't look away. He didn't dare—this was a man who could put a knife between his ribs and Dais wouldn't even know it until he was already on the ground.

"A spy," the Warlord said again, in a smooth, deep voice. He smiled at Dais, a feral curl of his lips. "Nothing more, and not a particularly good one, I'd wager. After all, you were caught."

Dais bristled. It hadn't been that long ago when he'd been one of the most valued assets in Anqar's army, even though most of them knew nothing of him. He'd also been one of the most respected men in the rebellion—leading a double life and doing a damn fine job of it, too. For close to forty years.

Until Morne—damn the man.

And Lee. Kalen. Damn them all to hell.

He made a conscious effort to relax, waiting until he knew he could speak without the knife-edge of anger apparent in his voice. "What I am, or what I am not, isn't the important issue here, my lords. The important issue is the information I've given you. Precious information."

"Precious." The Warlord began to pace around Dais in a slow circle, moving ever closer, until even a slight shift would have their bodies brushing. Dais held himself rigid—the thought of allowing this man to touch him in any way seemed about as foolish as drinking poison.

"Precious information," the Warlord murmured.

The Warlord was damned creepy. From the corner of his eye, he tried to watch the other man, but it was hard to watch him without turning, and he didn't dare give the other Warlords his back. He couldn't afford to let any of the others recognize his unease.

"You must admit, my lords, a female that can bear your power, surely the idea is enticing."

Circling to stand before Dais, the Warlord stopped. A smile curled his lips as he studied Dais's face. "Of course, we have only your word that this female, this daughter of Raichar, can actually use Gate magic. That she actually *is* the daughter of Raichar. No proof. Just your word."

"The word of a spy," somebody within the tent said in a voice thick with derision.

"The word of a spy," the Warlord murmured, shaking his head. "How much faith do we place in the word of a spy?"

Mouth gone dry, Dais forced a smile. "If she were delivered into your hands, perhaps then you would believe?"

"How do you plan to do that?"

Dais started, caught off guard as one of the other Warlords spoke. It was the older one, one who had silver starting to show in his reddish blond hair. Lines fanned out from his faded gray eyes, but although the years showed on him, so did strength and power.

"My lord?" Dais asked.

"How do you plan to deliver this so-called female Warlord into our hands?" He watched Dais with no expression. "Do you think we shall let you go? Leave you to this fool's errand simply at your behest?"

Dais was hard-pressed not to react to that.

He couldn't very well go on his "fool's errand" without their permission. They had more or less captured him. Instead of him approaching them as an equal—or at least approaching them from a bargaining position—they had taken him off guard and now he was their prisoner.

He gave the eldest Warlord a cagey smile and said, "Truly, my lord. What is the more appealing prize? My mangy hide? Or the possibility of a young, *powerful* woman?"

"Hmmmm. You do make a good point."

* * *

They watched as he left.

They remained silent and motionless long after the flap of the tent swung closed behind him, aware he was skulking about in the shadows. He made no sound, but he was there nonetheless. They continued to wait, until he finally withdrew.

After all, he couldn't stay there forever, not if he wanted to find this so-called female Warlord to turn over to them. Not if he wanted to live. Warlords rarely lost their prey, and if he did not deliver as promised, his life was forfeit.

"What is your opinion of the man?" the eldest Warlord asked, his voice indifferent. As though the answer mattered less than nothing.

"I do not trust him." With a deferential bow of his head, the youngest Warlord spoke.

"Of course you don't," Reil said, amused. "You trust nobody."

"No, there are a specific few whom I trust."

Reil imagined he knew who the few were—they didn't include the spy, or even himself.

He didn't trust the fool, either. Ironically, he did trust the Warlord before him. He came from a long, proud line—with a few exceptions, this man's family was held in high regard. They were merciless without being brutal, commanding without being domineering. Traits well admired in Anqar.

Unlike the cagey, conniving cur they had allowed to walk away.

Was it a fool's errand? Or could it possibly be true?

Dais Bogler was a desperate man, and desperate men did desperate things. Desperate men often did foolish things.

But whether Reil trusted him or not, they had a decision to make.

"He isn't to be trusted," he murmured, more to himself than anything. He came to his feet, knees aching as he did so. He shouldn't have come on this final raid. Every year was harder for him—the damp, heavy air in Ishtan wreaked havoc on aging bones. After three hundred years, time was catching up with him. But two of his offspring had been selected for the raiding parties, and he'd wanted to be with them. One more journey, before he retired to his lands to live out the rest of his life in relative obscurity.

Both of the boys were dead now and he may never see his estate again.

He grieved the loss of his boys—his great-great-grandsons. He grieved for them and awaited the time when he could lay his arms down and join those who had passed on.

He was weary.

But there were others depending on him. More sons, even a few daughters back in Anqar, and he couldn't protect his family if he was trapped in this world. Getting back was key. Anqar would be in turmoil and too many of his people preyed on any and every perceived weakness. Without him there, his family might be perceived as weak. He feared for them.

They must return home.

If by some chance this elusive "female Warlord" existed, she might prove useful.

Very useful.

There were other options, however. Reil didn't believe in limiting his choices. He'd been laying the groundwork for possible courses of action well before Dais Bogler entered their camp. If Dais was correct . . . He found himself smiling as he pondered the possibilities there.

Still, he hadn't gotten to his station by entertaining possibilities. He'd gotten where he was because he made things happen and left nothing to fate or happenstance.

He stroked a thumb down his stone as he studied the Warlord before him. He was well-known for being something of a diplomat—but a deadly one. He could, and had, easily cut the throats of his enemies. A swift, silent arrow in the dark.

A useful man to have at his hand.

"I want him followed," Reil said quietly. "I want him watched. If it seems he's right about this *female* Warlord, then I want her. She could be the very thing we need to return home."

They'd need all the power they could gather, if they'd even have the chance.

***

Night came, and with it, there was a blissful respite from the humid, heavy heat that had plagued the region for much of the summer.

It had been another long, tedious day, one Xan was glad to see end. That was the way of it, though. The days stretched on, one slow hour ticking by followed by another and another, with nothing to relieve his monotony.

Nothing but the few times each day he saw the captain. Every day during hand-to-hand, and at odd intervals with weapons training. Those hours seemed to dance by without him even realizing it, leaving him waiting for the next time he'd see her.

Two weeks. He'd been in the base camp for two weeks, and he measured time by how often he got to see the captivating captain each day.

He was becoming far too much like a lovesick boy, and the woman barely seemed to realize he was alive—or that he could serve as anything else but a target.

By the time he started making his way to his assigned dormer, darkness had fallen. The pathways were lit with solar-powered lights that did little to dispel the gloom. Just ahead, he could make out the dark shadow of the dormer he shared with nineteen others.

Strangers—every last one of them. For the first time in his life, he was completely and utterly surrounded by strangers. Any other time in his life, he'd either been with friends or comrades . . . or he had been alone.

Twenty bodies, packed into one crowded room. What he wouldn't give for some solitude.

The sounds of a struggle caught his attention. Solitude forgotten, he followed the low but unmistakable sounds. A woman—his attention sharpened and he realized he was snarling, his lips peeled back from his teeth. He drew the long knife from the sheath he wore at his back as he followed the sounds.

Brighter lights cast long shadows on the ground as he rounded a corner and ended up part of an audience at a sparring match. Feeling like a fool, he slid the knife back into place and started to turn away, but the opponents in the circle caught his attention.

The woman had a banner-bright head of blond hair, pulled back and woven in a tight tail that trailed down her back. The man was the commander, Kalen Brenner. Curious, Xan found himself moving through the crowd to take a place near the edge of the circle, staring at the combatants in the sparring circle.

The base camp had twelve different training areas, each one complete with a sparring circle. He had yet to see one of them empty for more than a moment or two.

This one was far from empty as well, and quite a few people stood off to the side, watching the participants with rapt interest.

He'd yet to see the woman's face. She stood with her back to him, facing the commander. She was long and lean, standing on the balls of her feet. Brenner was watching her with a grin on his face. It was the only time Xan had seen him with any sort of true expression on his face.

The light glinted in his eyes, and he rushed the woman. Xan felt something inside him clench, and then the woman spun out of the way at the last second, using a move that was oddly familiar. He was quite certain Syn had used a move similar to that one of the times she'd taken him down.

The women in this camp were just plain evil, he decided, watching as the commander hit the ground.

He hadn't been down a second before the woman joined him. Light fell across her face as she crouched down, one leg on either side of his hips. A grin curled her lips, and she said, "You're down, pal."

Her voice—the words, they had an odd inflection to them.

Her eyes were blue and the light in them was just a little wicked, just a little wanton, as Brenner shifted and moved, putting her under him on the ground. They grappled, fighting for control, barely aware of anything besides each other.

Somebody in the crowd called out, "Maybe we should leave the two of you alone."

"Maybe you should," the woman responded.

Kalen rolled away from her and came to his feet, smirking at the woman. "I've got five on you now."

"You do know that bragging is never sexy, right?" the woman asked, circling around him.

She moved well. The commander was better, but she was . . . sneaky. Yes, sneaky described her right as she let him close in on her. She gasped and when he paused, she used his momentary distraction to hook her ankle behind his.

They both went toppling to the ground, the woman on top of him, with her knee poised high between his thighs.

One of the spectators called out, "We do need him functional, ya know."

"Oh, don't worry." With a slow curl of her lips, the blonde smiled down at Kalen. "I like him functional myself."

"Yes, Lee. We can tell."

Xan recognized that voice. It was Syn. Following the sound of the voice, he found her standing on the edge of the circle. He hadn't seen her outside of training for close to a week. And he had looked. Often. More often than he wanted to think about.

Willing his tense muscles to relax, he made his way to her side, watching the two fighters in the circle.

"Who is she?" he asked as he stopped next to her.

"Lee. His wife." Syn didn't look up at him as she responded.

"Lee." He murmured the name to himself and frowned. He hadn't heard anything about the commander of the Roinan camp being married. "Wife?"

"Yes—fairly recent. They were married not long ago— maybe two weeks before you showed up."

"Not long after the Gate fell, then. Strange time to wed."

"If we waited for a more ideal time, none of us would ever marry. None of us would ever have any sort of life outside the damned war." Syn grimaced. Her features smoothed out and she gave him a questioning look. "Are you getting around the camp okay?"

"Yes. I was on my way to my dormer when I heard them." He looked back at the sparring partners.

* * *

"She's very much taken," Syn said dryly, following his stare and wondering why the intensity of it left her feeling a little edgy.

It's because of Lee, she told herself. Lee was still getting acclimated. Syn considered Lee and Kalen her friends. They had a new marriage, and although it seemed solid, it just wasn't right that they had some big, sexy brooder paying too much attention to Lee.

It was a perfectly logical way to feel.

It was also a lie. He was a big, sexy brooder, but what bothered her was the fact that she wanted him paying attention to *her*, not Lee.

"Taken?" Xan turned to look at her, cocking his head. He had to turn his head completely to see her—she was standing to his left, on his blind side.

"Yes. Taken—you do remember the part about them being married, right?"

"Of course. It's only been a minute since you mentioned it." A black brow arched over his eye and a faint smile tugged at his lips. "Why do you ask?"

Syn shrugged and focused back on Lee and Kalen. "You just seem very keen on staring at her."

"She's a beautiful woman."

Lee was beautiful. There was no denying that. She had the gilded, golden looks of an angel, the wiry, quick strength of a born fighter. It wasn't any big surprise that Xan had noticed her.

No, the surprise was that Syn was *jealous*. Screw being protective of her friends—she wasn't worked up over Xan noticing her friend Lee, who happened to be married.

She was worked up because *Xan* had noticed *Lee*.

Hell. She really did need to find a man and work off some of this tension.

But getting away from him was priority number one because the longer she remained this close, the worse that tension got. She gave him a tight smile and said, "You have a good night, Xan." Then she turned and tried to lose herself in the crowd.

Tried.

Failed.

Because he followed her.

Once more, he was at her side, and now they were alone, no longer in a very, very public place.

Not good.

"Have I done something that's offended you, Captain?" he asked, his voice level.

She shot him a glance and silently said, *Offend? No. Bother? Hell, yes. Everything you do manages to bother me somehow.*

Out loud, she just said, "Of course not."

"Then why is it that anytime I try to speak to you, you move in the opposite direction as quickly as possible?"

Syn was thankful the sol-lights weren't very bright. All they did was give off enough illumination to make out the paths in the base camp. Nowhere near enough light that Xan would see her blushing. Keeping her voice level, she said, "Do I? I haven't noticed."

"You also do not look at me unless it's to give me an

order to get in the circle or inform me that my knowledge on tech weapons is disgustingly shoddy," he said, his voice dry, referencing a comment she'd made the day before.

Syn stared straight ahead. "I do look at you."

No, she didn't.

"No. You do not." He reached out and caught her arm, pulling her to a halt.

Syn looked up at him and immediately tried to pull away. The grasp he had on her arm prevented it, though. He didn't hold her tight enough to hurt, but he wasn't letting her pull away.

Glaring up at him, she jerked on her arm.

A smile curled the harsh line of his mouth, softened it. "Now you are looking at me.

"Is it this?" He reached up and touched the patch covering his eye. "More than one person has had a hard time meeting my gaze because of it. Although I would have thought you were more accustomed to those with unsightly scars."

There was no inflection in his voice, and though the light was dim, she could see his face well enough to know there was no expression on it.

"Your scars don't bother me at all. They aren't unsightly— I've seen far, far worse. God knows, we all have our share of them." She jerked a shoulder and said, "Some of us have scars much uglier, although many carry them on the inside."

"Then why do you never look at me?"

Syn felt the blush once more start its slow climb up her neck, staining her cheeks, her face. "I do look at you. I *am* looking at you."

"Because I've all but made you," he replied, his brow arching. "Truthfully, if I wasn't touching you, if I wasn't asking you for a straight answer, what would you be doing?"

"Truthfully?" She tore her gaze away from him. *Truthfully*—she didn't want to tell him truthfully. But what was she to do? Lie? Somehow, she suspected that unless she gave him an answer, he would wait forever.

She could break his hold, and she knew he wouldn't force it, but she would feel foolish doing that.

Swallowing, she looked back up at him and said flatly, "If you weren't touching me, if you weren't pushing for an answer, I'd be clear on the other side of camp." *On the other side of camp. Alone. And cold. Again. Always cold. Except when you touch me.* How sick was it that the highlight of her days now centered on when there was training and she could put herself in the circle with him? She'd spar with him, and only him, every damn day if it wouldn't have looked so suspicious.

"Why? Again, I ask you, have I offended you?"

"No." She forced the word past her tight throat.

"Then if it isn't that, if it isn't my scars, perhaps it is just me."

"No." The word slipped out before she could stop it. *Idiot.* If she was half as interested in self-preservation as she should be, she should let him think just that. If he thought she had a personal problem with him, maybe he would leave her alone.

But I don't know if I really want him to leave me alone. And her body already knew it didn't want to be left alone.

"Then what is it?"

He was closer now, Syn realized. When had he moved closer? She swallowed, aware that her throat was terribly dry, that her heart was racing. Her head was spinning, too. Damn it, he smelled good.

She had to tip her head back to see him now. She could feel that seductive heat of his, shimmering between them. The heavy intensity that made up his being had surrounded her, slammed at her shields. Through them, she felt something she really didn't need to feel. Not if she wanted to keep her distance.

He was every bit as aware of her as she was of him.

Every damn bit.

Her control shattered and she reached up, hooked her

hand around the back of his neck and pulled his head lower. As she slanted her mouth against his, she felt his surprise—it lasted all of two seconds before he wrapped both arms around her body and hauled her close. He straightened and her feet left the ground.

Their mouths opened, and she shuddered as she traced her tongue along his lower lip. Male. The heady male taste, his scent, all of it flooded her, and she wrapped her other arm around his shoulders, straining to get closer.

* * *

Want . . . *need.*

It dominated Xan's every thought and he was just a heartbeat away from forgetting everything—himself, where they were—a heartbeat away from forgetting everything and everybody who wasn't Syn.

She tasted like honey and heat. Her mouth was soft under his, but there was nothing hesitant in the way she kissed him. She kissed him like she craved him. Like she absolutely had to do it or die.

Off in the distance, he heard voices. Instinctively, he moved, walking blind until they were lost in the shadows between two buildings. There, he backed her up against a wall and leaned into her.

Syn wrapped her legs around his hips and rocked against him.

Xan was utterly convinced the top of his head was going to come off if she did it again. Sliding a hand down her side, he cupped her hip and growled against her lips, "Do that again."

She did, smiling against his lips as he shuddered.

Gripping her hips in his hands, he held her steady and rocked against her, over and over, striving to get closer, despite the clothing that separated them. She whimpered low in her throat. Tearing his mouth from hers, he raked his teeth down her neck and bit her where her neck curved into her shoulder.

"Is this why?" he demanded, lifting his head and staring down at her.

The light was dim, so dim, all he could make out was the shape of her face, the glitter of her cat's eyes. And her mouth . . . Damn it all, her mouth. She licked her lips and he was hard-pressed not to dip his head and catch her lower lip in his mouth.

"Is this why?" he asked again, nudging his aching erection against the warmth between her thighs.

"Yes," she whispered. She closed her eyes, and her body shuddered as she sucked in a deep breath. "This is exactly why."

"You're attracted to me."

A wry grin curled her lips and she asked sardonically, "Isn't that obvious?"

"Is there a problem, you being attracted to me?" But even as he asked it, he wanted to kick himself. Of course there was. This might not be recognized as a "formal" military unit in the outside world, but they ran it as such.

"There is a problem," she admitted.

Clenching his jaw, he reached behind and unhooked the ankles she had wrapped so tightly around his waist. "Then I'll apologize. I would do nothing to endanger your position here." He went to move away.

But she grabbed his arm. Staring up at him, she shook her head. Some of the light from the path outside their narrow alley filtered in, falling across her face. "This wouldn't cause a problem with my position. Only my actions would do that and the commander would personally kick my ass from here clear into Anqar if I let personal issues affect how I did my job.

"When it comes to certain areas, we don't operate like the formal military would—we can't. This *is* our lives, and if we were never allowed anything outside our jobs . . . Well, we need to remember why we fight." She sighed and brushed her hair back from her face. "Lee and Kalen, they have something between them that might not exist if we insisted there be no 'fraternizing' among ourselves. We outnumber the civilians four to one and if it came down to only having . . . ah . . . relationships with civilians, we'd have a lot of infighting and animosity over it. We're allowed to do whatever we wish on personal time."

He narrowed his eyes, trying to follow her thinking. Unsuccessfully. Women. They were incomprehensible. She was attracted to him but wouldn't pursue it. Not because it posed a problem with her job, though. So why?

"If it isn't that, then why? What is this problem?"

Syn glanced away, once more pushing her fingers through her short, dark hair. A nervous habit, he was coming to realize. "You don't understand the idea of asking easy questions, do you?"

"If the questions are easy, likely so are the answers, and I can find them on my own." He cupped her cheek in his hand and stroked his thumb over her lower lip. "If it isn't because of some law within the base camp, and if it isn't because you are not attracted to me, then why?"

"It's *because* I'm attracted," she admitted softly. "I don't know if I need the complications it can bring me."

"So you need time to . . . what, decide if you want these complications?"

Unsmiling, she nodded.

Something inside his heart clenched and knotted. Then, as bizarre as it might seem, he felt as though some small part of him started to die. It took everything he had to let his hand drop. It took even more to make himself take a step back. He reached down and caught her hand, lifting it to his lips. Pressing his mouth to the back of her hand, he murmured, "Then take that time. Should you decide you want . . . complications . . . I am not hard to find."

* * *

Absolutely fucking wrong, Syn decided three days later.

Xan *was* hard to find. Very hard.

Should you decide you want . . . complications . . . I am not hard to find.

Syn wasn't entirely convinced she wanted complications, but she did want him, and it was growing painfully clear if she didn't decide to risk those complications, she could say farewell to a decent night's sleep. For quite some time.

Not to mention that the chill was worse now. It was like those few brief touches had done something to her inside, and now she felt the cold in a way she could no longer ignore. Although it was still smoldering hot outside, she was so chilled, she'd taken to wearing long-sleeved tunics under her cavinir vest. She couldn't handle it much longer.

She needed to feel that heat of his. She needed him.

She'd made that decision yesterday. But when she went to look for him after they'd finished training and their various job rotations in the evening, he had been nowhere to be found. He was serving on weapons detail, learning more about the tech-based weapons and repairing them. She'd already been assured that at some point, he'd likely be helping design the weapons. It didn't surprise her. She knew he had a canny mind. But she wouldn't address this while one or both of them were supposed to be on duty.

Now she couldn't find him outside of the job, and it was only irritating her even more.

In the past three days, ever since she'd lost her mind completely and kissed him, she had been having a very hard time not thinking about him. While she worked, she could make herself focus. It wasn't hard to do . . . Matters like sex and need did manage to pale next to matters of life and death. Both of them definitely had jobs that dealt with matters of life and death.

So while she was busy, she could deal with the cold that ached inside her, and she could deal with how acutely empty and lonely she was. Until he touched her, she hadn't realized just how cold, just how lonely, she was.

But when she was no longer focusing on her job, in the nights when she lay awake and longing for him, he dominated her thoughts.

She needed him to touch her, to chase that cold loneliness away.

Gritting her teeth together, she strode out of the common area where she'd hoped to find him. It was time for the evening meal—why in the hell wasn't he eating in one of the common areas provided for just that?

Frustrated, and getting more so with every passing second, she followed one of the lesser-used paths and tried to figure out just where she might find him.

And what do you intend to do when you find him? she asked herself silently.

Her belly clenched. "Is jumping him an option?" she mumbled.

"Jump who?"

Even the sound of his voice, low and smooth and deep, made her shiver. The icy knot inside dissolved, just like that. Just that easy. Just that simple. He hadn't even touched her.

Just the sound of his voice thawed the ice.

But the aching loneliness lingered.

Stopping in her tracks, she turned her head, following the sound of that voice. He was in the very outer edges of the camp, sitting with his back to the camp's inner wall, with a knife in his hand. He stared at her, and the heat in that one dark, dark eye was unmistakable.

Her knees threatened to give out.

Swallowing, she started toward him, placing one foot in front of the other and trying to decide if she should really do this.

Then he leaned his head back at the camp's inner wall and a faint smile curled his lips as he stared at her. "You are utterly beautiful," he murmured.

Oh, hell yes, she wanted to do this. And not because of the compliment, although it did further serve to weaken her knees. But because when he looked at her, with that intent, probing stare, it made her feel as though all he saw was her. It made her see nothing but him.

It made her forget she was anything, anybody, other than just herself. She was simply Syn . . . and it made her want him that much more.

Sinking to her knees beside him, she eyed the knife in his hand. He was carving something. She eyed it curiously and glanced up at him. "What are you doing?"

He brandished the bit of wood in his hand. "Trying to occupy my mind so I do not come looking for you. And you . . . I do not need to ask what you are doing. You are avoiding giving me an answer." A grin curled his lips and he added, "Again."

"Avoiding giving you what answer?"

He lowered his lashes, staring at her from under them, and murmured, "You said something about jumping someone. I asked who. You haven't answered."

"You already know the answer," she said slowly. She flexed her hands and then rested them on her thighs. Hopefully, it would keep her from reaching for him. Hopefully.

"So you want to jump me . . . What exactly does that mean? Have I not been the good little soldier boy for you, Captain?" As he asked, something glittered in his eyes.

Something wicked. Something hot.

Her heart started to race. "You know, I've never once felt the need to strip naked when somebody calls me Captain. Until now."

"Are you feeling the need to strip naked?"

She bit her lip. Curled her fingers into the thick, durable fabric of her pants, gripping it desperately. "Yes."

"Does this mean you want complications?"

"I want you," she said, forcing the words out of her tight throat. "I can't think about the complications because all I can think about is you. So I guess that means the complications don't matter as much as I thought they might."

***

She looked so nervous, Xan realized. He understood it completely. From the moment he'd glimpsed her wandering aimlessly in his direction, he had been dealing with all sorts of nerves and anxiety. What if she was coming to tell him that she had made her decision and she wanted him to stay away from her? What if she told him the opposite?

But now, as she stared at him, need and nerves warring in her cat's eyes, he decided none of it mattered. Not right now. She wanted him. That was what counted.

Doubts tried to rise inside him, but he shoved them away. Nothing mattered in just this moment. Save her.

Slowly, he slid his blade into its sheath and tucked the small bit of wood he'd been working into one of his pockets. Then he pushed himself to his feet and held out a hand.

She placed her hand in his and stood. As small as it was, there was strength in that touch. Her palm was calloused, her nails brutally short and naked. Lifting it, he pressed his lips to the inside of her wrist. Her pulse leaped at his touch and he felt his own do the same in response.

She twined their fingers and tugged on his hand. "Come with me."

"Where?" he asked, lifting a brow. Not that it mattered. He'd follow her to the ends of the earth if she asked. That realization should have shaken him to the core, and it might—later, when thoughts of touching her, when thoughts of mounting her sleek, slender body weren't threatening to drive him mad.

A feline smile curled her lips and she murmured, "Being one of the people in charge does on occasion have its benefits. I've got my own dormer. As charming as your bunkmates may be, I'd rather not have an audience, and I'm also not much for having sex in the grass. Leads to bug bites."

"I love the way you think."

He followed along beside her and tried not to rush. He had no idea where her dormer was; otherwise he might have scooped her up and run the entire way. Need pounded inside him, pulsed in tandem with his heart and echoed through every fiber of his being. How in the hell was it possible for a walk to take so long, and how was it possible that he grew more aroused with every step?

Every fucking step.

He grew more aware of her, noticing how her chest

rose and fell as she breathed, noticing how gracefully she moved. The way the faint light glimmered on her hair, dancing off the blue-black highlights.

What in the hell was taking so long? Did she have a dormer built on the other side of the mountains?

Then they reached it, and abruptly, he realized he didn't know if he was ready to do this. Didn't know if he should. Somehow, he knew deep inside that touching her would be unlike touching any other woman in his life. She was unlike any other woman, with her strength and her confidence, yet there was vulnerability that was also part of who she was.

Once he touched her, once he had her, could he let her go?

Did he even have a chance of keeping her? Deep inside, the answer to that question made itself known. No. He could never keep her . . . and he shouldn't even think of touching her.

Then she tipped her head back and smiled at him and all those questions faded away into nothingness. It didn't matter. In that moment, only *she* mattered. She led him inside, and the moment the door shut behind them, he grabbed her and whirled around, pressing her up against the door.

Over the past three days, he'd envisioned how he might handle it if she came to him like this. A slow, careful seduction—that had been his ultimate plan.

But plans often fell apart, and his had just crumbled. Slanting his mouth against hers, he fisted a hand in her short, dark hair and tugged, arching her head back to deepen his kiss. She opened for him even as she worked her hands between them and went to work on the utility vest he wore over his tunic. It went flying across the room and then she reached for his belt. Heavy with his knife and other weapons, he should have handled it with more care but he had no patience, no finesse, as he nudged her hands away and all but ripped the blasted thing off. It fell to their feet and the rest of their clothes followed.

When he had her naked, he forced himself to take a step

back. He needed to see her, needed to at least once see that slender, strong body completely. His chest heaved as he gritted out, "Bed."

"No." A smile curled her lips and she reached for him. "Here." She drew him back to her and reached up, twining her arms around his neck.

Xan groaned and cupped her hips in his hands, lifting her. He braced her back against the door and leaned into her. She wrapped her legs around his hips, an action that opened the soft, sleek folds of her sex.

He nestled his cock against her heat and rocked against her. They both shuddered. The scent of her rose to tease him. Hot. Musky. Perfect. Ripe . . . Gritting his teeth, he lifted his head and muttered, "Are you . . . Should we . . ."

He couldn't think—

Her lashes drifted low. "I won't get pregnant if that's your concern. Unless there are other concerns . . . ?"

"No." No. Other than that, the only concern he had was just having her. Reaching down, he wrapped his hand around the base of his cock, steadied himself and pressed against her. Then he stilled and shifted his grip, catching her knees over his elbows and lifting her, opening her.

"I want to see," he muttered. "Want to watch as I take you."

She whimpered, a hungry female sound that did bad, bad things to his already shaky control. Then she lowered her gaze, and they both watched as he entered her. She was wet and slick, but tight, flowering open around him as he forged deeper.

By the time he had buried his throbbing dick completely inside her, they were both sweating, both shaking, and Syn was making hot, sexy little sounds deep in her throat. Hunger rode him, hard and demanding, but he resisted the urge. This wasn't going to last long enough as it was, and he needed it to. Needed more than a fast, quick fuck that ended nearly as soon as it began.

So instead, he withdrew as slowly as he'd entered. And he continued to watch her. Her mound had tight, black curls. Her clit, swollen and red, peeked out from the folds of her sex. And where she stretched so tight around him, her flesh glistened with dew. His mouth watered, and if he had any semblance of control, he might have pulled away and gone to his knees before her, pressed his mouth just there to see if she tasted as hot, as sweet, as he thought she would.

She whimpered and strained against him, arching in his arms. "More," she demanded. She didn't wait for him to respond, though, sliding her hand down, her slender, pale fingers seeking out the stiff bud of her clit and stroking it. The sight of her touching herself had his balls drawing tight against him and he swore as hot and cold chills raced down his spine. He let go of her legs, groaned as she wrapped them around his hips. Then he caught her wrists and pinned them over her head—if he had to keep watching as she stroked herself, this would end far too soon. Excitement flashed in her eyes even as she jerked against his hold.

He smiled at her and leaned against her, carefully tightening his hold and watching as her lashes fluttered over her eyes. "You like that, Captain?" he teased, dipping his head to rub his mouth against hers.

She responded by biting his lower lip, then sucking it into her mouth. "More," she demanded. Then she clenched around him, using her internal muscles to milk his cock.

Buried inside those snug folds, his cock jerked demandingly. Growling against her mouth, he said, "Stop—I want this to last."

"Why? We have all night."

"Excellent point." Then he let go of his fragile hold on control, riding her soft, sleek body and listening as she sobbed out his name.

Her breasts flattened against his chest, her nipples tight, hard points. The muscles in her belly spasmed and clenched and she trembled. All over, she trembled, shuddering as though she might fly apart in his arms.

He wanted that—just that—wanted to watch her fly

apart and be there to hold on to as she came back to her-self. Back to him. Letting go of her wrists, he worked his arms around her body and caught her, held her close.

His climax rushed up on him, demanding—insistent. He felt her tightening, felt the tension mount in her body just as he felt himself falling, faltering. Her arms wrapped around his neck, held him, just as securely as he held her.

"Come for me," he rasped. *Please . . . before I fall alone.*

But it wasn't necessary because even as he whispered the words, she was flying apart in his arms, a low, hungry moan falling from her lips. It rolled through them both, echoing, emptying them both.

Everything else fell away and for him, there was just her.

Just her.

***

Hours later, they lay on her narrow bunk. He had his back to the wall, with her wedged between his body and the edge of the bunk. It shouldn't have been comfortable. Not one bit, but Syn was rather certain she hadn't ever felt this satisfied, this right, in quite some time. Possibly ever.

She felt warm. She felt safe. She felt wanted. And that ache in her heart didn't even feel like a memory.

She rarely lingered with a lover once the moment passed. All she had ever looked for was a brief escape, some pleasure, some release of the tension that built inside so many of them who had spent most of their lives on the front line of a war. After that was done, the silence that often built was uncomfortable.

This, though, this felt right.

Utterly right. In a way, it terrified her. Not enough, though. Because she couldn't imagine pulling away from him just then.

He nuzzled her hair and murmured, "It is getting late."

She glanced at her windows. Her internal clock told

her what time it was without her bothering to check her timepiece. "It's already late, past midnight."

"Should I leave?"

She covered the arm resting around her waist and hugged him. "Hell no."

She could almost hear the smile in his voice. Then he nudged her backside with his cock. Even as tired as she was, even after making love with him three times, she felt the heat once more begin to build. "If we stay like this all night, will either of us sleep?"

"Yes." She glanced over at him and smiled. "We should sleep now . . . so we can wake up and do it again before the day starts. Morning sex is always a great way to wake up the brain."

He chuckled and nudged her again. "My brain is already rather awake."

But then he tugged her a bit closer and Syn snuggled back until not even a whisper of air could come between them.

As she drifted off to sleep, she decided she'd been right.

No matter what, this night had been worth the complication.

FOUR

It was too much to hope for that his gear hadn't been discovered.

In under a minute, Dais knew that his belongings had been found and confiscated—Morne, Kalen and the lot, no doubt.

A snarl twisted his face, but he didn't linger. He couldn't risk it. If they'd found his gear, it was likely somebody might still be watching the area. He'd done a search around the immediate perimeter, but lingering was foolish.

He had other caches hidden within the forest and nearby mountains. He'd find one of them, gather his weapons, and take a bit of time to lay down some sort of plan. A good, solid plan—he needed one that had a half a chance of working, and he didn't even know if it was possible.

If he didn't turn Lee over to the Warlords, they'd kill him.

If he was caught by the rebels, he'd *wish* they'd kill him. Ishtan's people rarely resorted to torture, but somehow he doubted Kalen would be satisfied with a quick death when it came to Dais.

Losing himself in the trees, he began following an old, rarely used trail. It was a familiar one. It would lead him to an area well outside the range of the army's patrol, a place where he could rest easy for a night, possibly two, while he developed some sort of plan.

"You can do this," he muttered. He'd managed the impossible for decades—evading discovery for his people as he fed information to the enemy. Surely he could get his hands on one mouthy witch.

***

There were times when Laithe envied the people of Ishtan. His kind eschewed any form of technology—the War-lords and their people had risen above such pursuits. They were above the petty wars that often tore worlds apart, the power struggles, the inability to care for every last soul in their world.

The perfection of magic—that was the ultimate desire of his people.

But Laithe possessed only Gate magic, and it was use-less here. He was neither sorcerer nor seer—he had no ability to see the future, no skills to rival the talents of the Ishtanian witches. All he could do was manipulate Gate energies, and since the Gate's collapse, that gift had been rendered useless. He could feel the energies, but he could no longer touch them.

However, he could have a great deal of use for some of the technology used by those in Ishtan. The ability to send word back to his fellow Warlords in just moments—ah, yes, that would be useful.

He kept to the shadows, silent and still, as he watched the traitor. Warlords had superior eyesight and he used it now to keep watch on the man from a safe distance. This far away, Dais couldn't hear him, couldn't smell or see him.

But Laithe wasn't such a fool to think the man was unaware of him. Despite his arrogance, the traitor hadn't survived all these years by being careless. Laithe knew of the man. Until yesterday, he hadn't known the man's name, but many of those who'd served the High Lord's family knew that Raichar Taise had a spy within the rebel army.

Now the spy promised to deliver a *female* Warlord. One who had the blood of both Warlord and witch in her veins and could harness both powers. It was unthinkable, so far outside the realm of possibility that Laithe couldn't understand it.

He wouldn't put it past Dais to lie, but there had been nothing of a lie in the man's eyes, in his scent, in his voice, when he'd made his claims. Either he truly believed in the existence of some female Warlord . . . or she truly did exist.

The daughter of Raichar Taise.

Laithe idly stroked his fingers against the stone he wore around his neck. It barely pulsed at his touch. Once, it had held enough power that it had throbbed, all but vibrated under his touch.

That power was useless now, scattered. Lost in the chaos of this world's tumultuous energy.

Witches could touch that power. Harness it. Calm it.

A female Warlord with a witch's power . . .

The possibilities.

***

There were times when being in charge had its benefits; Syn had no doubt about that. Having a private dormer was absolutely one of them, and one she'd put to her advantage over the past few weeks.

But there were also times when it absolutely sucked.

She pored over the reports, even though the numbers threatened to make her eyes cross. Her dormer also served as her makeshift office, and she'd been stuck inside it for half the day, trying to figure out if she had enough men to safely send a unit back east for supplies.

They needed more material—for weapons, for clothing. Food would be nice—they had plenty to eat, but what she wouldn't give for some sort of variety. She was tired of the basic rations they existed on. It was supplemented to some extent by the food found by the hunting and gathering parties, but Syn had no idea how long much longer that would last.

True to their goals, the rebel army had focused on culling the demon population, and as expected, the demons had ramped up their aggressiveness. It was getting too dangerous outside the walls—how much longer before Kalen decided they couldn't afford to send people outside the gates for food when they had rations inside the camp?

If they couldn't drive the demons back . . . "No. We'll find a way," she muttered, forcing her thoughts away from that path. They'd figure something out. They had to.

"Focus on the supply report, girl." She pinched the bridge of her nose, ignoring the grumble of her belly. She'd missed the noontime meal, and none of the food she had in her dormer appealed. She'd almost sell her eyeteeth for a cache of sweets she had to share with no one. Greedy—she was absolutely greedy.

There was a knock at the door, and she absently called out, "Come in."

The door opened, and she didn't even have to look up to know who it was. Heat rippled through her and she looked up, found herself lost in the dark depths of Xan's gaze.

Although her heart stuttered under that look, she forced a smile and kept her voice calm as she said, "Yes?"

A smile curled his lips and he lifted a small bit of paper. "A message from Gunner." Gunner—a nickname for the old bastard that ran the weapons detail.

She grimaced and muttered, "It had better not be bad news. I'm already trying to figure a way to get the supplies he needs."

He crossed the floor and handed it to her, eying the reports spread across the scarred surface of the narrow table she used for a desk. "You haven't been outside much today. Is there a problem?"

She shrugged and said, "Not a new one. Just trying to cover everything we need to cover." She winced and reached up, rubbing at the back of her neck. Numbers made her eyes cross.

Xan lifted a hand and nudged hers away, covering her neck with his rough, broad palm. He did nothing else until she leaned back into his touch. Then he lifted his other hand and started to massage her shoulders and neck. Syn groaned and her head fell forward.

"You are tense."

She slitted her eyes and glared at the paperwork that lay there. All but mocking her. "I hate numbers. I have to juggle the numbers. The problem, though, is that they aren't really *numbers*. They are people. Have to figure out a way to send a unit back east without losing any of them—which means a larger contingent has to go, but we can't send so many it leaves us spread too thin here."

"Why couldn't those who escorted the convoy bring back the supplies?" he asked.

"Several reasons. One, none of those who escorted the last convoy out are coming back. They are done. And second, the supplies we need come from a different area, and heaven forbid those fools back east make our lives easier by having the stuff we need shipped to a drop-off point." She closed her eyes and muttered, "Bastards. They've just gone and forgotten about us."

"People often take those they need for granted."

There was another knock at the door. Syn didn't know why, but when he went to pull away, she reached up and caught his wrist, holding him in place as she called out, "Come in."

The door opened to reveal none other than Vena.

Xan resumed his massage of her shoulders without speaking as Syn arched a brow and met the other woman's eyes. If she wasn't mistaken, there was no small amount of irritation in the other woman's gaze.

"Did you need something?"

Vena smirked. "Damn, no wonder you like being the supreme bitch in charge if you get on-the-job sex bonuses." A malicious glint lit her eyes. "Does the commander have any idea how you spend your days?"

I knew this bitch was going to be trouble, Syn thought. But she didn't let any of her irritation show. She gave Vena a nonchalant smile. "The commander hasn't felt a need to check up on me for quite a while, Saurell. However, if you feel the need to enlighten him over the fact that you saw Xan in my office, feel free."

"You think he won't *care*?"

Now it was Syn's turn to smirk. "No. I *know* he won't care."

"You are telling me he won't care that you're spending your days screwing around when we're *supposed* to be dealing with the demon threat—that's why you sent so many back east, because we don't have the manpower to protect everybody and still deal with the demons. Yet you can spend your time getting fucked?"

"Oh, come off it, Vena." Syn gently nudged Xan's hands from her shoulders and shoved back from her desk, facing the other woman. "I've known the commander for most of my life—we've fought together; we've bled together. He's left me in charge of the camp more than once when he's had to leave or when he's out of commission due to an injury. He trusts me, and he knows I let nothing interfere with getting my job done. And, more to the point, he's also aware that getting fucked involves some level of nudity and a lot more contact than what you see in front of you."

Vena shot a venomous look at Xan and then leveled it on Syn. "You honestly expect me to believe you two aren't screwing each other?"

"Oh, we are." A smug grin curled her lips. She couldn't help it. "We just aren't doing it right now—we'll save it for when we're officially off duty, which is still a good three hours away."

Vena went white, then red. "You walk around like you're so damned important, expect everybody to follow *your* rules, but you don't have to. Some leader you are."

Syn shook her head. "I do follow my own rules—has anybody ever once told you that you're not allowed a personal life once you join this army?"

"Military leaders don't fuck those serving under them."

"If that military leader has spent her *entire* adult life fighting a war, she does—especially if she wants to maintain some semblance of sanity." Syn shook her head and said, "But that's not even the issue. You're not mad because I'm involved with somebody serving under me—you're mad because I'm involved with the one you set your sights on—and he's not interested."

Vena's pretty face twisted into an ugly scowl, and her blue eyes glinted with rage. Jealousy didn't set well on the woman. Not at all. "Of course he's not going to be interested in *me*. I can't help his position here, now can I?"

Through it all, Xan had remained silent, his arms folded over his chest, his expression unreadable. Now, though, he moved, pacing forward to stand in front of Vena. "My interest in the captain has nothing to do with my position in this army. Just like my lack of interest in you has no bearing on your lack of influence. My apologies if you cannot see that."

Vena flinched. Muscles in her cheeks worked as she clenched her jaw. "Some fucking military unit this is—no wonder the outside world doesn't view this place with any modicum of respect, if this is how you run things."

She stormed out of the dormer, her shoulders rigid, hands clenched into fists at her side. "And I was so certain she and I could be friends," Syn said, a sardonic smile twitching at her lips.

"I'm sorry."

Syn glanced at him and shrugged. "I'm not. Something tells me that Vena comes from a background where the world seemed to revolve around her. She might be a talented fighter, but she's not soldier material—this isn't the place for her."

A strange look crossed over his face.

Syn scowled at him. "What?"

"It is nothing," he said, shaking his head.

"The look on your face tells me it's something. What is it?"

A muscle pulsed in his cheek and he stared at her, that one-eyed gaze heavy with intensity. "As skilled a warrior as you are, as fine a leader as you are, part of me still feels this isn't the place for you or any woman."

Her belly knotted. His mind-set wasn't an unusual one—it really wasn't. It was one she'd faced time and again throughout her life, and one she'd have to face in the future. Repeatedly.

Pulling her gaze away from him, she seated herself back at her desk and made herself stare at the reports. Even though her mind wasn't on them, even though her attention wasn't on them. Quietly, she said, "Without some of the women who have served in the various rebellions through-out the world, we would have lost long ago, Xan. Anqar would have won—we would have become little more than a breeding house. Before the Gates fell, our best weapon was to disrupt the energy flow when we felt them flicker— something only a witch can do. By disrupting the energy flow, we could shut the Gate down. Sometimes. We didn't always get there in time. But every time we forced a Gate to close, we averted a raid. We averted the loss of life. We averted losing our sisters, our mothers, our daughters, aunts and friends to a life of slavery."

She lifted her eyes and looked at him. "You don't like seeing a woman in battle. Some part of me does under-stand that—in full, straight-out battle, we aren't as strong, and unless we're the better fighter, it's easy to lose. But without *us*, the rebellion as you know it wouldn't exist."

She looked back at the spread of paperwork and made herself focus on the words, the names, the numbers. "Now, if you don't mind, I need to put my female mind to work and see if I can't find a way to get the supplies we need without losing too many lives."

She didn't look up until she knew he was gone.

His point of view wasn't necessarily wrong—she knew that. More often than not, the first to fall in direct conflict with the enemies were the women. Physically, they were weaker. More than one attack on various units throughout the years had been focused on the units that had a higher number of females—the gifted ones, always the gifted ones. Eventually, they operated by only sending out witches like Syn, Lee, or Elina who had a knack for the combative magics. Magics like calling fire, the ability for a witch to focus her gift and use it to disrupt the very ground the enemy stood upon without endangering her unit, or the other offensive magics.

Those who had gifts closer to healing or sensing disruptions were kept protected within the base camp.

He wasn't exactly wrong. Women were more vulnerable, and those with gifts were more highly prized by the enemy, and that only increased their vulnerability.

But they were also necessary.

Syn's gift had saved the lives of her men countless times.

Elina's gift had saved the lives of the entire camp.

And Lee's dual gifts—her father's Warlord blood and her mother's witch gift—had been the key in shutting the last remaining Gate.

They were needed here. And they had a right to be here.

Of course, she'd feel more useful in the long run if she could use her damned gift again. She felt naked without it. Naked, cold . . . and in that moment, rather lonely.

* * *

With his back to a tree, Morne Ramire sat in the night-dark forest and stared at absolutely nothing.

The camp . . . so close. What in the hell had he been thinking, letting himself come this close? If he had realized how it would affect him, he would have stayed far, far away. At least he wanted to think so.

He shouldn't be here. No, he should be out there, continuing his search for that bastard, Dais Bogler. Find him, choke the life out of him.

But he found himself here instead. So close to the camp, he could smell the smoke from the fires. So close, he could all but feel the life there. Feel the presence of those he'd called friend.

And *her* . . . But no, he wasn't going to let himself think of her.

They still searched for him. It had been close a couple of times. Once, Bron had walked by, close enough that if Morne had breathed too loudly, the other man likely would have heard him.

As careful as he was, as cautious, if he lingered too long this close to the base camp, then he was going to be found.

He didn't want to be found.

Not yet. Probably never.

They'd want him to come back. He already knew. Though he hadn't stepped foot back into the camp since the day he'd walked away, he knew he was missed. Kalen, damn the bastard, hadn't allowed Morne's absence to sway him.

Rarely a week went by when the commander didn't send out a psychic probe and force Morne into talking.

It was odd, realizing that he was missed. Almost as odd as discovering he missed his friends.

Lousy thing, sometimes, having friends.

Yet it was also a lovely thing. If he would just get up off his ass, he could sleep within the camp tonight. It was a tempting thought. A bed. A few familiar faces . . . one in particular.

Her.

He closed his eyes and brought her face to mind.

Elina. She dominated his thoughts, crept up on him in the darkness, haunted his dreams. That is, she haunted what few dreams he had that weren't centered around what he had done, the dreams that weren't designed to kill him with the guilt.

He welcomed the guilt. Needed it. Deserved it. Deserved to see every last horrifying moment of his brother's death. Needed it to remind him how abysmally he'd failed the one person who had always stood by him.

He deserved to suffer.

But the dreams of Elina weren't suffering. Unless suffering could be a sweet, hot torture. Unless it could include dreams where he put that body of hers beneath him—long and lean, but still so damned female.

Of course, after the dreams, he woke with an empty ache in his heart, one he couldn't hope to ease.

Perhaps he did deserve them. They served as a taunting reminder that he would never have her.

Living in hiding in the forest, barely scraping by, and dreaming of a winsome witch he could never have. Fitting.

"How the mighty have fallen," he murmured to himself. The ache in his chest threatened to destroy him.

Once, he'd been only days from the preparations that would have taken him from Sirvani to Warlord. As a high-ranking Sirvani, a respected healer, his control had been absolute, control over his powers, control over those under his command, control over his emotions.

Now his powers had splintered, the thought of being around others was intolerable and he couldn't control his emotions any easier than he could control the weather. He could do nothing to ease the ache in his heart, or the guilt, or the need, or the pain.

The pain . . . it welled up inside him. Finally, something eclipsed his rather pathetic desire to see the witch once more. From the pain came memories, memories swarming up out of the night and pulling him down.

His brother's face, so like his own. Arnon. Grief and acceptance in his eyes as he told Morne to kill him.

Do it, Morne.

If I do, she'll likely die. So will you.

I have been dead inside for years, my brother. You know this. It will come as a blessing.

Brother . . . I can't.

You have to. Do it now before her power wanes.

You made an oath to me, brother. You will keep it.

He pulled away from the memories, but not in time.

Deep inside his soul, he relived the very moment he felt his brother, his twin, die. Like something inside Morne had been wrenched out with brute force, and the emptiness inside him filled with ice.

For days, he had hovered on the brink of madness. It wasn't until he accidentally came across Dais's back trail that he realized he wasn't ready to give in to madness or grief yet. Not while he still had revenge.

It gave him a goal. A focus. As long as he remained focused, he no longer teetered on the very edge, but now, he was once more just a breath away from oblivion. It took everything he had to simply exist and not . . . shatter. Explode. Fade away. Maybe even all three. Although the fading away bit seemed to be happening anyway. He wished it would hurry the hell up. Tonight would be ideal.

An end to the pain, the guilt, to needs he would never be able to ease.

You didn't use to be so quick to give up, my brother. The voice, a ghostly whisper, echoed in the back of his mind. He hung his head, rubbing at the back of his neck. If he believed in ghosts, he might have believed Arnon was haunting him.

He didn't believe in ghosts, though. This was naught but a trick of his mind, possibly one more sign of how close he was to madness. Yet another sign was the fact that he responded.

Lips quirking up in a smile, Morne said, "If I was quick to give up, I would have done so years before now."

No, you wouldn't. Not while you had a purpose. A goal. It's easy for you to fight when you have a reason, and you always had that. But your fight isn't done. This isn't over.

But it was.

Lelia lived. Arnon was gone.

Morne had kept his promise.

What was left to him? He could give in to madness now and do it with a clear conscience.

No. He made himself climb to his feet, made himself walk away from the camp. His job wasn't done—not yet. Not until he'd satisfied a blood debt. Dais's blood would run red and then, maybe then, Morne would give in to the lure of madness.

He walked away from the warmth of the camp. Tonight, tomorrow night, and the next, the next . . . he'd warm himself with thoughts of vengeance and dreams of a woman he'd never have.

* * *

She dreamed of him.

Sleeping alone on a narrow cot in the peace and quiet of Granna's old dormer, Elina Corsairs dreamed of a man with pale blond hair, the face of an angel and eyes deeper than midnight.

Sighing in her sleep, she rolled over and snuggled deeper into her blankets. In her dream, she wasn't on the cot, she wasn't alone and it wasn't a pile of blankets keeping her warm.

It was the strong arms of a man who had never touched her, had never really shown any interest in touching her.

She was on the beach, in one of the grand lodges that no longer existed—except in ruins—in a bed that was as wide as a lake and soft as angel wings. Next to her lay Morne. He was leaner, and although it was difficult to imagine, he was harder. Harsher.

Sadder, too. But then, sadness had always been a part of him, although he was unlikely to ever admit it. Although it was unlikely anybody else had noticed.

His dark blue eyes were shadowed and he stared up at her as she lay over him. He toyed with her hair, twining it around his long fingers. "You've stayed away a long time," she murmured.

"A few weeks. A few weeks is not very long. You've been gone much longer. Years."

"I had to." Elina shrugged and grabbed the sheet, tucking it under her arms. "I couldn't raise my kids in the middle of a war zone. They'd already lost their father . . . I couldn't risk anything happening to me. Besides, this was the last place I wanted my daughter."

"Of course." He reached up and brushed a lock of hair behind her ear. "She is safer in the East. *You* would be safer in the East."

Heat shimmered through her body as he cupped her cheek in his hand and stroked his thumb along her lower lip. "Do you plan to remain in New Angeles? Or will you go back east?"

"I don't know. Part of me wants to leave here." Elina sighed and lay back down. Resting her head against his chest, she snuggled close. "I had something that resembled normal back there, although it was getting bad when I left. Now that the Gate is pretty much out of commission, I guess things will settle back down there. I could start teaching again. Have a life."

"But?"

She grimaced. "I'm needed here. The magic . . . we have to do something about it."

"Like what?" He stroked a finger down her cheek and said, "It is in chaos—we've both seen it. A maelstrom. You cannot fight that kind of chaos."

"No. I can't." She pinched the bridge of her nose and muttered, "There has to be something."

He laid a hand on her belly. "Perhaps you are trying too hard. Perhaps you need to simply adjust to the changes before you try to fix them."

She opened her eyes and peered up at him.

"Adjust to the changes." Pursing her lips, she frowned thoughtfully.

Morne nuzzled her neck. "Whatever it is you are thinking about, think some other time. You're needed here right now," he whispered, raking his teeth along her smooth, golden skin. "Right here."

"Yes." She pressed a kiss to his lips and whimpered as he reached between them, pulling away the sheets. Now nothing separated them as he aligned his body with hers.

Elina groaned as he nipped her lip. His hands, those beautiful hands, stroked over her body. He left fiery trails of heat in the wake of each touch, filled a need even as he stoked another. "Make love to me," she whispered, pressing her lips to his shoulder.

"As you wish."

* * *

Elina came awake with a ragged gasp, her body hovering on the razor's edge of climax. Gritting her teeth, she rolled over and buried her face in the piss-poor excuse for a pillow. Her slender, willowy body acclimated to the ridiculous cot that served as a bed even as it protested. She could still feel the luxurious softness of the bed from her dreams . . . still feel the warmth of Morne's hands on her body.

Still feel him as he moved over her, in her.

"Why in the hell did I have to wake up *now*?"

She had half a mind to finish the job herself, but it was a waste of time. She'd been sleeping alone for too long, and after a while, it got to the point where nothing was going to ease the ache inside, save for a man.

That posed a problem, though.

Elina didn't want just any man.

She wanted Morne.

Craved him.

That wasn't anything she couldn't handle. She was used to wanting what she couldn't have. Craving what she'd never know. She'd dreamed about Morne for years, and she had always dealt with it. It had been easy, because there were always miles separating them or a war to be fought.

It wasn't so easy now, though, and she wasn't entirely sure what that meant. It might not mean anything . . . or it might mean everything.

She closed her eyes as a sigh shuddered out of her. *Don't think about him.*

But thinking about him was getting to be a lot like breathing—something she couldn't control.

Just don't think about him . . .

But even as she tried to push those thoughts out, she found herself remembering what he'd said.

Adjust to the changes.
Adjust.
Don't try to fix the changes.
Adjust.

FIVE

"So what do you think?"

"I think we'll be lucky if we don't end up getting our asses handed to us on a platter," Syn said grimly. "And in my case, I'll be lucky if I get through with my sanity intact."

"If I thought it was that big a danger to you, Syn, I wouldn't ask." Elina tucked her hair behind her ear and gave Syn an easy smile. "I can handle the magic for short periods of time, certainly long enough to see if this is even possible. If it doesn't feel like it would work, or if it's too dangerous, I don't pull you in."

"I want to think it can work," Lee said softly. She glanced from Elina to Syn, a self-deprecating smile on her face. "But I'm hardly the ideal person to ask. All the magical theory classes you two took, I never had them. Do you think it sounds plausible?"

The question was directed at Syn. With a grimace, she flicked her hair out of her eyes. The thick black strands were getting too long. She needed to find some trimmers and take care of the mess. It was getting in the way again.

Meeting Lee's gaze, she shrugged and said, "I think it sounds like madness, and that it goes against every law of magic I've been taught. But I also think it's got a real chance of working, so take that however you want."

"Man, you sound just like this voice I keep hearing over and over in my head," Lee muttered. "This is crazy . . . *and* crazy as it sounds, I think it could work."

The stronger witches could anchor themselves but tired quickly.

The weaker witches couldn't anchor themselves at all.

But together . . .

Together, they could create a web and anchor one another, let the power flow through them, and the power would boost that anchor. They didn't know if it would work, though. And only one way to find out. Try it and see what happened.

Syn, Elina and Lee were breaking a direct order from their commander, but they didn't see any way around it.

In theory, each of them was too important in their own way for the penalty to be that bad. Kalen couldn't risk sending any of them back east, and for a diehard soldier, that was the worst possible outcome.

Elina was the instigator and she'd be the one taking the biggest risk. Not just because it had been her idea, but because she had more power than Syn, and she had more experience than Lee.

Lee's gift was amazing but she was still too new to it.

It was something that confused the hell out of Syn, because she had memories of Lee serving in battle with her dating back to when she wasn't much more than a child. But until a few short months ago, Lee had never truly *been* in their world.

Just her shade. A physical manifestation of her being, and the memories of those times, had been hidden deep inside her subconscious. She'd managed to merge her split selves—her shade who fought as a warrior to the woman she knew she was. Once she'd crossed over into their world, she'd had to relearn her magic from the ground up.

She'd uncovered most of her memories, but some of them were still less than clear.

But there were other reasons Lee couldn't take the biggest risk. Other reasons that would keep her on the sidelines for this experiment. At least until they had an idea of what could happen.

Lee's father had been a Warlord, one of the bastards from Anqar, the realm on the other side of the Gates. He'd claimed her mother, one of the witches in Ishtan, after she'd been kidnapped in a raid, and he'd fathered Lee.

Lee's mixed heritage combined the two powerful magics, the Warlord's abilities to manipulate Gate energies, and her mother's witch gift. That dual heritage would make her one very, very fine prize to any Warlord that still lurked in the forests at the base of the Roinan Mountains.

If she used her magic, they might sense her. None of them could take that chance, especially not until they knew if the magic was reliable again. If the energy that fueled their magic couldn't be used, they couldn't even use it to defend themselves in an attack.

Syn stood by the side, her arms crossed over her chest. She hoped neither of her friends could feel how terrified, how anxious, she was.

For close to two months, she hadn't been able to use her magic.

There were times when she felt like she was dying inside. She wasn't as strong as Lee or Elina, but the magic was a part of her. It was second nature for her to use it to probe an area before making a decision on whether to advance or fall back. It was instinct to use the magic as a defensive tactic when they were battling the demons that prowled the forest. It was natural to use it in an offensive when they corned a cache of the fucking monsters.

It was part of her, and ever since the Gate's collapse, she hadn't been able to so much as make sparks flare.

She'd tried. Once.

It had been a week after the Gate's collapse, and she'd been in the forest with her team. Bron's team wasn't far away and they'd been closing in on a small contingent of Raviners. Things went bad and then from bad to worse quicker than she could blink. And if she'd had less effective troops with her, she'd be dead. Or at least insane.

She'd reached for the magic and it had responded by reaching back and trying to suck her in. One of her seconds had struck her in the head with the butt of his pulsar, knocking her unconscious and breaking her connection to the energy. It had been instinct, and a gamble, but it had worked.

Now she couldn't reach for the earth's energy, and she needed it to use her magic. But she couldn't do it . . . and Syn feared it was slowly killing her.

The Gate's collapse had set the earth's energies into a state of chaos. It was no longer safe to merge with the energy, and until they could reach it safely, they couldn't rely on their magic.

That was a huge part of the reason Syn had felt so chilled over the past weeks. She was hemorrhaging inside. But it wasn't blood she was losing. It felt like part of her. Not being able to use her magic made her feel like she wasn't the woman who'd helped lead the rebel army to their somewhat questionable victory.

She felt like she had lost herself.

***

Laithe's people might lack the technology of the Ishtanians, but they didn't lack simple resources. He'd been trailing after Dais for five days when he first sensed the presence of one of the others.

He recognized the crackle of power, the restrained energy, and knew who it was even before the Sirvani approached him that afternoon.

"Lord Reil wishes an update," Corom said after bowing to Laithe.

Laithe sheathed the knife he'd held and dropped down out of the tree. "It took you long enough to find me. By the time you return to him, it's likely the situation will change."

Corom simply inclined his head. "Has the traitor made any attempt to secure this reputed female Warlord?"

"No. He hasn't fled, however. Nor has he tried to establish contact with the rebels. If it was sabotage he was about, he would either have fled or already contacted one of his previous acquaintances."

Corom was quiet for a moment and then he asked, a trace of curiosity in his voice, "Have you seen this woman?"

"No." Laithe shook his head. They might be close to the rebel camp, but the rebels rarely left it, unless it was in large numbers. This was their territory and Laithe wasn't about to place himself in their path just to see if this woman existed.

Corom's face showed no change, but there was a flash in his eyes—disappointment. "If this man has lied to us, if she doesn't exist, what chance have we of returning home?"

It wasn't entirely an unexpected question—Laithe had pondered it more than once himself. Could they return home? How?

"I do not know, Corom," he said finally, turning his head to the west, staring in the direction where the Gate had once stood.

"I've heard talk."

Laithe cocked a brow. They'd all heard talk, but he must admit, he was surprised that Corom would discuss this with him—this particular Sirvani was known for being reticent, talking only when relaying orders or addressing his superiors. "What sort of talk?"

"Some of the other Warlords, including Reil, seem to think they could coax enough energy from the witches to forcibly open a small Gate—the Gate's pathways still exist, but we haven't the ability to open the portal."

"Coax the energy," Laithe murmured, smiling despite himself. "There will be no *coaxing*. It would be taken, and taken in a way that would likely kill them."

Corom's lids flickered.

"If we're to be talking of something that would kill whatever woman we laid our hands on, let's not be soft and dance around the issue. We're talking of returning to our world—and the price is the life of another."

"Does that bother you?" Corom asked.

Judging by the look in his eyes, it bothered the Sirvani.

"I will do whatever I must do." Laithe shrugged. "Although, it may not even be an issue. The only place we could possibly hope to lift a Gate is here. That's where the strongest pathways lie and the Gate's destruction threw everything into chaos. Trying to force a small Gate up in a new, untried locale would be foolish, and likely a death sentence for all involved. Besides, I've yet to feel the power of a single witch. It's been more than a month, and not a one of us have sensed any witch magic at all."

"Most of them have already fled this region," Corom said, nodding. "And we haven't a chance in the frozen hell of kidnapping one from another place and forcing her here. We'd be caught and killed."

"Yes." It was practically a nonissue.

Corom opened his mouth to speak—no sound came out, though. Both of them heard it. The faint whisper of sound, a foot gliding over the uneven earth. Farther away, a murmured voice. This far away, neither of them could hear the words . . . just the voice itself.

But it was a female voice.

A female voice outside the camp.

And through the trees, they could both see a familiar head as he cut back and forth through the forest.

Dais.

On somebody's trail.

* * *

They followed him.

Not one now, but two.

Dais smiled in hot satisfaction.

Good. Damn good. It was her. He hadn't seen her, but in his gut, he knew Lee had slipped outside the camp.

He caressed his pulsar lovingly, thought about jacking up the power so that when he shot her, it would boil her blood from the inside out—she'd die horribly, painfully. Relatively quickly, but he could handle quick, as long as it was painful.

Instead, he set it to stun. Stun the bitch, and then have her trussed up and tied like a beast when the Warlords showed up.

They'd have to make haste. And he knew she probably wasn't alone. But there were only a few people with her. The path they followed wasn't one that allowed for large parties—at least not quietly. It was a scout's trail, narrow and uneven, winding up into the foothills.

If it was one of the larger units, they'd take an alternate route.

So Lee would be mostly unguarded. A few soldiers at best. Drawing his secondary weapon, he tossed his primary to his left hand. He'd take down whoever accompanied her and then stun Lee. It would be over in a matter of seconds. Damn good thing, because he knew Kalen—the bastard wouldn't have allowed Lee to leave alone, which meant she'd slipped away.

Once that was discovered—no, there wouldn't be much time.

Dais crept ever closer, listening to his back trail, well aware the Warlords were closing the distance.

Finally, he was close enough to pick up a clear, distinct voice and he paused, swore.

Of all the fucking individuals to be with the bitch— Elina, her aunt, and Laisyn Caar.

Syn.

She'd been one of Dais's subordinates right up until the last few conflicts—now she was a captain. She'd taken *his* place.

Damn the bitch.

Damn all three of them.

Witches. They were mounted on some of the battle-trained baerns, and those beasts were viciously protective.

He could take down ungifted soldiers in a heartbeat, but a witch . . . no. He had to proceed with more caution.

Especially with Syn. Her gift wasn't as strong as Elina's or Lee's, and because of that, she trained harder, pushed harder—it resulted in a connection to the earth that outmatched all others—maybe even Eira, the old goat, may her soul rot in hell.

He wouldn't be able to catch Syn by surprise. She was more a soldier than the other two combined, and all she'd need was one glimpse of him and she'd flame his ass.

No. If he had any chance of taking them out, it would have to be a united attack, him and the two Warlords. He'd have to share the glory in claiming this prize . . .

However—

A smile curled his lips.

The Warlords would love to get their hands on a female with Warlord blood, there was no doubt of that.

With the possibility of two more witches . . . and the loss of these three women would cripple Kalen.

Yes.

This could work.

Most definitely, it could work.

He would wait, let the Warlords know he was aware of their presence.

As they made their way to him, he put together a plan.

Lee *and* the two other witches. He knew Warlords—they wouldn't be able to resist getting their hands on a couple of skilled witches. The fact that all three women were young and attractive simply sweetened the pot. They would very much appreciate the boon he was about to offer them.

Finally.

After all these weeks of chaos, uncertainty and strife, he found himself once more in a position of bargaining.

* * *

Laithe listened, his arms crossed over his chest, his mind spinning furiously as Dais outlined his plan.

"You're certain it is her—this Warlord female—the

daughter of Raichar Taise?" he demanded, his voice flat, his blood starting to pump hot in his veins.

Part of him didn't want to believe it possible.

The other part of him burned—he sensed something. Something strange. Something new. Power, the likes of which he hadn't felt before. It was cloaked—if it came from the woman, it wasn't because she'd used her power. She was hiding too well, and if he had been any farther away, he never would have sensed it.

The feel of it had his skin itching.

Dais gave him a small, pleased smile and nodded. "Of course I'm certain it is her," he said, giving him a deferential nod even though the look in his eyes clearly said, *Yes, I'm certain, you arrogant bastard.*

Laithe flicked his wrist. Dais's eyes widened at the sight of the blade in his hands. Laithe tossed it in the air, making the silver weapon dance, all without taking his eyes from the man before him. "You realize this is your life you are bargaining with, do you not?"

***

Lee leaned forward, peering at Elina as she sat on the ground. Syn recognized the vials, powders, potions, but she imagined it looked very strange to the other woman. Lee was still struggling to connect with some of her memories, so it was entirely likely she'd forgotten much of her earlier magic training.

"What is she doing?" Lee asked, frowning.

"Making a barrier." Syn rubbed her hands down her arms and glanced around. They were outside the base camp's walls, inside an old shelter that was seldom used. It was built for the scouts to use if the weather took a bad turn on them, but not many chose to stay here. They'd rather make a run for the base camp than linger outside.

Syn wouldn't mind making a run for it, either.

She felt far too exposed out here. Far too vulnerable.

But they couldn't do this in the camp.

"We have to keep this contained when we try, thus the barrier."

Lee planted her hands on her hips, her brow furrowed. "I've never seen anybody use *sand* to build a barrier."

"Yes, you have." Syn's lips twitched as she glanced at her friend. "*You* have done it. I remember. It was in your earlier training."

She shrugged restlessly and started to pace the squeaky wooden floorboards. "We're going back to the basics here. Not taking any chances. Which means a lot of mental preparation, focus and whatnot. She's constructing the barrier the same way she'd teach a first-year trainee. Basics."

"How does using sand construct a barrier for *magic*?" Lee muttered.

Without looking away from her work, Elina called out, "We could try using it to plug our ears so we don't hear the nattering of my niece, for starters."

Lee made a face at Elina's back and moved away, joining Syn in her pacing.

Syn smiled. Keeping her voice low, she said, "It's not the *sand*—it's the mental process. She's grounding herself—we use the physical images to help strengthen our connection."

"Considering how the energy has gone all kablooey, I don't think strengthening that connection is all that wise an idea." Lee leaned back against the wall and absently toyed with the end of her long blond braid. She watched her aunt with concern in her eyes.

Syn wasn't entirely sure what *kablooey* meant, but she got the general idea. "The energy is still there. It recognizes us, somehow. It has to—otherwise, it wouldn't have tried to grab me. We still need that connection if we're to do the magic."

"You really think this will work?"

Syn glanced at Lee and whispered, "I hope so."

They fell silent, watching with anxiety and hope as Elina finished her preparations. When she was done, she heaved out a sigh and then said, "Okay, Syn. You're up."

Syn crossed the floor and settled on her knees across from Elina. "I hope you haven't lost your mind," she said grimly.

"And I hope you haven't lost yours by trusting me not to have lost mine," Elina replied. She held out a hand.

Syn laid her palm in Elina's and then glanced at Lee. She flashed the other woman a grin and said, "Wish us luck, Lee."

Then they closed their eyes. Syn stretched out her senses, watching Elina. Elina fought through the chaos of energy like a swimmer struggling to navigate a flooded, raging river. She was strong, though, strong and steady, and didn't falter as she made her connection.

It echoed—a minute click—through both Elina and Syn. Then Elina whispered, "Now."

Syn reached.

Reached . . . and fell. The energy grabbed her, sucked her in, and she struggled, desperate to surface before it was too late.

Then Elina was there. Within the earth's energy, Elina was there and she reached for Syn. The second their gifts united, the chaos eased and Syn realized she wasn't drowning in the chaos.

It worked—

They opened their eyes and stared at each other, both of them grinning. Elina had tears in her ears, and there was a knot in Syn's throat that robbed her of speech.

"It's working, isn't it?"

As one, they looked at Lee. "It's working," Elina said quietly. She pulled her hand from Syn's and held it out. Fire sparked. From nothing, it grew until it danced in the air above Elina's palm.

Syn could feel the heat. Her fingers itched and she lifted her own hand, stared at it nervously. Did she dare?

There was a crash.

Syn looked up as Lothen came barreling in. She saw him lifting his pulsar, but she wasn't quick enough. He caught Elina across the side of her head, knocking her

unconscious. The connection between them shattered
and Syn's magic recoiled back inside herself. She felt the
greedy, desperate draw of the earth but somehow, she
fought free.

Surging to her feet, she sidestepped as Lo turned to her.
"You touch me with that thing and I'll ram it up your ass,
soldier," she said, her voice icy.

"At ease, Lo." Kalen came inside and the look on his
face was one of pure fury.

Syn glanced at Lee and then at Elina.

Hell. They'd known there would be trouble if they were
caught. She could handle it.

Then she caught sight of another face—Xan.

He stood at Kalen's back and the look on his face froze
Syn to the core.

* * *

Torn, Morne lingered in the trees just a few hundred yards
from the small shelter. He'd been trailing Dais when he'd
sensed the presence of the women.

It had made him pause, and now he couldn't seem to
pull himself away. Even from this distance, he could make
out familiar faces. It made his heart hurt in a way he hadn't
expected.

Bleeding sands, he missed his friends.

Not just Elina—all of them.

Most of all, though, Elina. She was there. He could all
but feel her.

Did he join up with the rebels? Somebody had been
hurt—he didn't know who, but what if it was her?

Or Lee. Syn.

Thoughts of the others paled in comparison to his need
to see Elina, though.

Only one thing kept him from following.

Dais.

The bastard was close, and he wasn't alone.

Morne trailed his fingers along the bark of a nearby tree
and focused, reaching out with his gift. Dais was no longer

operating on his own. He had two other men with him, and that wasn't good.

Dais, the fucking traitor, wouldn't come this close to camp without good reason. There was only one likely reason—Lee.

Morne closed his eyes and focused on the sounds of the rebels. They were heading back to camp. Distantly, he thought he could hear Kalen's voice, Lee, Lo. He could sense the emotions, vaguely, even through his shields. Anger. Irritation. Fury. Fear. But the emotions were all focused—no adrenaline-fueled terror, nothing of desperation, no emotional cries for help.

They could do without him.

Which was damn good, because as much as he wished to be with them, he suspected he needed to be elsewhere.

Dais.

As he started through the trees, he brushed his hands down the trunk of a tree and whispered, "I'm getting close, dead man."

The earth would carry his message.

Moments later, he sensed the fear.

Dais had heard him.

***

Dais swore as he heard something through the trees.

No time. They'd wasted too much time.

He needed to pull back. It was the only wise decision.

Grimly, he caught the Warlord's gaze and bowed his head. "My lord, it would appear there will be others joining up with the female. I feel it would be wisest to pull back before our presence is discovered. We can try again when we have a better chance of success."

"Success?" The Warlord arched a brow.

The Sirvani stood off to the side, waiting in silence. He had his hands clasped at his back and he stared at Dais with unreadable eyes.

"Yes, my lord. We have time. We will get her. But we cannot risk—"

A wind whispered through the trees.

A chill raced down Dais's spine as he heard the words. Eerie, disembodied . . . *I'm getting close, dead man . . .*

It echoed around them, and the wind faded away, the air still, undisturbed. Dais swallowed and laid a hand on his pulsar, instinctively backing away even though he had no idea where the threat lay.

Morne—

One look at the Warlord's face told him they had heard the warning as well. The Sirvani looked at the Warlord and then back at Dais, but remained silent. The Warlord didn't flicker a lash as he said, "It would appear somebody else had plans for you as well, spy."

Dais opened his mouth to respond.

But the words died on his tongue. He had good eyes—he was a damn fine marksman, a damn fine tracker. Still, all he could see was a flash of silver as the knife hurtled through the air.

Then the Sirvani lay on the ground, a blade protruding from his chest.

Dais jerked up his pulsar, aimed it at Laithe. Confused, he stared at the Warlord. Yet again, that safe position he'd been scrambling for was crumbling away under his feet. So close . . .

"Stay back or you're dead," he warned the Warlord. "Hell, you're dead, anyway. Your lord will gut you."

"No." Laithe smiled, a humorless twist of his lips. "He'll kill you, assuming you live long enough. After all, you're the one who just killed one of his servants."

Dais's eyes widened, comprehension dawning. "Double-crossed. Was this the plan all along? Set me up . . . No, that doesn't make sense."

Despite the fact that Dais had a pulsar leveled square between the man's eyes, Laithe continued to watch him with that amused little half smirk on his face. With the weight of the weapon pulling at his arm, Dais fought to keep his hand steady. It was hard, though. Death breathed down on him from multiple directions—both Morne and Kalen would gut him where he stood.

The Warlord before him looked as though he had similar inclinations.

"I'd hardly kill a comrade in arms just to set you up, scum." Laithe cocked his head. In just that moment, something about the man seemed very, very familiar. "Unlike you, I actually understand the concept of loyalty."

"If you're so fucking loyal, then why did you kill him?"

"Because it was the only way to protect the one thing I'd die to protect . . . Nothing is thicker than blood. Nothing." Muscles in the Warlord's body tensed.

It was like watching one of the ed-discs about natural predators when he was back in school, in what seemed like another life.

Although the Warlord still appeared unarmed, Dais had the worst feeling he was utterly outmatched . . . and death was only seconds away.

"Desist."

The order came in a familiar voice—the tone bored, as though Dais's death meant less than nothing.

He knew otherwise. As Morne stepped out of the trees, Dais stared at the man. He used his thumb to adjust the pulsar's settings—one setting would kill the person who took the blast. There was another setting, though, that had a broader scope—strong enough to disable several people with one blast. He might have a chance against one Warlord, but not against two.

Hell, he doubted he had a chance against Morne, period.

If there was anything Morne wanted more than to see Dais's blood spill red on the forest floor, it was to do it himself.

Laithe barely glanced at Morne. They looked as though they'd been cast from the same mold—was this the family the Warlord had spoken of? The reason he'd killed one of his own men?

But they looked at each other with no sign of recognition. "Desist?" the Warlord demanded in the native tongue of Anqar.

Dais followed the conversation haltingly—they spoke too quickly for him to translate as easily as he'd like. Still, he understood enough.

"Yes."

The Warlord's lips curled in a smile as he studied Morne, from the top of his shorn hair to the very battered soles of his boots. Morne looked more like a rebel soldier than an Anqarian Warlord. "On what grounds?"

"That of a blood feud." Morne looked at Dais and said coolly, "My brother is dead because of this man. I call a Warlord's vengeance on him."

The words froze Dais to the core. They had an effect on the other Warlord as well. With a displeased look on his face, the Warlord stared at Dais for a long moment before shifting his attention to Morne. "Warlord's vengeance. What is your line?"

"I'm a blood-son of the Ramire line. My brother—my *twin*—lies dead, and this man had a hand in it. His blood is mine."

"Ramire . . . The only Ramire I know was a Sirvani. He served under Raichar Taise." Laithe's eyes narrowed. "I question the truth of your words."

Morne cocked a brow. "Would I lie? To what purpose? I want the man dead, and it's my right to end his sorry existence."

Dais saw his death in Morne's eyes. The other Warlord looked less than pleased as he slanted a glance at Dais. "Then end it now."

"You can't trust this man," Dais said, shifting his pulsar to Morne. "He's fought in the rebel army for nearly three decades."

"And this coming from the man who betrayed his own people for money?" Laithe asked, that amused smile returning to his face. "I don't care if he's served tea and sweets to the devil himself—we both want you dead. I do not need to trust him to watch him send you straight to hell."

Dais wasn't a foolish man. He knew things had just gone bad in a major way, and he knew he didn't have a saint's chance of surviving this. Still, he wasn't going to stand still for his death sentence, either. Curling his lip in a sneer, he said, "I may well be going to hell, but I'm not interested in a straight trip."

He fired, and without waiting to see the results, he dove into the woods.

* * *

Morne gritted his teeth as the lingering effects of the pulsar's blast tore through him. It burned like hell—agony that tore at every last nerve ending, fire that buzzed through his veins. Digging one hand into the earth, he rode through the pain and emerged from its grip in time to see the other Warlord still fighting it.

Taking a full-body blast was less than pleasant, to put it mildly. He knew he'd be feeling the lingering numbness and alternating chills for the next several hours. He could do nothing to ease his own pain, though. Healers rarely had much effect on their own injuries—he could direct energy to serious wounds, enough to slow bleeding and possibly save his life, but that would do nothing for this sort of pain.

He could function through it, though, and it was the only reason he still lived. Dais wouldn't have forgotten that detail. Sucking in a deep breath of air, he shoved himself upright and managed to draw his own pulsar within seconds of hitting the ground. Clutching his weapon in a sweaty grip, he managed to shove himself upright, keeping watch.

Dais—what if he lingered? If ever he would have a chance to kill Morne, it was now.

With his free hand, he dug his fingers deep into the earth and asked, *Where . . . ?*

The answer came to him in a rush of images, and as

his mind processed them, Morne sagged, torn between relief and disgust. Dais was fleeing. He wasn't a foolish man—he hadn't lingered to see if his gamble had paid off. Morne had dealt with enough blasts that he could focus past the pain, at least enough to disable the treacherous bastard. If he had lingered, Morne would have found a way to kill him.

The fuck had eluded him once again.

The pain cleared enough for him to shove himself to his feet. Giving the other man a disgusted glare, he braced his weight against the nearest tree trunk. Still holding his pulsar, he waited.

SIX

"You could have gotten all three of you killed."

Syn stood before the commander with her hands linked behind her back, staring straight ahead.

In the back of her mind, there was a mix of relief, guilt and exhilaration.

But she didn't let any of it show on her face.

Kalen was beyond pissed, and if he had any idea that part of her was figuratively rubbing her hands together in glee, he'd only rail at her for that much longer.

As it was, she'd been confined to quarters for the remainder of the day while he seethed. It wasn't just her, though. Lee was also confined to her quarters, and Elina was confined to a bunk in the medicon. She was under observation—the medics didn't seem overly worried, but head injuries were chancy things.

Of course, if they hadn't been interrupted the way they had, Elina wouldn't have gotten hurt at all. Lo had found them first and he'd panicked, striking Elina the same way he'd struck Syn back when she'd almost gotten lost in the energy maelstrom. Knocking her out had cut the connection.

Of course, there hadn't been any danger for Elina, and Lo had given her a concussion for no good reason. But somehow Syn doubted Kalen would appreciate her pointing that out.

"Do you have anything to say for yourself?"

Cutting her gaze to meet his, Syn inclined her head. "Nothing that you would care to hear, Commander."

It had been a long time since the two of them acted like commander and subordinate . They were comrades— friends. He was Lee's husband. He was one of Syn's dearest friends.

But right now, he couldn't act like the frightened friend, a horrified husband. She could understand that. And even though it was hard to keep quiet, she understood his fear, and she understood his position.

She also understood her own, and she couldn't very well expect those under her to treat her with respect if she couldn't show it to the commander.

So she kept the words behind her teeth. Or rather, that was her intention.

He glared at her, his silver eyes flashing. "I want an answer, Captain Caar. I don't give a bloody damn if it's one I want to hear or not. What do you have to say for yourself?"

Syn looked away.

Kalen rarely yelled. He didn't need to. His anger was like a cold blade, and now was no different. He advanced on Syn and she stiffened her spine, met his gaze dead-on. "Captain?"

"You want to know what I have to say for myself?" Syn narrowed her eyes at him. Spinning away from him, she stalked over to the window and stared outside. The paths were empty and the common area she could see was empty. Considering how early in the evening it was, that was rather unusual.

Except it made perfect sense.

Every last soul in the camp probably knew what happened and every last one of them knew that Kalen wasn't going to react well. They were keeping out of the line of fire.

Smart.

Looking at Kalen over her shoulder, she said flatly, "It worked."

Kalen slashed through the air with his hand and growled, "I don't *care* if it worked. I said *no magic*. That means *no fucking magic*."

"That's easy for you to say," Syn responded. "You're not the one who has to live with it. You're not the one who is dying inside from that damned edict."

His silvery eyes turned to winter ice and he shook his head. "Don't, Captain. You know damn well I understand how hard—"

"No." She turned back to face him and crossed her arms over her chest, fighting the chill that had lived inside her ever since the day she realized she couldn't use her magic anymore. "You don't understand, Kalen, because it doesn't touch *you*. You don't understand, because you've never been where we are, and even though I know you sympathize, it's not enough. Sympathy doesn't equate understanding, Kalen."

A muscle jerked in his jaw. "I know this is hard."

"Hard?" Syn shoved a hand through her hair. With a humorless laugh, she said, "You know this is *hard*? Kalen, this isn't hard—this is like dying inside."

"You think I haven't thought about that?" he snarled. He spun away from her and stalked over to stand by the narrow table she used as her desk. He braced his hands on it, stood with his head bent low. "You think I can't see how hollow this leaves you? How hollow it leaves my *wife*? Lee is suffering the same way you are—dying inside, bit by bit. That woman is my heart—my soul. When she suffers, I suffer. So don't *tell* me that I don't know how hard it is. I damn well do."

"No." Syn shook her head.

He straightened and turned to look at her.

"You don't know, Kalen. You *can't*. Both of us have gifts, but psychics grow into theirs. It comes with puberty, or it comes with trauma. You grow into it—like you learn how to use a pulsar." She gestured to the weapon at his side. He was never without it, at least not that she'd seen. She imagined it was close to his hand even as he slept. "And I know that weapon feels like part of you. But magic *is* part of the witches. It's who we are. It's *what* we are. And now we're not supposed to use it, and it leaves us feeling splintered inside. Broken. I'm not *me* right now, Kalen. The only time I feel complete . . ."

She cut her words off, blushing even as she realized she'd been about to share some very, very personal details with her very pissed-off commander.

"Kalen, I am sorry that we went behind your back," she said, once more turning to stare out the window. "But whether you like it or not, we had no choice. We cannot just wait and see. We can't. It leaves us weaker, it leaves us confused and it leaves us uncertain. And bit by bit, it's killing us. We're hemorrhaging, Kalen. We're dying inside."

She slid a look at him over her shoulder and asked, "Is that really what you want from those you've chosen to help lead this army? Is that really what you want for your wife?"

"Damn it, Syn." He gave her a disgusted look. "That's a low blow, and you well know it."

She did. But it was also a calculated one. Whatever it took to win, that was how Syn fought. That was how she survived. Fairness didn't play into it.

"You can't expect us to wait forever. It's been two months, Kalen. We had to do something—we can't stay crippled like this. And it's damned cruel, damned unfair for you to expect us to, just at your say-so."

The commander's mouth twisted in a snarl and he stalked toward the door. "You broke orders, Syn. Don't expect me to forget that."

"I'm sure you won't. But if you would be a little more

reasonable when it came to discussing the problems your witches have, it wouldn't have been necessary."

He stopped and looked over his shoulder at her. "I've tried discussing these problems, Syn. Remember?"

"I remember the one meeting we've had since you passed the no-magic rule, Kalen. All you did was shut it down without evening listening to what any of us had to say. That's *not* discussing the problems. It's ignoring them."

She looked away from him and continued to stare out the window.

Even when the door slammed shut behind him, hard enough that the windows rattled, she continued to stare outside at absolutely nothing.

***

"Should have known better."

Morne cocked a brow as the Warlord forced an eyelid open and managed to glare at him.

"Regarding . . . ?"

"You. Dressed like a damned primitive, yet you speak my tongue. Shouldn't have trusted you." He forced his other eye open and then shoved over onto his back, staring up at Morne.

His face was impassive, but Morne imagined he knew what the man was doing. Taking mental stock—could he fight? Could he run? Could he even *move*? Not well, at least not for a few more minutes. Leveling his pulsar at the man's prone figure, he said, "The effects will linger for some time. If I see you so much as twitch a finger, I finish the job."

"Then finish it already, but if you do, you'll get to know a Warlord's vengeance, personally."

"I understand it personally already. I lay claim to nothing not rightfully mine." Morne's mouth quirked in a smile. He studied the Warlord. Despite himself, he was curious. "What is your line?"

Surprise flickered in the man's eyes. "My line?"

His voice was impassive, but Morne sensed his surprise. "I'm a blood-son of the Ramire line, from the High City." In Anqar, blood-sons were the direct patriarchal descendants. If the matriarchal ancestors were higher in their society, one would claim a pledge-son.

In Anqar, power was all.

Whichever familial line yielded the most power was the familial line a Warlord lay claim to.

"So you claimed. But again, I question the truth of your words, *Ramire*." The Warlord's eyes narrowed. He scrutinized Morne from the top of his head to his feet and then shook his head. "There is only one blood-son to the Ramire line in the High City and he cannot lay claim to a Warlord's vengeance. You're not him, either."

"No." Morne's mouth twisted as grief ripped through him. "He was my brother. He lies dead because of that bastard's treachery—his blood is mine."

One thing that killed curiosity damn fast—grief. As it settled inside him, Morne found himself unconcerned with this man's line. He holstered his pulsar and shoved away from the tree. His body reacted well enough. Minor weakness remained but it was nothing that would slow him much. "Dais Bogler is mine, and I'll gut the Warlord who dares interfere."

He caught sight of the dead Sirvani lying nearby and he paused. "Best bury that body or get gone before the sun falls. The predators in these woods care little if there is a pulse or not. To them, meat is meat."

* * *

Laithe damned the weakness that plagued him as he shuffled through the forest. He hadn't the energy to make the journey back to where his kinsman waited, even if he did have the inclination.

His priorities had taken a drastic shift in recent hours, and he'd yet to decide on a course of action.

He had no doubt he could convince Lord Reil and the others that Corom had died at Dais's hands. It would even be sweet irony—Reil would unleash his men and Dais would be lucky to live another night.

But Laithe was loath to take that route. He'd taken what he knew was a necessary action, and he didn't relish lying about it. Nor did he relish the idea of dying for that necessary action.

More, he didn't want the Warlords this close to the base camp.

His priorities and all.

Sagging against the trunk of a tree, he stared through the trees. He couldn't see the rebel camp from here, nor could he hear them. But they were close.

And if they were close, that meant she was close.

***

Syn was still staring at absolutely nothing when the door opened sometime later.

There was no knock.

Xan came inside and shut the door behind him without saying a word.

She didn't need to look to know it was him. It was him, and he was pissed. Just as pissed off as Kalen had been, it seemed.

No. More.

His anger came off of him in huge, pulsating waves, battering against her shields.

It had been like that back in the old shelter just hours ago when the three witches had been interrupted, and she didn't think he'd cooled down one bit.

Syn sighed and rested her brow against the glass. It was warm from the sun and seemed almost painfully hot against her chilled flesh. "Didn't you hear the word, Xan? I'm under restrictions for the rest of the day and if the commander knows you're in here, he'll have your ass."

"The commander can go fuck himself," Xan said, his voice harsh. And directly behind her.

She managed to keep from jumping. Barely. Damn, he moved quiet. It went deeper than silence—it was like he didn't even disrupt the airflow when he moved. Forcing her face to settle into a blank mask, she turned and faced him. "I've already had the commander launch into me, Xan. I don't need this from you."

She went to go around him and he shot an arm out, blocking her.

"You little fool," he muttered. "Do you have any idea how dangerous that was?"

"Yes. I know full well how dangerous it was. But we needed to do it."

"You needed to do something that could have alerted every last Warlord within a day's travel of your presence. You needed to do that." Xan's dark, one-eyed stare glowed hot with fury.

Belatedly, she realized it was the first time she'd ever seen him angry.

Actually, it was one of the few times she'd ever seen any emotion from him period. Unless he was inside her. When he was touching her, he let that guard down. But any other time . . .

Folding her arms over her chest, she glared back at him. "We were *careful*, Xan. I would like to point out that I'm not a beginner—I'm well experienced with magic and how to use it. We created a barrier, and except one brief flash, nobody would have felt it, unless we had a Warlord in the very same room with us."

"You think they need to be that close to feel it?" Xan said, his voice thick with mockery. "They are like sharks, Syn. They can scent it from miles away, barriers or not."

She gave him a withering look and said, "And who made you the expert on witches and Warlords?" Shoving past him, she stomped away from him and flopped down on her bunk. "Elina's a damn good witch, Xan. One of the best our world has ever seen and probably the strongest alive, except for possibly Lee. She knows what she is doing."

"And if a Warlord had caught the scent? Made a move?"

"We would have handled it."

"You sound so utterly certain," Xan muttered. "So convinced. You arrogant fool."

Kicking her legs over the edge of her bunk, she came to her feet and gave him a venomous look. "Listen, my friend, I'm getting tired of having men question my intelligence when they don't have any stake in this matter."

Xan watched her, his gaze narrow and hard. "You think I have no stake in this issue?" With two long strides, he closed the distance between them and reached out, snagging the front of her tunic, hauling her against him. "You're wrong in that, *Captain*. I very much have a stake in this issue."

His mouth came crushing down on hers, swallowing any protest she might have made. She went to pull back and his hand cupped the back of her head, holding her still. He didn't hurt her, but his grip was relentless.

His tongue stole between her lips, and she stopped thinking about pulling away.

Abruptly, her own anger, all of the adrenaline trapped inside her, exploded—changed. She met his kiss with one of her own and as he fought to remove her clothes, she did the same to his. He took her to the floor, wedging his hips between her thighs.

"Open for me," he growled as he tore his mouth from hers. He reached down between them, steadying his cock. His gaze bored into hers as she wrapped her legs around his hips.

The thick, round head of his cock pressed snug against her entrance, and Syn groaned, arching against him, desperate, dying. But he didn't move to enter her. He held still, steady, and watched her face.

"I smell your skin on me while I lie in bed at night," he whispered, his voice deep and dark, his breath drifting warm across her mouth as he spoke. "I feel you next to me even when you are not there. I need only to think of you, and I want you. I need only to think of you, and I have to see you, have to be with you. For this . . . and more. And yet you tell me I have no stake in your safety?"

Syn stared up at him, shuddering, shaking with need. "Xan, please . . ."

He brushed against her, settling his cock, thick and smooth, against the cleft between her thighs. "Please . . . please you. I will please you. But is this all it is?" He caught her lower lip between his teeth and bit her gently. Then he started to rock against her, using his body to caress and tease hers. "Is this all we have, Syn? This and nothing more?"

"What . . . ?" She squinted up at him, trying to think beyond the need, trying to focus on his words and not just his body. The words connected inside her head and then, as she started to get his meaning, they began to ricochet through her.

How in the hell did she answer him? And how could she do it *now*?

She was confused, terrified and even a little pissed off. Or rather, some of her was. There was another part that wasn't confused or terrified. It was a part of her that she kept hidden. It was her heart that guided her as she laid a hand against his cheek, feeling the rough scratch of his stubble against her palm and the warmth of his skin.

His warmth . . . he'd managed to warm her all the way through from almost the very second she laid eyes on him.

It went deeper than skin. It went deeper than sex. It went deeper than need. If she didn't fully understand it right then, that was fine.

In her heart—that part of her that wasn't terrified—she knew. There was more than this.

Stroking her thumb across his mouth, Syn lifted her head and kissed him, soft and slow. Keeping her mouth pressed to his, she whispered, "This isn't all . . . nowhere close."

"I have a stake in this—I have *you*." He sank inside her, deeper, deeper, until they were as close as a man and woman could possibly be. "You are becoming everything, Syn . . . Don't take that away from me."

Tears stung her eyes. Reaching up, she cupped the back of his head and pulled his face down until she could kiss him. "I won't. Make love to me, Xan. Please . . . I need it. I need *you*."

"Need." A smile tugged at his lips, and he bussed his mouth against hers. "Let me show you *need* . . ."

He did just that. He showed her need. He showed her pleasure. He showed her all the things she'd been missing in her life . . . until him.

And, she suspected, here was the beginning of love.

Their bodies rocked together, his rough hands tender and teasing on her body, his mouth wicked and warm, chasing away the cold, chasing away the loneliness. Hot and greedy, she clutched at his shoulders, sank her teeth into his lower lip when he would have drawn it out.

"Now," she demanded.

He caught her wrists and pinned them overhead. "Shhhh." He caught her protest with his mouth and shifted higher on her body. Now, as he sank inside her, he pressed against her clit, riding her, pushing her closer, closer.

Need cramped her belly. Jerking against his wrists, she arched her hips, clenched down around him. As he stole her breath away with his kiss, she tried to show him with her body what she needed, but just when she was almost there, almost flying, he shifted his angle, slowed his pace.

Snarling in frustration, she tore her mouth away and glared at him.

Xan chuckled and nipped her lip. "See how mindless you make me? You drive me to insanity every day, until I think of nothing but you."

Working his arms under her, he clasped her head in his hands and held her still as he crushed his mouth to hers. At the same time, he slammed into her. Hard, deep, driving past her gripping muscles, deeper and deeper, until he'd buried his length inside her.

Syn cried out against his lips and came, hard, fast and brutal. She felt him tense, heard him swear, as he started to come. Her own climax lingered, and with every stroke of his hands, every thrust of his hips, it set off a new series of aftershocks that wracked her body, trapping her in a storm of pleasure.

When it ended, he collapsed against her and rolled to his side, cradling her close.

"You're everything," he whispered against her hair. "Everything, Syn. Do not take that from me."

* * *

With his lips peeled back from his teeth, Kalen Brenner unleashed every last bit of his energy on the solid, weighted bag hanging from a crossbeam. Alone inside one of the interior training rooms, he gave in to the fury and pounded until his knuckles were red and swollen, until his arms hurt with every move, and still he pounded away.

"Damned women," he muttered under his breath. Worried for all three, but terrified for his wife.

What in the hell had they been thinking?

The brush on his mind was unwelcome.

At nearly any other time, he would have welcomed the familiar presence inside his head, but not now.

Without bothering to tamp down his skill, he projected his thoughts. *"Leave me the hell alone, Morne,"* he ordered. He knew from experience that it was likely his mental voice came through loud enough to have Morne's teeth aching, but he didn't give a damn.

"You seem perturbed."

Morne's voice came through as clearly as if he'd been standing in the same room with Kalen. Through no skill of Morne's, though. The man might be a damned wicked fighter and a fine healer, but his psychic skill was nonexistent.

Kalen's, however, was nearly off the charts. He was a skilled receiver and projector—all he needed was to tune in somebody's mind and he could speak to them. And in the case of others, all they had to do was focus their thoughts to him and he could likely pick them up.

It came in handy during battle.

Not so much in that moment.

"I. Am. Not. Perturbed," he spat out. He pushed the thoughts out with his mind as well as his throat, knowing Morne would hear him.

He wasn't *perturbed*. He was fucking pissed. Pissed. Terrified. Frustrated.

But perturbed? It made him sound like a little mite a bit put off because he'd missed a feeding.

He was mad enough to spit nails, and he'd be damned if he knew what to do about it.

Morne's presence lingered and Kalen spun away from the bag and started to pace. "Elina used her fucking magic. She had Syn and Lee in on it with her—they were *right there*. If anything had gone wrong, a Warlord could have grabbed all three of them."

There was only the briefest pause; then Morne responded, *"Are you so certain of that? None of them are fools, and none of them are weak. I cannot think of three women more capable of handling any Warlord fool enough to confront them."*

"And what about five Warlords fool enough to confront them? Ten?"

"Do you think they wouldn't have called for help if they needed it? Do you think Elina would have hesitated to have the earth swallow them whole? The energy's in chaos, but she can still use her magic, Kalen. If it came down to their safety, she'd use it without blinking an eye."

"Their safety was in danger *because* she used it," Kalen growled.

What in the hell had she been thinking?

"Tell me, my friend, how long is she to not use it? Lelia? Laisyn? Would you have them live their entire lives only half alive, with some part of their hearts withered and dead . . . useless? Is that what you want for your wife, Kalen?"

Snarling, Kalen grabbed a towel from a hook and the wall and used it to sop up the sweat from his face and neck. "You know damn well it isn't what I want. I just want things to be safer before they do something that could put them in danger."

*"They are witches, first and foremost, Kalen. Without
their magic, you leave them crippled. Crippled, they are in
danger, whether you want to see it or not."*

"They aren't crippled." Kalen hurled the towel against
the wall and turned, staring out one of the narrow windows
into the night. He braced fisted hands on either side of the
window and fought against the urge to start pounding on
something again. The muscles in his arms jumped, jerked
and twisted as he battled not to let the rage take over.

It was well past midnight. It had been hours since he'd
seen Lee. Although they'd woken in each other's arms,
lately there had been a distance between them, one that left
him sick at heart.

That distance had been between them for some time,
and every day, it grew. Now it had become a chasm, one he
didn't know how to bridge.

*"They are, Kalen. If you could no longer speak into
the minds of your men, if you could no longer hear their
thoughts with ease, wouldn't that leave you crippled,
Kalen? If I could no longer heal with a touch and Lee
was grievously injured, wouldn't you view me as such?
Gifted people rely on those gifts, like the sighted rely on
their sight, and the hearing rely on their hearing. Take
those gifts away, and you leave them all but blinded, all
but deafened."*

In the silence of the training room, Kalen's sigh echoed.
Leaning forward, he braced his arms on the wall and muttered, "Damn you, Morne."

* * *

She dreamed.

In her dreams, Syn was home—that place she still
thought of when she thought of *home*. Where her mother
and father had raised her and her brother, where her mother
had been taken from her.

It was that night, all over again.

But this time, she wasn't a child to be tucked away

into a hiding place, wrapped snug in her older brother's arms. Back then, he'd covered her mouth with his hand and begged her, pleaded for her to be quiet.

But when their mother started to scream, both of them had sobbed.

The Sirvani had been too far away to hear them, or perhaps their mother's screams had simply been too loud.

She stood in front of the hidden room their father had made while Mama tried to push her into the room. "You must hide, Laisyn, you must hide now and be quiet."

"No, Mama. I won't hide." Syn shook her head, staring into her mother's face as she tried not to weep. She didn't hide anymore. She fought.

If she had fought then . . .

"Laisyn, you will obey me," Crea Caar said, her voice low and firm. "You must hide, and hurry—I need to warn the Trell family, tell them to hide."

Behind her, Syn heard her older brother Con say, "Mama, you can't. They are too close."

They. Not the Trells, the neighbors who had kids almost the same age as Syn and Con. But *them*—the monsters that hunted them—not just the demons, although they certainly *looked* like monsters. But the Warlords and their servants.

They were close, too close. If Mama went outside, they would lose her.

"Mama, you hide," Syn said, reaching out, grabbing her mother's wrist and hauling her into the hidden room. "I'll warn the Trells."

But Mama talked to Syn like she was a child, not a grown woman. Not a trained soldier. Not a witch. Just a silly, useless child. "You will hide *now*."

Then they came through the door—that wasn't how it happened, but Syn knew, even as she dreamed, how dreams took on lives of their own. The Sirvani came— they came for Mama, and they came for her.

Syn laughed at them, because they didn't know.

They didn't realize what she was. What she could do.

Perhaps they looked at her and saw a silly child, too, just like Mama.

But Syn wasn't a child. She lifted her hand and whispered, called to the sleeping power in the earth. Called it, claimed it.

And when it came, it came in the form of fire, and the fire swallowed the Sirvani whole, burning them where they stood, leaving behind nothing but charred husks.

"You see, Mama? I didn't need to . . ."

Syn turned. Horror froze her throat.

Her mother, her brother . . . dead. Burned to death, by her hand.

Deep inside the earth, the sleeping power started to laugh.

You cannot claim me anymore, witch . . . You are nothing. Once more, nothing. Just useless, silly Syn . . .

Backing away, she stared at the dead bodies. And then time flashed forward, and she was no longer home, but in the forest.

Even before she lifted her head to look around, she knew where she was. She knew when.

She'd relive this horror as well.

She was already reliving it—the fire was tearing through her, wild and unfettered, and try as she might, she couldn't control it. Couldn't focus it, and the fire was spreading, spreading—the demons were dead, but the fire still hungered, reached for more bodies . . . the bodies of her men. She screamed in rage and tried to wrest control back from the bowels of the earth, but it fought her.

The power, it was too big for her. It had always been too much for her to handle, but until this very moment, the power had welcomed her—had allowed her to use it, to shape it and form it.

Now it threatened to shape and form her into the image of a killer—a woman who lost control and let her own magic kill the men who followed her.

"No, no, no, no . . ." It was her voice echoing inside her

ears, her voice, underscored by the screams of those trying
to evade the power that sought to kill them.

The fire, so close . . .

Then—pain—

***

In his arms, she shuddered, shook and wept silent tears.
Her mouth opened in a silent scream and Xan felt his heart
twist inside his chest. Dipping his head, he nuzzled her
neck and whispered, "Syn, come back to me."

Where was she?

What dreams held her so thoroughly trapped?

And then she was awake, a harsh gasp slipping free.
She struggled to break away from him, sucking in air as
though starved for it. Xan let her go, watched as she sat
up on the side of the narrow bunk, her head lowered, her
naked spine bowed.

"You dreamed," he said softly.

"Yes."

Stroking a hand down her back, he asked, "Can you
talk about it?"

She glanced at him over her shoulder, her narrow face
grim. "It's over. Was just a dream."

Xan sat up and settled himself behind her, drawing her
still-trembling body into the curve of his own. He wrapped
an arm around her, pressed his palm flat against her belly.
He used his other hand to wipe away the tears on her face.
"You cry. You fought. You wouldn't wake up. It was more
than just a dream, Syn." Pressing his lips to her shoulder,
he murmured, "Tell me. Let me help."

Please . . . please, let me help.

She sighed and another shudder wracked her body. "It
was about the night my mother was taken from me," she
murmured. Shaking her head, she added, "I don't like
thinking about it."

"The night she was taken," he echoed. "In a raid."

"Yes. We had a hidden room . . . no surprise, I guess.

Most homes, especially those near a Gate, have places to hide. Mama put me and my brother in there. We wanted her to come in, but she wouldn't—we had neighbors. They were like family. She insisted on checking on them. But the Sirvani were too close. They caught her." She leaned her head back against his shoulder and murmured, "We could hear her screaming. Through the walls. We heard her screaming."

Xan stared down at her, his heart aching. Automatically, he moved his head so that his hair fell and hid most of the scarred half of his face. "You were in that little room—hidden—alone."

She looked at him. "My brother was with me. He was thirteen. But yes. We were alone."

"I'm sorry." Sorry . . . half sick, furious. Sorry didn't even cover what he felt.

Her mouth twisted in a grimace and she shrugged. "It's not an unusual story. Most of us have lost people close to us, because of a raid. Haven't you?"

"Yes." He turned his head, staring out the narrow window set high along the wall. The full moon spilled silvery rays of light inside, easing the darkness. "My mother was captured in a raid, too."

He barely remembered her. But he remembered that he'd loved her. He could remember her arms, soft and strong, holding him close, as she sang to him and told him she loved him so.

Syn sighed and turned around in his arms, snuggling close. She kissed his shoulder and whispered, "So we have that in common."

"Do you dream about your mother much?"

She shrugged. "Some. It's not usually this bad." She glanced at him from under her lashes and said, "There was more, too."

She shifted back and lifted her hands, staring at them as though she didn't recognize them. She flexed her fingers wide, then balled them into a fist, over and over. "About two months ago, I almost killed half of my team, Xan.

We were coming up on a cache of Jorniaks when another group of demons came at us from behind. Raviners. It was so strange, almost like they were working together. And we keep seeing it happen. But Jorniaks lack the higher brain function to work as a *team*. I don't know . . . Maybe the Raviners have been trailing them and waiting until the Jorniaks attack, then slipping in during the aftermath. All I know is that they were slaughtering us, picking us off one by one."

His heart started to pound in hard, slow beats, tension mounting inside him. There was horror in her eyes. Horror. Hatred. Self-disgust. "I reached for my magic—I'm not the strongest witch around, nowhere close. But I've got a knack for fire. If I can see something, I can make it burn. And that's what I did. I burned the Raviners, the Jorniaks, and when I tried to cut the fire off, I couldn't."

She lifted her head, staring at him with haunted eyes. "The earth's energy, Xan . . . it's like it's damaged. Whatever happened when the Gate collapsed affected the energy—reshaped it. It reached inside me and it came out through the fire, and it killed and it wanted to keep killing. I kill demons without blinking an eye, but this time, the fire wanted to kill everybody. It wanted to use me to do it. I couldn't turn it off. No matter how I tried, I couldn't shut the flow down."

She reached up and brushed the back of her head. "Lothen was with me. He used his pulsar, hit me in the back of the head. He saw that something was wrong—figured it out on his own, because I couldn't even speak to tell him. He knocked me out and that broke my connection. The fire stopped. But I almost burned my team to ashes."

His heart ached for her. Cradling her face in his hand, he murmured, "That wasn't your fault."

"It doesn't matter if it is my fault or not—I almost did it." She took a deep breath and shook her head. "I know you don't understand. But we have to find a way to fix things so we can still access that energy, still use our magic."

He was hesitant to say it, very much so. Syn's magic

was part of who she was. Like his skill with a blade. He loved the feel of a blade in his hands, loved crafting one, giving it life.

But the words had to be said. He had to understand—if he didn't understand, it would fester between them.

He slid his fingers through her hair, cradling the back of her head. "If the energy has become so dangerous, it can't be used, wouldn't it be best to just leave it alone? You are a warrior, Syn, with or without your magic."

"Yes, I'm a warrior." She turned her head away and stared at the wall. "But I'm also a witch—it's every bit as much a part of me as being a warrior. And not being able to use it is crippling me. I feel it . . . like there's a part inside me that is fading away and dying, bit by bit. A part of *me* is dying. I'm not meant to be like this, Xan. None of the witches are, and I don't know what's going to happen to us if we keep trying to suppress it like this."

She ran her hands up and down her arms, then crossed them over her chest. He wrapped an arm around her, easing her close. "You're cold."

She rested her head on his chest and murmured, "Not so much. When you're touching me it isn't bad." She snuggled close and slid her arms around his waist.

"What isn't bad? Being cold?"

"Hmmmm. When you touch me, I don't feel the cold."

The cold . . . He frowned, thinking back. He almost always saw her standing in one way—when she stood still, it was with her legs spread wide and her arms crossed over her chest. It was a somewhat arrogant, defensive stance, sometimes. But now something occurred to him. "You feel cold a lot."

"Almost always." She sighed.

"Is it the magic?"

"Yes. It wants out, Xan. It needs out. Keeping it trapped inside is terrible," she whispered.

"And that's why you did this thing with Lee and Elina."

"That's why. The magic is kind of like a conduit. It

connects me to the earth and lets me draw the earth's energy in." She shifted around on his lap and reached for his arm. She held his hand in one of hers, with the palm turned up. "Picture a lake, right here. Your hand is the earth, and cupped inside your hand is the energy. Like a lake, deep, still and peaceful."

She laced her fingers with his and looked up at him. "In a lake, it's easy to drop an anchor—to secure yourself."

"But now the energy is like a raging river, sweeping everything along as it goes. When the waters are rough, even the stronger watercrafts have a harder time staying anchored, although they can usually manage it."

Eyes narrowed, he said, "So basically, the energy is trying to suck you in . . . because you're not strong enough?"

"I'm not an overly powerful witch, Xan. I've mastered what I can do, but I'll never be as strong as Elina or Lee. I just won't. Right now, if I try to make that connection, to anchor myself, I get swept away."

"I do not want to think of that. Give me a few moments before we go down that path, if you would." He grimaced and shook his head.

She smiled and traced a pattern on his chest. "I don't really want to think of it, either. But we have to think about finding a solution. That's why we did it, Xan. It's not just because we're mad over not using our magic. We *need* to use it, but the lesser witches, if they tried to use it now, it could kill us and others."

A choice between dying inside or dying in reality, and possibly causing the deaths of others—neither option held much appeal.

"What exactly were you trying to accomplish?"

She peered up at him, cocking her head. "Do you really want to know? Or are you just humoring me?"

"If I didn't want to know, I would not ask. Help me understand. Please."

"We want to make a net—to forge links between the witches. All of us. We'd be our own anchor, and for those who aren't as strong, the net would act to help stabilize us."

She licked her lips and shrugged. "It *could* work. I didn't study magical theory as in depth as Elina has, but it could work."

Then she grimaced and added, "It *was* working—I felt it. Then we ended up having our little party broken up and Elina took a blow to the head because Lo was too quick to jump to conclusions."

"So that is how she ended up wounded."

"Yeah." Syn sighed glumly. "It was working, Xan. We could make this work . . . I could have my magic back; we'd be able to provide those magical defenses once more. But the commander has a stick up his ass over this."

"He has a hard road to walk," Xan said, his voice soft. "He wants what is best for his followers, including those with magic. But he must keep his people safe, as well. It isn't an easy choice."

"I know that." She had a disgusted look on her face. "But we've tried explaining, and he won't even listen. He has a blind spot about this, because of Lee."

Xan crooked a grin at her. "I can understand that blind spot, Syn. A leader needs to look after the interests of all his people, but a man's gut insists he protect his woman, first and foremost. He is trying to do both, and it cannot be easy for him."

"I know it's not easy for him. But he's *not* protecting her—Lee, even more than Elina and I, is being hurt by this. And he doesn't even realize just how much it is hurting her. I don't think Lee even understands." Syn sighed and stroked a hand down his chest, running the tip of her finger over a long, thin ridge of scar tissue that bisected his right pectoral.

Xan covered her hand with his and lifted it to his mouth, pressing a kiss to her palm. "How is it hurting her more than you? More than Elina?"

"It's complicated." She stroked her fingers across his lower lip, along the firm line of his jaw. Reaching the narrow strap that held his eye patch in place, she stroked it. "Will you tell me how this happened?"

"A knife."

Syn rested her fingers on the black shield that covered his damaged eye and asked, "So I guess you're completely blind in the eye?"

"The eye is no longer there. Infection settled in. It was either lose the eye or risk dying."

"I'm sorry."

He turned his head and nuzzled her hand. "There is nothing to be sorry for. It happened a long time ago. I've lived longer without the eye than I lived with it. I adjusted."

"How old were you?" Syn frowned, studying his face. He might be a few years older than her, but not that much, she didn't think.

"Ten."

Her jaw dropped. *"Ten?"* she demanded. Shock recoiled through her and she sat upright, staring down at him with horror.

"Yes."

"Exactly how does a ten-year-old get hurt that badly with a knife?" But even as she voiced the question, she realized she could imagine just how. "Well, maybe that's not a good question. Kids very often run around carrying things they shouldn't."

Xan's mouth twitched in a smile. "It happened during a training session."

"Training session." Syn narrowed her eyes as something cold and hard settled inside her belly. "You were *ten*. You shouldn't have been *training* with knives."

He sat up and settled behind her, drawing her stiff body against his. He stroked a soothing hand up and down her thigh as he rested his chin on her shoulder. "And how old were you when you started serving in this army, Syn? You were orphaned at age ten . . . What did you do after you lost your mother?"

"I sure as hell didn't start training with knives." Tears stung her eyes, and she turned her head, pressing her lips to his cheek. Under her mouth, she felt one of the narrow lines of his scarred face. Shifting around on his lap, she slipped her fingers under the strap, slowly. She waited for him to pull away, but he sat there passively as she eased the patch away.

The scarring was much neater than she'd expected; most of it was one long, thin line that bisected his eye, starting at the outer edge of his eyebrow down to the bridge of his nose. The lid to his eye was closed, permanently—and unless she was mistaken, they'd stitched it.

"They stitched it closed," she murmured. She could just barely make out the faint lines where the stitches had been placed. "Did they actually use old-fashioned stitches? Why not las-sutures?"

His lips twitched, that small smile she saw from him so rarely. "I was but a child when it happened, Syn. I barely remember anything other than the injury itself. It became infected, and there was a fever. After the fever came on me, I don't remember much of anything until I woke up one day and the eye was gone."

She scowled. For all its surgical neatness, it seemed borderline barbaric. She leaned in and pressed her lips to his eye, running her mouth along the scars and then easing the patch back into place. "Why do you wear the patch? The scarring is actually rather minimal."

"Yes. I've just always worn it. A child tends to shy away from any unusual attention—I guess it just became habit." He ran a finger along the narrow, raised ridge still visible around the patch and shrugged. "People stare, with or without the patch. But the patch makes them more comfortable than the actual scarring would."

"And you're really all that concerned about people being comfortable?" Syn asked, smirking.

"I couldn't care less if people are comfortable." He flashed her a grin—a real smile, there and then gone. Reaching up, he tapped her nose and added, "But I prefer not to be bothered when the insanely curious see the scars and ask what happened."

She arched a brow. "Am I being insanely curious?"

"Perhaps." He reached up and curled a hand over the

back of her neck, drawing her in for a kiss. "But you may ask me anything."

There was a hard, perfunctory knock at the door. Syn grimaced and kicked her legs out of the bed. Grabbing a tunic from the foot of the bed, she tugged it on and crossed to the door. She peeked through the small viewing hole and then shot Xan a disgruntled look. He remained silent as she spoke through the door. "Yes, Commander?"

"Get your ass out here and in my quarters. You have ten minutes." There were a few seconds of silence and then he added, "And bring Xan with you—it will save me the trouble of pretending to look for him when I already know where he is."

Syn made a face at the door and listened to the faint sound of his footfalls as he walked away. Then she turned and met Xan's gaze. "He may decide to tear into you for being here. He's still pissed off at me . . . You might end up catching some of it now."

Xan shrugged. "I can handle it. I heard the order go out and I chose to ignore it." He stood from the bed and grabbed his clothes. "Although I don't have time to go to my dormer and grab anything but the clothes I wore yesterday."

"Not an issue. If we're lucky, all he'll do is assign us to latrine duty for the next few days, and trust me, you don't want to mess with clean clothes on that job rotation."

Xan's face twisted with disgust. "I'll take your word on it."

"You're probably going to end up in trouble." Syn sighed and flicked her hair back from her face. "I'm sorry."

He caught her hand and lifted it to his lips. "Do not be. There is nowhere else I would rather be, I promise you."

Syn felt the blood rush to her cheeks and her heart fluttered. Forcing a smile, she said, "Let's hope you don't regret those words."

***

They weren't alone in Kalen's quarters.

Elina and Lee were also there. Elina sat on one of the

narrow, hard-backed seats. She must still feel lousy—Syn had seen the goose egg covered by her hair. There was no way the woman couldn't have a massive headache.

But she looked serene—completely undisturbed. It came from years of practice and Syn had already put on her mask as well. She'd be damned if she let anybody see how tangled she felt inside. Never show weakness—it was a lesson she'd learned early in life, and one she adhered to.

Lee hadn't quite perfected the art of hiding her every emotion. She stood there, leaning against a wall and looking miserably unhappy. She was pale, dark circles under her eyes, and her mouth was a tight, narrow line. She glanced at Xan and then at Syn. "If he's here for moral support, I gotta say, I'm impressed, Syn. I love you, but there ain't no way I'd be here if I didn't have to be."

Xan stroked a hand down Syn's shoulder. From the corner of her eye, she could see him smile. "He's here at the commander's orders," Syn said, shrugging.

Lee cocked a brow and studied Xan curiously. "Oh?"

"Apparently breaking orders is contagious," he said. "After word went out that you three had been confined to quarters, I ignored it and went to see Syn."

"Moral support?"

"Hardly." Syn snorted and glared at Xan. "He came to yell at me. I'm getting very tired of males yelling at me over this when they can't really even understand what it's like for us." She softened the words with a light brush of her fingertips down his cheek.

He caught her hand and kissed it.

Aware of the curious gazes from her friends, she battled down the urge to blush through sheer will alone. Facing Elina, she cocked her head and studied the other witch. "You look like you're feeling well enough."

"My head hurts like a bitch," Elina said, a cool smile curling her lips.

"I bet." Glancing around the dormer that served as living quarters and office for the commander and his wife, she said, "Where is his lordship?"

Lee sneered. "Out lording it over his obedient subjects. Jackass."

Under the heavy sarcasm, Syn heard the hurt. Closing the distance between them, she caught Lee's hand and squeezed. "Bad?"

"Bad enough," she said softly, her voice husky. "I didn't get any sleep. He stayed away all night."

The door opened and all four of them turned to look, expecting to see the commander.

It was Vena Saurell. She looked at Syn, a devious smile on her pretty face. "Hello, Captain."

Lee pushed Syn and narrowed her eyes, glaring at the other woman. "Excuse me, but who in the hell are you, and why are you in *my* quarters?"

"Why, the commander requested my presence, Lea." She widened her eyes dramatically, staring at Lee innocently.

"It's Lee." With a brittle smile, she said, "If the commander requested your presence, so be it. But this *is* a private dormer and you aren't welcome in *my* home without knocking. Get your ass out. Now. When Kalen is here, you can come in."

With a pretty frown, Vena said, "I am very sorry if I've offended you, Lee. I realize it must be hard sharing your husband's attention with . . . others."

The innuendo was unmistakable.

If Lee hadn't been so tired, so miserable, Syn doubted Vena's comments would have had any impact at all. As it was, though, her summery blue eyes darkened with doubt, with hurt. Syn opened her mouth to say something—anything—but Vena had already seen the look on Lee's face, and a smug light appeared in her eyes.

"If the commander was sharing his attentions with a camp tramp, then he wouldn't be worth grieving over," Xan said, his voice cold and harsh, much like the look on his face as he stared at Vena. His voice softened as he shifted his gaze to Lee. "But the commander isn't a foolish man—he's got more sense, and more taste, than that. I know it, and likely so docs every soul who's ever had any contact with him."

Syn could have kissed him. And she would, later. But right now, she was enjoying the look on Vena's face too much.

"Excuse me?" Vena glared at Xan, her face red, her hands clenched into fists at her side.

"I'm quite certain you heard me," Xan said levelly. "I do not know why the commander requested your presence, but I'm very certain he'd be less than pleased if he knew you were here insulting his wife."

Finally breaking free from her silence, Lee shoved away from the wall and stalked to stand between Vena and the rest of the room. She gave Xan a quick glance and said, "The commander's wife does have a name. And while she appreciates it, she's also capable of handling this particular camp tramp on her own."

Vena glared at Lee. "You call me a tramp? You fucking slut, you whored your way into his bed. You whored your way right up through the ranks; everybody knows that."

"Do they?" Lee grinned. "I must be good if I convinced a die-hard soldier to marry me, just because I'm good in bed. Must suck for you—did you come here with that plan in mind?"

"You're leading him around by his dick." Vena's voice shook with her fury. "There's no other reason he would have married the bastard daughter of a Warlord."

"You're so certain of that?" Lee pursed her lips thoughtfully. "Okay, I take it back. I'm not good. I'm fucking amazing."

"Yes." Kalen's voice came from the doorway. "You are amazing. There is no doubt about that."

Lee started visibly, but Syn had known he was coming, and once more, she had to admit, the man had excellent timing. He'd heard Vena's comments. The woman was up to something, and while she suspected Kalen was too clever to fall for any tricks she might have, Syn felt better knowing the man had seen her for what she was.

Recovering, Lee inclined her head and said coolly, "Good morning, Commander. I hope you slept well."

"No, you don't." A smile tugged at the corners of his lips. "But don't worry, I didn't sleep any better than you."

Lee's eyes narrowed. "Good."

He came inside, ignoring Vena, ignoring everybody but his wife. He stopped in front of her and laid his hand on her cheek. The look that passed between them was one too intimate for words, too intimate to be shared with others. Wistful envy curled through Syn, and she found herself staring at Xan. And he was returning her look.

Kalen dipped his head and pressed his brow to Lee's. For a moment, they just stood like that.

Then Lee eased back and crossed her arms over her chest. "I'm not going to apologize, Kalen." She glanced at Elina, then Syn, before looking back at her husband. "We can't keep going on like this . . . It's destroying us inside."

To Syn's surprise, he nodded. "I know." He reached out and brushed a hand down her arm. "We'll work through it."

Then he strode to his desk and settled behind it. Settling once more into his position as commander, he studied Vena Saurell.

"When you have several thousand people living in one place, you're going to have your share of troublemakers." He had a bored tone to his voice, a bored look in his eyes. He studied Vena as though she had about as much significance to him as a gnat. "You're not the first troublemaker here; you won't be the last."

She flushed, but in a fairly steady voice, she said, "I apologize, Commander; however, I'm not sure why you would think I'm trying to cause trouble."

"Because you are." He glanced at his wife and then at the other women in the room before once more meeting Vena's gaze. "Now . . . you're here because you told me you had concerns about Captain Caar and Xan. Would you care to explain those concerns? In front of them?"

Her eyes flashed, hot and bright. Her mouth tightened.

Then her features smoothed out. "I prefer to discuss any personal concerns I have in private."

"Too fucking bad." His face impassive, he said, "I haven't the time or the inclination to listen to *personal* concerns. If there's a matter that can affect my camp, my men, those under Caar's leadership, speak—have the guts to lay your *concerns* out before those involved. But if it's personal, don't waste my time."

"I don't feel a person can fairly lead when she's screwing one of her subordinates."

"Oh, puh-leeze." Lee snorted. She shoved off the wall and moved to stand in front of Vena. "While I don't really consider myself one of Kalen's subordinates, he is in charge and he screws me on a regular basis. Are you questioning *his* ability to lead?"

"You aren't an active member of his army."

Lee widened her eyes. "I'm not? Then what am I?"

"His wife," Vena said, her mouth twisting in a sneer. She spat it out like she'd just taken her first sip of insian tea.

"Really? Just his wife?" Lee glanced at Kalen and then back at Vena. "Wow. Then can somebody explain why in the hell I'm routinely dragged out of bed at an ungodly hour, why I have to take my turn doing the damn job rotations, why I'm dragged to weapons training, why I get sent out on—"

Kalen interrupted, "Lee, I think she gets the point."

"Everybody knows she's not a real fighter in this army," Vena said. She wouldn't look at him. She stared straight at the wall over his shoulder.

Somehow Syn suspected this meeting wasn't going exactly as Vena had planned. But that didn't surprise her. Vena hadn't ever struck her as somebody who'd fight fair in the open—she'd come at somebody's back, while doing everything she could to avoid a head-on confrontation.

"What I find massively entertaining is this . . . 'everybody knows . . .' crap," Elina said. She lounged on the hard, ladder-backed chair like it was a silk-covered throne. She wore her fighting gear with ease and elegance. Ease and elegance . . . it described Elina from the top of her head down to her feet. She studied her nails, as though she couldn't be bothered to look at Vena as she spoke. "If everybody knows, as Saurell here implies, then why does Lee regularly have people either ordering her about or coming to her with concerns? More important, if she's not a *real* fighter—that would imply she has no use here other than warming the commander's bed."

Now she looked up, pinning Vena with an icy, green stare. "But if she has no other use than that, then I'm curious . . . who destroyed the Gate?"

Confusion danced across Vena's face. It was echoed in Xan's. Syn said quietly, "Vena, do you know what happened in Sojourn Gap?"

"The Gate collapsed."

"It didn't collapse," Kalen said and for once, he looked at Vena with real emotion. The look in his eyes was one of utter disgust, complete disdain. "Lee leveled it."

Lee flushed as she became the object of Vena's disbelieving stare and Xan's intent interest. Jerking a shoulder in a shrug, she said, "I didn't exactly level it, and if it wasn't for Morne, I probably would have killed us all. It was blind luck."

"No. It was instinct, and it was a damned good one," Elina said, rolling her eyes. She came out of her chair and closed the distance between herself and her niece. She gave the younger woman a light pat on the shoulder. "Modesty is nice, honey. Really, it is. But you did a good thing. You saved a lot of lives. Deal with it."

Then she turned and looked at Vena, eying her with more than a little irritation. "Commander, as fascinating as this is, I thought you'd called us in here to rail at us more, not to have a little gossip session with this twit. Am I wrong?"

"Oh, I definitely plan on railing," Kalen said darkly. "But since it was word from Saurell that informed me of the plan the three of you hatched, and since she's also been muttering to various individuals about her 'concerns' regarding Syn and one of her subordinates, I decided it would be more effective to clear the air."

"Word from Saurell?" Syn echoed. She narrowed her eyes and focused on the other woman. Lee, Elina and Syn had met to discuss their plans only once—in Syn's quarters. Elina shared her grandmother's old dormer with a medic. The medic, the young woman who'd showed up in camp the same day as Xan, had a promising healing touch, and Elina was teaching her some of the potions and brews she'd learned from her grandmother, Eira. Since Lee shared her dormer with her husband, their best bet at privacy had been in Syn's quarters.

They'd discussed it there. Only there. And only once.

"You little bitch," Syn said, utterly disgusted. "You've been spying on me." And doing a damn good job of it—Syn hadn't once detected the presence of another, and it wasn't likely Lee or Elina had, either, because they would have mentioned it. It wasn't that easy to spy on a witch—hell, at one time, Syn would have said it was almost impossible to eavesdrop on a witch, but that was back when they'd still had full use of their magic.

Vena didn't bother denying it. She said nothing. Absolutely nothing.

Looking back at the commander, Syn said, "Commander, respectfully, I want this woman out of my unit. If you have no concerns with that, I'll talk to Bron and see if he can find a place for her. I don't want her near me or my men."

Kalen grimaced. "Respectfully, Captain, request denied." He held up a hand before Syn could argue. Shaking his head, he pointed out, "This woman was assigned to your unit for a reason. You train your soldiers to fight either as a unit or in small groups of two or three. You help those used to fighting alone integrate into fighting as part of a team. Saurell is woefully in need of that particular ability. She's best suited to your unit, and you know it. Bron works better with the larger teams. If I place her with him, she's too likely to end up dead. Or cause even more dissension."

Vena opened her mouth, only to snap it shut when Kalen

glanced at her. He lifted a brow and quietly asked, "Did you have something you wanted to say?"

"It's very clear the captain has personal issues with me."

"Do you?" Kalen asked, looking at Syn.

"Respectfully, sir? Hell, yes."

"Don't blame you." Then he shrugged. "Too fucking bad. Captain Caar, you're a professional and I expect you to carry on as such. You've never let personal issues interfere with your job before and I don't expect that to change. I'm not concerned over it."

He paused for half a beat and then asked, "Should I have reason to be concerned?"

Syn wished she could lie about it. She did not want Vena Saurell in her unit. Period. But she knew how to work with people she didn't like. And Kalen was right. Vena, wherever she'd learned how to fight, didn't know how to function as part of a team. Here, that was something that could get a person killed.

"No, Commander. No reason for concern at all."

"Good." He glanced at Saurell. "You're dismissed."

With her back and spine stiff, Vena headed for the door. Just before she opened it, Kalen said quietly, "Saurell, this is the only warning you'll get from me. I don't tolerate this type of bullshit from my men. At all. One more incident like this, and you can expect to find yourself eastbound."

Vena gave a single terse nod. "Of course, Commander."

It sounded a lot like, *"Fuck you all,"* Syn decided as the door closed behind Vena. Giving Kalen an irritated look, Syn settled onto one of the other chairs in the room. Spinning it around, she straddled it and rested her arms on the top of it. "Was that some weird way of entertaining yourself, Kalen?"

"So it's Kalen again, Captain?" he asked, cocking a brow at her.

"Unless you plan on being an ass all day. Then I'll call you Commander again."

"Oh, I'm sure I'll do something that rubs you wrong." He reached up and pinched the bridge of his nose. As he glanced at his wife, something sad and heavy moved through his eyes. "There are days when I'd give anything to turn this job over to somebody else."

"Nobody else here is crazy enough to do it," Elina said, shrugging.

"Agreed." He slanted his gaze to Xan. "I'm trying to decide if it's even worth the hassle of addressing the fact that you disobeyed a direct order."

Xan gave him a small nod. "Perhaps if it makes it easier, I do not recall being told that when one was confined to quarters, it also meant that they could have no company."

Kalen stared at him. "You truly think I'm going to buy that line?"

"Whether you buy it or not, it doesn't change the fact that never once has anybody told me that when one of us are confined to quarters, I'm not allowed to enter those quarters." Xan looked unconcerned.

"Captain, did you fail to discuss this with your soldier?"

Syn pretended to think. "Perhaps not in those direct terms. I think I said something along the lines that you'd have his ass if you knew he was violating the confinement order. He was a bit distracted at the time—seeing as how he'd come to tear a few more strips off my hide. Perhaps he didn't make the connection."

"Not buying it," he muttered, under his breath. Then he blew out a heavy sigh and said, "Fuck it. Xan, you've lost your off-duty day for the next week. For the next ten days, you're picking up two hours of extra duty each day, to be carried out in the stables. Consider that your punishment, although if I get pissed off, I may just assign you to work with Saurell, one on one, for the next month."

Syn had to bite her tongue to keep from saying anything. She shouldn't have bothered. Kalen saw the look in her eyes, and he laughed. "That idea bother you, Captain? Maybe I should do it just for the hell of it."

Syn said nothing. Kalen had enough of a mean streak in him to do just that.

He waited, watching her with a grin, until Syn looked away.

Shoving out of his chair, the commander made his way to the dented metal carafe resting on the hot plate in their small cooking area. Most of the dormers didn't have one. The soldiers tended to share their meals in one of the communal dining areas. He eyed the carafe and glanced at his wife. "You drank it all already."

"I needed the caffeine," she said dryly. "I had trouble sleeping."

He reached into the shelf overhead and grabbed the bag of kava beans they used for brewing kion. "Yes, I know. I keep hearing you yell about me. Damn near all fucking night." He rubbed his temple, a dark glare on his face. "It's damned annoying when a psychic can't rely on his psychic shields for some peace inside his mind."

"Yes . . . it's damned annoying not being able to rely on one's gifts," Lee said with a syrupy smile. "However do you cope?"

He ignored the comment as he added some water and got the kion to brewing. It wasn't long before the rich, heavy scent filled the air. Syn was glad his mood seemed a little less stormy, because she badly needed a cup of that kion.

"I will be honest. Your rather loud thoughts weren't the only ones filling my head last night."

"Really?" Lee looked puzzled.

Curious, Syn studied him. "You usually have no trouble blocking voices out of your head, Kalen. You're a talented receiver, and you figured out a long time ago how to keep from catching unnecessary thoughts."

"True. But there are a few specific individuals who have always managed to establish a connection with me when they needed it—whether I want it or not."

Syn couldn't help it. A grin curled her lips. To her knowledge, that described only a handful of people. He *could* hear anybody, but these few were people he trusted, people he respected. He wouldn't cut off communication with them for anything short of life or death.

Other than herself and Bron, she could only think of a few people who fit that list. Syn hadn't contacted him, and somehow, she doubted the other captain had.

One of those other people was dead. It had been Eira—Elina's grandmother, the woman who had had a hand in training nearly every witch who had served under Kalen's command.

His wife was another. Their connection was one born of the bond between them.

The only person left, that Syn could think of, was Morne.

"So . . . who was this other person?" she asked.

Absently, she noticed Elina sitting up straighter, saw something flash through her green eyes.

Kalen smirked. "That's not really of any importance." He poured himself a cup of kion and then settled behind his desk. Pinning Elina with a flat stare, he said, "Okay, witch. You have my attention—explain to me *exactly* what you were trying to do, and why in the hell I should allow it."

SEVEN

The encounter with the unknown Warlord had thrown Morne too far off Dais's trail. Skittish now, and justifiably paranoid, the traitor wasn't operating with any sort of logic Morne could understand.

He was moving deeper into demon-thick territory, the huge expanses of land Kalen's army currently fought to free from Anqar's demon hordes.

It was damn foolish. There had been more than a few times when Morne had brushed far closer to death than he liked.

Death wasn't necessarily unappealing to him, but he'd rather not go down under a mess of Jorniak bodies.

But despite the danger, every step Dais took led him, and Morne, deeper into their midst. Too often he came across stands of trees that had been scorched by the presence of the fiery Ickado demons, or land all but sapped of life—both plant and animal, the lingering trace left behind by Raviners. The worst were the half-eaten carcasses—humanoid, demon, animal, anything foolish enough to get too close to a Jorniak.

With bile churning in his gut, he crouched down beside one small body. Malnourished, thin. Young . . . possibly even a child. It was hard to tell, but Morne suspected the girl might have already been dead before the demon took her. Jorniaks were eating machines—living, dead, it mattered not to them.

It wasn't much comfort, though.

He wished he could bury her. But he had no tools, and as much as it hurt his heart to leave her there, the pragmatic side of him knew she was beyond caring now. Beyond his reach.

Dais, on the other hand, wasn't.

Dais had to be his priority, especially if he was trying to align himself with Warlords once more. The man knew too much, had too much knowledge of this world, of Kalen, Lee, the camp. All of it. Too dangerous.

"I'm sorry," he said quietly before straightening and scanning the forest, searching for some visual sign that might clue him in on Dais's direction.

There was nothing. Nothing in the forest to whisper, no physical signs that he could see. Nothing.

Bitter, he muttered, "Did you expect anything else?"

Dais had put his time to good use, getting far, very far, away from the camp, from Morne, diving deep into territory where only the foolish and the desperate would dare follow.

Morne wondered what that made him—a fool? Desperate? Both?

Likely both.

He strode away from the girl's body, leaving the path and taking to the cover of the trees. He listened, ears pricked, for any slight sound that might betray the presence of another.

There was nothing, not even the sound of the wind blowing overhead.

The air was heavy, thick. Rain was moving in. He needed to get closer to Dais before a storm came in. A heavy storm would wipe out any sign of Dais's presence and right now, Morne needed all the help he could get.

Flexing his hands, he knelt in the undergrowth, brushing aside the vegetation that grew in thick, heavy clumps. Something swarmed near his ear, settled on his neck. He ignored it as he knelt in the dirt. Laying his hands on the ground, he reached out. Searched.

He had to fight past the taint of the presence of the demons left, had to fight to remain steady in the heavy swirl of power.

Lee would say, "You're searching for a needle in a haystack."

She would be right.

***

Lee, Elina and Syn took up the center of the room, seated on the hard ground with their legs crossed.

Elina's face was serene.

Lee's face was a flat, hard mask, concealing the nerves Syn knew jumped inside her.

Syn did her best to look bored, unconcerned.

It couldn't be farther from the truth.

They weren't alone this time, and they weren't in a small shelter outside the camp's walls. Kalen, Bron and Xan waited with them, each of them in charge of one witch. Kalen had lowered his shields and he was in direct psychic contact with all three of them, but he was specifically focused on Lee.

If one thing went wrong, all three of the witches would feel it and Kalen would end this.

They wouldn't get another chance, either, Syn suspected.

They were in Elina's quarters, the old dormer her grandmother Eira had called home for decades.

It was the most secure place they had.

Eira had trained untold witches here, and even months after her death, the protections she'd laid within the earth still held. Waiting and ready. Just walking into the dormer set Syn's skin to buzzing. It was torture, feeling the warm kiss of magic but not being able to reach for it.

Not for much longer, she told herself. She wouldn't even let herself consider that this might fail.

Failure simply wasn't an option.

Taking a slow, deep breath, she rested her palms on her thighs and looked at Elina. "I'm ready."

Lee gave a curt nod.

"Relax," Elina murmured as she reached out and linked their hands. "Everything will be fine."

Syn wished she had even half as much confidence as Elina had. From the corner of her eye, she saw Xan, watching her with that heavy, intense gaze, as though she was the only one around for miles. He caught her glance and the corner of his mouth quirked up in a faint smile.

Oddly enough, the butterflies in her belly eased and she found herself looking at Elina with anticipation. "Let's do this."

Syn could remember the first time she'd actually tapped into the earth, reaching for the energy.

She'd been four, and under her mother's strict, careful hand, she'd hesitantly reached for the magic and then utterly freaked when it reached back. She'd felt it, sensed it, and in her mind's eye, she'd seen it—welcoming hands, reaching for her, drawing her close.

Terrified, she'd jerked away and her mother had been waiting, there to steady her, there to comfort and reassure her.

As Elina made the first connection, Syn fought to control the fear inside her as once more, the magic reached for her. There was no welcome, though. Just hunger. A thirst for more.

Panic flared inside but she tamped it down. She couldn't be afraid, couldn't give in. Had to be in control.

Elina made the link and then turned to Syn. Lee was the stronger witch, but they were all still leery about drawing Lee in until they knew it was safe. Or rather—until they knew they could use the magic to protect the camp if the need arose.

Adrenaline pulsed, sizzled inside her veins as she caught Elina's exploratory grasp and linked. A gasp fell from her lips and then she was drowning, swirling in the ebb and flow of energy.

It was hot. Wild. Unlike anything she'd ever felt before. Always before the energy had been a peaceful well—now it was hot, edgy . . . almost erotically so. Under her tunic, she felt her nipples swell as her breath caught in her throat. Blood rushed to her cheeks and she forced her eyes open, staring at Elina—it was like looking at one scene laid over another. Her physical eyes saw Elina, sitting just a few feet away with her legs crossed, her hand linked with Syn's. Her golden skin was tinged a light pink and Syn could see the hot light burning in Elina's gaze, one that she was certain was echoed in her own.

With her inner eyes, she saw Elina, standing in a vast, open space, neither night nor day, surrounded by a torrent of power. A silvery glow, edged with veins of purple and pink, the power pulsed and ebbed, swirled and spun, wrapping around them. Elina's hair drifted around her face, the strands all but crackling with the echo of energy, and her eyes seemed to glow.

"Touch it," Elina said, lifting her hand, letting it hover about the tendrils of power swarming around them.

Back inside her body, inside the cabin, Syn felt Elina's hand—twined with her own—lift.

In the energy plain, she lifted her hand and glided it just above the energy. She didn't touch, but she felt it warm her skin nonetheless.

"Take it," Elina ordered.

Syn sank both of her hands into the energy. Part of her mind warned of caution, but Syn couldn't be cautious, not now. The power . . . it called her now. And through the power, she could feel Elina.

"Reach for me." Elina extended a hand, although it wasn't a physical hand. In the energy plain, they were not touching. Elina offered a link, a connection to her own strength. As the power pulled and tugged at Syn, she reached out and joined her power to Elina's.

Their energies merged, and immediately, Syn felt the energy steady around it. It continued to wrap and wind about them, but she felt *connected*—connected in a way she hadn't felt since the Gate went down. Grounded. Secure.

"It's working," Syn murmured.

The two grinned at each other and then they focused and reached out for Lee.

* * *

Syn felt drugged.

With a wide, wobbly smile on her lips and her heart racing, she slipped inside her dormer and leaned back against the door. A laugh bubbled out of her as she cupped her hands together. She focused, and there . . . right in her hands, flame danced. A small, fiery little ball. The grin faded from her lips as she focused, and slowly, the little ball of fire began to spin. Her eyes narrowed and the ball constricted, then expanded, responding to her unspoken commands with ease.

"It worked . . ."

Abruptly, she realized she wasn't alone. Her skin burned, and without seeing him, she knew who it was. Through her lashes, she cast a glance around her dormer and found him leaning in the doorway that led to her small, personal bathroom. He had his arms crossed over his chest, and he stared at the flames she held in her hands, an unreadable look in his eyes.

She closed her hands, banishing the flames just before the fire would have burned her flesh. Holding his eyes, she lowered her hands to her side and stared at him.

"I never realized just how fucking erotic it would be to see a witch using her magic," he mused, shoving away from the door and starting toward her.

Syn blushed. "Erotic?"

"Hmm. Erotic. Earlier, when the three of you were doing this, right before Elina and you started on Lee, you had this look on your face." He stopped in front of her and trailed a finger across the line of her mouth, down along her neck, tracing the line of her cavinir tunic and stopping at the fastener, centered between her breasts. He caught it and started to drag it down, slowly, bit by bit revealing more of her flesh. Syn brought her hands up, resting them on his hips.

"You had this look . . . It was almost the exact same look I've seen on your face when I'm inside you. I still can't decide if I'm jealous or not."

Her breath caught in her throat and her heart skipped a couple of beats as he reached up and pushed the tunic off her shoulders. It caught on her elbows, but when she went to tug it away, Xan caught her wrists and dragged them overhead, pinning them to the wall.

Against her belly, she could feel the hard, thick ridge of his cock and she groaned, rubbing against him. Xan shuddered and leaned in, using his weight to still her body. "Stop it," he muttered.

"Why?" she asked, turning her face and pressing her mouth to his neck. She licked him, tasting salty sweat and man.

"Because I've got a mind to seduce you, but I can't do that if you turn me into a slobbering, raving maniac in the next five seconds, now can I?" Shifting her wrists to one hand, he reached inside her open tunic and cupped her breast. He circled the nipple with his thumb and murmured, "I was watching you—terrified that something would go wrong, and you'd get hurt. Then you started breathing fast, heavy . . . like you are now. A blush turned your cheeks pink and you smiled, the same way you're smiling now. You were aroused, and it drove me mad. There I stood, worrying that you were in danger, and you were aroused."

He pinched her nipple and raked his teeth down her neck. "Were your nipples hard like they are now?"

"Yes . . ." Her breath hissed out of her, and she jerked against his grip, desperate to touch him.

He stroked his hand down her middle, toying with the waistband of the formfitting cavinir she wore, then slipping his hand inside.

Syn groaned as he pushed two fingers inside her aching sex.

Xan growled against her neck and rasped, "You're already wet. So fucking wet . . ." He jerked back and let go of her hands abruptly. Syn wobbled, caught off balance, reaching out to brace her weight on his shoulders. He removed her tunic and flung it across the room and then he went to his knees in front of her, jerking her boots off, and then her trousers. She was naked before him in under a heartbeat.

She fisted her hands in his silken, midnight hair and whimpered as he leaned in, pressed his mouth to her. "So wet," he muttered, circling his tongue around her clit. "So sweet."

Her face flaming, Syn closed her eyes. As quiet as he was, it never ceased to amaze her how much he liked to talk at certain times . . . like now. When he was licking her flesh, when he was pushing two fingers in and out of her body in a quick, steady rhythm, he liked to talk. Dirty, wicked words that were almost as erotic as the feel of his mouth on her, as the feel of his tongue circling around her clit.

"I want you to come," he said gruffly. "I want to taste it. Want to feel it. Come for me, Syn."

She whimpered and arched closer, desperate to be as close as possible. He caught her thigh and guided it up, draped it over his shoulder. Her other leg threatened to buckle and she swayed. Then he used his hands to steady her, hold her as he shifted lower, lower . . . replacing his fingers with his tongue.

Syn cried out as he stiffened his tongue and started to fuck it in and out her pussy. He was growling, pausing every now and then to mutter something against her flesh. But her brain couldn't process it—couldn't think. All she could do was feel . . . All she could do was feel *him* just before she flew apart.

She was still struggling to catch her breath when he stood and caught her in his arms, carrying her to the bed. She sank against the thin mattress, closing her eyes as she labored for air.

He joined her, catching her sigh with his mouth as he rolled on top of her and settled between her thighs. "Wrap your legs around me," he whispered. "Pull me close."

She did, shuddering as it brought them together. He throbbed against her, thick, hard and hot. "Xan . . ."

Against her chest, she could feel his heart, beating fast and heavy. Forcing her eyes open, she reached up and covered his heart with her palm. Staring into his gaze, she said, "Make love to me."

As he sank inside her, they watched each other.

As he started to rock against her, they watched each other.

As their climaxes burned ever closer, they watched each other. Syn's lashes drifted low and she whimpered, arching and rocking her hips, needing more, needing all. Xan caught her chin in his hand and angled her head back. His voice a rough, insistent growl, he rasped, "You look at me."

She forced her eyes open, staring at him from under her lashes.

It hit her low and hard, rippling and echoing, dancing through her body, pulsating inside . . . like a drug.

Staring at him, she reached up and caught the back of his neck, dragging his head down and kissing him. Hungry. Desperate for his kiss, for his taste. For him.

Xan was becoming her drug, she realized.

Something she needed every bit as much as her magic. Maybe even more.

***

"Commander, if we're going to do this, now is the best chance we're going to get," Syn said, spreading the map flat on Kalen's desk and indicating the route she'd chosen for the next supply run.

"How many soldiers are you planning to take?" Kalen eyed the map. His face revealed nothing, but she knew he dreaded these supply runs.

Cautiously, she said, "I only want one squadron."

His eyes flashed silver, but that was the only change in his expression. His voice was flat as he asked, "Have you gone and developed a death wish recently, Captain?"

"Not hardly." She lifted a hand when he opened his mouth again and said, "Please. If you'd let me explain. A smaller unit will move quicker, make less noise. And . . . I want to go with them. Now that the magic is available to me again, I can provide far more in the way of offense than a full-sized unit."

A troubled look passed over Kalen's face. "You're so certain that it's safe."

"I am." Syn knew he wanted to believe that, knew he wanted to trust her . . . and she also knew his fear for Lee made him wary. "I know it's safe for *me*. For Elina. We'll have to proceed with caution with Lee, because we don't know what's going to happen when she uses her gift—if it will react differently since she has Gate magic—and we don't want anything alerting the Anqarians. But I'm stable. Lee's stable. Elina's stable. I can feel it. I'd know if something was wrong, and that's not arrogance, or wishful thinking—I'd just know. I'd feel it."

She glanced down at the maps in front of her and then back at the commander. "We need these supplies, Kalen, and you know it."

He nodded. With a heavy sigh, he rubbed the back of his neck. "This net—what helps you, Elina and Lee anchor one another. Is *it* stable?"

"Yes. It's like a shield, almost. We'll reinforce it and add to it over time, and when the time comes that we need to add more people to it, we'll have to adjust, but the net itself, it's very stable, and maintaining it—it takes nothing from me. It's fueled by the same energy that fuels my magic."

Long, heavy moments of silence passed. A muscle ticked in his jaw and then abruptly, he nodded. "So be it. You're the witch, Syn. If you say it's safe, then I have to trust that."

She stared at him, not entirely certain she believed what she'd just heard him say.

"You've never let me down yet, Syn." A faint smile tugged at his mouth. "I shouldn't have let myself forget that."

Then he settled in his chair, studied the maps. "Let's go over this. And you'd better make it good . . . I still don't like the idea of such a small team."

Before he could change his mind, she outlined the plan.

"We can make better time, get through the forest quicker. We'll take the baerns, one for each of us and a few extra to help bring back the supplies."

When she was done, he gave her a narrow look. "You should have made it better, Syn. Still don't like the idea."

Syn didn't particularly like it herself, but it was a good plan. It was a solid one. Choosing her words carefully, she explained that. "Kalen, whenever we make a supply run—or go *anywhere* more than a few hundred yards from the camp—we tend to lose men. Sometimes, it's just a few; sometimes, it's a lot. Every once in a while, nobody dies. We take larger numbers because those larger numbers give us more strength when confronting the demons, yet when we have larger numbers, we have a high casualty rate, too. But I can provide that same strength, and if we have half the men we usually take, we can move quicker. We can make it safer when we stop for the night and I can set up defenses that will keep the demons from catching us by surprise while we sleep."

"I know the positive aspects, Syn." Kalen leaned back and stared off into the distance, brooding. "I used to lead scouting teams, remember?"

Of course she remembered. That was where she'd met him—for the first few years, she'd dressed as a boy and just made herself useful around the camp. Then she was finally assigned to act as one of the scouts, and Kalen had been in charge of her unit. The two of them had been working together for close to twenty years.

In this little pocket of the world, that was probably close to setting a record.

"I still don't like this," Kalen said again, tugging the leather strip from his hair. The long, dark hair fell loose around his face as he bent over the desk, staring at the map. "But it's a better solution than what we've been doing. Have you picked your team?"

Syn just barely managed to keep from gaping at him.

He was going to go along with it.

Just like that?

* * *

With one small exception, Syn figured her hand-selected team was ideal.

The exception came with the name of Vena Saurell, the resident pain in the ass.

Vena's presence was almost enough to make Syn rethink the squadron she'd chosen for this run, but Syn hadn't ever let her personal likes and dislikes affect her job decisions. She wasn't going to start now.

According to the squadron's leader, Vena was doing well enough working with others. She also had experience with the baerns, something that would definitely come in handy—and it had been the deciding factor in allowing Vena to come on the trip.

She was the newest, and the only one with little to no experience—that acted as a mark against her, but the rest of the soldiers in Gering Squadron were experienced and tough, quick and silent, exactly what Syn wanted for this little trip. Vena was handy with weapons and she knew her way around baerns. Despite Syn's personal misgivings, she knew Vena was a good fit for the assignment.

Blowing out a breath, she turned away from the squadron and made herself focus on the upcoming run.

Kalen studied the squadron with a measuring look and gave her a single, satisfied nod. "Who are you taking as your seconds?" he asked.

"Lothen and Xan."

Kalen's brow winged up. "Xan. He's rather new to be acting as a second."

"He's very new . . . to our unit. But the man has military training. You can tell that just by looking at him."

"There's no denying that." He glanced around and located Xan by one of the supply houses, speaking with Lo. "Have you spoken to him?"

She nodded. "He's fine with it. Lo, as well."

"What about the rest of your unit?" Kalen asked, his voice dry. "You can't tell me hundreds of soldiers with more time in are fine with you picking him to act as a second on this little outing. He hasn't been here long at all."

"I selected my seconds based on who displayed the most skill, the most leadership abilities and the ability to make decisions under pressure. Xan fits the bill on all three, better than damn near anybody else in the camp, save for a few." Tilting her head to the side, she gave Kalen a wide grin and said, "I could always request Elina or Lee accompany me and act as my second."

"Fat chance," Kalen muttered. He didn't want the three of them together for more than a few seconds right now. He was probably being paranoid, but Syn appreciated his caution.

"Well, that marks off two of the others I'd considered. Bron was one, but we can't afford to have both him and me away from the camp at the same time. Unless of course you want to take over the training . . . ?"

"No." He crossed his arms over his chest and waited. "Who else did you consider?"

"The only other person I'd even think about having at my back out there is Morne, and as you know, Commander, he's not exactly available right now." She shrugged and rubbed at the back of her neck. She had the start of a tension headache brewing, and it was going to be an ugly one if she didn't relax. Come sunrise, they'd head out on their supply run, and although she wouldn't admit it, she was terrified. "Xan and Lo are the best choices . . . I suspect you know it as well as I do."

Kalen grimaced. "Of course I know it. I just want you prepared to explain your reasoning to those who bitch about it once you return." He jabbed a finger in her direction and said, "You'd best be prepared to handle those explanations, too, because I already know I'm going to have people at my door demanding it. I'm sending them your way."

"I wouldn't expect anything else," she said levelly.

"Good." He gave her a critical stare and then jerked his head to the side. "Get the hell out of here, Syn. I'll brief the squadron on things and then they can have the night off to rest and get ready. You go do the same."

"Respectfully, Commander, I'll do that after we dismiss the squadron." She gave him a faint smile and added, "Besides, the last thing we need is for me to look like I'm slacking in my duties."

Kalen hadn't admitted it, nor would he, but there had been some backlash from Vena's machinations. More than once, Syn had found herself being challenged by some of those who either were unfamiliar with her or just didn't care for her all that much.

She could handle the face-to-face confrontations, but if there were those giving her grief in public, then she knew there were probably twice as many who were taking their grievances to Kalen in private.

The debriefing took close to an hour. Lo and Xan were called up to stand by her. Kalen remained on hand, giving his silent, unwavering support. He may let her handle those who bitched about her choice in seconds, but just by staying there as she outlined the planned run, he showed he backed her decisions.

She appreciated it.

There were a few people watching Xan from the corner of their eye, but by the end of the debriefing, the faint hostility she'd sensed had faded. Some of them still weren't thrilled, but they were professionals—most of them.

"So . . . does anybody have any questions? Concerns?" she asked, wrapping things up. She hooked her thumbs in her utility belt and stood with her legs braced wide, studying the squadron.

A few hands went up. The general questions. Concerns expressed about the route, whether or not they were taking a large enough unit.

Vena's hand went up and Syn braced herself for whatever stupid commentary that woman might offer. But to her surprise, it was a fairly legit—and fair—question. "How can you be certain your magic is steady enough to rely on?"

"If I wasn't certain, we'd be going forward with a different plan," Syn replied. "We've used this method before, back before we had trouble channeling the magic, and it's always worked. The magic is channeled differently now, but it's still there—I can still use it, still rely on it. It won't fail us."

"Hope not." Vena scowled and looked off into the distance as she added, "Since it's our lives you're playing with."

"Your lives aren't a game to me, Saurell. I take the safety of my unit very seriously. If I had even the slightest doubt, this wouldn't be happening."

Kalen spoke up, his voice carrying to the back of the squadron and beyond. "Captain Caar has my utmost trust in this matter. I know her skills, and I trust them. I'd trust them with my life, and I have. I also trust those skills with *your* lives." His gaze skimmed over the unit as he continued. "This doesn't mean there's no risk involved in this run. There is risk and if you forget that for even a moment, it could very well be the last mistake you make. The demons are getting more aggressive. They can no longer travel back and forth between the Gates, and as you well know, they are predators. Game is getting scarce. They are starving and they are getting more desperate—to them, we are nothing but food. That only ups the risk to our men. However, we can't hope to combat that risk by sending ever-larger units on the supply runs. That presents an all-new danger. Larger units move slower and it's harder to conceal a large group of men. There is risk involved in this run, but there is risk involved in this no matter what. If you want a life without risk, let me know; we'll get you eastbound as soon as possible."

Nobody spoke.

"Well, then. I'd say we've covered everything," Syn said. She nodded to the squadron and dismissed them. As they all filed out of the hall, she turned and faced Xan, Lo and Kalen. Giving them a bright smile, she said, "That went rather well."

Kalen snorted. "That smile would terrify a sane man, Captain."

EIGHT

As much as he might dislike it, Laithe had come to the conclusion that he couldn't return to his unit.

Guilt over Corom gnawed at him, although he'd had little choice. Corom would have reported back to Reil, and Laithe simply couldn't have that.

Few things mattered more than his duty to his superiors, his duties to his brethren.

This was one of those things, and he'd acted as he must. That it had cost the life of a good Sirvani would keep him awake at night, however not as much as the alternative.

Like it or not, he couldn't return. Deserting his people certainly came with risks, though. If by some slim chance the bastard Dais returned to the High Lord and spoke of what Laithe had done—assuming they believed the off-worlder—then Laithe's life was forfeit.

But he doubted Dais would attempt to return to Reil.

So hopefully, he was safe. At least he hoped so, because he couldn't leave here now. Not after what he sensed going on the past few days.

It was the buzz of magic. Witch magic hit his senses
like strong, undiluted alcohol, and he reveled in it, almost
drunk on it. This was part of the reason why his kind
hunted witches. Having that power so near, it was almost
as pleasant as foreplay.

It was also something that had been absent until just
very recently.

A day or so after he'd killed Corom, that was when he
first sensed it. It was faint, and hidden almost as quickly as
it had flared to life. If he wasn't so close, he never would
have sensed it before they had concealed it.

From everything he understood about witches, they
used their gifts the same ways others used their eyes or
their ears. It was as natural as breathing. So why hadn't he
felt it before now?

He'd certainly been close enough.

At night, he could even see the faint light from the
campfires within the base's walls.

So it wasn't a matter of distance, or anything else . . .
They simply hadn't been using their magic.

He wondered why, but it wasn't a puzzle he could dwell
on, at least not right now.

There were soldiers moving in his direction, and more
than just a few. They weren't on foot, either, so they were
moving rather fast. They rode big animals—Laithe couldn't
remember their term for the four-legged creatures, but the
things were big, fast and rather effective guards, as well.

Laithe gathered what little gear he had and wiped away
all signs of his presence with the ease born of habit. It
took only moments and then he was melting into the trees,
withdrawing until he could no longer hear the soldiers,
no longer catch their scent on the wind, no longer feel the
burn of magic humming in the air.

* * *

He was closer—getting closer.

It had taken him close to a week. Another long, frustrat-
ing week, but Morne was finally closing in on Dais. Just that

morning, he'd found where Dais had made a quick camp for the night. He'd left early, well before dawn, almost as if he knew he couldn't afford to not keep moving.

He'd finally circled back around, though, moving out of the more demon-dense parts of the forest. For that, Morne was glad. Not just because he could relax a bit over his own safety, but because now he had less need to worry that a demon might get Dais before he had a chance.

That would be a serious disappointment.

Morne studied the path before him, brushing his fingers against the earth. With his eyes, he couldn't see any sign of Dais. But when he looked using his connection to the earth, he could feel the very path Dais had taken. The disturbance in the ground. Where he'd brushed against leaf, branch or rock.

Then he sensed another disturbance.

Violent rage.

Anger.

The lust for blood and deep, deep hunger, the kind that turned the belly into knots.

Demons. Moving about in the damn day again, like they no longer cared about the sun burning in the sky.

Damn it.

There was more, though. They were still too far away from him to see, or even hear. Curling his fingers into the earth, he reached farther, expanding his senses until they were stretched paper-thin.

There . . . Syn. He recognized the feel of her magic. Lo . . . Warlord.

Recognition flickered in his brain and he swore, shoving upright and glaring into the distance.

The rebels were moving in this direction and somewhere in between lay monsters.

He didn't hesitate. Reaching out, he established a link with the commander of the rebel army.

"Commander, you have a problem. You have a team out in the forest, and they are about to become demon fodder."

Morne's mind buzzed as Kalen reached out, projecting his voice. *"Location?"*

He projected a rough guess as he started to run through the trees. He dodged and swerved to avoid the branches that reached out as though to grab him, anything to slow him down.

People were going to die. He didn't even know how he knew, but he did. People were going to die, and if Kalen didn't get men there quick . . .

"Bloody hell. It's the supply run."

"It's about to become a massacre," Morne bit off. *"Unless your get men there quick."*

"Bron's already on the move with backup." There was a brief pause, and then, *"There will be wounded. Will you help?"*

Out loud, Morne muttered, "You already know the answer to that. I'll be there as quick as I can, but I'm not close and I'm on foot."

* * *

"You realize that doing that could be construed as making sexual advances toward your commander, right?" Syn barely managed to keep her moan behind her teeth as he stroked a hand down her back and rested it on her hip.

It was past midday and they stopped for a quick break and to let the baerns drink their fill from the nearby stream. She leaned against one of the trees, staring out at her unit and trying not to blush as Xan stood behind her.

Through their clothes, she could feel the warmth of his body. The scent of him flooded her head. She wanted to turn around and bury her face against his chest, rub herself against him—lose herself in him.

Not an option, she reminded herself.

This was the only time they'd stopped during the day. Tonight, they'd make camp—the location Syn had selected as a fortified area, one of the many shelters the rebels had built over the years. It was in an easily defensible place. Once they got there, maybe she'd breathe easier.

In the morning, they'd hit the trail at first light, and if they were lucky, they'd reach the outer limits of their territory before noon.

From there, they'd be safer. Until they were safe, she wasn't indulging in anything that included Xan's body and hers.

Voices rose and fell around them. With a sigh, she made herself step away.

Xan chuckled and moved to stand beside her.

"If that could be construed as a sexual advance, what would your good little soldiers think if they'd seen us last night?" he asked, his voice so low only she could hear it.

Memories of last night rushed through her, and to her horror, she felt a blush creeping up her cheeks. She was a captain in the Roinan rebellion—she'd faced down demons, Warlords and testosterone-laden soldiers who were convinced no female could possibly lead them as well as a male.

But this man managed to make her blush like a schoolgirl.

Syn narrowed her eyes at him. "*You* are one of my good little soldiers, remember?"

"One of the good ones? I want to be the best." His lips curled in a slow smile.

She wanted to lean in, kiss him until that smile faded. Kiss him until they both forgot everything but each other.

But duty wouldn't let her. More, neither would her gut. She was nervous as hell, but she was always nervous when a supply run went out. Even when she wasn't in charge, she was nervous.

This was more than nerves, though, and that was enough to have her resting a hand on the butt of her pulsar in readiness. She trusted her instincts. Even when she didn't trust much of anything else, she trusted her instincts.

It had been a quiet morning and already they were miles from the camp. Traveling by baern wasn't as quick as using more modern methods of transportation, but it was the safest.

Safest, because it didn't attract the wyrms. Wyrms—
yet another blight brought into their world by Anqar—are
giant feeding machines that lived in the ground, growing
to sizes untold. The big behemoths were drawn to anything
engine-powered—the roar of an engine was the equivalent
of a dinner bell for them. Gliders weren't loud enough to
attract them, but the things moved too damn slow and just
weren't effective for anything of this nature.

So they rode the baerns, and they were making good
time.

Once they reached the outer limits, they wouldn't have to
worry about the wyrms, period. The land there was rigged
to blow at the presence of a wyrm. The line stretched for
miles, all along the base of the Roinan Mountains. It was
one thing their world's formal military factions had finally
gotten right.

There would be sol-fueled caribins waiting, wicked fast
two-seated transports. From there, they could ride the rest
of the way to the military base where they collected supplies from grudging hands. They'd be in relative safety—
for a time.

If they made it to the outer limits.

If . . .

Syn's heart beat slow and hard against her rib cage.
Beating out a warning.

The hair on her arms, on the back of her neck, stood on
end. *Get ready . . .*

She sank her senses deeper into the tumultuous energy.
Through the earth's energy, she felt her link to Elina
strengthen and solidify, steadying her. Lee's presence was
also there. The two women gave Syn the one thing she
needed to tap into the energy again.

An anchor.

In the privacy of her mind, she reached out and demanded,
"Show me."

The response was sluggish. Slow.

"Syn?"

Although Xan stood at her side, his voice seemed to

come from over a long distance, faint and thready. Focusing her eyes on him, she said grimly, "Do a circuit. Something's wrong."

Immediately, the concern left his face, and he went from lover to warrior in seconds. He stepped back and reached for the pulsar at his side, drawing it. Syn didn't bother stopping him.

"What is it?"

She shook her head. "I don't know. I just . . ." Her words trailed off and she just shook her head again. "Just do the circuit for me, okay?"

He nodded and melted into the trees.

Once more, she focused on her link, stretching farther, farther. *Come on,* she thought impatiently. *What is it? Where?*

She couldn't really *feel* anything yet. Yet . . .

Stop it. You're going to bring the bad on just by thinking about it overmuch. Negative energy loves negative energy.

Sweat trickled down her neck, between her breasts. The cavinir garments she wore were flexible and breathable, but cavinir was designed to be armor. The ultimate in hot-weather wear, they were not. And it was hot—damn hot. If only there was a breeze, the heat might have been tolerable.

As it was, the heat only added to the tension mounting inside.

In the back of her mind, she could hear her men, talking quietly among themselves. The two medic-trained fighters who'd accompanied them were traveling near the middle.

None of the others seemed ill at ease. Just her. She kept her pulsar at the ready, focusing on the forest instead of the people behind her.

Finally, she felt a little click as her tedious search yielded results.

Demons. Moving on them—fast.

The air was heavy. Dark with death. She could feel it. Taste it.

Did they try to make the run back to camp? Yes. They had no other choice. They were only twelve and if they stayed here, they'd all end up dead. At least if they made a run for it, the baerns had a chance at outrunning the demons.

From the corner of her eye, she saw one of the beasts throw his head, skittish. He'd scented the things, too. Damn. Damn. Damn.

She'd led them into death.

She battled back a shudder as that knowledge rolled through her. A sure, eerie knowledge she couldn't hope to explain. Taking a deep breath, she distanced herself from her link to the earth and focused on her soldiers.

Quietly, she called, "Lo."

"Captain?"

"Problems," she said softly. Then she raised her voice to address the rest of the rebels. "Mount up, my friends. Ride like hell back to camp, but stay *together*. Trouble is coming."

She mounted her baern. She called him Kerr and he'd been her companion on treks like this many times. Stroking a hand down the big stallion's neck, she murmured to him. The little nubs of his ears flicked back at the sound of her voice, and he leaned into her hand, as though he sensed her fear and wanted to soothe it. "We'll get through this, won't we, Kerr?"

Syn tilted her head back and drew in a slow breath, trying to pick up something other than the scents of the forest and the people around her, and the warm, musky scent of the baerns. She smelled moss, pine, oak and wildflowers. She smelled the herbal soaps a lot of the people in the camp used. She smelled the stink of tobacco and sweat.

Under all of that, she caught the faint trace of demon. How close?

She reached out with her mind, focusing on Kalen. He responded but with a faintly distracted manner—she recognized it. He was talking mind to mind with another. *"Commander, we might need reinforcements."*

"I'm aware. Give me one minute, Captain, and you had better be hauling ass back to the base camp."

"As we speak." As she waited, she reached for her link to the earth. It welcomed her, wrapped her in its strength and whispered knowledge to her. It offered its energy. Only days before, she would have shied away. But this time, she let it flood her. The energy and relief swamped her. Control—she was in control.

And damn, she was going to need it. Opening her eyes, she stared into the woods.

Her men, all mounted now, started back down the trail, two by two, sticking close together.

"I've got Bron putting together a team. Where are you and how close are they?" Kalen barked, his mind voice harsh and abrupt—others might not recognize it as such, but Syn knew it was a sure sign that he was worried. It didn't help her state of mind.

Syn projected an image of their surroundings to him, all the while scanning the forest.

"I'm not sure how close the demons are, just yet, but there are quite a few," she said, trying for a deeper connection, wishing she could give a more concrete answer. *"Raviners, for sure, though. I can feel them trying to block me."*

Raviners were power thieves. While Jorniaks fed off flesh, Raviners fed off of power, and they were able to hide themselves, to some extent, from the witches.

"Haul ass," Kalen said again and then he broke the connection.

Seconds ticked away into minutes, and nothing happened. She could feel the edgy looks from her men, felt the skittishness of the baerns, how the big beasts tugged against their reins and tried to run rather than trot. Not good ground for running, though. Couldn't risk it.

But soon, the terrain smoothed out and the trail widened just enough. "Pick up the pace, men," she said, tapping her baern's sides with her heels. Obediently, he settled into a quicker pace.

They'd made it halfway to the camp when the Jorniaks came boiling out of the woods. Big, strong and stupid, they were base predators, nothing more. They were vaguely humanoid—as in walking upright on two legs, with two arms and a head with all the expected features one would expect on a humanoid. Mouth, eyes, ears, nose . . . teeth. Very big, very sharp, ugly teeth that protruded from a mouth designed to rip and tear.

Their skin was a leathery, putrid shade of gray, their bodies hairless and often covered with a variety of bulges and bumps that made them look even more grotesquely disfigured. They were big, as well, nearly half as big as the average male warrior in the rebellion.

Big . . . and dumb. Syn counted six of them—they could handle six Jorniaks. They could do that without her needing the magic, even.

The low hum of pulsars filled the air and then a nauseating stench filled the air. A dead Jorniak stank like nothing else—cut them open and it was guaranteed to leave you fighting the urge to puke.

Kalen's voice hit her mind just as she cut one of the demons down. *"Report."*

"Busy," she snarled out loud, knowing he'd hear it anyway.

"Backup is en route. Hold the line, Caar. I've got men on the way. Elina's with them."

"Elina—"

He'd only send Elina for one reason. Adrenaline buzzed as she watched three of the monsters go down in a heap before they even cleared the woods.

Syn took down a fourth and as she swung to take aim on a fifth, she caught sight of the demons she'd sensed.

The Raviners.

Raviners and Jorniaks. Again. Working together . . . and in broad daylight. Jorniaks might be too stupid to recognize their lesser strength under the sun, but Raviners? Not again. Not fucking again.

"This is no damned coincidence," she muttered, changing her aim to one of the higher demons. Somehow, the Raviners had figured out how to control the Jorniaks. Or at least point them in the right direction.

With her heart racing in fear, she called out an order. *Hold the line,* Kalen had said. She'd hold the line, damn it. She just hoped the magic would hold, too.

"Left flank," she called out.

As one, a third of her fighters turned to guard against the Raviners. The demons appeared from the shadowy forest, their robes hanging on gaunt, skeletal bodies. They were flanked by more Jorniaks. A dozen, easy. Through her shields, Syn could feel the confusion from her fighters, the dread . . . and something else. Something hungry. Something that knew what she was and wanted her. She flinched as she sensed it reaching for her.

Slamming tighter shields into place, she let her gut lead her and she aimed for one of the Raviners. Nothing about him marked him as leader—not the cut of his robe, no physical adornments, nothing. But he was the leader, and he was the one casting out a psychic net and hoping to find the vulnerable mind of some talented soul.

Syn was talented, but her mind was anything but vulnerable. Still, just the feel of him was enough to turn her heart to ice. She sighted on him and fired—his head disintegrated under the blast.

But he wasn't the only one.

There were more. Too many.

She heard the death scream of one of the baerns and swore, seeing from the corner of her eye as the beast went down. It was followed by another. The big creatures were being hampered by the close press of the demons—they couldn't get the room they needed to fight, leaving them vulnerable.

Through the melee, she could see Xan, a pulsar in one hand, a wicked long blade in the other. He was no longer mounted—she didn't know if he'd lost his baern or just preferred to fight on foot. He used the pulsar to take down anything he could get a bead on and the blade was reserved for anything stupid enough to cross his path.

The man was death personified.

Stay alive, she thought desperately. For all of them. For herself. For Xan. For her men and the medics who wouldn't stand much chance against the demons.

Her men knew how to fight.

They knew how to fight against ridiculous odds.

But they were being overrun. If they didn't get help soon . . .

"Damn it, where are they all coming from?" Lo growled. Then he looked at Syn and said, "If you're going to do something, now's the time, Captain."

She nodded and dismounted. Her feet had barely hit the ground when her baern launched his massive body into the throng of demons, stomping, crushing, using his powerful jaws and neck to grab one of the Jorniaks and send it flying. She hoped he'd make it. She loved the animal.

Taking cover behind her men, she took a deep breath. "Cover me," she said, her voice flat and hard. Hopefully none of them sensed the fear inside her.

Staring at the demons, she started to gather the energy. In her mind, she spun a web of flame. They came boiling out of the woods like ants, more and more. Dozens of them. She waited until they were as close as she dared let them get—the more of them she could see, the more of them she could kill.

Then she flung the fire net at them.

Screams filled the air. Enraged, filled with pain. It echoed around them and Syn continued to call the fire, until she sensed no more life in the demons in front of her. But there were more. Coming from all around.

So many more.

The time would have passed quickly—logically, Syn knew that. But it felt as though she'd been fighting for hours. Gather the energy, form the fire, force it on the demons, burn them to ash and then start all over again.

But even with the earth feeding its energy into her, she could only call the fire for so long. After setting a third line of demons ablaze, she had to stop. Her control was too shaky, and even with an anchor, she had to be able to direct the fire or she could kill her own men instead of the monsters.

Adrenaline fueled her muscles and she relied on her weapons instead of her magic. Somehow, she found herself fighting shoulder to shoulder with Vena, guarding the fallen as best they could.

Lo was one of them. Although blood gushed from a nasty, jagged bite on his arm, he was on the comm-unit, contacting Bron.

Bron—with the reinforcements. Where in the hell were they? And Xan . . . she hadn't seen him.

"Syn—Commander—drop." Lo's voice was ragged and harsh with pain.

They dropped as one and over their heads came a wide, pulsating burst of light. She felt the heat of it singeing her skin, close—too close, but she didn't let herself flinch. Both the heating blasting over her head and the Jorniaks were just an arm's reach away now.

Lo was a wizard with weapons—whatever piece he'd invented this time, he would have tested it and he trusted it enough—

The stink of burning Jorniak flooded her nostrils, and she swallowed the bile that climbed up her throat. Their bodies were in a burning, grotesque heap in the ground as she stood and turned to face yet another line of the monsters.

And another.

To her left, she heard a sharp female scream and she turned, jerking up her pulsar, but she was too late. Vena was down, blood bubbling from a vicious wound in her throat. A Jorniak grabbed her ankle to drag her away and

Syn unloaded on him, reaching deep down for some remnant of her magic and delivering a fireball straight into his face.

The demon went down. But Vena was already dead, her throat laid open in a vicious, bloody smile of death.

It seemed forever before she heard Lo's voice say, "Backup is here."

It seemed almost as long before she was able to lower her weapon without fear of having her own throat ripped out the second she relaxed her guard. Bleeding from gashes in her right arm and left leg, she stumbled to a tree and leaned against it. Fumbling in her pack, she pulled out a couple strips of leather.

The injury on her thigh was ugly and painful, but not too deep.

The one on her arm was a different story. It was still pumping out far too much blood.

"Let me help."

She looked up, dazed, to Xan.

Dazed, she reached up and touched his face. "You're okay."

"More than I can say for you, Captain," he muttered, his voice nothing more than a growl. He reached for the strip of leather in her hand, and she let him take it.

He was bleeding, too. Under the gore splattered on his face, there was a long, sliver-thin cut. "You got that pretty face of yours cut up even more," she said. "Gonna have more scars."

"I'm told women like scars on their warriors."

He wasn't gentle as he tied her arm off. She bit her lip to keep from crying out. Focusing on the ugly mess of her arm, she said, "Well, the girls are just going to love me, then. I'm going to have some damn pretty scars when these heal up."

He used the bandages in her kit to field-dress her major injuries, but when he moved on to the lesser ones, she waved him off. "I'm good. We need to stand guard in case they come back."

"They won't come back," he said.

"Don't be so sure."

Famous last words. With the blood still roaring in her ears, she could barely make sense of the clamoring inside—whispers. Voices whispering to her. She squeezed her eyes closed and concentrated, focused.

She wasn't a strong witch.

For short periods of time, she could burn things like nothing else but that was it. She knew her gift, though, had honed it to a razor's edge, and right now, it was screaming.

The demons were doubling back.

"Elina . . . Where's Elina?"

She came striding out of the bloody melee, dressed in the casual clothes she wore when she wasn't on duty. She had her weapon belt strapped over it and blood splattered her arms and face. "I'm here." She reached out a hand, caught Syn's. "You feel it?"

Syn squeezed. "I feel it. We need more than just firepower if we want to make it out of this."

Elina nodded. "I'll do it, though. You can't handle it right now."

"I can—"

"No." Elina shook her head. "When it comes to the magic, I outrank you, and you can't maintain." She gave Xan a hard look and said, "Get her to camp. I don't care if you have to throw her over your shoulder and haul her ass out of her. Get her to camp *now.*"

Xan nodded.

Elina called to Bron across the field. He was barking out orders but at the sound of Elina's voice, he stopped. She gave him the signal to fall back and he nodded.

With Syn wounded, he was in charge.

"Round up the wounded and haul ass," he called out.

One of the medics said, "We need to stabilize—"

"Now," he interrupted. He glared at the medics and said, "If we don't move, it won't matter if the wounded are stable or not—they'll die."

***

Xan didn't know what Syn had sensed—it was something. He had seen the naked terror in her eyes before she locked it down. He boosted her into his arms as she ineffectually shoved against him. "I can walk—we need your hands free."

He pushed his pulsar into her hands. "You be my hands—you can't walk fast enough to keep up."

"Then put me down, damn it. I'll guard the retreat."

Like hell. The ice-cold fear he'd seen in her eyes had him tangled into knots. He ignored her weak struggles, blocked them out of his mind. If she was so weak she couldn't dislodge him, then she must have lost a lot of blood.

They almost made it.

Bringing up the tail, Xan cradled Syn against his chest and whispered, "Hold on. We're almost there."

He could see the walls of the camp. Could hear the voices just ahead.

But then he heard the growling behind him. He shot a look behind him just as the demons broke through the trees. Swearing, he grabbed his pulsar and looked around, searching for somebody who could take Syn. But there was nobody.

Elina—where in the hell was the witch? But then he figured out the answer. Within the woods, smoke billowed. She was burning them, and from the amount of smoke, she was burning up a whole hell of a lot more than the eight or nine demons at a take like Syn had been doing.

She hadn't gotten all of them, though—too many of them were still rushing the ragtag, injured fighters.

The buzz of her magic thundered through the air, hot and powerful. Shit, every Warlord within a day's walk would feel her power this time. There was nothing hidden about it. She had her hands full, wherever she was.

Bron was all but dragging a soldier toward the camp

gates, and all of those able to walk were doing the same thing as Xan and Bron—aiding the injured. One of them tried to come up and help Lo, but the red-haired soldier shoved him off. "I'm on my own two feet, damn it. Find somebody that isn't."

Xan caught Lo's eyes. The man was pale from blood loss, but the look on his face was grim, hard and determined.

"If we buy them a few minutes, they can get a team out there, protect the gate," Lo said, his voice grim.

Buying them time against that many demons—it was a suicide mission.

"Syn won't make it," Xan said quietly. He glanced at the gate and then back into the forest. He might make it—if he ran. But more of the soldiers would die if they didn't cover their retreat. He eased Syn to the ground—she was unconscious now, her face a deathly shade of gray.

It all but ripped his heart out as he stood over her body.

Lo lifted his pulsar and said absently, "Do me a favor—if you make it through this, tell Janis I love her."

The two men began firing as one. Others joined them. Shrieks filled the air.

Not all of them came from the demons. Hot, red blood splashed against his face. He couldn't turn his head to see—couldn't take his one good eye from the enemy coming at him.

But it was human blood.

Jorniaks didn't bleed red.

Hurling his pulsar down, Xan reached for the blades at his back. Pulsars were nice little weapons to use if you had some distance between yourself and the target. He had next to no distance. Besides, he preferred the bladed weapon over the blasting kind any day.

He fell into a fog—a fog made of his own driving need to keep the demons from Syn and their fetid, hungry breath clogging his every breath.

Then there was only one demon.

He lifted his blade to take it down, but it hit the ground before he could strike.

A man stood there, just behind the demon.

A blond man, with midnight eyes and fresh, black demon blood splattered across his face.

The feel of him made Xan's skin crawl.

Power—a Warlord's power, and this man had it in spades.

The stranger glanced behind him, his gaze lingering on Syn.

Lips peeling back from his teeth, Xan lifted his blade. "You can't touch her."

"And you can barely stand, you fool." The blond circled around him and knelt beside Syn, tearing away the makeshift bandages.

Warmth pulsed through the air.

It knocked Xan back—a palpable force. From the direction of the camp, he heard voices calling out. He looked away from the man for just a moment—good—help. Thankfully. Finally. Gripping his blade, he went to attack the unknown Warlord, although he barely had the strength to stand.

When he looked back, it was just in time to see the back of the blond man's head as he disappeared into the forest. "Get the hell out of here," he muttered. Away from Syn.

Swearing, he crouched down by her side and reached for the discarded bandages. But when he went to press them to her wounds, he realized they weren't needed. The deep, gaping gashes in her arm were no longer deep, gaping . . . or open. Fine ridges of deep red scar tissue were there instead.

Startled, Xan lifted his head and stared into the trees. He couldn't see the other man anymore.

A healer . . . ? Not a medic or some sort of herb witch, but a real healer.

He lifted his gaze and looked around. A healer—they could use a healer.

But then he realized . . . no. They couldn't use a healer.

Syn was no longer bleeding and those still standing might need medical attention, but a healer's gift would be wasted on them.

And nothing could help the fallen.

Including Lo.

NINE

Syn came awake to find Elina leaning over her.

A familiar, unwelcome smell filled her nostrils, and she promptly closed her eyes. "I'm still asleep," she said baldly.

"Nice try. Now sit up or I'll pour this shit down your throat." In a taunting voice, the witch added, "And you're really not strong enough to stop me."

Syn hated to admit it, but the bitch had a point. Popping one eye open, she glared at Elina. "I don't need that stuff. I'm fine."

"You're not. You could have lost your arm and there's an infection settling in the bite wound in your leg."

"My arm?" Now Syn sat up. Elina moved back but more to keep the hot tea in her hand from spilling onto Syn's chest. She lifted both arms and stared at them. She saw right away which one she'd almost lost. Her left arm had three raised ridges high on it. Deep inside the arm, she ached. She could feel the pull of healing muscles and the itch of healing flesh. It looked like an injury that was a few weeks old. But she hadn't had it that morning.

A memory flashed through her mind.

She could remember Xan, hauling her back to camp even as the Jorniaks and Raviners swelled around them. It was bizarrely dreamlike—just outside the camp, Xan had stopped, put her on the ground.

Lo had been there. A few others. She heard screams. Heard howls. Smelled the blood.

Then nothing—a brief flash of darkness, followed by one startling clear memory. A man's face, surrounded by a shock of pale hair, followed by the rush of a healer's touch.

"Morne."

Elina cocked a brow. "I assumed as much. Nobody else around here can do what he does. All the smart healers do the same thing the smart witches do—stay very, very far away from the Gates."

Syn closed her eyes and slumped back against the jela-pad. One nice thing about getting injured—the patients in the medicon got all the good beds. The bed conformed to her body, cradling her. "Guess that means he's not as smart as we always thought he was." With a smirk, she added, "And neither are you. After all, *you* left and then came back."

"Yes. I guess that means I'm either very, very foolish or just a glutton for punishment."

The smell of the insian tea grew stronger, and Syn could feel the heat of the cup close to her cheek. "Come on, Syn. Drink up."

Syn turned her head aside and held out a hand, grimacing. She could either drink the shit and feel better shortly or fight Elina, feel like a fool when she lost, and she'd still have to drink the damn stuff. "Fine. Give me the damn thing, and go find Kalen. I want a report on the losses."

"He's already on his way. I buzzed him when I knew you were waking up."

Forcing her body upright, she gulped the tea down in four big swigs. It was hot, burning her tongue. Not enough to kill her taste buds, though, unfortunately. It was like drinking water laced with mold and fecal material—utterly vile.

But it worked.

Within a few heartbeats, the pain in her arm eased, as did the lingering headache she hadn't even been aware of. "You would think there would be something to make that crap taste better."

"There is—grinding it down into a powder and making tablets out of it." Elina smirked and added, "But we kind of lack the technology to do it out here and the bastards back east are too stingy to share the good stuff, I guess."

Syn was only marginally aware of Elina's voice. She was remembering—trying to work past the cloud of pain that fogged the memories.

Xan.

Lothen.

The cloud of death she'd sensed, even before the attack had begun.

Somebody had died.

"Elina."

The blond witch sighed and settled down on the bed next to Syn. "What, honey?"

"You do know that you're about the only person with the guts to call me honey, right?" Syn smiled, but it wobbled and faded as she looked up and met Elina's gaze. "How bad was it?"

"Pretty bad. From all accounts, there were a couple dozen Jorniaks, at least, probably more. There were also Raviners."

Syn swallowed and said, "I remember calling for everybody to fall back. The demons doubled back, didn't they?"

"Yeah. They didn't catch up until your men were almost at the camp—we sent men to get the injured. I was able to catch some of them with fire. Still, we would have lost even more, but . . ." Elina stopped talking and swallowed.

Screams echoed in Syn's ears. She remembered.

"Xan and Lothen guarded the retreat," Syn said softly.
"I remember it. I was going in and out, but I remember him
carrying me. Then he put me down and I heard them—
heard one of them scream; then I was gone again."

Elina reached over and covered Syn's hand. "Lo's
dead."

Syn nodded. Lo—one of Bron's best friends. A guy
about her age—he was goofy and liked to tease, liked to
laugh. Fought like a demon. Had a thing going with one of
the medics—Janis—he'd adored that woman.

Now he was dead.

"Was it quick?"

Elina nodded. Under the warm gold of her skin, she
was pale. Very pale. Grim-eyed, she said, "The secondary
units went out to sweep for survivors. They brought his
remains back. He died fast. Very fast . . . and I . . . Well, he
didn't hurt much."

Syn blew out a breath, tried to breathe past the pain
knotting inside her chest. "What about Xan?"

Elina nodded her head toward the medicon doors.
"He's standing guard outside. Very grim look on his face.
I've got to tell you, Syn, he's a sexy piece of work." She
wiggled her eyebrows and gave Syn a wicked, somewhat
forced smile. "And the way he watches you, it's something
else. I'm kind of surprised he's not already in here."

Syn didn't have a chance to even think about how to
respond to that one, because the door opened and Kalen
came striding in. He stopped in the middle of the room,
arms folded over his chest, a dark look on his face.

"We have two men unaccounted for—two confirmed
dead—Lo and Saurell," he said bluntly.

Syn nodded. "I saw Saurell go down. I heard about
Lo—Elina told me."

He stared off over her shoulder, but he wasn't seeing
the plain white wall, she knew. Lo had come to the Roinan
camp about the same time she had. They'd trained together,

fought together. "I'm giving Bron a day or two off. You're taking a week."

Syn scowled at him. "I don't need a week."

"You're lucky you're not being shipped out," he snapped. He gave her arm a pointed look.

It felt like the bottom of her stomach just dropped out. Okay, she hadn't quite managed to get her thoughts around to that point. Absently, she reached over and ran a hand down the ridge of scars. "Don't suppose Morne showed up in the camp, did he?" she asked softly.

"Briefly." His mouth twisted in a smile, but it wasn't a happy one. "Not that anybody saw him. He attended to some of the other wounded and then disappeared—not a damn soul saw him. Didn't linger around to say two words." He glanced at her arm. "Did he say anything to you?"

Syn grimaced. "Hell, I don't really even remember *seeing* him. I thought maybe he was there, thought I sensed him. But he could have been dancing with the Jorniaks for all I can tell you."

"Well, I'm pretty sure he wasn't dancing with the Jorniaks." Elina wrapped an arm over Syn's shoulders.

Something in the other woman's voice had Syn looking at her. "He's okay, Elina."

"Okay enough to come in, heal three of our more critically wounded and then disappear, alone, into the forest again." Elina sighed and rose, moving to stand at the foot of the bed. She slipped her hands into her pockets and stared up at the ceiling. "Yes, he is okay . . . for now. But for how much longer? Not even he can hope to fight every last demon out there. The longer he is out there alone, the more likely it is he will die."

Huh. I'll be damned, Syn thought. There was something there. Slowly, she pushed herself to her feet and went to stand by the other witch. Now it was her turn to wrap an arm around her friend. She couldn't reach Elina's shoulders so she settled for hugging her waist with her uninjured arm. "Morne will be fine. He's a survivor. I'm sure enough that I'd bet my arm on it. The bad one—I need at least one good one or I can't kick Kalen's tail until he lets me back on duty."

"You're off duty for a week." Kalen didn't look at all fazed as she turned and gave him a pitiful look. "You need it. Hell, we *all* need it. Go back to bed. Sleep. Take your week off and heal."

"I want to know more—"

Kalen narrowed his eyes. The silvery gray darkened to pewter and he said, "You'll obey orders, Captain, or I'll have you confined to quarters for the week—*without* your self-appointed bodyguard."

He'd do it, too. Glaring at him, she made her way to the bed and sat down. "I'm sitting down on the bed because I'm tired—*not* because you ordered me to."

"Oh, trust me. I believe that."

* * *

The commander left.

Eventually Elina left.

Xan needed to see her—*had* to. But he had to protect her, and when he saw her, saw that she still breathed, still lived—

There was chaos within him. In his mind, his heart, so much chaos and he didn't know if he could hold himself together once he saw her. But he had to—

Finally, after waging a war with himself, Xan slipped into her room. Just for a few minutes. Just long enough to reassure himself she had survived. That she was safe. That the Warlord hadn't crept into the camp somehow and stolen her away.

Her room was barely the size of a closet, large enough for her bed and that was it. It wasn't a large bed, but her slender form looked lost inside it. Stroking a finger down her cheek, he studied her wan, pale face. The sight of her was like taking a blow—straight to his heart. She was so pale. And weak—

Syn might not be hovering near death.

She might not have a gaping wound that should have cost her her arm.

But she was still weak, vulnerable, and that Warlord was in the area.

Healer or not, that man had been a Warlord. There was no denying what Syn was, what Elina was. After the power storm Elina had unleashed, any Warlord in the vicinity would know there was at least one witch left in the rebel camp. There was a buzz in the air, one that would take some time to fade, if he knew a damn thing about magic.

They were too vulnerable. No matter how strong they were, how well they trained, they were viewed as a prize the Warlords would do damn near anything to get their hands on, especially now.

The healer . . . who in the hell had he been? Why had he healed Syn?

He'd saved her arm, quite possibly her life. But why? Possibly because he had plans for her that didn't include dying.

There were circles under her eyes, huge, dark circles that gave her face a bruised look.

So pale. She was so pale—her ivory skin had a grayish cast and her lips looked colorless, as well. She'd lost a lot of blood. He could still feel the heat of it as it pulsed out of her body and spilled onto his hands as he tried to staunch the flow.

In her sleep, Syn sighed and then she shifted. Pulling his hand back, he remained by her side as her lashes lifted, revealing her green-gold eyes. "Hello."

He didn't respond.

Syn yawned and reached up, rubbing her eyes. "If they have put you on bedside duty for the time being, we might need to rethink that. You're not very good at it."

"I'm not on duty." He frowned as she started to ease upright. He braced a hand against her shoulder and said, "You need more rest."

"I just want to sit up," she said, rolling her eyes. "Don't worry, I wasn't about to get up and dance or start plotting out my plans for world domination. I can handle sitting up."

She narrowed her eyes and shifted her gaze to the hand he still held against her shoulder. "Stand down, Xan. I may be out of action for the next few days, but I'm still a fucking captain in this base, and I'm not going go to be forcibly kept to bed."

"As you wish," he murmured.

Her gaze shot to his and he bowed his head, falling back precisely two steps. If all she wanted to do was sit up, she could probably do it. But if she tried to stand . . . well, Xan wanted to be close enough to catch her when she fell. Despite having a healer deal with her arm, she was still weak from blood loss. Nothing but rest, water and food would help that.

But she didn't stand up. All she did was sit and draw her knees to her chest, smoothing the sheet down around her lower body. Under the simple white gown they'd given her, she looked incredibly frail—breakable.

The look in her green-gold eyes didn't help. She stared off into the distance despondently.

He didn't need to ask what had her so unhappy. She'd lost a friend in the attack—not just someone she knew, but a close friend. During this unending war, all of them had lost friends or family . . . both. But loss was something people never grew accustomed to—and if they did, they weren't any better for it.

"You could have died, staying behind to lug me along," Syn said quietly, looking at him from under her lashes.

"And if I hadn't stayed to lug you along, you *would* have died." He crossed his arms across his chest and stared at her with a resolute expression on his unyielding face.

* * *

Resolute. Unyielding. They were words that described Xan, Syn figured. From the top of his head to the bottom of his booted feet. He had as much give to him as some of the sheer rock walls that bordered the camp.

"It wouldn't have helped us any if you had died, you know. We need all the able bodies that we can get."

"If you had died, you'd leave this camp weaker. You're needed here." He closed the distance between them and stroked his fingers down her cheek before cupping her chin in his hand and arching her head back. He brushed his mouth against hers as he spoke. "The people in this camp need you. *I* need you . . . Captain."

Somehow, when he said it, it felt like a caress. Felt like something intimate. How was that possible? Something warm fluttered inside her chest, but she shoved it aside. People had died because of her arrogance.

Lo was dead . . . because of her.

She didn't deserve his warmth or his comfort.

"I'm far from indispensable. Perhaps if you hadn't slowed to help me, the survivors could have reached the camp more quickly and Lothen would be alive."

"That's absurd." Xan shook his head.

"Is it?" She glared at him, jutting her chin up. She was trying to pick a fight with him, and she knew it. Even as she knew it was stupid, she couldn't stop. "You were in charge of the team if I went down, and you were supposed to take care of *all* of them, not just me."

"Are you angry with me because I saved *you* or because I didn't save Lo?" he demanded, his voice harsh. Something glinted in his eyes, gone almost too quick to identify.

But not quick enough. Grief. Guilt. The same emotions threatening to choke her. Abruptly, her anger faded and tears burned her eyes. She buried her face against her knees. In a voice thick with tears, she whispered, "They keep winning, Xan. No matter what we do, no matter how hard we fight, they always manage to find a way to beat us."

"You're wrong."

Was she? She honestly didn't know anymore.

She didn't hear him move, but she sensed it. The heat of his hand curved over her neck, comforting and gentle. "You haven't been *beaten*."

"It certainly feels like I have," she muttered, her voice harsh and bitter.

"You've suffered a loss. But that's not the same as being beaten. You continue to fight, and you'll continue to do so for as long as you live. People die in war, Syn. People die in battle. You know this. Lothen risked his life to buy the rest of the unit time to get to the camp—he knew what he was doing, and he did it of his own free will. Don't dishonor his memory by questioning his choice. He deserves better than that." He cupped her chin and lifted her face to his. Quietly, in a hoarse voice, he said, "You would have made the same choice, and we both know it. If it was Lothen standing here instead of you, would you want him beating himself up with guilt?"

"No."

He dipped his head and kissed away her tears. "He laid down his life for his friends—for this army. And if I know anything about the man, he was honored to do it."

"Yeah. That's Lo, all right." She forced a smile at him and wiped away her tears. "But even knowing that, it doesn't make it any easier." She clenched her hands into fists, tight—so tight her nails bit into her flesh and drew blood.

"Nothing makes it easier . . . including giving up." He gave her neck one last, lingering stroke. He pressed his lips to her temple. "You need to rest, Syn. You lost a lot of blood. Lie down for me now."

Because he asked, and because she was damned weary, she let him ease her body back until she was lying down. "Will you sleep?" he asked quietly.

"Will you stay with me?" She caught his hand and twined her fingers. She couldn't stand the thought of being alone right then. Even though the bloody dreams would haunt her no matter what, it would be easier to tolerate them when he was close.

"I am not going anywhere," he promised. He drew the blankets back up and then stretched out next to her. It was a tight fit—the narrow bed was barely wide enough to accommodate his body, much less his and hers. Easing onto his side, he drew her close. Syn turned into his heat, one arm around his waist. He cuddled her close and nuzzled her brow. "Sleep."

TEN

"As far as my area goes, supplies are damn low."

A grim look on his face, Kalen listened as Gunner gave a quick report of weapon materials. It was in line with the reports he'd gotten about rations, too. They had other supplies. They were still running fine as far as food went, but with winter coming, they needed more if they wanted to make it through in good shape.

Syn, Elina and Bron were seated across from the commander. It had been a week since the attack and despair continued to cling to the camp like a heavy, wet cloak.

They were in bad shape. Very bad.

"What are we going to do?" Syn asked quietly.

Kalen pinched the bridge of his nose and said, "I really don't know. I'll keep sending word back over the sat-comm but . . ."

"It's a waste of time." Elina sat with her arms folded over her chest, her legs crossed, one foot swinging angrily back and forth. Her eyes glinted like green ice and right then, her face showed about as much emotion as Syn had ever seen. She looked like an enraged queen. Regal fury.

"Your military contact is paying about as much attention to us as the rest of the world. They've forgotten about us."

His voice a low growl, Kalen demanded, "Do you think I'm not *aware* of that?"

"It's the damned barrier the military got set up," Bron said. He stared off into space, brooding. "They put it up to keep the wyrms out, but it also works to keep the rest of the demons trapped inside this area, too. I bet my ass they've got it rigged so that anything with nonhuman DNA gets vaporized when it tries to cross. They don't think they need to worry about the demons anymore, which means they don't give a damn what happens to us now."

Syn closed her eyes. God above, she didn't want to think he was right, but deep in her gut, she suspected he was. "Again, what are we going to do?"

"I've got an idea or two," Bron said, a nasty smile curling his lips. "I say I grab a couple of the techs and we go screw that barrier to hell and back."

Kalen slanted a look at Bron. "We'll hold off on that. Appealing as it might sound, I'm not going to do anything about that barrier—it's protecting millions of lives by keeping the demons trapped here. Still, we need to figure out something."

"I have an idea."

Everybody turned to Elina. She had a hard smile on her face, hard enough to cut through glass. "It involves blackmail and unsavory things like that, but if it works, it would take care of our supply issues."

Kalen leaned back in his seat. "Blackmail and unsavory things . . . I like it already."

"I'd need a vis-comm because I'm not having the conversation on a sat-comm. I want it recorded and I want copies." She uncrossed her legs and rested her hands on the arms of the chair, her fingers curling around the wood as though she wanted to gouge it with her nails. "We're going to record the whole bloody discussion and if we get screwed over, I'm sending it to the media contacts I have back east."

Kalen winced.

Once upon a time, the media had fawned over the broody, sexy leader of the Roinan rebellion. Sat-images of him had been streamed across many media-sets, flashed on the front screen of digiports. Over the past few years, after the Jivan and Yorkton Gates were destroyed, people waited with bated breath to see if Kalen Brenner could pull off a similar miracle. But then their interest waned, and when the Roinan Gate finally did fall, it barely made a ripple in the outside world.

The world had indeed forgotten them.

Cocking her head, Syn studied Elina. "Exactly what is this plan? From what little we've heard, the media doesn't talk about us much anymore."

"That's because there's just not enough to sensationalize anymore," Elina said with a shrug. "But if we give them a scandal . . ."

"What kind of scandal?" Kalen narrowed his eyes. "I'd just as soon not have everything about this camp spread all over the evening reports, Elina. If that's what it takes to get a supply drop, I'd tolerate it, but we need to think long range. Something more reliable, something steady."

"That's my plan exactly." Leaning forward, Elina braced her elbows on her knees. "I've got a friend in the military's para-science division. I studied magical theory with her when we were both in university. She's fairly high ranking, and she has contacts like you wouldn't believe. I suspect people on the outside are still having trouble reliably accessing the magic and it's got to be causing all sorts of problems for them. The demonic issue may be localized, but the energy problems will not be. If it's affecting us, it's affecting all. That's because the earth's energy is *all* connected. What problems we faced here a year ago, they faced. Five years ago? They faced. Which means . . . those in the outside world are still struggling to adapt to the disrupted magical flow, and chances are there have been casualties—witches injured, or killed, when the magic spiraled out of control, and innocent bystanders."

She flexed her hands wide, and Syn shivered as a ripple of magic flickered between Elina's hands. The burst of power was a warm caress.

"We've got one hell of a weapon here, Kalen . . . We know how to tap into the energy again. We can show them how. They may well figure it out on their own soon, but I know Geina—she's not going to want *soon*, especially not if I have the way *now*. I want to contact her and one of her superiors—let them know we've figured out how to tap into the energy and we'll share the knowledge, providing the military signs a contract for regular monthly supply airdrops."

"Like some of the higher-ups are actually going to honor a contract for any longer than they want to," Bron said, shaking his head.

"That's where the media comes in." Elina smiled tightly. "I'm going to send encrypted files of the discussion and the contract to several media contacts. And after the contract is signed, I'll inform Geina and her superior. Now, I trust Geina to honor any deal she's involved in, but I don't want her in a bad place. If she doesn't know, she's in the clear. Once the contract is signed, if even one supply drop is missed, I'll contact them to go to the public with the information. Let the world know we're still here, and while we're fighting to get rid of the monsters, the military is ignoring us . . . starving us, while we fight a fight that belongs to them every bit as much as it belongs to us." She brushed the corner of her eye and said, "I could even manage a few heartfelt tears as I make my impassioned plea to the masses."

"Cagey, crafty woman," Kalen muttered, shaking his head. He looked at the others and cocked a brow. "Thoughts, my friends?"

"Do it," Syn said. She jerked a shoulder in a shrug and said, "I'm tired of feeling like we're flying solo here. They want to ignore the ugly truth here; let's force them to look at it."

Lee nodded.

Bron drummed his fingers on his thigh and said, "At this point, I don't think it can hurt. And if anybody can work those bastards, it's going to be Elina." He glanced at her. "No offense."

"None taken." Elina smiled. "Because of my husband, my grandfather, I know how the military is playing this, and I think I know how they will react. Any unwise decisions on their part will reflect badly on them and the elected officials in the government who have control over the military factions. They won't want the world's population aware of the fact that they've abandoned us."

The smile on her face grew sad and she sighed. "These people know who I am, too. I may not have been the focus of the media the way you were, Kalen, but the world knows who my family is. They know Eira; they know of my husband, my father, my grandfather. If I go public, the world is going to listen. Trust me."

* * *

Syn had the pleasure of watching as Elina delivered her ultimatum to the head general of the AMC, Aishen Militia Corps. He was flanked by his counterparts from the Aishen Navy and the Aishen Air Corps, as well as several high-ranking government officials. Elina's contact from the para-science division was visible on the monitor as well.

Elina had planned well, and it took only three minutes of the "plea for help" vid she'd created before the general agreed to routinely drop shipments of food and the various supplies they needed for weapons, clothing, repairs.

He also requested that she destroy the vid, but Elina had just smiled. "Now, why would I do that? Not that you'd trust my word anyway. Rest assured, General. It's in safe hands, and as long as you uphold your end of the bargain, my contacts won't share that footage with a soul."

"What guarantee do we have of that?"

Elina smirked. "My word. Which is a hell of a lot more reliable than *your* word, General. I remember when you were assigned to your position—you promised to defend all the citizens of Aishen, with fervency, with passion and with respect. But you've left us here to rot. I'm quite certain we're still citizens . . . unless this area defected without my knowledge."

A few more comments were exchanged, Elina with a cool smile and the general's face hard as stone. A date, time and location were established and then Elina ended the vid-conference in the middle of a comment from the general. She flipped the monitor off and murmured, "Oops."

Kalen snorted. "I'm sure you've endeared yourself to that man, Elina."

"Oh, he hated my guts before he heard my demand." She shrugged and added, "My grandfather had more than a few run-ins with the general, back when they were both serving in the infantry. The general always had his sights set high and had no problems trampling on the backs of others or wading through their blood."

Kalen grunted in acknowledgment and moved to stand by Syn. She was studying the map, particularly the coordinates Elina had given the general for the drop. Slanting a look at him, she murmured, "I don't particularly like taking this route, you know. I wish there was another option."

"As do I." He ran a hand down his stubbled jaw. "But I like the thought of my men starving even less. And the idea of us running out of powercells and the materials needed to repair and build new weapons."

"Damn." Syn glanced over her shoulder at Elina and said, "Next time you speak with them, suggest that we could use some 'new' weaponry here. *New* weapons—not just the raw materials we need to make our own."

"Getting greedy."

"No. It's a matter of being practical. Why waste so many men on repair detail, trying to patch together pulsars that were outdated five years ago? They'll have newer weapons, better weapons."

Elina grimaced. "He agreed to all the 'extras' you already added in. Let's just be thankful for that."

"Oh, I am." She smiled and stared at the map, but she was no longer studying the coordinates for the drop shipment. She was studying the lands west of the camp. She had a plan, one that she had been thinking through for quite some time. But she'd never given it serious thought—they lacked the materials needed and had no way of getting them without outside help.

Or rather, materials she didn't have *yet*.

In another seventy-two hours, however, the rules were about to change.

***

"Will it work?" Syn asked as Gunner continued to study the info on the data pad.

"Hmmm." He made a noncommittal grunt under his breath and pushed back from his desk, leaving the small office in front of the weaponry storehouse. He started making his way through the materials that had been dropped into the camp the day before.

It wasn't enough—nowhere near enough, but it was a hell of a lot more than they'd had available to them twenty-four hours earlier. Off in the workroom, some of the weapontech men were making progress on the needed repairs that had been piling up over the past few months.

She'd seen people grinning at one another as she made her way to the weaponry. Elina's little plan had managed to restore some of the hope that had been dying bit by bit.

Tapping her foot, Syn watched as Gunner stopped by one crate and lifted the lid, peering inside with a thoughtful expression. "Hmmm," he muttered again, tugging on his lower lip.

"Gunner."

He glanced up at her, a distracted look on his face.

Narrowing her eyes, she said mildly, "If you don't give me some sort of answer, I'm going to scream. Just so you know."

"No, you wouldn't." He smiled at her and pushed his spectacles back onto his head. Age was starting to show on the older man and he could no longer see close objects with clarity unless he wore the corrective lenses. His faded blue eyes danced with humor as he slid a look toward the workroom. "Your man is in there. If he hears you scream, he's going to come running. You're too much the soldier to distract him unless it's really necessary."

Syn rolled her eyes. "Damn it, Gunner, would you stop being so damned obtuse and just give me an answer?"

"Am I being obtuse?" he mused, cocking his head. He pushed the lid back onto the crate and made his way back to the entrance, stopping just a few feet away. He held her data pad up to her and said, "It's an idea with merit, there's no doubt about that. But it's risky. I don't completely understand the technology they used to rig the barrier line and from what I can see, these devices you want to build work on a fairly similar platform."

He sighed and ran a hand through thick, grizzled gray hair. "I'm self-taught on damn near every weapon we currently use, Captain. You know that. Now, my second, Egan, he attended the Air Corps Academy, and he knows his way around all that tech—far better than I do. Perhaps you should talk to him."

"I plan to." She took her data pad, studying the notes and sketches she'd made. Then she looked up at him. "But I wanted your input as well. This is . . . well, it's a gamble. There's no way to know how many we could take out until we do it. And it's dangerous."

"Yes. But these days, it's dangerous simply to leave the base camp." He flicked a finger toward the data pad and said, "If the Raviners are trying to unite the rest of the demons, trying to get them to work against us, we have so many problems, I don't even know where to start. This could be that start—one that cut down on their numbers substantially. And for those of them capable of higher thought, it will serve as a warning. They think they have us cowed. That's not good for us. You know that."

* * *

Kalen eyed the huge whiteboard across the room and then closed his eyes. With his head leaning back and his eyes closed, he looked like he was in the mood for a nap. Syn had to shove her hands into her pockets to keep from fidgeting.

Xan leaned by one of the windows and he shot a faint smile in her direction.

Elina and Lee were studying the whiteboard. Lee looked curious. As always, Elina's face was about as easy to read as a blank sheet of paper—her expression revealed nothing. But Syn could feel her excitement.

She liked the idea.

Both of her fellow witches did.

Egan waited by the desk, side by side with Syn.

He'd liked the idea, and more, he had a design in mind for some detonators that would work ideally. They could be rigged to have a limited, focused range, so they could hopefully minimize the damage.

"Getting them all planted in the key locations is going to be very dangerous," Kalen said quietly, finally opening his eyes and studying Syn. "We wouldn't be able to send out large units—too likely we'd clue the Raviners in that something was going on."

"Absolutely."

He nodded and then leaned forward, bracing his elbows on the desk. He glanced at Elina and Lee, then at Syn. "Somehow, I get the feeling you don't have my witches in here just to keep them updated."

"The outer points are going to be the most dangerous, and the witches are best equipped to protect a small group."

He grimaced. "How small?"

"Just two." She swallowed and pulled her hands from her pockets. Her palms were damp with sweat, and she resisted the urge to swipe them down the front of her pants. "One witch, one combat-trained soldier. I want to take the caribins as well."

The caribins were rocket fast, but they were also dangerous. The vibrations from their engines were noisy—the sort of noise that attracted wyrms.

Kalen's mouth twisted in a scowl. "I like that idea about as much as I like the idea of having my eyeballs plucked from my skull, you know."

"I don't like it, either." She met his eyes, held his gaze. "But we need to move quickly with this; otherwise, it won't work. The baerns just aren't quick enough and if the devices work, the blast will terrify them. The caribins are the best choice." Kalen nodded, then looked away from Syn, and studied Elina, then Lee.

Shoving away from the wall, Lee moved to stand by his desk. "This could work," she said quietly. "I mean, I'm not the military genius in this room, but it could work, right?"

He looked at Lee, then at Syn. Then he stood.

"Yes. I think it could." Shifting his focus to Egan, he said, "Get to work on the detonators. We're going to blow those demons straight to hell and back."

ELEVEN

Syn rested a hand on the comm-unit at her waist. She checked the time, made sure they were still moving on schedule. She guided the caribins through the woods with ease, following the familiar path that would take them around the heaviest pockets of demon life, while hopefully keeping them far enough out of reach that the demons didn't make any move to pursue them.

So far, so good.

The caribins moved fast enough that the only real concern were the wyrms, and fortunately the big, ugly bastards didn't move as easily in this isolated part of the forest. Like Sojourn Gap, the soil was thinner, rockier. The forest life here mostly consisted of skinny, tall pines that could settle deep roots despite the lousy soil and smaller vegetation. The soil itself was littered with rocks, some no bigger than pebbles, but there were sheets of rock in the earth the size of a small house.

"Check the reading," she said to Xan.

He pulled a palm-sized scanner from his belt and flicked

it on, studying the readings. "No sign of any life other than humanoid."

Humanoid could be Anqarians, demons or rebels—not the wyrms. The wyrms were too fucking big, and nothing remotely humanoid. The only thing they really resembled were colossal, armored earthworms. Brought over by the Anqarians, the ugly behemoths had dug into their soil, and with little competition as far as predators, the things had grown so huge, just one of them could decimate an entire settlement in seconds. They could grow upward of a hundred feet long, and Syn had seen them almost twenty feet wide.

The one good thing about their existence—they might be able to burrow through dirt and mud, but not rock. They couldn't go too far west because of the Roinan Mountain range, and the barrier on the outer limits would vaporize any wyrm . . . or demon . . . that crossed it. As the major Gates fell, the world's military forces were able to eradicate the population until only the Roinan range still suffered the infestation. Syn had hopes they could do the same here, but first they needed to deal with the demons.

She flicked another look at the time and then glanced up, feeling Xan's eyes on her. "We're making good time, Captain," he said, a soft smile on his face.

"Yeah, I know." Then she glanced at him and added, "You know, we don't have anybody around. You could call me Syn."

He stroked a hand down her back. "I like calling you Captain." Then he leaned in and pressed a kiss to her neck, murmuring, "I like calling you Captain and thinking about how you tore up my back with your nails last night."

"Pervert." A blush rose up to stain her cheeks red and she was damn glad they were alone right now. To distract herself, she grabbed her comm-unit and sent out a relay to Elina and Lee. Elina had Egan with her, and Kalen had accompanied Lee, despite arguments from some of the other high-ranked leaders within the camp. They felt the commander should be in the camp . . . safe.

Safe, while his wife made a dangerous run into demon territory.

He'd told them what to do with that idea, and it wasn't anything pleasant.

Leaving the camp in Bron's capable hands, he accompanied his wife to their designated location.

"Report," she said after Elina responded. Lee checked in a few seconds later.

"I'm almost to my location," Elina said. Through the unit, Syn could hear her voice lower as she murmured to Egan, and then Egan's voice respond back. "ETA less than a half an hour."

"Lee?"

"Forty-five minutes," she responded.

"I'm at forty-five minutes, too," Syn said, checking her monitor. "Report back in when you hit your location, Elina. Lee, the same to you."

Elina ended the relay. Lee lingered long enough to say, "Don't know why I need to report in, since I know you'll be sending another relay out in fifteen minutes, give or take."

Syn rolled her eyes and ended the relay herself. So she was nervous—it was perfectly understandable.

She continued to maneuver the caribin one-handed through the undergrowth, aware of Xan's eyes. She slid him a look and saw the grin on his face. "I'm entitled to worry."

"Yes." His smile faded and he said softly, "It sounds as though the three of you are close."

"Elina, Lee and me?" She jerked a shoulder in a shrug. "Yeah, I guess. Common bonds and all of that."

"How long have you been friends with them?"

"With Elina, most of my life. She was the one who found me and my brother after my mother was taken." She focused on the path ahead, refusing to let herself think about that time. "She was a teacher of mine for a while, up until she decided she wanted to take her kids back east. She offered to take me, too. But I didn't want to leave. I already knew I belonged here."

"And Lee?"

"Not long." She frowned absently, thinking back to her encounters with Lee over the years. Up until Lee had shown up in the camp in the middle of broad daylight a few months earlier, Syn had only seen Lee sporadically. She'd thought maybe the other witch was something of a recluse, living alone in the forest and only showing up to kick a little ass from time to time. She hadn't established any kind of friendship with the woman, not until recently. "Right up until things started to come to a head with Anqar, I hardly ever saw Lee. She didn't come here very often."

He grimaced and said, "Please tell me that woman wasn't living in these mountains alone. That's suicide."

"It's a long story," she said, shaking her head. One that seemed to go better when accompanied with a nice, cold glass of wine. Wine . . . A grin curled her lips and she said, "Hey, I wonder if we could get Elina to request the general send some wine with the next drop. Something other than the home brew we can make around the camp."

"Wine."

Syn sighed. "Yes. Good wine. I miss a good glass of wine every now and then."

Xan stroked a hand down her back and kissed her shoulder. The caribin hummed as she slowed it down. Just ahead, the trail narrowed. The wind kicked up, bringing with it a familiar stench—rotting flesh. The foul odor tended to appear in areas thick with Jorniaks. Syn lifted a hand and pressed her finger to her lips, catching Xan's eye.

The Jorniaks might or might not associate the loud purr of the caribin with human presence, but she wasn't taking any more chances than necessary.

The rest of the trip dragged on. The forty minutes seemed to take three times longer than normal. She flicked a glance at the time as they jumped off the glider. Xan had the device in his pack, and she took up position at his back as he got to work.

She kept her senses peeled, listening for any slight noise, a breath, a tree branch.

Her heart almost jumped out of her chest when Xan touched her shoulder just moments later. "Done?" she asked quietly. He nodded.

Just as she lifted her comm-unit, the others chirped.

Elina and Lee, almost in sync, each said, "Done." Lee added in, "This baby is locked and loaded."

Syn shook her head and muttered, "Don't refer to the device as a child, Lee."

Lee just laughed.

"Just need to get this set," Syn said, ignoring Lee.

"Once we set them, we have forty-five minutes to get clear and then these little bastards go boom."

"I'm ready," Elina said.

"Me, too. Let's get this done."

Syn caught Xan's eye and nodded.

With one flick of his wrist, he armed the device. A timer flashed onto the display as they ran for the caribin.

Forty-five minutes. It should be plenty of time to get away safely, as long as the devices weren't disturbed. They'd been set to detonate immediately if they were disturbed after being armed. For the next twenty or thirty minutes, Syn knew her heart was going to be somewhere in the vicinity of her throat, just out of nerves.

If a demon so much as touched one of those devices while they were in the area, they were dead—the demon *and* whatever team was unlucky enough to be in the area.

But as they drew closer to the rendezvous, nothing happened. She kept having Xan check the monitor and it showed the device was ticking away the minutes exactly as it had been programmed, and no life-forms showed up even remotely close.

They had eight minutes left when they hit the rendezvous. Elina and Egan were already there.

Off in the distance, she heard the quiet hum of Kalen and Lee's caribin. They had two stops, setting the fourth and final device, the one that would be closest to the camp, but they'd planted that one earlier and the monitor showed it to be in sync with the other three.

"Went off without a hitch," Egan murmured, meeting her eyes and smiling.

But even as he said it, something cold settled in the bottom of Syn's belly.

The monitor in Xan's hand started beeping, sending out a warning.

Demons. Moving fast.

The wind kicked up, bringing with it the stink of brimstone. Death. Slowly, she turned and stared through the trees, in the direction she and Xan had come from.

Black-robed figures. Raviners.

"Shit."

Elina was at her side before the word even left Syn's mouth. She met the older woman's gaze and said, "We should have known it couldn't be that easy."

"As long as your little boomers go boom, then we win," Elina said, her voice flat. "Might be a bloody victory but who the hell cares?"

Bloody.

Yes. It got very bloody. The Raviners were alone this time, but there were nearly two dozen of them—and they were enraged. Even once Kalen and Lee arrived, just minutes later, the rebels were outnumbered.

Separated from Xan, Syn fought against two of the Raviners. She fought with both metal and magic, using her knife because they were too close for her to use her pulsar without injury to herself as well. She used small, focused bursts of fire, afraid to use anything larger for fear it might beckon to any other Raviners that lingered nearby.

He came out of nowhere. One moment he wasn't there. The next moment, he was. He wore his blond hair in a club down his back and carried nothing but bladed weapons. A fighter that cut through the Raviners with the flash of metal. For one second, Syn thought it was Morne. He moved like him. He bore a vague similarity to the healer. Was it . . . ?

No. It wasn't him. As he turned to take down the Raviners coming at her, she caught full sight of his face.

Syn hadn't ever seen him before in her life and every instinct inside her screamed as he used his blade on one of the remaining Raviners, laying the thing's neck wide-open, nearly severing the head with one powerful blow. He moved like a pale shadow. Like death.

She couldn't watch him, though, because she still had one of the power-hungry creatures to deal with, close, too close, slashing at her with a blade of some foreign black metal.

The next time she saw the blond man, another Raviner had joined the mess of bodies on the forest floor.

Off to her right, Lee screamed and Syn turned just in time to see her friend go to her knees, clasping her head. A Raviner stood behind her, one pale hand lifted. Inside the depths of the thing's robes, Syn could just barely make out the faint glimmer of its eyes.

Power. The thing reeked of it.

She jerked her pulsar up and aimed.

But before she could pull the trigger, a brawny arm came around the Raviner and then blood flowed as his neck was laid open. The Raviner collapsed to the ground, his blood bubbling out of the gaping wound in his throat. Xan . . . alive. Covered in grayish Raviner blood, but alive. Then he was gone, losing himself once more in the battle.

Fear left a metallic taste on her tongue. She didn't fight it. She welcomed it. If she didn't use the fear, it would use her.

Her gift whispered to her, begged to sink into the earth, to be set loose—to forge something larger than a ball of fire. Syn resisted. Not here. Not out in the open—using the bigger magic called too much attention. Instead, she lobbed fire into their faces, one after another, and just hoped they'd burn like mad.

She shot a glance at the time and swore. Raising her voice, she bellowed, "Duck and cover!"

The ground started to rumble. What few remaining Raviners were there froze and then they darted into the forest. Seconds later, a deafening boom echoed through the woods. In seconds, the sky was obscured by smoke and debris.

Syn huddled against a tree, Xan's body pressing into hers.

The earth shuddered, heaved. She caught the stench of wood burning—hot, acrid smoke flooded her head. Distantly, she heard inhuman shrieks. And deep inside, she felt the first wave of death.

Minutes passed.

It could have been hours. Days.

Thunderous cracks echoed through the forest as trees succumbed and went crashing to the earth. Ash choked the air.

After an eternity, all went still. Struggling to breathe, Syn shoved against Xan's chest and rasped out, "Need air, lover."

Two seconds later, she was on her feet, with his arms wrapped tight around her waist. In that moment, she didn't mind a bit. She let herself take a few seconds and then she eased away, looking for the others. The air was thick with dust, ash and debris, and she grabbed a small, folded mask from her pocket. The thin mask would filter out the worst of the debris, and she just hoped it thinned closer back to camp.

They were still miles away and the winds were blowing to west; hopefully it would carry most of the debris into the mountains.

Squinting to see through the clouded air, she searched for her friends. Kalen was leaning against a tree, holding his unconscious wife close to his chest.

Egan climbed to his feet and swiped at the blood trickling from a gash in his head.

Elina was in the middle of the small clearing, staring off into the west. Under the dirt and blood, she was smiling.

"How's Lee?" Syn asked.

The commander stroked a hand down her face, resting his fingers in the hollow of her throat. "Her pulse is fine and I can feel her."

Syn knew he wasn't talking about physically. He shot Syn a relieved smile and said, "I think she's going to be fine. The fuck didn't have her long enough to do any real damage."

Syn nodded. "Elina, are you hurt?"

"No," she murmured, still smiling that strange, fey smile.

Shifting her gaze to Egan, Syn cocked a brow. "I'm good, Captain."

With the exception of Lee, all of them were conscious and nobody looked to have any serious injuries.

Peering over her shoulder, she stared at Xan, touched his face to reassure herself he was well. He caught her hand and pressed a kiss to her bloodied palm. The sight of him hit her hard and fast, leaving her head spinning and her heart racing. It was hell, having feelings for a guy when she might have to send him to his death on any given day.

She moved to stand by Kalen, placing herself at his side if he needed her. Lee was unconscious—helpless. Uneasy, she kept her weapon at the ready as she did a head count.

Seven humans, quite a few Raviner corpses. Or rather . . . six humans, quite a few Raviner corpses . . . and one fucking Warlord. They were miles from the base, one of their witches was unconscious, and most of them had some form of injury or another. Syn narrowed her eyes. Even if she wasn't a superstitious witch, that would have had her instincts howling.

The Warlord had no earthly business here.

Keeping her weapon ready, she stared at the man.

"Warlord." Kalen said the word as though it left him with a bad taste in his mouth.

It certainly had that effect on Syn.

He didn't bother to deny it, just inclined his head. Even if he'd tried, even if he wasn't wearing a Warlord's garb, he couldn't hide himself from Syn. She could feel the Gate magic in him. He might not be able to *use* it, but it was still there. Her gift recognized his—his kind hunted hers. His kind enslaved hers. Her fingers itched to draw her pulsar and kill him—*now*. But curiosity, and perhaps something else, stayed her hand.

Xan came to stand at her side, but she didn't so much as glance at him, unwilling to look away from the threat.

Kalen glared at the man. The Warlord's gaze flicked to Lee, and Syn moved to stand in front of her, blocking the man's gaze of her friend.

"Why are you here, Warlord?" she asked. *Does he even understand me?*

He flicked a disinterested glance around him and then looked back at Syn. "At the moment, it would appear I'm standing here with the lot of you while you linger and wait for more demons to appear."

He spoke flawless Ishtanian with no trace of an accent. Hell, if it wasn't for his clothing, if it wasn't for the way her gut screamed at the sight of him, she could have mistaken him for one of her people.

"How considerate of you, showing such concern for us." She bared her teeth at him. "Any other reasons why you're darkening our doorstep?"

His brows came together, a puzzled frown on his face. "I've yet to darken a doorstep, witch."

"You're too damn close to our territory—too damn close to a whole lot of people who'd sooner gut you than look at you. Why in the holy hell are you here? Where are the rest of your men?"

With a humorless smirk on his lips, he said, "It doesn't look as though I have any men."

"Not buying it." Syn shook her head. "Warlords don't travel alone. Where are the others?"

"There are none. I'm what you would call a . . ." He paused, his head cocked as though he was trying to find the word. "A deserter," he finished, his voice cool and regal.

Off in the forest, they heard another ominous crack and the ground under them shuddered as one of the forest giants went crashing to the ground. They were going to be dealing with downed trees for a while, she suspected.

Glancing up into the canopy, she hoped none of the trees around them gave out just yet.

Unless, of course, one of them fell on the Warlord's head.

Xan lifted a hand, rested it on her shoulder. He dipped his head and quietly said, "It isn't safe to stay here, Captain."

"Agreed," Kalen said, his voice flat and hard.

Damn it, she *knew* that. But damn it, she didn't know what to do. Tersely, she said, "What about *him*?"

She glanced at Kalen, one quick glance, because she wasn't looking away from the Warlord for any longer than two seconds.

He didn't answer out loud. His voice, hard and harsh with worry, blasted into her mind with enough force that she almost flinched. *"I don't know what in the hell to do, but I don't think it's wise to just leave him here."*

"How do we know he's telling the truth about being a deserter? And what in the hell does that mean anyway? Why did he help us?"

Kalen's silver flashed. *"I don't know. You or Elina need to* look *at him. I can't do it—if he's ever encountered a psychic before, he'll know how to modify his thoughts, but he can't alter his basic emotional landscape.* Look *at him—if he's a threat, kill him. Here and now. Otherwise, he comes with us. But he doesn't leave here alone."*

Shit. Heaving out a sigh, she focused on the Warlord and looked. Looked deep—but not with her eyes.

It came at her in a rush of images. He had heard the fight. She felt his need to intervene—felt an altruism from him that she didn't dare trust. There was that one desire to help, and beyond that, his presence was nebulous. She sensed nothing good, but nothing evil. *Not* what she'd expected—she'd been prepared for a moral cesspool.

Frustrated, she pulled back. She didn't want to trust what her gift whispered. But she couldn't lift her pulsar against him, either.

"Captain?" Xan said.

She gave Xan a quick glance and then looked at Kalen. "Nothing." Shoving her sweaty, soot-and-blood-stained hair back from her face, she said, "He comes with us."

The Warlord cocked a brow. "And if I choose not to?"

Now she lifted her pulsar. With a cool smile, she said, "Please do. It would make my day so much easier."

"Indeed." He glanced at the others and then nodded. "Very well."

"I want him restrained."

The Warlord's dark blue eyes narrowed. "Restrained."

Metal whispered against leather as Xan drew his blade and leveled it at the Warlord's throat. "Restrained. Unconscious would probably work as well for her. Actually, I think she'd be happy with you dead. Take your choice."

***

He didn't like the way the Warlord was looking at Syn.

Like she was some delicacy placed before him after weeks of famine.

In all likelihood, that was exactly how the man felt.

Xan kept an eye on the Warlord during the journey back to camp, and the Warlord, in turn, kept his eyes on Syn. Xan didn't like it. At all.

Since Kalen couldn't pilot the caribin and hold his wife, they'd left one of the vehicles behind. They made good time, even with the extra passenger and Lee's unconscious body. Elina was in the caribin with Kalen and her niece, piloting it while Kalen held Lee.

"I don't like this." Syn shot a narrow look at the restrained Warlord. He was on his butt next to Egan's feet, a rather unceremonious position to be in, but he could have been reclining on a golden throne. Arrogance clung to him.

"You can always just leave him here," Xan said. He would have felt better if she had done just that.

She sounded more than a little disgusted as she said, "Not an option."

The trip to the base camp passed without incident, but

it didn't do much to soothe Xan's raw nerves. His instincts were screaming, wailing out warnings. Having a Warlord this close to Syn . . .

Even before they pushed through the gates, he could hear voices—the low, indistinguishable buzz of too many people talking at once.

As they stumbled through into the camp, people swarmed up. Nobody save the necessary people had known about Syn's plan, so the smoke and flames visible in the distance had probably caused some panic. Bron seemed to have gotten that under control, but now the rest of the army waited for an update.

At least they did—until they caught sight of the Warlord.

The low hum of voices quickly changed into a heated, angry roar.

Syn and Kalen shoved to the front, placing themselves between them and the unspeaking prisoner. Syn must have recognized the disaster in the making because she was already gathering up men, placing them in a perimeter around the Warlord. Xan waited in silence, his muscles tense.

The man wouldn't stop staring at Syn, and with every passing second, Xan could feel his patience fraying more and more.

Damn it.

"What in the hell is he doing here?" one of the soldiers asked, forcing through the crowd and squaring off with Kalen.

Kalen narrowed his eyes and in a low, flat voice, responded, "The last I checked, I was the commander." His silver gaze skimmed over the growing crowd and then he looked back at the soldier. "Has that changed?"

The man opened his mouth, then snapped it closed.

"Well?"

"No, Commander. That hasn't changed."

"Then do yourself a favor and do not make *demands* of me. When I feel the need to explain my decisions, I'll do so." He looked away from the soldier, seeking out Syn's gaze. He jerked a head toward the Warlord and said, "Deal with him. I want you in my quarters within the hour."

"Yes, Commander." As Kalen strode away, Syn stared at the crowd. "Unless you have permission to be away from your assignments, get your asses back to work. And if you *do* have permission, it better be for a damned good reason; otherwise both you and your superiors will be receiving a visit from me shortly."

She didn't bother waiting to see how they'd respond. She turned, and Xan caught sight of her face, the grim set of her mouth, the unyielding green-gold of her eyes. Not a happy woman.

She strode in their direction. From the corner of his eye, Xan could see the Warlord's face.

The bastard was smiling.

Syn stopped in front of the Warlord, a cool look on her face.

Xan had a good idea of what the Warlord saw when he looked at her. It was the same image he'd seen in those first days. An image he still had to wrestle with at times.

She looked too delicate for the job she did. But Xan knew from experience she was anything but. The sleeveless black cavinir tunic clung to her form, outlining her slight curves, revealing the tightly toned muscles of her arms.

Crossing her arms over her chest, she met the Warlord's eyes and said, "I don't know what we're going to do with you."

"Is it up to you?"

A faint smile came and went but she didn't answer.

It wasn't solely her decision, Xan knew, but if she told the commander the Warlord's presence created a threat, Kalen Brenner would have no trouble killing the man.

Her fellow witches would likely agree with whatever decision she made. Only a fool would ignore a warning from those three.

Their commander was no fool.

She caught Xan's gaze and said, "We're going to escort our *guest* to the west hall. You will remain with him for the time being."

The west hall—which, ironically enough, was located adjacent to the detention area.

Facing the Warlord, he said, "You might want to enjoy the next few minutes. They may be the last free ones you have for a while."

"I'm hardly free," the Warlord said. His muscles tightened, reminded Xan of the bonds at his wrists.

Xan gestured to the man, and they started off.

They'd made it ten feet before a rock came flying through the air. It hit the Warlord's temple with a solid thud. Xan turned in time to see him take one staggering step before he righted himself.

Blood trickled down his cheek and already a knot was forming. The Warlord didn't speak, didn't do a damn thing. If it hadn't been for the blood and that one staggering step, Xan might have wondered if he'd even noticed.

Others noticed.

The crowd that had yet to clear.

And Syn.

She was already striding in the direction the missile had come from and she stopped in front of the small cluster of soldiers. "Who did it?" she demanded.

Nobody spoke.

Syn crossed her arms over her chest and said again, "Who did it?"

When the silence continued, she smiled. "If that's how you want to play it, fine. I will ask one more time, and if I do not get an answer, the lot of you are confined to quarters for an undisclosed amount of time. You will leave only for job rotations, which will be latrine duty for the next six months. You will not leave for meals, you will not leave for your free day, you will not leave for any reason unless your dormer catches on fire. Am I clear?"

A few nodded.

"All right. Let's try this again. Who did it?"

The culprit didn't step forward—he was shoved forward with enough force that he almost fell flat on his face. As he righted himself, Syn studied him.

Xan did the same. Young. Just barely old enough to be considered an adult.

And he looked pissed as he faced the Captain. "What the hell is the problem?" he demanded, his voice angry.

"There are several of them," she said, her voice as cold as winter ice. "The first is how you're addressing me, soldier. The rules in this camp haven't changed—you address your superiors in the proper way. I'm rather certain 'What the hell is the problem' doesn't qualify as proper."

A muscle jerked in his jaw. He shuffled his feet and looked away. "I apologize, Captain."

"That's better." Then she gestured to the bound Warlord. "I believe there is another requiring an apology."

The man's jaw dropped. Several others echoed his surprise. "You want me to tell that bastard I'm *sorry*?"

"You should. You assaulted a man in restraints—those restraints render him helpless."

"He's a fucking *Warlord*," the soldier spat.

"Yes. And we expect *Warlords* to attack the helpless. However, we aren't Warlords, and I will not tolerate any soldier of mine attacking somebody incapable of defending themselves."

A dull red flush stained the soldier's face red. "I'm not apologizing to *him*. He's nothing but a fucking animal."

"So you have no problem throwing rocks at animals, then?" She curled her lip at him and said, "If you wish to engage in violence, then perhaps I should have his restraints removed, and you can face him in the circle. Get as bloody and as violent as you want. Would that suit you?"

The color leeched out of the soldier's face, leaving him white.

"Well?"

He glanced from Syn to the Warlord, skimmed the faces of those around him. Most wouldn't look at him. Too many had the same mind-set as this soldier, Xan realized—nothing was too dishonorable, nothing was uncalled for when it came to the Warlords. But some looked as irritated as Syn.

"I'll take your silence as a 'no.' What's your name, soldier?"

He stuttered it out, still staring at his feet. Syn backed away and gestured, "You're confined to quarters for a period of two weeks. You're on latrine duty for the next month. You've lost your free day for the next two weeks."

As he left, Syn faced the others. There was still a very large crowd, people meandering away at a slow pace, as though they couldn't bear to miss a second of the drama. The captain raised her voice and said, "Let it be known—the next person caught assaulting a prisoner will have to deal with me, and I can assure you, you will not like the consequences. Additionally, with the exception of my team, if there is even one soul here in the next three minutes, the entire fucking camp will lose their free days for the next *month*."

That cleared the area. Within the allotted three minutes, the common area was empty, save for Syn, her team and the Warlord.

***

Man doesn't even seem to notice he's bleeding, Syn thought, heaving out a sigh as she turned to face him.

He didn't look at all affected by the blood. There was a goose egg swelling up on his temple and she imagined it probably hurt like a bitch, but he gave no indication of discomfort. Hell, he barely gave an indication of *life*. Striding toward him, she glanced at one of the soldiers in the escort and said, "Fetch a medic to the west hall, if you would."

She looked back at the Warlord and inclined her head. "I'll apologize for that, Warlord."

"Would you?" he asked, cocking a brow.

He had a deep voice, she realized. She hadn't really noticed it earlier. Deep, smooth . . . her heart skipped a beat and she was horribly afraid she might start to blush. Horribly afraid somebody had noticed—

Noticed what? She gave herself a swift mental kick. In a flat voice, she said, "Yes, I'll apologize. We do not mistreat prisoners."

"A few moments ago, I was a guest."

Something glinted in his eyes—heated interest. The sight of it had her reaching deep, very deep, for control. It was enough to strike terror into her heart. No witch ever wanted to catch the attention of a Warlord.

Syn had to resist the urge to back away—get as far away from him as she could. Preferably hide behind Xan.

Settling on the strength of will that had served her well most of her life, she just gave him a cool smile. "I imagine you're quite aware of your status here, Warlord."

Turning on her heel, she continued to make her way to the west hall. She wasn't going to throw his ass in the detention center—*yet*. He'd saved their lives, and imprisoning him wouldn't rest easy on her honor.

But she would have him heavily guarded while she spoke with Kalen and tried to figure out what to do. And if Kalen wanted to make it easier on her and just make the call, she was all for that.

From the corner of her eye, she caught sight of Bron and smiled tightly at him as he fell into step with her.

"Interesting company you're keeping," he said.

Syn grimaced. "Tell me about it."

"I get the feeling this could get very, very ugly."

"You and me, both." Syn sighed and shoved her hair back from her face.

TWELVE

"What in the hell are we going to do with him?" Syn demanded some twenty minutes later.

Kalen sat at his desk, staring at a monitor with heavy intensity. "The Warlord isn't my chief concern just yet, Captain."

"Maybe he should be," she bit off.

"You know, I'm getting very tired of being told how I should do things, what things I should do, what things I shouldn't do." He flicked a glance at her and then focused on the monitor once more.

"Damn it, Kalen . . ."

He held up a hand. "Relax, Syn. Just give me a minute— Egan is fine-tuning one of the sats and he's trying to bounce an updated therma-map of the strike zone . . . There." A pleased smile curled his lips and he gestured to Syn. "Come here a minute."

She joined him behind the desk, absently resting a hand on the back of the chair as she bent over and peered at the image. Therma-maps showed signs of life, by displaying colored specks for any life force. All of the demons had a distinctive life-signature. Ickado demons were vivid, dark red—so dark a red it was almost black. Jorniaks had an orangish yellow signature on the therma-maps, and Raviners were orange. Humans and Warlords were displayed as reddish purple, undifferentiated. Their genetic makeups were pretty much identical, to Syn's disgust.

Lifeless body forms were black.

Right now, the only colors she could see on the therma-map were reddish purple and a *lot* of black. The black was all centered in the strike zone. She pushed a button on the monitor, widening the range. Off to the west and north, she saw a few clusters of demon life. But not much—nothing compared to all of the black in the center of the strike zone.

"It worked," she murmured, a pleased smile spreading across her lips.

"Damn straight." Kalen was smiling as well, a wide, rather savage grin that echoed the glint in his eyes. "Damn straight."

Thinking of Lo, her smile fell away, and she sighed. Backing away, she stared at the window. Flicking her hair back away from her face, she murmured, "Too bad I didn't have this strike of brilliant thought before we lost Lo. And others."

"We only now had the means to do this, Syn."

Feeling the weight of his gaze, she glanced at him and shrugged. "Maybe we could have pushed harder from the supplies. Maybe we could have planned better—"

"And maybe the bastards back east could have done better to help us out," Kalen said, his voice gruff. He shoved out of the seat and rested a hand on her shoulder. "You know as well as I do—there is no guarantee of safety here. Hell, not anywhere. Lo knew what he was doing, and it was no less than what you would have done, what I would have done." Gently squeezing her shoulder, he added, "And he'd be damned happy with what we managed to do today. Lives were saved today, Syn, because of your idea."

Tears stung her eyes, but she blinked them away. He

spoke nothing less than the truth and she wanted to take comfort in it, but she couldn't. Not right now. The wounds from all the losses were just too new.

Forcing a smile, she looked at Kalen and asked, "If you're that pleased with the results, then maybe you'd like to deal with the Warlord for me. It would be a reward of sorts."

"No." Kalen curled his lip. "If I say so much as two words to him, I'm going to gut him, and I'd like to know why he bothered to help us before I kill him."

"It was worth a try." She started for the door, saying over her shoulder, "I'll update you if I learn anything."

Not that she expected to learn much.

As she started toward the west hall, she ran through all of the other chores awaiting her attention. She had to get together a team to go gather information on the damage in the forest. They had managed to clear out the areas with the heaviest demon infestations; according to the reports Kalen had pulled up, they'd managed to kill quite a few.

Now they just needed to evaluate the damage, and figure out how to kill the rest of the things.

She managed to put together the recon team before she reached the west hall. Bron had already selected men and once she got on the comm-unit, he gave them the order to head out.

By the time she reached the west hall, the majority of the soldiers were finishing their daily rotations. With the exception of those on active guard and scout duty and those in food prep, most of the camp was done with work for the day.

And little surprise—many of them were gathered at the west hall.

She could have happily gone her whole life without having this mess dumped in *her* lap. Shouldering her way through the crowd gathered in front of the hall, she mounted the steps and turned to face the soldiers.

The low rumble of voices stopped and all eyes moved her way. She met the gazes of those standing nearest and then moved, from one row to another to another. "Did I request your presence?" she asked, singling one of the fighters out.

"Captain?" He blinked.

Cocking a brow, she repeated, "Did I request your presence? I'm thinking I didn't. So why are you here?"

He glanced over her shoulder and gestured toward the front of the hall. "Well, we heard you all caught a Warlord," the fighter said.

"We didn't catch him. He walked right up to us—after he assisted in a Raviner attack. That doesn't explain your presence here. Leave." She raised her voice and called, "All of you—leave. If you are not here at my orders or orders from the commander, you don't belong here."

A rush of whispers lifted in the air. Syn narrowed her eyes. She was getting damn sick and tired of having her orders questioned today.

With a disgusted sigh, she crossed her arms over her chest and did a quick count. Probably close to a hundred people were there and more were trickling in. *Fine, you idiots. Have it your way.* She glanced over her shoulder and caught the eye of one of the guards.

It was Kiri, a wiry, redheaded female with a big mouth, a quick temper and an even quicker pulsar. "Kiri, call the security detail. I want an entire squad dispatched to this location."

Kiri pulled her comm-unit off and made the request as ordered. While she did, Syn faced the crowd. "Anybody still in this area when the security squad arrives will be detained. They will be placed in detention—screw being confined to quarters, because apparently that isn't enough to deter you."

She hadn't even finished speaking and probably a tenth of the group had already disappeared.

Those lingering shot her varying looks of surprise and anger.

One of them, a medic, pushed free from the crowd and said, "With all due respect, Captain, I wasn't made aware this area is off-limits." She gestured to the soldiers and said, "We just want to know what is going on."

"And when the commander and I have an answer, we'll make it known," Syn snapped, not bothering to temper the edge of her voice. "Have you all forgotten what you were told when you arrived? This is a military unit, and you will carry yourselves accordingly. If you were serving in the AMC, would you *dare* go to your commanding officer and demand an answer?"

"You're asking us to blindly go along with whatever you say," the medic bit off.

"That's generally how it works." Syn jumped off the steps and faced the medic. "This is *not* a democracy. It's a military base—the commanding officers make the decisions. You all follow—if you don't like that, you *are* allowed to leave. There is no penalty for deserters here. You are all here of your own free will. But there damn well is a penalty for disregarding a direct order, and you've been ordered to evacuate this area."

From the corner of her eye, she caught sight of the sunlight flashing off clear plastin—the shields the security squads carried. She hadn't called for riot gear, but apparently somebody had deemed it necessary. And it just might be, she realized.

Please don't let it come to that, she prayed.

She should have just executed the Warlord, she realized. Just ended him and been done with it.

For some reason, though, the thought made her belly twist.

She'd killed before. Always in the heat of battle, but still, this was just a Warlord. This was the enemy. Killing him would have saved her this headache, wouldn't have left her wondering if she was endangering herself, Lee, Elina . . . not to mention the rest of the camp.

Killing him would have been easier.

Yet even thinking about it left her feeling cold and queasy.

Confusion flooded her, and she shoved it aside, focused

on the medic. The door behind her had opened, and she was being watched—she already knew by whom. Her body recognized Xan's presence easily. She took some comfort in it.

"Security is here." Raising her voice, she called out, "Last chance. Either disperse or spend the night in the detention center." A mean smile curled her lips. "And since there's a whole hell of a lot of you, you will not go into the few cells created for human prisoners. You'll go to the pit where we used to hold Jorniaks."

The pit was huge and it would hold all of them. But it wouldn't be fun. The pit was exactly that—a huge pit where the prisoners would need a ladder to reach the bottom without breaking bones, and without a ladder, it wasn't possible to escape it.

As they dispersed, she turned and mounted the steps. Xan met her halfway, eying the retreating backs of the soldiers. The hostility in the air wasn't lost on him. "Was that wise?" he asked quietly.

"Maybe not. Ignoring it would be even less wise." She took a deep breath and said, "We shouldn't have brought him here, Xan. It was one huge, motherfucking mistake."

This was *not* how she wanted to handle this mess.

"What else were we to do?" he asked. He shook his head. "The commander wouldn't have let him go—his presence raises too many questions. But could you have killed him? He helped us." Xan brushed his fingers down her cheek. "Some of us—*you*—could have died without his aid. Could you have killed him?"

Syn muttered, "I wish I knew." Muscles knotted in her neck, and all she wanted to do was sit down. And bathe. Damn it, she wanted a bath, to get rid of the blood and gore still splattering her clothes from the earlier Raviner attack.

The most she'd been able to do was wash her hands, face and arms. But she needed a bath; she needed to burn these clothes. It was a luxury that would have to wait. Turning, she gestured to the highest-ranked in the security squad. He approached, his face void of any emotion.

"Contact your officer—I want a security squad in this location around the clock for the time being. I'll clear it with the commander. Nobody save the assigned squad, the commander or one of his seconds are allowed in this area unescorted until further notice. I'll draft up a notice once I'm done here."

"Yes, Captain." She stepped away as he made the call.

Unable to put it off another second, she went inside.

The prisoner stood at the far end of the west hall, staring straight ahead. He didn't seem at all concerned with his current situation. The soldiers guarding his sorry hide might as well not have existed for all the attention he gave them.

But when he saw her, his demeanor changed.

A smile curled his lips, and he inclined his head—an oddly regal action.

"Captain . . . It is Captain, yes?"

Syn ignored him. "You realize that I've got about fifteen hundred men and women in this base and most of them would just as soon slit your throat as look at you, correct?"

"Yes. I'm quite aware of that." His smile widened and he said, "Perhaps I should thank you for taking such care of my sorry self."

"I'm not *taking* care of you. I'm seeing to the safety of a prisoner—we do not mistreat prisoners." She curled her lip at him and said, "We leave that to your kind."

His blue eyes went midnight dark and the smile faded from his stare, replaced with a flat, unyielding stare. He said nothing.

Syn returned his stare and fought the knee-jerk instinct to flee.

His kind hunted hers.

From the time she'd even known how to form words, she'd had a fear of Warlords. She dealt with them from a distance as often as possible—burn them to ash, put a blade through the heart, using a pulsar to cut them down from twenty paces away, anything that kept her from being close.

This was the closest she'd ever been to one outside the heat of battle. She'd much rather face one in battle, she decided. Then she knew what to do. Cut them down. Kill them. Move on. Thwart whatever raid they'd been involved in and then get the hell away before reinforcements arrived. The bastards let the demons do most of the dirty work as far as battles went. With the exception of raids, they rarely dirtied their hands to engage in any sort of combat.

Syn hadn't ever spoken to one.

Well, except Morne.

But Morne was a unique case—he wasn't one of *them*—he wasn't the enemy.

Syn doubted she could say the same for this man, no matter what her senses told her.

Breaking eye contact, she sauntered across the raised platform and settled behind the narrow desk. It was designed to seat only three or four people. Settling in the middle chair, she forced an air of calm as she studied him. "Now we need to decide what to do with you."

The table between them served as an effective barricade and she reached down, drawing a blade from her boot. It helped, the solid weight of the metal in her hand.

"What are you doing here?"

That faint, amused smile curled his lips again. "It appears I'm being detained."

"Yes, it does. If that doesn't bother you, then be as much of a smart-ass as you please. I can leave you in restraints for the rest of your life. Doesn't bother me. But if you'd rather have a chance to get out of those restraints, answer me."

The humorless smile on his mouth did nothing to light the dark depths of his eyes. "You won't let me out of these restraints as easy as that, madam. I'm not a fool."

"That's still up for debate. After all, you put yourself pretty deep into enemy territory."

"I'm in an alien world. I deserted my men, my captains and my High Lord—no matter where I go, I'm in enemy territory."

"Let's start there, then. Why did you desert? When did you desert?"

Deserters in any army were pretty much unwelcome; however, Syn couldn't find it in herself to get worked up over somebody walking away from a Warlord's army. Assuming he had, of course.

A muscle jerked in the man's jaw. "It is a personal matter." Something flashed through his eyes.

There was determination in his eyes, but also something else, an emotion she couldn't identify.

If he wasn't a Warlord, she might have just thought it was grief. Loss.

Did Warlords know how to grieve? Did they even understand emotion?

Just beyond her shields, she felt the echoes of the emotion she glimpsed in his eyes, but she didn't want to lower her shields, try to understand it better. She didn't want to understand *him* better.

"Why did you help us?" she asked, shoving aside the issue of why he'd deserted, *if* he'd deserted. She'd need to think that through later, but right now she was just trying to wrap her mind around having him here. And the fact that she could have died, might have lost friends in the attack, if it hadn't been for him.

"You needed the help."

Syn scowled and leaned back from the table. She crossed her arms over her chest, drumming her fingers against her arm as she stared at him. "We've needed help quite a bit over the past few decades—more and more demons coming through the Gates raised by *your* kind. They wouldn't be here if it wasn't for *your* kind, so I'm curious as to why you felt the need to do a damn thing." She gave him a tight smile. "I doubt there is anything altruistic in your motives."

"There isn't." He stared at the wall just past her shoulder, but somehow, she didn't think he was seeing the wooden walls.

He said nothing else.

Staring at him, she felt a headache creeping up on her. He was going to be one major pain in the ass. Taking a deep, controlled breath, she leaned back over the desk, resting her elbows on the scarred surface. "So you admit you didn't act out of altruism. So my question remains unanswered—*why* did you help us? If some of us, all of us, had died, what would it matter to you?"

His lashes lowered, shielding his eyes. "The loss of life always matters, Captain."

"Yes, because I've noticed how very sacred life is to the Warlords—so sacred you have no trouble enslaving women, killing their spouses before their eyes and dragging them away to serve as your personal whores." Ice edged its way into her voice and she gripped her blade harder, tighter. "Try again, Warlord. Why in the fuck are you here?"

He just stared at her.

Syn took it for about five seconds and then she shoved back away from the desk. Gesturing to three of the men guarding him, she said, "Escort him to a containment cell. Three guards on duty, at all times. I'll draw up a rotation."

Without looking at him a second time, she left the west hall.

***

The door slammed shut behind her, and Xan turned to study the Warlord. He was still staring at the door, although Syn was no longer in sight. He was smiling. Xan drew his blade. It caught the Warlord's eyes and as their gazes met, Xan tossed it in the air, making the silver metal dance and twirl about his fingers.

"I'm tempted to cut you, just for looking at her at all," he said mildly.

"Should I close my eyes when I speak to her, then?"

Xan slid the knife back into the sheath. "Might be the wiser choice. But wise doesn't describe your actions, does it? You shouldn't have come here."

The Warlord smirked. "And yet . . . here I am."

"Yes. Here you are." Moving closer to the Warlord, he

said in a quiet voice, "Touch her, and I'll bleed you. No way around it."

* * *

He was half delirious with hunger, lack of sleep.

Stumbling through the forest, Dais kept his knife in his hand, watching for anything that might be slow enough for him to kill. He was so hungry now, so desperate for food, he'd eat nearly anything.

But there wasn't anything here that he *could* eat.

Burned. Everything was burned. The stink of cooked demon flesh, rotting and sour, flooded his head. He almost tripped and ended up crashing into a charred tree. He'd been higher up in the mountains when the devices exploded, so close that he'd felt the heat of the blast, so close that the ash had choked the air and all but blinded him.

"Should have just stayed in the mountains," he muttered. He didn't know why he'd left—at least in the mountains, there had been enough vegetation around for him to eat. Not that he enjoyed chewing on leaves, seeds and the like, but it provided some nourishment.

If he'd stayed there, he wouldn't have gotten trapped with no food, no water.

There was nothing here. Nothing he could use for food, no place he could hide, no soul to offer him refuge.

Bloody hell, if he'd been just a bit closer to the blast zone, he'd be dead.

"Should have stayed in Anqar," he muttered. So many times, he'd been tempted. Raichar Taise had paid him well enough; he could have survived there. Taise could have found a use for him. He'd had plenty of men serving under him, that was certain. Powerful men always had a use for clever, clear thinkers. Dais would have been set.

But greed had made him push for more and more.

Now he was trapped here, trapped. Hunted like an animal—

Had to get away. That was why he'd left the mountains. Couldn't stay there, not come winter. Needed to get south. Couldn't go back to the band of Warlords, thanks to that one backstabbing, double-crossing bastard. Might even have a price on his head, courtesy of the Warlords. Fuck . . . what if one of their damned mercenaries were here?

If they had one of the Insar . . . Oh, damn.

"South," he muttered, shoving off the tree trunk and stumbling down the path. Needed to head south, needed to get out of this ruined land, find some place with game, with clean water . . . had to . . .

* * *

"Clever little witch." Morne stood at the outer edges of the blast zone and stared at the devastation with a smile. He had no doubt who had been behind this plan. It had Laisyn's name written all over it.

Kalen had warned him a few days ago to stay clear of this area. Morne had been miles away when the blast hit and he'd still felt the earth shaking, seen the smoke billowing up into the sky. The ash had cleared from the air, but some of the fires still burned. The damage stretched across an area of five miles, with the worst of the damage in the center and gradually lessening on the outer edges.

Morne had come to satisfy his curiosity. He'd done that—and more. Standing in the skeletal remains of the trees, he stared at the man a few dozen yards away, hardly able to believe his eyes.

Considering how much time he'd spent looking for Dais Bogler, Morne felt more than a little disappointed. It seemed too anticlimactic.

Just ahead, through the trees, he could see Dais, stumbling around like a drunken fool. Though that wasn't the case. Morne didn't need physical contact with the man to realize why it was so easy to catch him unaware.

"Life's not so easy when you're on the run, is it?"

Dais was starving, dehydrated and exhausted. So exhausted, it almost made Morne's teeth hurt before he shielded himself.

Morne had seen others in a similar state—many of the refugees who'd come into the base camp over the years had been like this. Dying of thirst, starvation and a bone-deep exhaustion that went beyond mere weariness. If something wasn't done, Dais would be dead in a few more days.

"Can't have that," Morne muttered. Too easy a death for that bastard. He'd cost the lives of too many people. Resting a hand on his blade, he debated about whether he should just slit the bastard's throat or let the fool wander around until he was simply too weak to walk another step.

Maybe he'd end up Jorniak fodder. Would serve him right.

However, it was more likely he'd end up catching the notice of a Raviner.

Though the blast had killed quite a few demons, not all were dead, and sooner or later, they'd be drawn back to this area. Demons were creatures of habit.

The last thing Morne wanted was a Raviner getting his hands on Dais. There was enough rage, enough fear, to feed several of those things for days. Nasty things would come about if that happened.

So Morne either needed to just end him here or haul him into the camp and let the rest deal with him.

He stood there, torn. Then, abruptly a smile curled his lips. Sheathing his knife, he drew a leather cord from the pack at his waist.

"Hello, dead man."

THIRTEEN

Syn was so tired, the words were blurring together before her.

She yawned so loud, her jaw cracked. Feeling Xan's eyes on her, she glanced up and found him watching her with a smile. He stroked the tip of his finger down her cheek and murmured, "You should rest."

"I'll rest when the next rotation arrives."

Since they'd brought the Warlord into the base camp, there had been three attempts to kill him. Two of those attempts had been stopped by the guard detail. One of those attempts had been stopped by the prisoner himself.

Syn had ended up moving him into one of the secure containment pits, for his own safety. It didn't sit well with her, although she couldn't figure out *why*. It wasn't as though she was mistreating the Warlord. She was actually trying to *protect* him.

He hadn't so much as fought when they'd led him to the pit and he'd leaped down into it of his own volition, not waiting for the ladder. She'd flinched when he jumped, half thinking he'd done it with the hopes of breaking his own neck. But seconds later, she'd remembered some basic Anqarian physiology—they were physically stronger than most humans, their bones denser. It was theorized that the force of gravity in Anqar was greater than in Ishtan. They had the same genetic makeup as people from Ishtan, but one of them could make a twenty-foot drop with no injury. The same couldn't be said for people from Ishtan.

She'd peered over the edge at him and seen him settle himself down in the corner of the narrow, tomblike pit, his face expressionless, his emotions carefully hidden deep inside. She still couldn't get much of a read on him—no overt maliciousness, no rage, none of the negative emotions that would have made it easier for her to have him executed. All she could sense from him was a deep, abiding sense of determination.

He had a goal.

Until she knew what that goal was, she wasn't going to trust him.

But she also wasn't going to leave him alone, either.

Sooner or later, either he'd get tired of people trying to kill him, or one of the attempts would be successful.

They'd moved him into the pit after the third attempt. This particular pit had been designed for "unique" prisoners. It was smaller than the main pit and built under one of the dormers. To get to the Warlord now, it would require going through whoever was on guard duty.

Syn had selected the guards herself, and she was almost certain the only threat to the Warlord now was himself.

In all the years the rebellion had been in this location, there had been a few occasions when they had managed to take a Warlord alive, and smaller pits like this were where they'd keep such prisoners. Or at least, where they'd keep them until the Warlords found a way to commit suicide. They didn't tolerate captivity well. Rather ironic— they had no trouble enslaving others, but would rather die than have any sort of captivity forced upon them.

"Think he's down there trying to figure out how to

kill himself?" she asked, glancing at the wooden floor as though she could see him through the planks.

"No." Xan was whittling away on a piece of wood, and he paused to glance at her face. He shrugged. "If he was going to kill himself, he would have already done so. He figured he was going to get locked up once he got here, and if he didn't want that, he would have just found a way to make you kill him right then or he would have escaped."

Syn grimaced. It wasn't like either of them could be experts on Warlord personalities, but she'd arrived to the same conclusion herself.

"So we just have to keep up this game until Kalen decides what to do with him." Shoving a hand through her hair, she yawned again and glanced at the dented carafe. "Is all the kion gone?"

"Yes. You drank the last cup about an hour ago." He rose, tucking away the butt of wood he'd been carving. "I'll go to your dormer, bring back more. I need to stretch my legs."

Then he smiled at her and stroked a hand down her neck. "Although I can think of more pleasant ways to wake up, ways that would also help both of us stretch . . . loosen up." He bent over her and nipped her earlobe. "Wake up."

Syn swatted at him. "We're on duty, remember." Then she hooked a hand over the back of his neck and hauled him down for a kiss. "But later."

Definitely later.

"After you sleep a good twelve hours," he said. He cradled her cheek in his hand and stroked his thumb over her lower lip. "You're pushing yourself too hard, trying to take a shift in here every other day on top of your other duties. You need to let yourself rest."

"I can rest when I'm dead." She shrugged and waved him toward the door. "Go on already. Get me some caffeine, I'm begging you."

The door closed behind him, leaving her alone. Leaning back in her seat, she stared at the faded wooden beams overhead, counting them just to keep her mind from wandering, drifting off. If she let her mind drift for even five seconds, she was going to fall asleep.

Xan. She'd think about Xan. It was one way guaranteed to have her blood pumping hot enough to chase the exhaustion from her mind. Although he hadn't been on rotation here tonight, he'd been with her. She hadn't even been surprised when he showed up on the doorstep only moments after she'd taken over guard duty. She was getting way too used to having him around, she knew. It was something she kind of wanted to talk to him about, although she wasn't sure how.

He had come to the camp to join the army. What would he do when it was over? She wanted to know where things between them were leading—and was there even anything between them other than sex?

You're becoming everything . . .

Yes. There was something between them besides sex. Smiling, she recalled how he'd whispered that in her ear. There was more. And maybe she needed to just lay things out between them, see if she couldn't get a better understanding of it.

Syn scrubbed her hands over her face and muttered, "Not really the ideal time to talk of the future, is it?"

But as she'd told Xan close to two months ago—if they waited for an ideal time to live their lives, well, none of them would have a life.

At the sound of the door closing quietly, she came to her feet almost instantly, drawing her pulsar and leveling it at the doorway. Xan—?

No.

Syn's jaw dropped and she found herself staring at a familiar face. Morne's midnight blue eyes dropped to the pulsar she held and then back up to her face. A smile tugged at his lips and he said, "Should I just surrender now?"

Blinking her tired eyes, she stared at him. "Morne?" She lowered the pulsar, not quite sure she was awake.

"In the flesh." His smile took on a hard slant, and he said, "I even come with a gift."

With that, he reached out the door and grabbed something—no. Somebody. Dais. The man, his hands bound
and his mouth gagged, was thrown summarily at her feet.

A rush of adrenaline and anger chased the exhaustion
from her mind, and Syn lifted the pulsar once more, aiming it at Dais. "And what a fine gift, too. Is he all mine or
do I have to share?"

"I'd suggest you share, unless you want the commander
to tan your hide," Morne said.

Dais glared at her, hitching his shoulder up and rubbing
his jaw against it in an effort to dislodge the gag. When
that didn't work, he settled for grunting and sputtering at
her from behind the cloth. His eyes, opaque with fear and
fury, narrowed on her face. She didn't need to hear the
words—she suspected she understood him just fine.

"If it isn't my onetime captain . . . my friend." She
sheathed her pulsar and came around the table, crouching
down beside him. She lifted a hand and called the fire. It
spun and danced in her hand and without taking her eyes
from Dais, she asked Morne, "Do you think if I burn him a
bit here and there, you could heal him up before I turn him
over to Kalen?"

Morne clicked his tongue. "Bloodthirsty. I like that."

Dais shrieked behind the gag.

"Don't care for the idea, *friend*?" Syn laughed. "Too
fucking bad. I find it very appealing."

And she did—enough that it left her stomach twisting.
Clenching her jaw, she quelled the fire and stood over Dais.
He swung out with his feet, trying to knock her down. She
backed away, eying him narrowly. "Watch it, old man. I
may be above torture, but I'm not above beating you senseless if you so much as touch me."

Dais tried a second time. Snarling, Syn went to bend
over—she had half a mind to grab the front of his filthy,
threadbare shirt and pound her fist into his face until
she broke all the bones in her hand—and his face. But
Morne beat her to it. He placed a booted foot on Dais's
neck and said, "Try it again and see what happens,

treacherous coward. Laisyn may be above torture. But I am not. Although I prefer to think of it as *justice*."

The man went white, and when Morne pulled his foot away, Dais curled away, huddling up against the wall to glare at them both.

Morne glanced at Syn and then at the closed opening to the pit. "I'd planned on throwing him in there before reporting into the commander—preferred not to drag him through the streets. Most people are sleeping, but I didn't want to risk a riot if somebody saw him." He paused and lifted a brow. "But the pit isn't empty, is it?"

"No." Syn curled a lip. "We have a fucking Warlord in there."

"Do you, now?" An odd look entered Morne's eyes, and he cocked his head. "May I?"

Syn gestured toward the pit. "By all means."

Morne started toward the pit and then paused, looked back at Dais. "If you so much as try to stand, I'll beat you bloody. *Then* I'll heal you . . . and do it all over again."

Dais returned his stare sullenly. There was defeat written all over the man's face, Syn decided. She was almost disappointed. All that was left was to kill him. There was no hunt, no capture, no fight left. Nothing.

No. Not nothing.

Keeping Morne in her line of sight, she approached Dais and crouched down in front of him. "Try to kick me, attack me in any way, and I will burn you this time," she warned. Then she yanked the gag out of his mouth. "Why?"

Dais worked his jaw, not responding for a few seconds. He looked like utter hell, she decided. Thin, almost skeletally so, his hair lank and grimy. He stank to high heaven as well, and the clothes he wore had seen better years. They were threadbare and hung loose on his gaunt frame.

His mouth, dry and colorless, remained stubbornly closed.

Staring at him through slitted eyes, she lifted a hand and cupped it in front of her. "Answer me, you bastard. You owe us that much."

Now he laughed. It was a rasping echo of the laugh she remembered. Dear God, had it been just a few months ago that this man had stood at her side, fought with her? Grieved right alongside her as they buried the bodies of their fallen?

"I don't owe you a damn thing, *Captain*," he said. His voice, like his laugh, was harsh and rasping. "The only person I owe a damn thing to is *me*. I was watching out for my own hide, and the fact that none of you saw fit to do the same is why you're so pissed."

"Watching out for your own hide?" Syn echoed. She smirked and shook her head. "Yes, and it looks like you've done a fine job of it. When's the last time you had a good meal, old man? Clean clothes? A warm bath? When's the last time you slept without wondering if you'd ever wake again?"

He spit at her. Syn retaliated by driving her fist straight into his nose. Cartilage crunched and blood fountained. Pain jolted up her arm, and without bothering to replace his gag, she straightened. "Keep your fucking mouth closed. If anybody hears you in here, they'll come to investigate, and I warn you—many of them are more likely to peel the flesh from your bones and see how long it takes you to die. If you scream, if you try to escape, I'll let them have you."

Unable to look at him another moment, she turned to face Morne. He was staring into the pit. He must have been waiting for her attention, because the moment she looked at him, he lifted his midnight gaze to hers and said, "I don't think this man is any threat to you, Captain."

Her gut agreed.

Her mind didn't want to.

"No threat?" Her mouth twisted in a smirk, and she moved to stand beside Morne, looking down into the pit. The lone prisoner was staring ahead, not bothering to acknowledge the people standing over him. No surprise there. He hadn't bothered to look at them at all, not even when she lowered food and water into the pit or clean clothes, rags and water for washing. "He's a damn Warlord. He's all kinds of threat."

"No." He said something to the prisoner.

Vaguely, Syn sensed the Warlord's surprise, but she was too busy trying to understand what Morne had said. She understood basic Anqarian—most of the rebels knew a handful of words and the higher-ranked soldiers could carry on a stilted conversation.

But the words coming from Morne's mouth were beyond foreign. It *almost* sounded like Anqarian—*almost* but not quite. Just when she thought she'd grasped a word or two, it was lost again.

The Warlord's eyes narrowed and he stared up at Morne, something like shock written on his features for the briefest moment. But then it was gone, replaced by that smooth, unreadable mask.

Morne said something else—a question, Syn thought.

Her guess was confirmed when the Warlord gave a brief, terse nod. He gave Morne a regal nod and then said in a cool voice, "Laithe."

"I thought as much," Morne muttered under his breath. Then he looked at Syn. "He is no threat to you, Syn. Nor to this camp."

"How so?"

"His name is Laithe Taise—son of Raichar Taise." He waited just a moment and then said softly, "It's Lee's brother."

Syn gaped at him and then shifted her gaze, staring down into the pit. Her heart slammed against her ribs and her lungs felt tight, closed off. "Her brother." She rubbed her eyes.

Syn caught a movement from the corner of her eye and she turned her head, staring at Dais. Morne did the same. Dais froze. He had been in the process of shifting his weight so that he was sitting upright, but one look from Morne had the man lowering himself back down. Syn shifted around to stand on the other side of the pit so she could keep Dais in her sight line.

Her head was pounding, she realized. Pain flared behind her eyes, but she shoved it aside. No time for headaches now. Splitting her attention between Dais and the

Warlord—Laithe—Lee's *brother*, she said, "Just because this is Lee's brother, *if* you are right, doesn't mean he is no threat. Hell, her own father tried to kidnap her."

"In his own way, her father tried to protect her," Morne said.

Syn opened her mouth to argue, but Morne lifted a hand, cutting her off. "Believe as you wish, Laisyn, but her father did not seek to bring harm to her—he wanted her with him—safe. A Warlord gives loyalty, protection and allegiance to only three things—family, the High Lord and his liege lord. Lee was his family, and he did want her safe. He simply could not comprehend that his version of *safety* is naught by imprisonment."

Jabbing a finger in Laithe's direction, she demanded, "And how do we know that won't be *his* idea of providing safety?"

Laithe, his voice cold and hard, said, "My father wasn't always a wise man. His arrogance couldn't let him see that bringing Lenena among Warlords would be akin to leading a sheep to slaughter. Warlords ceased warring among ourselves centuries ago, but her presence would reignite those wars. There are those who would level entire cities, nations, to have one such as Lenena under his control."

Lenena—that was the name Lee's father had given her. Curling her lip at the Warlord, Syn said, "She doesn't go by that name. Her name is *Lee*."

"Lee," he said, giving her that regal, polite nod once more. "As you wish."

"As I wish." Syn shook her head and swallowed the knot in her throat. Just being this close to a Warlord terrified her, left her feeling half sick. What she *wished* was for these bastards to leave her world and never return.

She couldn't have what she wished, but she'd damn well have some answers. Studying the man Morne insisted was Lee's brother, she asked, "And what would be your idea of *protecting* somebody that valuable to your kind?"

"She is my sister—my blood. I'd lay down my life to protect her. It is my duty, my honor . . . my *right*."

She could feel the truth of those words—not just *sense* them, but feel them. Blowing out a shuddering breath, she said, "I want to trust you. I want to believe the brother of one of my friends wouldn't bring harm or heartbreak on her. But according to Morne, her father wanted to protect her, too, and I'd rather die than have *that* kind of protection. I suspect Lee feels the same way. What are your plans? Tell me now why you are here."

"I seek only to watch out for her. I wouldn't bring heartbreak or harm on her, not if it was within my control, and I would do anything within my power to keep others from bringing it, either." He looked away. A sad, heavy sigh left him and for the first time, he seemed as human as she. As capable of emotion as any other man. "I barely remember her, you know. I was but a child when she was taken from us. But I remember the way she smiled, and I remember how she loved to hear our mother sing. Our mother had a lovely voice."

That was the one thing about her mother that Lee remembered, Syn thought. Her voice.

"Damn it." Syn turned away, driving a hand through her hair. She glanced at the door. Xan would be back—should have already been back, she thought.

Giving Morne a narrow look, she said, "You've always had to complicate things." Then she stooped over and grabbed the rope ladder to the pit. She tossed it down in and said to Laithe, "Come out; you need to speak to the commander, and damn it, you need to be prepared to actually *give* answers this time. Because he's going to have a whole hell of a lot of questions, and he's not going to want to listen to a damn thing you say."

Laithe's mouth twitched. There was something oddly familiar about that smile. "And you did want to listen?" He wasted no time climbing the ladder, clearing it easily.

Syn looked away from him. His presence still made her skin prickle, no matter what Morne said. But he wasn't a threat. It was a truth she'd been denying for the past few days, but she couldn't deny it anymore. Thanks to Morne.

Focusing on Dais, she gave him a dark look. "I have your quarters ready, *Captain*."

He stared at her and then lowered his eyes to the pit. Something entered his eyes—fear. The man knew once he entered that pit, the next time he left would probably be to die. Assuming he left it alive.

"No."

Laithe and Morne both took a step toward him. Morne gave Laithe a narrow look and said, "I already own his blood, boy."

The door opened.

Syn lifted her head, resting her hand on her pulsar. But it was Xan. She moved her hand away from her weapon and gave him a weary smile. It faded fast, though, as his dark, enigmatic gaze settled on Morne.

His eye narrowed. His body tensed. "You."

Syn put her body between the two men from Anqar and Xan. "Stand down, Xan. It's okay. You haven't met Morne . . ."

"Actually, I have." Xan's mouth twisted in a cold smile as he drew the long, wicked blade from his back. "Please step away from him—"

"Insar!" Dais's eyes rounded, and he shoved himself to his knees, staring at Xan in shock. He started to babble in halting Anqarian, but this time, Syn understood the words.

"Please—Battlelord, aid me. I beseech your aid and in exchange, I offer up a prize any Warlord would pay much to acquire."

Battlelord—what in the hell?

Silver flashed. A knife hurtled through the air and buried itself in Dais's left eye.

Morne muttered, "Bleeding sands, Kalen will have all our hides." He moved to crouch beside Dais.

But it was too late. Dais was already dead. Syn could feel the echo of his passing—angry and bitter—as his soul faded.

Morne shot Xan a black glare. "Damn your aim, Insar. The commander isn't going to be pleased."

Xan wasn't looking at Morne. He stared at Syn. Only at Syn.

Something about the intensity of that look had her heart quivering. Insar—?

Licking her lips, she looked from Dais's lifeless body to Xan. "Why was he talking to you in Anqarian? Why did he seem like he knew you?"

A muscle twitched in Xan's jaw as he sheathed the long blade. His gaze fell away from her face, and his big shoulders rose and fell with a rough sigh. "I have seen the man before, Captain." His gaze flicked to Morne, then the freed Warlord, before returning to her face.

"How? When?" Her voice was shaking. Hell. *She* was shaking.

He clenched his jaw. Strong, broad hands opened, then closed into fists. "I believe you already know the answer to that."

Oh, God.

Oh, God.

"What does *Insar* mean?" she demanded.

"Battlelord."

With a sharp, humorless laugh, she snapped, "I got that much—thanks. But what in the hell is a Battlelord?" When he didn't answer, she looked at Morne.

He stared at her, his gaze softening with sympathy. He didn't say anything, but he did reach out, lay a hand on her shoulder.

Xan snarled, drawing his blade again. "Get your damned hands off of her!"

Syn ducked away when Xan would have grabbed her. The world—dear God, the world felt like it was rocking under her feet, spinning around her. The roaring in her ears got louder and the pain behind her eyes threatened to blind her.

Xan wasn't from Ishtan. He was from Anqar—he was whatever in the hell a Battlelord was. Reaching up, she curled her fingers around Morne's arm. Blindly, she looked in Xan's direction. "I'd trust Morne with my life—*Battlelord*. Which is more than I can say for you."

"Laisyn." Morne murmured her name gently, covered her hand with his. She felt him reaching out—not physically, but on the energy plain, on that level where they shared a similar gift. *This man will not harm you—part of you already knows that.*

Shaking her head, Syn backed away. Xan had already *harmed* her. He'd lied to her—all of them. But she didn't, couldn't, say the words out loud. In that moment, all she could do was run, because if she didn't run, she'd shatter.

Syn started for the door and Xan moved to touch her. "Syn, wait, please."

Then she realized she could speak. It was like forcing broken glass through her tight throat, each word painful. But she managed. "Get the hell out of my camp, *Battlelord*."

* * *

The door slammed shut behind Syn, and Xan flinched, closing his eye.

Syn . . . Aching, he reached up and rubbed the heel of his hand over his heart. *Bleeding sands, I should have told her.* He *knew* that . . . He just hadn't known how. *Dear one, I have a confession I must make—I come from Anqar. I am not a Warlord, but I come from a long line of them. My ancestors enslaved yours for centuries. Can you try not to hold it against me?*

"Damn it all to hell," he growled, whirling around and driving his fist into one of the stone support beams. His skin split and pain shot up his arm, but he ignored it, punching the stone a second time.

Should have told her . . .

And now, it was too fucking late.

"You'd best go after her."

Xan opened his eye and glared at the man she'd called Morne. Yes, Xan had heard of him. More often than he could recall, to be true. "She has no desire to speak with me." With a bitter laugh, he added, "All she wants from me now is my absence."

"Since when does an Insar let a trifling thing like that interfere?" Morne asked.

Xan shook his head. He'd betrayed her, all this time, he had betrayed her. Not because he had come here wishing to cause harm, but because he hadn't told her who . . . *what* he was. Grief and guilt swamped him—he couldn't think. He needed to, needed to make himself return to his dormer, gather his belongings and leave.

But he couldn't make himself take that first step. Couldn't think. There was no room inside him for anything but his grief, anything but his guilt.

He moved to stand at the window and as he did so, he caught sight of Syn.

She was at the stables, just across the path, guiding her baern out. It was dark—not quite dawn. Xan moved to the door, growling under his breath, "Damn you, woman."

She was already gone, the baern flying down the deserted paths as though he had wings.

It seemed there was room for something besides guilt and grief after all. Rage. Fear. Worry.

Behind him, Morne and Laithe echoed similar sentiments, but it was Laithe who moved to grab Xan's arm. "Whether she wishes your absence or not, it isn't safe for any woman, especially a witch, outside these walls—not alone. Lord Reil is in the forest, and it's likely his men will be near—no Warlord with any measure of power could have missed the magic that emanated from this area a few days ago. She'll be in danger."

He glanced at Morne and then back at Xan. "I shall go with you."

"No." Morne's mouth twisted. "Insar, it must be just you for now—I have to speak with the commander about Laithe." He slanted a look at Laithe and added, "If we do not do that *first*, we will have more trouble, and that will not serve Syn or this camp well at all. So we'll speak to the commander, and you had best be with me. Otherwise, we'll have another problem on our hands, what with half the camp combing the forest for *you*."

He gave Xan one quick glance and said, "I'll have Kalen send word to Bron to help you look for her."

Xan barely heard. He was already out the door, moving toward the stables himself. He didn't bother using one of the saddles, just searched for the baern that looked to be the quickest. In a matter of heartbeats, he was mounted and chasing after Syn.

***

Kalen grunted as a voice touched on the edge of his mind.

Snarling in his sleep, he rolled over and flung an arm around Lee's waist. She snuggled closer, absently stroking a hand down his side, caught within her own dreams.

The voice came louder and this time, Kalen came awake with a swear, jerking upright in bed.

Sighing, he rubbed a hand over his eyes and said, "I'm awake, damn it. But this had better be urgent—Morne, it's not even dawn."

"It is urgent. I'll be at your door in a few seconds."

At the door? Kalen scowled and kicked his legs over the bed, tucking the sheet around Lee and bending down, pressing his lips to her cheek. "Lee, wake up. We have company coming."

A sulky frown darkened her face and she rolled onto her belly, burying her face in her pillow. Sighing, Kalen stroked a hand down her back. "Come on, pet."

She turned her face toward him and popped open one eye. She glared at him through the tangle of her hair and said, "'M tired. 'S early. If there isn't a fire or attack, I wanna sleep."

"Me, too." He snagged a pair of his pants from the foot of the bed and said, "But it's Morne, which means it's likely important. He wouldn't be in the camp if it wasn't."

"Morne?" She shoved up onto her elbows, a position that pushed her very nice breasts together in a way that had

Kalen's mouth watering—he tore his eyes away before he pounced on her. "Did you say Morne?"

"Yes."

She was out of the bed and shimmying into her own clothes. As she pulled on a thin undershirt, there was a knock at the door. She went to lunge for it and Kalen blocked her, shoved a tunic at her. His eyes flashed hot and bright as he brushed the backs of his knuckles over one nipple. It hardened, stabbing against the skimpy material of her undershirt. "Please, let me be a jealous boar here— I'd rather no man see these quite so clearly."

Lee blushed and rolled her eyes, jerking the tunic on. "Open the damn door."

He did.

No sooner had he opened it than Morne was inside, shoving a man in before him and closing the door quickly at his back.

Kalen's hand flexed.

It was the Warlord. He slanted a look at Morne and, without saying a word, grabbed his pulsar from his desk and raised it, leveling it at the Warlord. "You've got five seconds to explain why he is out of the pit, Morne. Five—"

Lee barely heard him. She found herself staring into a pair of eyes that were eerily similar to her own. Not just the shape, not just the color—*everything*—they were *her* eyes. Without understanding why, she reached out and shoved Kalen's pulsar down. Distantly, she heard Morne talking.

"I only need two. He's her brother."

Brother—

Kalen snarled and jerked the pulsar up again. "That's not good enough for me—remember what her *father* tried to do?"

Lee hissed and shoved the pulsar down, glaring at her husband.

He was speaking—saying something to Morne. Morne was talking back.

But none of it made sense. The words bounced around

in her head without connecting. They could have been speaking ancient Latin for all she understood. She shook her head and said quietly, "Kalen? Baby . . . please, for me. Shut up."

There was a harsh sigh. Kalen reached up, curled his hand protectively over her shoulder. "Damn it, Lee."

Absently, she reached up and patted his hand. "It's okay."

And it was. She didn't know how she knew—it *shouldn't* be okay. She could feel this man's power. It had rivaled the power she'd sensed in her father, but there was more . . . She sensed the echo of a person she barely remembered. Her mother.

Swallowing past the knot in her throat, she said softly, "I don't remember you."

The Warlord stared at her, his eyes intense and probing, studying her face as though he wished to memorize her. "I remember you. You were so tiny. You laughed and smiled and danced. And you loved to listen to our mother when she sang. As did I."

"Yes. I remember her singing." Tears burned her eyes. She blinked them away and took a deep breath, trying to get a grip on the rampant emotions whirling inside her. "My brother." She licked her lips and tried to manage a smile. It was wobbly and weak, but it was the effort that counted, right? "So, I feel really lame asking you this . . . but what's your name?"

"Laithe."

"Laithe." She whispered it and it echoed inside her mind, rippled, like somebody had tossed a pebble into a pond. Closing her eyes, she whispered it again. "Laithe." Something tickled at her mind and she frowned. "I recognize the name . . . I don't remember you, but I recognize the name. But wasn't there . . . ?"

Her words trailed away as she sensed a heavy tension in the room. Looking up, she glanced at Kalen and saw a familiar look on his face. It was the same one he always had when he was having one of his weird little mind-to-mind discussions. And if the look on Morne's face was an indicator, she had no doubt about who else was in on the conversation. "Kalen?"

He glanced at her and she reached out, touched his arm. *He's okay . . . I don't know what you two are talking about, but Laithe . . . he's okay.*

Kalen grimaced and stroked a hand down her hair. "I know, pet. Morne just more or less bellowed the same in my ear. But that isn't the problem. Syn left the camp and according to your . . . *brother* . . . there may well be Warlords in the area."

"Syn left? Warlords?" Her mind bounced from one extreme to the other. "Oh, thank God, I'm glad I won't have to separate you two right now. What . . . Wait, Syn left the camp? What in the hell for?"

Kalen had no problem following her disjointed train of thought. He slid Laithe a narrow look and said in a flat voice, "We'll talk, you and I. *Then* I'll decide for myself if we are 'okay.' But for now, Syn." He looked back at Lee and said, "Yes, Syn's outside the camp, and yes, there may be Warlords."

"Then let's—"

"*No.*"

All three men said it at once, with such intensity, Lee found herself backing up a step. Dismayed, she advanced on her husband and poked her finger into his chest. "Excuse me?"

"You can't." He reached up and caught her wrist. "Damn it, Lee. *Think.* Don't think like a fighter; don't think like her friend. Think like a leader—if you're out there, you give them *two* targets."

"I can take care of myself," she said edgily.

"Yes. You can. But you're still a damned target." He curled his fingers around her shoulders, eased her close. In a quiet voice, he said, "Lee, please. Don't. Stay here. Syn's out there, and right now, she's not thinking clearly—don't ask for details. I can't get into it now. But she's vulnerable, *and* she's unaware there may be danger. Please, for me, and for her, stay here."

Mutinous, she stared at him. He rubbed his mouth against hers, and she huffed out a sigh. "Fine. Shit. Damn it, slick, you're going to owe me big-time for this, you know."

"Your word?" He stroked a finger down her cheek, watching her closely.

"You have it."

He gave a terse nod. "I'm taking Bron with me as well. Until we're back, you're in charge. I'll leave word with Gunner and Elina."

The door closed at his back.

Lee attributed it to her befuddlement over her brother, her confusion and fear for Syn, but it wasn't until they were already lost in the night that she found herself thinking, *Why in the hell is she out of the camp* alone *at this hour?*

Syn had picked up a big shadow—one by the name of Xan. Lee didn't know him, had barely said more than a few words to him, but she'd noticed one thing—the man had a very hard time letting the captain out of his sight.

Very hard.

So how had she slipped away in the dead of the night without him at her side?

"Hell, if *I* tried to get a few minutes away, Kalen and me would be having it out," she muttered.

Puzzled, she reached out to touch her mind to Kalen's, but stopped. No. Right now, he needed to focus on Syn. She could bug him, or her friend, for explanations later.

***

They left the base camp on baerns, four units of ten soldiers each. Just outside the gates, Kalen studied the hastily assembled men, saw the looks being sent in Laithe's direction. They varied from surprise to outright hate.

I very often despise this job, he thought.

"Okay, listen up—I'm not going into details right now,

but this *Warlord* is here with my authorization. He is under *my* protection."

Now everybody was staring at him. Lifting a brow, Kalen rested a forearm on the pommel of his saddle and said, "Under *my* protection, and make no mistake, if even one of you forget it, there will be hell to pay."

"Why in the hell are you protecting a Warlord?"

Narrowing his eyes on the one who'd asked the question, he fired back, "That's none of your damned business, Cohl. However, do try to remember—you had a Warlord fighting at your side for years, one who saved your life more than once. Nobody seems to have a problem with Morne's presence. And there's also the case of my wife."

He grabbed the reins of his baern and guided the animal around. "Not all of them are the slaving bastards we despise. That's all you need to know."

From the corner of his eye, he glanced at Laithe and then shot a thought at Morne. *"You had better not be making any mistakes here, old friend."*

"If he was any threat, you know I would have already killed him. But trust Lee's instincts, even if you can't trust mine."

Kalen sighed. *"I trust both."* Out loud, he called for the men to break into teams, updating them on the current situation.

Kalen sent the Warlord—his fucking brother-in-law—with Morne. He couldn't deal with that worry just yet and wouldn't let himself get distracted by the man, either.

Not when one of his oldest friends was out in the dark forest, alone, unaware of the danger that may well lurk all too close.

FOURTEEN

Why didn't I know?

Tears streamed down her face. The betrayal lay inside her like a nasty, infected wound, burning hot and painful, spilling its poison inside.

The first time she'd seen him—had there been something about him that she should have recognized?

No . . . there had been nothing. Syn dashed a hand over her damp cheeks and bent over Kerr's neck. "Faster," she whispered. Right then, she didn't care where the baern took her, so long as he was far, far from here. If she ran fast enough, hard enough, maybe she could outrun her own stupidity, her own blindness.

Though it was dark, the baern's steps were sure. The clever, nimble creatures had the night vision of a cat, and the surefootedness. As he neared one of the trails that led into the mountains, he slowed and began to take the path, winding them up and up.

Coward. A voice inside jeered at her, mocked her. *You let him into your camp, into your bed—spread your thighs for him, and now that you know the truth, you run and leave him in the camp. Who knows what he might do?*

Her mouth twisted. At least *that* voice she could silence. He was with Morne. And Laithe—she might not entirely trust the man, but he'd protect Lee, and right now, protecting Lee would mean protecting the camp.

He's not a threat . . .

Now, that voice was harder to silence. Must be her fool heart, not wanting to believe the man could bring harm on them—on *her*.

But if he wasn't there under false pretenses, he should have come clean—should have explained. Should have said something.

Memories flashed through her mind. The day she'd forced him to fight her in the circle.

I don't believe in harming women. She'd forced him into it—had it been an act? The Anqarian bastards had no qualms on *harming* women—they routinely kidnapped them, forcibly bred them—*raped* them.

The day Vena had barged in on them, after she'd left, Syn had told him Vena didn't belong in the rebellion.

As skilled a warrior as you are, as fine a leader as you are, part of me still feels this isn't the place for you or any woman.

Her mouth twisted and she muttered, "Of course not. It makes sense now . . . He feels like we should be barefoot, probably with some prettily decorated slave collar around our necks, while we get impregnated with one babe after another—"

A sob tore out of her throat. She'd trusted him.

And all the while, he'd probably been using her—plotting against them.

You're wrong. The voice in her heart grew louder. *Wrong. He cares.*

The day Elina had been hurt, the day the three of them had first tried to forge the net for the witches.

His hands, so possessive, so demanding and protective. His voice rumbling against her ear. *I smell your skin on me while I lie in bed at night. I feel you next to me even when you are not there. I need only to think of you, and I want you. I need only to think of you, and I have to see you, have to be with you. For this . . . and more. And yet you tell me I have no stake in your safety?*

A harsh keen escaped her. Beneath her, Kerr slowed to a stop. Huddling against his strong neck, she wrapped her arms around him and sobbed.

I have a stake in this—I have you. You are becoming everything, Syn . . . Don't take that away from me.

You're everything. Everything, Syn. Do not take that from me.

But it had been lies . . . had to be.

Why was he talking to you in Anqarian? Why did he seem like he knew you?

I have seen the man before, Captain. No emotion had crossed that hard, impassive face. No regret. No remorse.

"Oh, God." She lifted her face to the sky, terrified the pain inside her would shatter her into a million pieces.

She covered her ears with her hands, trying to drown out the voices in her memory.

What does Insar mean?

Battlelord.

"This isn't happening."

After all this time, she'd found a man who *meant* something. He hadn't just pleased her in bed, and he hadn't just understood her. He'd been more . . . everything. Friend. Lover. *Love*—not just her lover, but her love.

"I love him," she whispered, exhausted. The storm of grief hadn't passed, but it had ebbed, and once more, she could think again. Sadly, she could still feel, and she felt completely broken inside, her heart and soul shattered.

Through the chaos in her mind, she felt people reaching for her. Elina. Kalen. And though she didn't understand how, she thought she'd sensed Xan's presence as well. Blocking it off, she straightened in the saddle and looked down to the valley where the base was nestled. Kerr had picked his way to an outcropping, high above the base.

Dawn had come and gone without her realizing it. Full morning sun shone through the clouds. She could see the camp, but she was too far away to make out anything save the buildings and the small specks that were the people. Duty demanded she return to the camp, but for the first time in a long time, possibly ever, Syn didn't give a damn about her duty. If she wasn't needed right now, she didn't want to be there.

Sinking just the barest bit into the energy plain, she sensed Elina's presence, Lee's. They were there, watchful, waiting, worried. But not the adrenaline-rush worry that came from danger. No, this was focused . . . at her.

Just before they sensed her, just before they could reach out to her, she pulled back.

Whistling softly to Kerr, she nosed him once more along the trail. They'd managed to drive most of the demons out of the more mountainous areas of their land. She'd go there. A day. She would take this one day for herself. They didn't need her right now—they didn't need Captain Lai-syn Caar, and right now, she needed to just be Syn. She needed to find someplace to try to gather up the ragged pieces of her heart, her soul, her pride.

* * *

The ache in his chest grew, echoed by an ache in his throat.

"Come on, witch. Slow it down a bit, won't you?" Xan muttered, staring all around.

He could scent her faintly. Logically, he knew he couldn't be too far away, but impatience rode him, burned through him. He needed to find her . . . *now*.

A breeze kicked up, chilling the damp streaks on his face, but when he reached up to brush it aside, his cheeks were dry. Cool. Dry. When he closed his eye, he could feel the ice of the tears, though. On both sides. Insane, because even if he had given in to the urge to weep, no tears would have fallen from the ruin of his right eye.

"What in the hell . . ." But he already knew. Syn's tears. He was feeling her tears. Bleeding sands.

Her gift . . . ? Yes. It had to be—the part of herself she'd always kept closed up and locked away. Somehow, it was leaking through, and he was feeling *her*. Now he had both his pain and hers lodged inside him. His heart stuttered, felt as though it would rend in two. "Syn, I'm sorry," he whispered.

He'd tell her that, too, not that it would ease the pain. But he'd tell her; then he'd get out of her life. "Just let me find her. Safe."

But even as he said it, a cold chill—arctic cold—raced down his spine.

***

Kerr tensed. Deep in his chest, he growled, a warning. It managed to pierce Syn's melancholy, and she lifted her head, looked all around. Closing her eyes, she breathed in the wind, but there was nothing of demon in it.

This far into the mountains, she should be safer. It was too cool for the Ickado, too sparsely populated for the Raviners—they preferred to loiter around the edges of the lands the rebels had secured in hopes of picking off the stray refugee or scout. Jorniaks sometimes, but there was no taint of death in the air, and where there were Jorniaks, there was always death.

Kerr picked up his pace, first a trot. Then a run that was damn near deadly. Baerns often seemed to be part goat—entirely too surefooted, even in this terrain, but this was madness. Something had the beast scared, though, and it was enough to have Syn's instincts humming. He darted to the side, as though trying to double-back.

She caught a glimpse of something in the brush. A flash of golden blond. Somebody's hair.

"Shit." The fear in her heart trembled, but then faded, died, replaced by a hot, burning anger. Lips peeling back from her teeth, she flexed a hand. Whispered to the power. "Just let me see you."

Kerr continued his dash back down the trail, but then the beast froze. In the middle of the narrow path, he stilled, his great body shuddering, trembling, as he sucked in air. He quivered. Syn stroked a hand down his neck. "We can handle this, boy."

A blond form dropped down from a tree. Followed by a second and a third.

"Witch." A smile curled the man's mouth.

Syn smiled back and drew her pulsar with her left hand. "Warlord."

Then she flung her right hand out toward him. It was empty when she lifted it, the ball of fire forming inches from her hand, halfway between them, arrowing toward him. It hit him square in the chest and he screeched as it engulfed him. She downed a second and third with her pulsar.

Shifting her gaze to the others, she said, "Next?"

"Can you hope to fight them all?"

Another stepped from the trees, an older man, his golden brown hair streaked with silver, his dark green eyes set in a face that had seen more than a few decades. Centuries, most likely.

"I don't know if I can hope, but I'll damn well try." Then she smirked. "Even if it means burning myself out, draining myself dry. It would be a pleasure."

Somebody rushed her from behind. Kerr tensed—it was the only warning she had before the beast bucked and kicked back with his hind legs. She felt the impact, heard the crash. But she didn't look away from the Warlord. He was the highest rank—she knew it even without asking. Unless he called them off, they'd attack until she'd either killed them all or killed herself trying.

I always suspected I'd go out fighting, she mused. "Hadn't planned on it happening for my own stupidity, though," she muttered out loud.

She felt the clamoring at her shields and this time, she dropped them. Kalen's voice, Elina's magical probe, the light brush from Morne, all of them bombarded her and she flinched, forced her focus not to waver. *"I'm an idiot, I know it, and I need help. Badly."*

They went silent and she relayed her location, never once taking her gaze from the line of Warlords and Sirvani gathered around her. Hoping to distract them, maybe even scare the hell out of them, she summoned the fire and let it dance around her hand.

"Help is coming—just hold your ground, Syn. We'll get there."

She tried not to let the fear swamp her. *"If you don't get here in time, Kalen, it's not your fault. It's mine."*

"We'll get there."

Then he was gone and she was alone in her head once more. Alone, to face her very worst nightmare. She could handle being killed by a demon. She could handle going down in battle. But being taken a slave, like her mother, like so many other women from her world, it left her sick with terror.

She spun the fire, let it grow, then shrink back in on itself, grow . . . It was hypnotic, she knew, and more than a few of the Sirvani stared, fascinated. But not enough. Not enough.

"Draining yourself dry. Wouldn't that be a waste of your skills, my lady?" he asked.

"Not a waste." Kerr was restless, shifting his feet, his big head swiveling as he fought to watch all of the men around them. She'd counted eleven. There was no way she could fight them all, not unless they all grouped up and stood in front so she could fry them all at once. But they weren't going to be that stupid, she already knew. "I figure if it keeps me out of your hands, it would be a good thing. Plus, I can tell you, it will be one hell of a ride."

Another started to edge in, from the corner of her eye. Syn lifted her pulsar, fired. There was a faint, choked scream and then nothing. As his life faded, she smiled at the leader. "I ask again . . . who's next?"

The sound of hooves beating on the earth drew their attention. Hooves—help. Thankfully.

The baern bore down, and when the Sirvani in the path didn't move, he leaped over them, barely clearing their heads. They moved then—a bit too late. If those hooves had been any closer, their heads would have been caved in.

Pity it hadn't happened.

Damn, Kalen . . . your timing.

But it wasn't Kalen or Bron or any other soul she'd expected. Sitting atop the baern's back was Xan. He barked out an order in Anqarian—perfect, flawless Anqarian.

"Stand down."

Her heart raced at the sound of his voice, at the sight of him. He didn't look at her, staring at the older Warlord as he hurled something into the dirt. One of the Sirvani dashed forward and grabbed it, turning it over to the Warlord before Syn could even make it out. It wasn't until the Warlord lifted it to the sun's light that she realized what it was.

A stone, set in a filigree of dark metal. A black stone, surrounded by black metal. She hadn't seen anything quite like it—it didn't much resemble any of the stones she'd ever seen worn by Sirvani or Warlords over the years.

The sight of it had the Warlord scowling—a dark, heavy scowl as he studied the stone. Finally, he looked up at Xan and said, "Why am I not surprised to see you here?"

"Because you're a wise man," Xan said flatly. "Now act like one and stand down."

"You know better than that, Xanthe Taise." He tossed the stone back to Xan.

Syn only barely heard the words, too busy staring at the stone, watching as Xan drew the long blade from his back—that knife of his that he was so damned fond of. He twined the chain around the hilt, still watching the Warlord. "Lord Reil."

The Warlord grimaced and crossed his arms over his chest. "Need I even ask why you expect me to stand down?"

Xanthe. Taise.

Xanthe?

Taise.

"No, you needn't ask, and I needn't explain," Xan bit off. He finally shot one look at Syn. Regret flashed in his eye, a muscle ticked in his jaw and then he looked back at the Warlord and said something. It was in the same language Morne had used to speak with Laithe, Syn thought.

Her heart skipped. What were they saying?

Her fingers itched, and she eased them toward the reins. She should flee—now.

Xan—no, *Xanthe* said something in that same, unintelligible tongue, but her mind picked up on one word that sounded familiar. *A-tiri.* She didn't recognize the word *a-tiri* but it sounded an awlful like like *tiris*—*tiris* meant slave of some sort. Snarling, she drew her blade.

But he wasn't even looking at her, rattling off more and more—hell, he'd spoken more to this fucking Warlord in three minutes than he spoke to her in a day.

The Warlord's eyes narrowed, and he demanded, "Have you formally claimed her? For yourself? For another?"

"I claim ownership over no living creature. I am Insar."

That word again—Battlelord.

"Insar. Yes . . . yes, you are Insar." The Warlord stared at the chain wrapped around the hilt of Xanthe's blade, his mouth twisting into a cold, satisfied smile. He jutted his chin at Syn and said in Ishtanian, "If you are truly Insar—then I call your services, mercenary. Name your price, if you'll help deliver that woman to my camp. Unharmed—"

"Over my dead body." Xan lifted his blade and pointed it at the Warlord. *"Eshera esen avi."*

Reil's brows drew together over his eyes. *"Avi."*

It was a word Syn had never heard. As the Warlord's eyes came her way, she swallowed, uncertain what in the hell was going on.

She tightened her grip on her pulsar. Some of the men at her left were edging in on her again and she lifted the weapon, leveled it at them. "I don't give a fuck what these two are saying—one of you makes a move toward me, I kill you."

"Even the two of you, a witch and a Battlelord, cannot hope to fight us all," one of the other Warlords said.

Both—as though he plans to protect me, fight with me . . . Syn wished she had time to think that through, but a sound caught her ears. The faint whisper. Cloth gliding against leaves. More Warlords. More Sirvani. Their number had doubled.

Her heart raced. Her mind did as well, coming up with one possible plan after another, rejecting each one as ludicrous, or impossible, or with too big a possibility of her surviving—surviving to end up a Warlord's slave—*not* a viable option for her, not for any amount of time. She'd die first.

Again, she felt an odd brush against her mind—*Xan*—no. It wasn't *Xan*. *Xan* didn't exist. The man before her was Xanthe, a Battlelord from Anqar, whatever that meant, and she didn't know him.

She shied away from his touch, uncertain how he'd managed it, uncertain of anything and everything except for one fact. She was in serious trouble, and if *Xanthe* wanted to act like he was on her side for these bastards, her best bet was to go along with it until Kalen arrived.

Shooting him a sidelong look, she saw that he wasn't looking at her, but he still held his blade in one hand, a pulsar at the other, gripping his baern's barrel with his thighs. He stared at Reil, his gaze unwavering, his face resolute.

One of the Warlords—the one who'd spoken earlier—drew his own blade and pointed it at Xanthe. "Why don't we settle this?" he asked, cocking his head. Blond hair fell over his shoulder. Around his neck he wore a stone of medium blue and he held his blade with ease. "Whoever wins lays claim to the witch."

"Are you so ready to die?" Xanthe asked, his voice dismissive.

"Elorn, no." Reil moved, putting his body between the men. "Insar, if none have laid claim to her, then by our ways, she is mine. I found her."

Syn snarled. "I belong to *no one*." She lifted her hand

and hurled the fire, aiming it so that it hit the ground at the Warlord's feet.

Two of the men at the Warlord's back started forward, but he lifted a hand. "Fall back." He flicked a glance at the burned ground near his feet and said, "Try that again, child, and it will not go well for you."

"If another of your men moves toward her, or if you try to *lay claim* to this woman, I start killing and I do not stop until you kill me or every last one of you lies dead." A smile flirted with the corners of Xanthe's hard mouth, and he added, "And I will start with you, Lord Reil."

There was a low rumble of voices. Syn didn't look away from the Warlord, but from the corner of her eye, she could see varying degrees of surprise, fear, doubt. Some of them believed every word Xanthe said. Some saw only arrogance. Syn wasn't sure, but she guided her baern around so that she was at his back, facing those who'd been behind them. They were trying to edge close again, and as her gaze landed on them, they backed away.

Off in the distance, she caught the faintest hint of a familiar sound. Hooves pounding hard and fast. And another sound, the pulse and roar of caribins, quite a few.

A Sirvani approached the Warlord from behind. His voice was low, but not so low Syn didn't understand his words. "Lord Reil, the offworlders approach. Have you any orders?"

Syn could just barely see the man's face if she turned her head just so. Something crossed his face and he inclined his head. But before he could speak, the roar of caribins surrounded them and Syn saw why only a second later. Kalen and Bron had flown theirs straight up the mountainside—as they cleared the edge, they leaped from the caribins, letting the transports crash to the ground.

Both of them were armed and they settled in flanking positions, one at Syn's side, one at Xanthe's. "You're in my territory, Warlord," Kalen said, baring his teeth at Lord Reil. "You know what I do to Warlords who invade my territory?"

* * *

As more of the rebel army arrived, Xanthe allowed himself to breathe. Adrenaline crashed through him, drawing his muscles tight, sharpening his focus. He ached for blood, but one man alone could never fight this many warriors. From the corner of his eye, he saw Syn's slender back, straight and unyielding. He hadn't been alone, though. Syn had placed herself at his back—ready to fight with him.

Did it mean anything?

Yes, you fool. It meant she figured out it was her best chance at evading capture.

"Lord Reil."

The Warlord turned his head at the sound of his name. Xanthe watched as the blond healer Morne broke through the rebels and strode forward, standing before the Warlord.

Reil's eyes narrowed. "Morne Ramire. You live."

"Yes. I do." He glanced at Kalen. Kalen's jaw clenched, but then he gave a short nod. Morne inclined his head and looked back at the Warlord. "Now the question is . . . will you? Your men, you, you can walk away. Or we can fight it out." Then he drew a blade and said, "But if we fight, know this—you will die. As will many of your men. So choose."

"Ah, so it's a traitor before me."

Morne shook his head. "I am no traitor—my allegiance lay with my brother, and he is gone. I chose who I ally with, and I've been allied with these men and women for nearly three decades. I offer you an honorable choice—an honorable bargain. We all walk away. If we fight, yes, we will have the loss of life. But you are not in your world. You have naught but the men at your side. We have hundreds in the camp below. You will be wiped out."

"And the price to walk away?"

"You're an honorable lord. I had heard this, even though I have been away from my home world for many years. I ask simply for your word. You walk away—and you make no move to capture any of our men, any of our witches, any of our people, period."

* * *

"A bloodless battle." After the Warlords had cleared out, Kalen turned and stared at Morne, his expression a mixture of disgust and shock. "I don't know if I should be shocked or pissed."

Syn understood completely. Warlords had walked away. They had *let* the Warlords walk away.

"They walked away," Bron said, echoing her thoughts with a disbelieving shake of his head.

"Lord Reil is not a foolish man." Laithe emerged from the gathered men to stand at Xanthe's side.

Xanthe kicked a leg over the baern's back. "Hello, brother."

Brother—

This is Laithe Taise—son of Raichar Taise.

Xanthe Taise.

Brothers. The look the two of them had shared just before Dais's words had sent her world crumpling around her. Brothers.

They clasped each other's forearms, and Laithe leaned in, murmured something soft, too quiet for even Syn's sensitive ears to hear. Xanthe backed away and shook his head.

Off to the side, Kalen had a disgruntled look on his face. "Brother. Fuck." He shot Morne a dark look and said, "Please tell me that is just a bloody way of greeting and that he is not in fact a *second* brother."

"They are twins." Morne looked all too amused as he returned Kalen's stare. "They were once the very terrors of the High City, when they were young."

Kalen swore, long and hard. Sheathing his pulsar, he turned and started to pace around the narrowing clearing.

If Syn hadn't been so tangled inside, she might have enjoyed seeing her commander look so out of sorts.

As it was, all she could do was stare at Xanthe. Twins—
they looked absolutely nothing alike. One light and fair,
the other darker than a shadow. But they moved alike, she
realized. And they both shared that faint, almost nonexistent smile.

And Lee.

Both of them were Lee's brothers. *Xanthe* was Lee's
brother. Whatever in the hell a Battlelord was, he was
Lee's brother, her blood. According to Morne, that meant
a whole hell of a lot.

"What's a Battlelord?" she asked, surprised she managed to sound somewhat calm and collected. Her voice
was slightly hoarse, but it hadn't been that long ago she'd
cried herself dry. She felt as though she had been *wrung*
dry, drained and so very empty.

Xanthe's gaze met hers. He stared at her as though
he wished to memorize her, commit every feature to his
memory . . . like nothing else existed for him . . . save her.

Seconds ticked away and finally he spoke, his voice
low. "A Battlelord is a Warlord who has renounced all
magics, all ties of loyalty, save for those of his family. I'm
a mercenary."

"A mercenary. Well, that's certainly a surprise," she
muttered, looking away.

Bron snorted and clapped Kalen on the shoulder. "Well,
a mercenary is a damn sight better to have as a brother-in-
law than a Warlord." He shot Xanthe a narrow look and
then shifted his gaze to Laithe. "I don't know how in the
hell we're supposed to deal with *that* one, though."

Kalen grunted. "We deal by getting back to camp." He
looked at Morne and said, "Will they keep their word?
They will not attack?"

"Not under Reil's authority. In time, there may be some
defectors, but nothing we cannot handle. He gave his word,
though, and once given, Warlords do not go back on a
vow." He glanced at Syn.

Her heart froze, as Morne murmured, "Warlords, Battlelords, they honor their vows unto death. They do not lie."

Memory swamped her.

There is nowhere else I would rather be, I promise you.

You are becoming everything.

Blood roared in her ears and she found herself staring at Xanthe, even though it hurt to do so.

Staring at him, lost in him. She didn't even realize the others were leaving until Kalen paused at her side and touched the back of her hand lightly. "I'm leaving men near the perimeter to guard." Then he slanted a look at Xanthe, a scowl twisting his hard mouth. "But take some time. He . . ."

Then he blew out a breath. A dull, ruddy flush stained his cheeks red and he closed his fingers around her hand, gripping it as he projected into her mind. *"Morne said he thought of nothing but getting to you—protecting you. Whatever, whoever he is, he cares for you."* Then he broke the contact and strode away.

Moments later, they were alone.

Alone, and Syn had absolutely no idea what to say to the man before her. A Battlelord—for crying out loud, she'd never so much as heard the term before. A fucking mercenary, she would just call him a mercenary. Now, *that* she understood.

"Why did you come to the camp?" she asked, forcing the question out, even though she already suspected she knew the answer.

Xanthe's lashes flickered. "My father sent word to me, only moments before he died. He knew where my sister was—a girl I'd long thought was dead. She was my blood—it was my duty to seek her out, see her safe. Once I learned what she was, there was little doubt in my mind— her only chance at safety lies *here* in this world. In Anqar, she'd be fought over like some coveted prize. Wars might even start over her. My mother would have abhorred the idea—*I* abhorred it."

"Why? You're a damn mercenary. What does it matter to you?"

His eye narrowed to a slit. "A Battlelord isn't a hired thug, Captain. I name my own price, and up until the price is agreed upon, I may walk away from any offer made to me. And I've walked away often. Unlike Warlords and Sirvani, I am not bound to a liege lord. I hold allegiance only to myself and my blood."

"Name your own price, huh? So that's what that bastard meant when he said you could name your own price if you turned me over to him."

Xanthe looked away. "Yes."

Pain tore at her. *Why? Why didn't you tell me?*

But in her heart, she knew she might not have listened. No matter how he came about it, she didn't know if she would have heard anything beyond, *I am from Anqar.*

"So what am I worth?" she asked, curling her lip at him, trying to find anger inside. Rage. Anything . . . *anything* would be better than this hideous, awful ache inside her soul. "A bagful of gold? Lands? Exactly what do your kind use when bartering over slaves?"

"I own no slaves. Battlelords renounce *all* authority, Captain. I have no authority over any soul save those I accept a contract on, and none have authority over me, outside of those contracts. I've never owned slaves."

"Why?"

His gaze went hot. "My mother was a slave. I never understood it until I was older—long after she'd left us, stealing Lenena away to protect her from that sort of life. But she was a slave, and she wanted better than that for her daughter—my sister. Because of how my kind live, I lost my mother *and* my sister." He brushed the tips of his fingers over the patch that covered his scars and missing eye. "You ask how this happened—I'll tell you now. The boy-children who show promise of any sort of Gate magic are removed from their mother's care young—very young—and placed into training. We start out fighting each other, and as we improve, we fight others who are older, faster. By the time I was ten, I was faster and stronger than most others in my faction. I was placed in the training arena to spar with an offworlder. I didn't know who he was—I was just told to fight him, and that is what I did. I fought him, and I hurt him. Then I was told to kill him. I wouldn't. The training master hauled him out of the arena and drew his knife—*he* would kill him, he told me. It would toughen me up, prepare me for the duties I had before me. I tried to stop him and his blade caught my eye. He killed the boy anyway and when I demanded to know why, I was told he was naught but a slave, and an offworld male at that. Training and death was all he had to offer."

Xanthe's mouth curled in disgust and he muttered, "*All* he had to offer. As I lay in my bed, half sick with fever, and then recovering from the surgery to remove my eye after infection settled in, all I could think about was that boy and what the training master had said.

"He was just a boy," Xanthe said, his voice achingly sad. "Just a boy, closer to manhood than I had been, young and scared, but strong. He could have beaten me—I knew it then. I knew it as I fought him that he allowed me to win. He did not want to harm someone younger. Even though he was terrified, even though he'd been forced into that arena, he had too much honor to harm someone younger and weaker."

He shot Syn a narrow glance and said, "That is why the training master wanted him dead, you see. The master *knew* he had been going easy on me. He thought it marked the slave as soft, so he sought to punish him for it. Because he didn't beat me senseless, he lost his life. I promised myself, then and there, I would never lay *ownership* to another living soul. I renounced all claim to my lineage, renounced all magic."

"All magic."

He gave a single, short nod. "Aye. All. Until I came into this world, I've never so much as seen it—or if I have, it was so long ago that I'd forgotten."

"I thought magic was fairly commonplace in Anqar."

"It was until the past few centuries. But it has weakened." Xanthe stroked a hand down the neck of the bäern, paused a moment to murmur to the big beast. "By kid-napping witches, they bolster that power and the magic remained level, but it is nowhere near as common as it once was, according to the histories."

"Then how come you've never seen it?"

He shot her a dark glance. "Because I chose not to. I do not relate *magic* to pleasant things, Captain Caar." A muscle jerked in his jaw and he muttered, "At least not until I met you."

Blood rushed to her cheeks, and she turned away. Cold, that bone-deep, aching cold settled inside her once more. "Don't keep up the charade . . . Xanthe." Staring off in the trees, she added, "There is no need. The commander isn't going to chase away his wife's brother if it's clear you mean her no harm."

"Charade." He rasped something in Anqarian, too low, too harsh for her to understand, but when she glanced at him, his face was impassive. "As you wish, Captain."

"How long have you been looking for Lee?"

"As I said, until right before my father died, I had no idea she still lived. Laithe and I were led to believe she died when she was a child. After my father died, I made plans to come here."

Disbelieving, she turned and stared at him. "You are telling me you have only been in Ishtan a couple of months?" Lee's father hadn't been dead for long before the Gate fell—Syn *knew* that because Lee had only first met him just days before the collapse. "There's no fucking way. You speak my language too well, and you know your way around weapons too well."

"My mother would only speak to me in this tongue. As my father would only speak Anqarian, I learned both when I was very young." He jerked a shoulder in a shrug. "It has been years since I have needed to use it, but I never forgot it. A boy isn't going to easily forget the language used when his mother tells him she loves him, right before she uses that same tongue to tell him good-bye."

There was pain in his voice. Syn stared at him and

wondered if he even realized it. Naked, raw pain, the kind that consumed, threatened to destroy. "You loved her."

"Even Warlords, even Battlelords, know love, Captain." A bitter smile curled his lips. "We may be just a bare step above animals to you, but we know how to love."

His gaze lingered on her and then he mounted the baern. "Come. I'm sure you would rather be free of my presence, but I'll not leave you alone here."

"Morne said it was safe."

Xanthe's mouth twisted in a smirk., "The healer can get fucked sideways. I care not what he says. I'll take you to the camp."

"And then what?"

He paused and looked at her. "And then . . ." He blew out a breath and said, "And then, I do not know."

Words burned on her tongue. Questions. Demands. But if she voiced them, they would reveal too much, and she was terrified of stripping herself bare before him.

He already had too much of her soul, too much of her heart. He'd had her trust as well, and though some part of her understood why he'd remained silent, her trust had been shattered. Syn doubted she could take any more pain from him, not if she wanted to stay sane.

So instead of voicing the questions, giving in to the demands, she clicked to her baern and pulled the reins around, guiding him down the path that would lead them home. "So if you can't do magic, does that mean you can't open a Gate?"

"None from Anqar can tap into the Gate magics now. Not since the fall."

"That wasn't what I meant." She frowned as he fell into line in front of her. His gaze never rested, she realized. Constantly, he remained alert and he carried that long blade of his even as he rode, as though he was ready and expecting an attack. "Could you use the Gates?"

"When they were still stable, I could travel through them, as the lower soldiers or demons could. But no, I cannot raise them. I never learned how. Trying to forge a Gate without training is sheer madness."

Syn smirked at his broad, unyielding back. "Lee managed."

"Lee is . . . unique," he murmured. In a quiet voice, he added, "But then, so are you. It would appear to be something many women of your world have in common."

"Considering you're used to women who probably broke under slavery, it's no surprise we seem unique," Syn said, her voice bitter. Women like her mother . . . Had her mother broken? Lee's mother hadn't. She'd stayed sane, stayed strong enough to give birth to two sons, and she'd passed along some semblance of decency to them. She stayed strong and after she had a baby girl, she'd known she would have to flee if she wanted anything better for that girl. Although it had meant leaving her sons behind.

"Not all of them broke." Xanthe brought his baern to a stop and guided the mount halfway around, staring at her. "I will not defend the actions of my kind—we've enslaved your kind to suit our own needs, desires. There is no way around that. Some did suffer, I do know that. But not all were mistreated. My father, in his own way, did love my mother. He grieved when she disappeared, even as he raged at what he viewed as a betrayal. But he sought her, and if he'd found her, he wouldn't have punished her for fleeing him. He did care for her." Once more, those big shoulders moved in a restless shrug and he said, "Perhaps had they met in a different world, a different life, she might have even returned his affections. He wasn't a dishonorable man."

"Yet he had no qualms stealing women away from their homes, their families." Syn stared back at him. "Because of men like him, my world has suffered."

"I will not deny that. Our world might have perished long ago had they not found a way to keep the bloodline of the Warlords strong." He glanced around, staring at the trees, the way the sun slanted through the leaves. "Your world is softer than mine, Syn, even with the war. Anqar is a harsh realm, often pitiless. There are places where the demons outnumber people by a hundred to one—just keeping that threat contained is a task you may not fully comprehend. We keep the demons in check through magic and strength of arms. Without Warlord strength, without the magic of the seers and sorcerers, they would have wiped us out."

He stooped down and caught a fallen leaf. It was still green and he stared at it with something close to wonder before looking back at her. "Until I entered this world, the only place I saw such greenery was in the royal gardens of the High City. Much of our world is arid—the rain you often curse, my kind pray for. Without those skilled in earth magic, many of our cities would have died because the well waters dry up and the earth workers are the only ones with the ability to call it forth from deep within the earth. Yes, we raided your world to save ours . . . but when faced with extinction, people will do much to live, will they not?"

She couldn't even begin to figure out an answer to that. Staring at him, she shook her head, searching for something, *anything,* to say. "Did it ever occur to them to *ask* for aid?"

"And after the way our ancestors had used your world for sport when they first discovered how to use the lines connecting our world, do you really think anybody from Ishtan would have listened to a plea for help?" He gave a humorless laugh. "You and I both know better."

"There is no defending what your kind has done to mine," she whispered.

"No. There is not. But take heart, Captain. Now that the pathways between our worlds are broken, unless some miraculous change has taken place in the past few generations, it is unlikely my kind will survive much longer. The magic will weaken in a few generations; then it will begin to fade away." He absently twirled his knife, spinning it in patterns with deceptive ease in the sunlight that filtered through the leaves. The rays caught on the blade's edge, flashing silver at her. "Once it is gone, my kind will have nothing more than steel to protect themselves against the demons. For some of those demons, steel is not enough."

"You're telling me you think they'll all end up dying in a few generations?" she asked, doubtfully. He was exaggerating—had to be.

"Unless the magic remains strong, yes. They'll die." He sheathed the blade and once more turned the baern around. "The Warlord lines, the sorcerer lines, the seer lines and the commoners." He shot a look at the sky and then said, "We have tarried long enough. You need to return to the camp."

Syn scowled at him. "I'll tarry as long as I damn well want. What are commoners?"

Impatience crept into his voice and he asked shortly, "Are you truly so interested in the culture of slavers, Captain?"

No—yes—hell. Glaring at his back, she gritted out, "I'm trying to *understand.*"

"Understand what?"

"All of it," she snarled. Kicking a leg over Kerr's neck, she dropped to the ground and stormed off the trail, through the undergrowth, until she reached the deep slope of the mountain. Staring down, she focused on the camp, made herself take a deep breath. "I know Morne. I never knew what he was until a few months ago, but I know him—and I'd trust him with my life. Lee is part Warlord, yet she's one of the bravest, kindest souls I've ever met. And then you show up. You and your brother . . ." Frowning, she turned and started as she realized he was standing only inches away.

He caught her arm, drew her farther away from the drop-off. Heat flared where he touched her, and even though he dropped his hand immediately, it seemed as though she could still feel his touch.

Shaken, she shoved past him. "So he really is your twin? You look nothing alike." She gave him a skeptical look and added, "You don't look anything like one from Anqar."

"You haven't seen the families outside the magical lines."

"What's that mean?"

"Those with magic in their blood tend to be more fair. Some think it is the constant contact with magic, rather like the sun bleaches the sand over time." He flicked a glance at her dark hair and shrugged. "But if that is the case, it only affects those in Anqar. Those without magic look the same as those you'd find here, all shades of skin and hair and eyes."

"So does that mean you don't have any magic in your blood?"

"I said those with magic *tend* to be fair, but that doesn't mean all." He flexed his hand, held it open with the palm facing down. "There is magic somewhere inside me, enough to let me sense yours, but I cannot use it. Even if I hadn't made a vow, I never learned how to train it—I learned how to suppress its very presence."

Syn shuddered. She couldn't imagine doing that. It hurt to even think of it. "Wasn't that rather extreme?"

"The only magic inside me and my brother is the magic of the Gates—the ability to call them forth. Since I had no desire to call them forth, it wasn't extreme at all." His fingers flexed; then, slowly, he curled his hand into a fist and lowered it to his side.

He stared off into the distance. "I did not come to this world with the intent to deceive anybody—not you, not my sister, nor any other witch, any of the soldiers. I simply came here to see if this sister of mine truly did live here, and if she did, I only wanted to protect her.

"But I did mislead you." His gaze returned to hers, deep and intent. "At any time, I could have told you what I was, who I was. I chose not to."

"Because you didn't want to get thrown out of the camp, away from your sister."

"No. I would have found a way—I'd heard of your commander. Brenner is a wise man, willing to do whatever he must to keep his soldiers strong and ready. More, I've come to realize there is nothing he wouldn't do to protect his wife. If I had gone to him, it might have taken time, but he would have realized I could be . . . useful." Moving closer, he reached up, tracing one finger down her jaw. "I did not tell *you* because I didn't want to see the look in your eyes when you knew. But it happened anyway . . . and it was worse, because I wasn't the one to tell you the truth. I would beg your forgiveness, if I thought I deserved it at all. But I do not. I hurt you, and for that, I'll know regret every day for the rest of my life."

***

Regret. Pain. Longing. Worse, so much worse, but Xanthe didn't tell her that. Instead, he backed away. The longer he was this close to her, the harder it was not to touch her. Not to skim a hand through her short, silky hair and pull her against him. He needed to be away from her, because being this close and knowing he no longer had any right to hold her was more pain than he could handle.

Mounting the baern, he waited in silence, hoping she'd finally asked her fill of questions. To his relief, she mounted as well and they continued the trek back down the mountain. Off in the distance, he could hear others, the men Kalen had left behind to keep watch. As they drew closer to the camp, the men fell into place behind them, following them back to the main gates. By the time they reached the camp, twenty men were behind them. Enough of an audience—possibly the reason Syn had given up on her incessant questions.

But she wasn't done, it would seem.

As the men milled closer to the gate, Syn looked at them and said, "You may go back into the camp."

A few hesitated and she rolled her eyes. "I am right *here*." She pointed out the guards stationed in the watchtowers and said, "And they can see me just fine. I'm perfectly safe."

They glanced from her to Xanthe.

Xanthe knew why they lingered, understood their reluctance. They hadn't only been guarding their captain from the threat in the mountains—they'd been guarding her from him. They no longer trusted him. It cut deep, he realized. He hadn't been prepared for that—hadn't been prepared for how it would feel to lose the respect of these men and women.

In a soft voice, he said, "Go on into the camp, Captain. They are simply trying to watch out for you."

Syn shot him a narrow look. "I'm fully aware of what they are trying to do, thank you. But if you had malicious intents, I would be bound, gagged and blindfolded, trussed up in some Warlord's tent, and we both know it." She jerked her chin toward the soldiers and added, "*They* know it, too, or rather they would if they would get their heads out of their asses."

With that, she turned her back on them. It was a very clear, rather pointed dismissal and Xanthe watched as the mounted riders began to nudge their baerns to the gates.

As they passed through the main gate, Syn kicked a leg over Kerr's neck and dismounted, taking the reins. She passed them off to the one of the soldiers.

Xanthe did the same, half prepared to have the reins thrown back in his face. He was mildly surprised when one of the men offered a hand. His voice stilted, he murmured, "Thank you."

The men disappeared through the secondary gates, leaving him alone with Syn in the relative privacy of the gallery, the empty stretch between the two walls built around the camp. The soldiers stationed in the watchtowers and along the wall could see them, but they weren't paying Syn or Xanthe much attention.

Feeling the weight of her gaze, he turned his head and looked at her. She looked pale and tired, dark circles bruising the delicate skin under her eyes. He was responsible for this. Last night, she should have finished her rotation watching over Laithe and gone to her bed for some rest. She hadn't rested at all.

"You are tired."

"I've definitely had better nights." She tucked her hands into her hip pockets, shrugging restlessly.

"Why did you release Laithe?"

"Because of Morne. Morne said he wasn't a danger,

explained who he was." Syn's mouth twisted and she shot him a narrow glance. "Just being related to Lee isn't really good enough for me, though. Her father would have forced her into Anqar, and he might have even had good intentions—but it would have been wrong."

"Yes." He looked away. "He would have been very wrong—he was a wise man, but his arrogance sometimes overcame the wisdom. He would have believed he could protect her—that only her *blood* had that right. But he would have been wrong. Lenena—*Lee* would never have been safe in Anqar, and she would have never been happy, either. I imagine my brother, my father and I would have spent much of our lives making sure she didn't give herself to the sands."

"Give herself to the sands?" Syn echoed slowly. A dark look crossed her face. "Does that mean what I think it means?"

"I imagine. Giving yourself to the sands means to run into the desert with the intention of dying there. Between the sandstorms, the sun and the heat, it doesn't take long." That scene implanted itself in his mind and his gut went cold. Yes. He could easily see Lee killing herself before willingly submitting to living her life in the gilded cage their father would have created for her. She would have been pampered, protected and, whether she realized it or not, adored. But she would have had all freedom stripped away. Eventually, she would have killed herself—unless the life broke her first.

It was an ugly knowledge, Xanthe knew. But little about his life had been pleasant in recent years. He found himself thinking of his sister, then his father. Curious, he turned to look at Syn. He'd wondered before, but he had never dared to ask for fear she'd become curious.

But now . . .

"Do you know how my father died?" Xanthe asked quietly. He didn't know. He'd been found dead in his lodge, but the bodyslave with him wouldn't speak and there had been no other witnesses. His personal servant had been in his own quarters when it happened. Arnon had been the one to find the body . . . *Arnon*. Arnon Ramire.

Narrowing his eye, he studied Syn's face. "There were rumors that his spy had been playing both sides and had assassinated him." Arnon had relayed those rumors to Xanthe when he gave word of Char's death. Until that moment, Xanthe hadn't heard much about any of his father's spies. He had wanted nothing to do with that aspect of his father's life. "Did you know if it is true? Did Dais kill my father?"

"No. Dais didn't kill him."

"You sound rather certain." Too certain.

"I am certain." She met his gaze levelly, her cat's eyes unreadable.

"Who killed my father?"

"Morne's brother, Arnon."

"Arnon. My father's most trusted servant." Xanthe growled, closing his hands into fists. "Why?"

"Because of Lee." Syn hooked her thumbs in her utility belt, her eyes staring off into the distance. "Morne can tell you this story better than I can. But from what I understand, Arnon and your mother were in love. They kept it secret—considering how powerful a man your father was, how highly ranked, I can understand why. They would have both been killed. After she had Lee, she knew she couldn't stay there. Otherwise Lee was going to live out her life the way all women in your world do. She wanted more for her child—I guess Arnon did, too. He helped her escape."

"Escape." Xanthe shook his head. "Arnon was no Warlord. He did not know how to raise Gates."

"No. But his brother did—Morne was just steps away from being made a Warlord, whatever in the hell that means. He knew how to raise a Gate, and he did, and he came through with your mother. Arnon knew if he disappeared, your father would know how to find him. But the same didn't apply to Morne—guess Morne didn't serve under your father."

"Arnon.

"Arnon . . . and my mother?" Xanthe saw red. He had realized that somebody had helped her . . . somehow, but he imagined it had been one of his father's enemies. Not somebody his father *should* have been able to trust . . . "Arnon. And Morne."

"They are the reason your sister isn't trapped in that gilded cage—she's lived out her entire life in freedom, and in relative safety for the most part." Her voice softened and when he looked at her, there was sympathy in her eyes. "You did lose your mother because of this war . . . just like I did. But yours wasn't stolen away—wasn't forced away. She left, and she did it because she wanted to protect Lee. It was a brave thing she did—an honorable one."

Syn's mouth twisted and she added, "It seems one thing that Warlords respect is honor. Hopefully you won't despise her memory now that you know what happened."

"I'd never despise my mother's memory," Xanthe said, his voice gruff. There was a raw ache inside, one that would linger for some time. But he expected a lot of lingering aches in the months and years to come, and most of them would stem from memories of this one proud, strong witch.

"Good." Syn looked away again. She sighed and reached up to rub her neck. He imagined the muscles were tight under her hand, and if the tightening around her eyes was any indication, her head was paining her once more.

If he still had the right, he'd touch her, stroke the tension away until she was soft and pliant in his arms. Then he . . .

Stop, he told himself, jerking his gaze from her. In a hoarse voice, he said, "I must go. If I may, I would like to see Laithe before I do."

"Where are you going?"

"I don't know."

She shot him a look from the corner of her eye and shrugged. "If you want to see your brother, by all means, go see your brother. You don't need my permission."

"I do not belong in this camp," he said.

"Your sister lives here, Xanthe. Kalen isn't going to

kick you out on your ass." Then she scowled. A flush stained her cheeks. "You're asking my permission because I told you to get out of the camp."

He said nothing.

Syn swore and spun away from him, pacing. "I take it back. Fine. You're welcome in the camp—I can't rightfully tell you otherwise. Other than not being truthful about your intentions, you haven't done anything wrong. Don't let anything I've said keep you from seeing your sister."

"I've done plenty wrong." He stared at her. When it came to her, he'd done damn near everything wrong. From touching her when he shouldn't have, to falling in love with her, to not being honest with her. With a bitter smile, he murmured, "I've done plenty wrong, Captain. But rest easy. I have no intentions of lingering."

"Going to be hard for you to watch over your sister if you leave," Syn said, an odd note in her voice.

With a sharp laugh, Xanthe said, "That woman doesn't need me watching over her any more than you need somebody watching over you. She doesn't *need* my protection."

"But maybe she'd like to have her brothers—both of them—in her life," Syn said gently. She licked her lips and opened her mouth as though to say something else. But then she stopped and shook her head.

For the briefest moment, there'd been something in her eyes. Something that wrapped a fist around his heart and squeezed.

"What is it?"

"Nothing." She jerked her head toward the camp and said, "Go find your damn brother. Have a happy reunion with your sister. After she decks you for not telling her sooner, she'll probably be thrilled to learn who you are. Don't feel the need to leave because of me—you do whatever in the hell you want. It doesn't matter to me."

Until that moment, Xanthe didn't realize he had actually been harboring some naive hope that she'd forgive him. That perhaps she'd even let him stay in her life. That perhaps she *wanted* him in her life . . .

You should have known better.

Xanthe shook his head. "I cannot stay here. Not now." There was no way he could handle living so close to Syn, without having her. It would drive him insane. "Perhaps I'll return to visit her. And Laithe, should he choose to remain." He closed the distance between them and reached down, caught her hand.

"Captain, it has been an honor and a pleasure." He brushed his lips against her hand and then backed away. He wanted to leave—*now*. Screw seeing his brother. Despite what Syn said, he doubted Lee was going to welcome him with open arms.

He needed to leave.

"Wait."

He paused and looked back at her. She was staring at the ground, her hands balled into fists. "I understand why you didn't tell anybody who you were. Especially at first. But I don't understand about me."

"I already told you why I didn't tell you," he said, forcing the words past his tight throat. There was pain in her voice, such deep pain. It tore at him, tore into his heart. Bleeding sands, he had never meant to hurt her.

"That's not what I'm talking about." She shot him a look from under her lashes. "What in the hell did I have to do with anything? You didn't need *me* to find out more about Lee. Just being in the camp you would have learned about her. So why . . ." Her voice faltered.

But she didn't need to say anything. Xanthe understood what she was asking, and it only made his guilt and grief worsen. "From the first day I saw you, I wanted you. I wanted you more than I'd ever wanted another woman in my life."

He couldn't help it. He had to touch her again. One more time. Just once. Slowly, giving her every chance to pull away, he cradled her chin and arched her head back. Staring into her green-gold eyes, he pressed his mouth to hers. "When I touch you, there is nothing else for me," he rasped against her lips. Then he kissed her, wishing he could tell her all the truths he should have already shared.

She sagged against him, sighing into his mouth as she opened for him. She caught his tongue and bit him lightly.

His hands ached. Itched. He burned to grab her and pull her closer, pull her close and never let go. But he touched only her face and when the need for more threatened to drive him mad, he pulled back, tracing his tongue along her lower lip, and then he stepped away.

"I touched you, took you, stayed with you, because I wanted it—needed it. It had nothing to do with anything or anybody else," he said raggedly. "It was just you."

* * *

Just me—

Syn stared at his broad back as he strode toward the main gate. Getting ready to walk out of her life. Forever. She knew it without even asking. He didn't plan on coming back, no matter what he said.

Abruptly, she called out, "What does *avi* mean?"

He stilled and glanced back at her.

Syn shrugged. "I understand Anqarian well enough. I've never heard that word before."

"It means soul." Once more, he began to walk.

Soul—

Her heart, frozen inside, started to heat, and something began to burn inside her. She thought it might be hope. *Eshera esen avi.*

That was what he'd said to the Warlord.

"What does *eshera esen avi* mean?"

This time, Xanthe didn't stop. Narrowing her eyes, she glanced at the gatekeeper and shouted, "You open that damn gate, I'll have your ass."

That caught Xanthe's attention. He turned, eying her, his face unreadable.

"Answer me, damn it. When the Warlord was trying to convince you to help capture me—to turn my ass over to him—you said something to him, and I saw the look on his face. I want to know what in the hell you told him."

Her palms were sweating. She swiped them down the

sides of her trousers legs. She wanted to move to him, wanted to lean against him—let his heat warm her body. She was cold again, all but aching with it. Slowly, she walked toward him.

"You said, '*Eshera esen avi*.' I want to know what it means."

Xanthe's chest rose and fell on a ragged sigh and he shoved his hair back from his face. "It means, *She is my heart, my soul*."

"Your soul."

He gave a short, terse nod. "Damnation, Syn, have you any more questions? Or are you done now? Would it speed things up if I just begged for forgiveness? Then would you leave me the hell alone?"

It *was* hope, she realized. Part of her wanted to laugh. Part of her wanted to dance. But she shrugged and said, "I'm kind of curious if you meant it or if you were just trying to talk him into walking away."

"If I say it, I mean it," he shouted. "Are you done *now*?"

"No." She stepped toward him.

He tensed. He stood so still, he could have been carved from flesh-colored stone. He didn't blink; he barely breathed. A breeze blew a strand of his long hair into his face, but he didn't appear to notice.

Syn pushed up on her toes and cupped his face in her hands. She smoothed her palms over the rough stubble, gently traced her finger around the patch he wore over his scarred eye. Staring into that harsh, unyielding face, she murmured, "One more question, Xanthe. If you mean it . . . then why are you leaving me?"

* * *

Elina gnashed her teeth as the soldiers filed back inside the camp. So far, no sign of Syn.

She was going to beat the younger woman. Clobber her bloody. Would serve her right, doing something so damned foolish—

Narrowing her eyes, she searched through the milling

bodies, but she wasn't there. Kalen had said she was fine—
she'd be there soon. So what was taking so long?

She hid it well, but Elina was massively impatient. For
the past thirty minutes, she'd been waiting at the main gate
for Syn to return, ready to lash into her. With every passing minute, she got more and more angry—and more and
more worried.

Finally, she caught sight of the other woman, just inside
the main gates, staring at Xan. They stood in the gallery, obviously intent on each other, and Elina debated on
whether to wait or just hunt the witch down later. She had
yet to hear all the details—Kalen could give her those just
as easily and it looked as though Syn was having some sort
of private moment with her sexy, brooding male.

But on rare occasion, curiosity got the better of Elina.

No—very often, curiosity got the better of her. Though
not many knew, she was inherently curious, inherently
hot-tempered, inherently prone to getting into trouble.
She'd just learned to curb those impulses, and save those
who knew her closely, most people believed the calm, controlled façade she presented to the world.

Keeping her mischievous impulses under control served
her better—as a mother, as a onetime professor of magical
theory at a well-respected university, as a soldier in the
rebel army. So most of the time, she didn't let her curiosity
lead her around by the nose.

This wasn't one of those times.

She couldn't get much closer without being obvious.
But she wasn't going to let that stop her.

Elina strode toward one of the watchtowers and climbed
to the top. The soldier on guard blinked, surprised to see
her, and she gave him a cool smile—*I dare you to question
why I'm here.* He didn't. After a few seconds, he ignored
her and went back to studying his section of the perimeter.

Elina rested her arms against the wooden railing and
stared at the two people down in the gallery. She couldn't
hear them, but she didn't need to hear a single word to
sense the tension, the emotion. Xan was busy staring at

Syn like she held the keys to his universe in her hands. Syn's face was unreadable, that carefully guarded expression she always wore when she fought to keep others from seeing her emotions.

Then something changed—Xan turned away and something flashed across Syn's face—heartbreak. She blanked her expression quickly, then called out to the gatekeeper. Elina just barely made out the words. "You open that damn gate, I'll have your ass."

"Playing the voyeur, Elina?"

She suppressed a shiver at the sound of Morne's voice and glanced to see him standing behind her. She hadn't heard him climb the ladder.

Realizing he'd caught her eavesdropping, she gave him a guilty smile. Blood rushed to her cheeks and she shrugged. "Yeah. I can't help it. We don't get much entertainment around here."

He moved to join her, also peering down at Syn and Xan.

"So what are you doing?" she asked curiously.

"Playing the voyeur," he murmured, slanting a look at her and giving her a quick smile.

Elina chuckled. "Morne, how . . . unexpectedly common of you." She looked back at the two below as Xan's raised voice drifted toward them.

"If I say it, I mean it," the dark-haired man bellowed.

Elina's brows arched. "What in the world is up between them?"

She didn't expect an answer, nor did Morne offer one.

Her breath caught in her throat as Syn approached Xan, rising up on her toes to cup his face between her hands.

"Oh." Elina's heart melted. Misty-eyed, she whispered, "Isn't that beautiful?"

"You've got a bit of a romantic inside you, don't you?"

Forcing herself to look away from Syn and Xan, she met Morne's eyes and smiled. "Yeah, more than a bit, I guess. Not something we get to indulge in very often, though." She sighed and shoved away from the railing.

"Give it time."

They descended the ladder, Elina going first, with Morne following. Her skin buzzed, having him so close. Keeping her voice level took more of an effort than she would have expected. Keeping her emotions under control took even more effort, but it was a must—she knew too much about Morne's gift and there was no way she wanted him picking up anything from her.

"It would seem the three of you have found a way to work with the energy again," Morne said, out of the blue.

She glanced at him. "Yes." She flushed as she remembered the dream. Doggedly, she forced her thoughts away from that. *A dream. Just a dream, remember?* "We were going about it the wrong way—trying to use the energy the same way we've always done it. We had to adjust . . ."

"You needed to adjust."

They spoke at the same time. Self-consciously, she laughed as the dream edged in on her thoughts again.

But she made the bad mistake of looking at him and realizing he was watching her with a weird look in his eyes.

On any other man, she would have called the expression *stunned*.

"Ahhh . . ." She backed away. "I need to catch up with Lee. There are some things, something, yeah, something—"

He caught her arm.

Under that hard, calloused touch, she froze.

Because she knew exactly how it would feel to have him touching her—*exactly*. Even though he'd never done it before. Not once, in all the years she'd known him.

"The dreams—you had them, too."

Elina jerked against his hold. "I don't know what you're talking about," she lied, her voice shaking.

"Liar."

He reached up, laid his hand against her neck. His dark blue eyes began to glow. Through her shields, she felt him—felt way too much, felt more than she could possibly handle. "Elina."

Her name was a rough murmur on his lips, and just the sound of it made her tremble. He slid a hand into her hair, tangling it. His face came closer and for one heart-stopping, breath-stealing moment, she thought he was going to kiss her. He was close, so close, she could feel his breath on her lips, feel his warmth.

But then she was cold.

And he was gone, striding away from her, as though he couldn't get away quick enough.

Confused, she stared at his back.

Elina didn't know whether she wanted to die of embarrassment or chase him down so she could grab him. She'd been dreaming about him for years, and now she'd finally *almost* had a chance to kiss him, and then it was jerked away.

She didn't know whether to be glad or furious.

They'd been sharing dreams. She'd heard of such before, although not often, and she'd never thought she might be sharing her dreams with him.

Blowing out an unsteady breath, she muttered, "Well, hell."

* * *

"You just said 'twins.'" Lee looked from Kalen's face to Laithe, dazed.

Okay, she was still adjusting to the idea of Laithe being around.

Adjusting to *two* brothers, though, she didn't know if she could handle it.

Adjusting to *two* brothers from *Anqar*.

"And Xan, his name is really Xanthe. And he's some kind of fucking mercenary. Exactly what does that mean anyway?" she asked, shoving her hands into her pockets to keep from nibbling on a fingernail.

"It means he sells his sword." Kalen leaned back in his chair, his arms crossed over his chest, his finger drumming out a rhythm against one biceps.

She knew him well enough to recognize the sign of

restlessness. It was the only sign that he was as surprised by this twist as she was. Hopefully, it meant he was just as confused.

Laithe looked like he might as well be lounging by a pool with a nice, tall glass of beer. No. Wine. He'd be a wine drinker. He looked unconcerned, unperturbed. Disgruntled, Lee wondered if that was a Warlord thing or if she could maybe figure out how to look that unaffected. Morne was like that, too. So was Xan . . . or Xanthe.

Scowling, she kicked at the floor and muttered, "Should have figured out there was something weird with him before now. *Nobody* can act that . . . stoic all the time. Nobody from this world, at least."

Sighing, she moved to the window, staring outside. "So where is he, anyway? Shouldn't we be having some happy family reunion or something?" she asked.

"I get the feeling he doesn't plan on hanging around," Kalen said quietly.

It hurt, Lee realized. She knew the man—barely. But she didn't know her brother. And he wanted to leave. Slowly, she turned and studied Kalen's face. "Why? I mean, he's more than welcome . . . Hell, he had *better* be welcome."

"He is, pet." Kalen straightened in his seat and shot Laithe an unreadable glance. "Both of them are. Morne vouches for them—as do you. And while I can't say much about this one, I've learned enough about Xanthe to know he's a good man. He's welcome here, should he decide to stay."

Lee forced a smile. "You can't make everyone else feel the same," she murmured.

"I know my men, Lee. If I tell them he's welcome, most of them will accept that. Those who don't . . ." He grimaced and shrugged. "Well, I'll cross that bridge when we get to it."

"Okay, so if that's not the problem, then what—"

"It's his witch," Laithe said.

Lee looked at him, scowling. "Syn?" She didn't understand, at first. But the longer she thought about it, the more she understood. After a minute, she slumped against the windowsill and muttered, "Shit."

Xan—Xanthe—whatever he called himself—had come here with an agenda, and it was one he'd kept hidden. Then he'd gone and gotten involved with Syn. While Lee couldn't speak for the other woman, she had an idea how she would feel in that situation.

Very much used, and very much the fool.

But she'd seen the way he looked at Syn.

Sighing, she crossed her arms over her chest and muttered once more, "Shit."

* * *

Xanthe reached up and caught her wrists, easing her hands down. "Laisyn, this is hard—please don't make it harder." He pressed a kiss to her hands and then let her go.

"Oh, I plan on making this damn hard," she snapped. She reached up and caught his tunic with one hand. The other, she twined around his neck. He didn't lower his head for her, but she wasn't going to let that stop her, it seemed.

While he stood there, trying to find the strength to walk away, she was pressing a hot little line of kisses all the way up his neck, pausing to nibble at his chin, at his jaw. "Answer me," she said, her voice challenging. "If you meant it, then why in the hell are you so determined to walk away?"

Then she pulled back and glared up at him, her cat eyes all but spitting fire at him. "And don't you dare throw my words back at me, Xan. Considering the surprise I had dumped on me, I was entitled to be a little bitchy."

How did he respond? What did he say? He needed to get her away from him—perhaps if he did, he might be able to make himself think. With that thought in mind, he rested his hands on her narrow waist—his intention was to ease her back. That had been his intention anyway. Yet he found himself pulling her closer, staring down in her upturned face and fighting the urge to kiss her.

"Got an answer?" she whispered, pressing her mouth to his neck, then drawing his face to hers.

Xanthe groaned as she kissed him, nibbling on his lower lip, sliding her tongue into his mouth. Shuddering, he tightened his hands and hauled her completely against him. She hummed against his mouth and brought her legs up, wrapping them around his waist. He raked his teeth down her neck and forcibly reminded himself they were standing out in the open, in full view of the entire camp. Anybody could see them—

He should care about that. Really, he should.

Tearing himself away, he forced a few feet between them and stared at her flushed face.

"What in the hell do you want from me?" he demanded. Need, love and guilt twisted through him, tearing into him, greedy little blades that threatened to shred his heart. "Damn it, what do you want?"

"Right now, just an answer," she said, shrugging. "You tell me I'm your soul, but then you walk away . . . but if I mean much of anything, how can you walk away so easily?"

"You think this is *easy*?" he bit off. He felt as though he had ripped his heart out, as though half of it lay at her feet.

"If it's not, you could have fooled me."

"I can't stay here." He couldn't. Why couldn't she see that? He stared at her, his throat tight and his blood roaring in his ears. He couldn't.

"You can. If you want to." She licked her lips and uncertainty flickered across her face. "If you want *me*."

She shook her head and said, "But I guess I can't really make you stay. I can't make you want me. If I'm your soul—whatever you meant by that—then I don't see why you wouldn't want to be with me. But since you're so damned intent on walking, I guess I'm seeing this wrong."

"If you think I don't want to be with you, then you are very much mistaken. But can't you see how impossible this is?"

"No. I see the man I love—I've waited my entire life for you," she whispered, and her voice broke as she spoke. "Whatever you think the problems are, we can work it out. But not unless you want it. I guess maybe you don't."

But Xanthe hadn't heard anything after the words, *I see the man I love*. Stunned, he closed his eye.

Her words echoed inside his head, danced through his blood.

Had she truly just said that?

Love. It wasn't an emotion he had much familiarity with. He had loved his mother. He did love his brother. And although he barely knew her, he thought he probably loved his sister. But until Syn, he had never known anything like this—never felt an emotion that destroyed even as it remade, never felt such pain even as he felt such pleasure, never known such hope even as he discovered what it was to feel completely hopeless.

She loved him.

The soft brush of a shoe over the broken road had him opening his eye. She was walking away . . . walking through the secondary gates.

"Syn."

This time, she was the one to stop and barely glance at him as she said, "What?"

The irony of the moment wasn't lost on him. He caught her by the arm.

She whirled around, glaring at him. With a twist of her wrist, she tore away from him, backing away. Her cat eyes gleamed behind a veil of tears. "What, damn it? You can walk now. That's what you wanted. So walk already."

"What I want is *you*," he rasped. He advanced on her, watching as she backed herself right up against the gate's wall. Bracing his hands on the rough surface, he caged her in and stared down in her face. "Did you mean it?"

Syn sneered at him. "Mean what?"

Narrowing his eye, he pushed his fingers into her hair, gripping the short, silken strands. "Answer me, Laisyn . . . did you mean it?"

"If I say it, I mean it." She fired his words back at him and gave him a tight smile. "Not that it matters. You want to walk away—you think this is impossible."

"What in the hell do I know?" He dipped his head and nipped her lower lip. "Don't you know? I can very often be an utter fool. You meant it."

Syn jerked her face away from him. "Oh, yes. I imagine you can be an utter fool."

But the line of her mouth had softened . . . he thought. He rubbed his cheek against hers, breathing in the scent of her. He wanted to kiss her, needed it. But self-preservation kept him from doing so. If he kissed her now, unless she had the presence of mind to stop him, he just might take her here, and now—right where any damn soul could see.

"You love me," he said, staring down into her eyes.

Her hands came up, hesitantly cradling his face. "Yes, I love you." A weak smile curled her lips and she shrugged. "I was actually sort of thinking about telling you soon, but life sort of got in the way."

"It has a way of doing that." He pressed his brow to hers. "You love me."

Syn blushed and rolled her eyes. "Yes." Her slender arms twined around his neck and he boosted her up, cradling her close. "I think we more or less got that clear."

"I could still listen to you say it again. Possibly another ten or fifteen times would satisfy me. For now."

Syn laughed. "You haven't even told me once . . . but I'm supposed to say it another ten or fifteen times?"

"Haven't I said it?" He eased her to the ground and reached up, laid a hand over her heart. It raced furiously, pounding against his hand in strong, fast beats. "In your language, love is linked to the heart. In mine, it's the heart . . . and the soul. *Avi* means heart, soul. You are my heart, my soul. I announced it in front of men I barely knew."

Her eyes went soft, a smile curling her lips. "Well, if you could announce it in front of a bunch of men you barely knew, men who really wanted to rip into you, by the way, then maybe you could tell me."

"Maybe I could." He brushed her hair back from her face. "My heart. My soul. You're my everything, Laisyn. I love you."

"Then why are you walking away?"

Cradling her face in his hands, he murmured, "In this moment, every last soldier here couldn't drag me away."

"Good." She smiled and arched up, pressing her lips to his mouth.

He turned his face aside. "Bleeding sands, not here," he muttered, glancing all around.

"Not what here?"

He grabbed her hips, held her close and leaned into her. "Touch me, kiss me, it's entirely likely I'll forget anything, everything but you. Should we give your men that show?"

"Ummm . . . no. Let's not."

* * *

It took more than an hour to get to her dormer.

They'd been waylaid—by Elina, who had looked unsettled—weird for her. By Lee, who had stared at Xanthe as though she'd never seen him before. By Kalen, who had glared at Xanthe and walked away with just a shake of his head. Bron, Gunner . . .

By the time they reached her room, she was ready to shriek, and when she closed the door, she sagged against it with a groan. "How can a ten-minute walk take an hour?"

"When you keep getting stopped every ten feet, it isn't a ten-minute walk."

"Yeah. Good point." She shoved away from the door, itching to touch him, but nervous . . . so nervous. "I didn't see your brother."

"He's near. Somewhere." Xanthe shrugged his shoulders.

"I imagine you two have some catching up to do. I get the feeling you haven't spoken in a while." *And exactly why am I talking about this now?*

"It's been some years." Xanthe unsheathed the blade he wore at his back.

The black stone glinted under the light, and she realized he still had that black metal chain wrapped around the blade. No—not just wrapped. It looked as though the chain had been designed to wrap around the blade's hilt. Slowly, he freed it and then he laid the sheathed blade on her desk.

"What's the stone for?" she asked, watching as he cupped it in his hand, stared at it.

He jerked a shoulder in a shrug. "In Anqar, it's a mark of what I am. Here? It's naught much more than a trinket." He tossed it onto her desk beside his blade.

"Looks like a fancy trinket." Then she looked at him. "But I really don't care too much about trinkets right now."

"Really?"

Xanthe stood in the middle of her room, staring at her.

Staring . . . but not touching. Nowhere close to touching, and that just wasn't a good thing, Syn decided. She unfastened her tunic, rolled her shoulders. It fell to the floor with a muffled thud. "Yes, really." Stroking her tongue along her lower lip, she murmured, "You made love to me when we woke up . . . yesterday. It was only yesterday. But it seems like years."

"Years." He crossed to her and pulled her into his arms. The feel of him chased away every last echo of icy cold, and she tipped her head back, smiling at him.

"Too long." She reached between them and stroked him. "Make love to me."

Their clothes fell away, littering the floor around them as they made their way to her narrow bed.

"Xanthe . . ." She reached between them, wrapping her fingers around his cock. "Now."

He stroked her, rubbing his thumb against her clitoris, then dipping inside, testing her.

Syn shuddered as he eased one finger inside her damp sex, flinched as he added a second. "You're not ready."

"I don't care." She steadied his cock, tucked the head of it against her entrance. "I don't care." It hurt and she shuddered,

forcing her body to relax, to accept him. She wasn't ready—
not ready enough, at least. But she didn't care.

Xanthe continued to stroke her, drawing forth the slick,
wet heat and watching her with a hooded gaze.

Under his touch, under his gaze, her body warmed and
began to welcome him. Bracing her hands on his chest, she
took him deeper, then stroked upward, each time taking
more until she'd taken him all.

Xanthe lay under her body as she started to ride him,
rocking back and forth, her nails biting into his shoulders.
"You'll drive me mad," he whispered, watching her with a
wide, wondering gaze.

"Hmmmm . . ."

He tugged on her clit and she jerked as pleasure jolted
through her. His cock throbbed, pulsating inside her as she
squeezed him with her inner muscles and then lifted up,
sinking back down on him, one slow inch at a time.

Xanthe banded an arm around her waist and fell back
onto the cot, dragging her down with him. She whimpered
as he caught one nipple in his mouth, teased the sensitive
flesh until it throbbed. Then he switched to the other side,
treating it to the same attention. "I never thought I'd have
this chance again," he rasped against her flesh.

"Kiss me." She tugged on his hair until he lifted his
mouth to hers and as his mouth slanted over hers, she
started to rock, riding him fast and hard, desperate for
him. His fingers bit into her hips, clenching her tight, so
tight she'd have bruises, but she didn't care.

Inside, she felt him jerk, felt him swell. She clenched
down, using her inner muscles to tease and stroke until
he growled against her lips and flipped them over, tucking
her body under his. "Teasing little witch," he rasped, biting her lower lip.

"Hmmm. You love it and you know it."

* * *

He braced his elbows on either side of her head and caught
her face in his hands. "Hmmm. I love *you*." He did, so

badly it ached, so badly it left him feeling dazed and drained . . . and complete. More complete than he'd ever felt in his life.

Swiveling his hips against hers, he caught her thigh and drew it up, opening her. Below him, Syn arched and shuddered. Her head fell back, exposing the long, slender line of her neck, and he dipped his head, sank his teeth into the sensitive area where her neck joined her shoulder.

At the same time, he moved higher on her body, angling his hips so that he touched her just . . . there. Her eyes fluttered and she whimpered. Xanthe did it again, using the head of his cock to stroke over that bundle of tissue buried deep inside her pussy. "I love you," he whispered again, muttering it against her lips.

Syn raked her nails down his side and closed them over his hips, arching close. "More," she pleaded. Begged. "Give me more."

"Anything," he whispered. He'd give her anything . . . everything.

But he didn't want this to end, and she moved under him in a way that threatened to drive him mad, rocked against him with a rhythm that was going to destroy him.

He wanted it to last . . . and last . . . and last . . . but then she tangled her hands in his hair, jerked his mouth down to hers. As her teeth sank into his lower lip, he shuddered and felt the threads of his control snapping, one by one.

Hooking his arms under hers, he braced her body and shafted her, driving hard, driving deep, until she wailed his name against his lips. She arched against him and demanded in a low, throaty growl, *"More."*

"Everything," he whispered to her. Everything. For eternity.

She shuddered and started to come, her pussy clutching and gripping his cock, milking him. Her arms held him close, and he tasted the tears in her kiss as he went over, falling with her.

Dazed, he sank down, collapsing her slight body into the cot. With a grunt, he rolled to his side, dragging her with him, cuddling her close. Her eyes opened, and she stared at him. There were tears on her lashes. His heart squeezed in his chest, and he leaned in, kissed the tears away. "You cry."

A smile curled her lips and she said, "I've gone and turned into my worst nightmare . . . a weak, weepy girl."

"Weak." He combed his fingers through her hair. "There is nothing weak about you." He caught her hand and lifted it to his lips, pressing a kiss to her palm. "Nothing." He nuzzled her neck and then pushed up onto his elbow, looking down at her.

Syn felt herself blushing under that intent, probing stare. He cupped her face in one broad, scarred palm and said, "You're the most amazing woman I think I've ever met in my life. Smart and stubborn, strong and proud. Amazing."

She fought not to squirm and shot for a cheeky smile, hoping to hide some of her embarrassment, her nerves. "Be honest—you probably never once imagined falling for somebody like me."

"Not in my wildest dreams could I have imagined somebody like you," he said, pressing his lips to the corner of her mouth.

"So what did you imagine?" she murmured, reaching up to cover his hand with hers.

"When it comes to this . . . nothing." He settled back down on the bed, and she rested her head on his shoulder. "I don't know that I ever spent much time thinking about a woman and whether I'd want to spend the rest of my life with her."

"Is that what you think about with me? Whether or not you'd want to spend the rest of your life with me?"

"No. I don't think about that." He crooked a grin at her. "I already know I want to spend the rest of my life with you. Beyond. So I do not need to think about it."

"The rest of your life, huh?" She caught a lock of his long, black hair and wrapped it around her finger. "So . . . does that mean you're going to stay? Here, I mean? With me?"

"For as long as you are here, I will be here." He lowered his mouth to hers and whispered, "Wherever you go, I will go."

"Hmmm. I like the sound of that."

There was smoke.

And there was blood.

The air was thick with the smoke and he was going to choke on all the blood. Couldn't breathe, but even if he didn't have all the blood pooling in his throat, he wouldn't have been able to take a breath.

The pain wouldn't let him.

It stole through him, turning everything to ice.

She was crying. He could hear her. She cried and wept and pleaded with him not to leave her. But he had no choice. Death was coming, coming to rip him away from the one person who mattered.

Even though he slept, he felt the burn of tears. Felt them well up under his eyes, felt them burn their way down his cheeks. He wanted to wipe them away. Wanted to wake from this awful dream.

But he was helpless, locked in his slumber, locked in his dreams.

Ah, Nessa . . . my beautiful, foolish, wonderful girl. I

*love you so much. I will come back . . . I will find you
again . . .*

***

BROWNING, IDAHO

"You're too pretty."

"Am I?" he asked, a grin tugging at his lips. It was a mouth made for kissing.

"Yes."

She was dreaming. Nessa knew she was dreaming. If she had any sense, she would lie back and just enjoy it.

Well, I already did that. And she had—three, no, four times over.

There was no way any red-blooded, straight woman could lie in bed with this man, dream or no dream, and not enjoy it. Not enjoy *him.*

His eyes were dark, rich as melted chocolate and framed by thick, curly eyelashes. His skin gleamed a soft, mellow gold. In the sun, she imagined that smooth, sleek skin would deepen to a darker gold. His hair was black, blacker than onyx, and thick. It had just the slightest curl to it, and when she ran her hands through it, the jet strands twined her fingers.

She knew that from experience—she'd spent half the night with her hands buried in his hair.

They hadn't spent much time standing up, but she guessed he was about five foot ten. He had a long, lean build, and she sensed strength inside him, massive strength. But when he touched her, he did it with gentleness. Reverence.

As well a dream lover should, she supposed.

He reached up and traced the line of her mouth with his fingertip. She shivered under that light touch and felt heat flicker through her. Catching his finger in her mouth, she bit lightly.

Hunger blazed in his eyes.

She felt a response and leaned forward, pressing her lips to his. "Well, if I had to dream you, I must say, it turned out rather well," she mused.

He laughed against her mouth and asked, "How do you know I'm not the one who dreamed you up?"

"Oh, believe me, I'm the one who is dreaming. There is no man out there pining for me."

No man waiting. No man longing. No matter what was promised.

I will come back . . . I will find you again . . .

"You're so sad," he whispered. "Why are you so sad?"

Nessa forced a smile. "Of course I'm not . . . Well, I won't be for long. That's why you're here, isn't it?"

***

"I will find you. No matter where you go. No matter how far."

With a snort, Nessa looked away from the TV and focused on Mei-Lin's hair. The teenager grinned up at her. "It's romantic, Nessa. You can't snort like that when Daniel Day-Lewis is on the screen saying a line like *that*." With a sigh, the girl rested a hand on her heart and gazed at the TV with rapt eyes.

The Last of the Mohicans was the girl's favorite movie. They usually watched it once a month.

Unless Nessa could see a way out. Today was Mei-Lin's seventeenth birthday, though, and she'd wanted to watch the silly film before she went out with some friends.

Weaving the girl's silky hair into a tight braid, Nessa glanced at the screen. Spectacular scenery. Strong, sexy men with big guns, innocent-looking girls with simpering eyes. Romantic bits like, *I will find you.*

It struck a knife in her heart.

Although it had been five hundred years, she could still hear Elias's voice.

I will come back . . . I will find you again . . .

Only God himself could keep me from you, love.

And God himself had spent the last five centuries doing just that. Nessa couldn't watch this damn film without reliving her memories. A time when she was torn away from her husband.

Not by pissed-off Natives, but by death.

By God.

God had taken her lover from her, and God had kept her from joining him.

She was alone and empty. So empty inside. Not even her dream lover could ease that ache. At least not for long.

She blew out a sigh and used an elasticized band to keep Mei-Lin's braid from unraveling. Rising from the couch, she gathered up the ice cream cartons from the floor and carted them into the kitchen to dump them in the trash.

From the corner of her eye, she saw Mei-Lin, and despite herself, she had to smile.

This girl had pulled Nessa back from the edge.

Hovering at the edge of madness, despair. Even as she tried to draw her mind away from the memories, she found herself caught in them again. It had been a few years since her life had been turned upside down.

One last battle . . . She'd been so sure when she went to face the young witch that it would be her *last* battle.

After more than five hundred years, she had been so very, very tired. So empty inside, but she'd become accustomed to the emptiness. The exhaustion, though, it weighed on her more and more, with each and every year.

The thought of just being *done* had been such a . . . sweet relief. She'd yearned for it, ached for it. Longed for it. She'd gone to battle with a young woman who used her magic to steal life and power from others—Morgan Wakefield had practiced blood magic and it was addictive. Once a witch gave in to that lure, it became a hunger, a need. Fighting it was almost impossible, and Morgan hadn't wanted to fight it. She'd craved the blood, craved the power.

The only way to keep that young woman from killing was to end her life—a sad, sorry fact, but one Nessa had been prepared to handle. She'd been prepared for all likely outcomes—including her own death.

She hadn't been prepared to live. She certainly hadn't been prepared to live like this.

Absently, she glanced at the ornamental mirror hanging over the sofa and studied her face.

Her face.

Morgan's face.

No. She hadn't been prepared for this. She'd fought the young, deceptive, bloodthirsty witch, and as she'd expected, her body hadn't survived the battle. But somehow, her spirit had. She hadn't planned for it, hadn't done a damn thing to make this happen—at least not consciously. Nessa had wanted death, craved it. Craved it the way Morgan had craved blood. The way a drug addict craved his next fix. She'd needed it.

But instead of the sweet relief of death, she lived. In Morgan's body.

For so long after it had happened, Nessa had been lost— trapped in a muddle of depression, despair, memories and madness. Even as she began to emerge from that fog, she'd hated it—she'd yearned for the sweet cloud where she'd lived.

Until Mei-Lin.

Mei-Lin changed things.

They had met just a few months ago, but already, this girl had settled inside Nessa's heart, forged a place there. Given Nessa a reason to believe again. A reason to hope. A reason to live.

She looked at Mei-Lin and saw the echo of her own youth. Kindred spirits, she supposed. That was why she'd felt so drawn to the girl, why she'd taken Mei-Lin under her wing instead of shipping her off to Excelsior.

Almost a year earlier, Mei-Lin's mother had died and the girl had ended up in foster care, only to run away after one of the other foster kids had tried to molest her.

The night they met, Nessa had been walking through the dark streets, looking for a fight, a drink, both . . . anything to occupy her mind.

What she found was Mei-Lin. Or rather, Mei-Lin found her. The girl had quick hands—she might not have even noticed the theft if the girl hadn't unconsciously used her magic as well.

Untrained witches—they were a danger to themselves. Nessa had planned to dump the girl back at Excelsior. She needed training, that was for certain, and she also needed to finish high school. She could do both at Excelsior. Kelsey and the other Hunters would see to it that Mei-Lin was trained and care for.

But in the end, it was Nessa who took the girl in. It hadn't taken but a few hours to realize she needed the girl as much as the girl needed her. Perhaps more.

The two of them, they were both lost, lonely souls.

Meeting the girl had pulled Nessa back from the brink— she'd reminded Nessa of who she was.

She'd reminded Nessa of *what* she was.

She might be a lonely witch still pining over her lost lover, but she was also a fighter.

Nessa was a Hunter—a warrior, a witch. She'd devoted her life to protecting the innocent from the monsters in the world. She'd never given up in her whole damned life.

Mei-Lin helped her remember that about herself.

She owed the girl.

More, she loved her.

Leaning against the counter that separated the kitchen and the living room, she tucked her hair behind one ear and watched as the teen finished watching the movie. As the credits started to roll, Mei-Lin patted her heart and said, "If you're still wanting to find me another birthday present, I want *that*. Gimme a man like *that*."

"I looked but they'd already sold out at the mall." Nessa rolled her eyes. "Darling, you are seventeen. You have plenty of time to find a man."

"They do still make them like that, right?" She wrinkled her nose and said, "I want a *real* man, not one who spends more time messing with his hair than I do. I don't want some dumb boy, either. Real men still exist, right?"

Nessa grinned and thought of some of the men she knew. Chortling, she tried to picture Malachi messing with his hair. The vampire had seen millennia come and go and while he was a vain bastard, he wasn't one to primp.

Images of other men, other friends—Hunters she'd worked with over the years—flashed through her mind. Would they stand in front of a mirror and primp? Tobias, Declan, Vax . . . no. Not a one of them.

Eli, perhaps, but he had always been a peacock.

She had a quick flash of her dream lover. That thick, silken hair, tousled by her hands. He wouldn't spend his time studying his reflection, either, she knew.

Of course, he wouldn't . . . he isn't real. He was just her dream lover, a man her imagination created to help with the emptiness inside her, to help while away long, lonely nights.

A dream lover . . . and he belongs in those dreams, only those dreams, so for the love of all things holy, stop thinking about him during the day.

She shoved off the counter and went to turn off the television. "Yes, Mei-Lin. I promise, there are plenty of men who are less than enamored with their pretty reflections."

Outside, Nessa heard footsteps and she tugged on one of Mei-Lin's braids. "Your friends are here."

"*How* can you hear them?" she asked, cocking her head. She squinted her eyes as though it might help her hear better.

"Practice." Nessa shrugged a shoulder. "You'll get there."

The doorbell rang and Mei-Lin moved to answer it. As a gaggle of giggling girls entered the small house, Nessa tidied up the living room. Living with a teenage girl, she was constantly picking up, straightening up, doing laundry.

She didn't mind, oddly enough.

Other than Mei-Lin's training, this was the closest to *normal* Nessa had ever known.

Mei-Lin reappeared in the door, surrounded by her friends.

"Hi, Ms. Chandler!"

Nessa managed not to make a face. *Ms. Chandler* was only one of the many names she'd used during her life— she'd much rather be called Agnes or Nessa than anything *Ms.* That made her feel as old as she truly was. Ancient.

Giving them a smile, she said, "How are you this evening, Kim?"

"Oh, you know." She rolled eyes heavily made-up with black liner and said, "I'm sort of on probation. Brought home a *C* on my final, and Mom said if it happened again, I'd lose the car until I brought home something better."

"You could have a better grade if you wanted." Nessa knew the line she should use and she used it. Mei-Lin's friends, the teachers, all the people they knew thought Nessa was Mei-Lin's stepsister. They even had legal papers to document it. "Your mother just wants you to do your best."

"I know." Kim sighed and shrugged. "Chemistry is just so *boring.* I can't wait until I'm done with school and don't have to worry about that sh . . . uh, crap, anymore."

Dryly, Nessa said, "Paying bills is quite boring as well. You'll have to do things you don't enjoy the rest of your life. The good comes with the bad." She gave Mei-Lin a bright smile and said, "Speaking of which . . ."

She dumped the armful of shoes, books, an iPod and socks into Mei-Lin's arms. "Before you go out, please put these away."

Mei-Lin rolled her eyes and obediently trucked up the stairs.

One of the newer girls asked Nessa about her accent, and another started rambling on about how *sssexxxy* accents were. Kim enviously told the others how Nessa had taken Mei-Lin to France for spring break.

The new girl—Ashlyn—rolled her eyes and said, "Man, Mei. You've got the coolest mom. Mine would never let me go that far away without her."

Mei-Lin appeared on the stairs and pain flashed across her face. Nessa gave her a gentle smile and whispered mind-to-mind, "*Are you okay*?"

Mei-Lin gave her a tight smile.

An awkward silence fell and one of the girls leaned over and in a loud whisper said, "Way to go, Ashlyn. Mei's mom died last year. Ms. Chandler is Mei's stepsister."

Ashlyn went white. Nessa patted the girl on the shoulder. "It's okay, Ashlyn. You didn't know, now did you?" Then she gave her a smile and said, "I imagine your mom is quite the protective one. I'm sure you find it quite irritating, but she loves you. Enjoy it . . . enjoy her, because you never know how long you'll have her."

Ashlyn gave Mei-Lin a slightly sick smile. "I'm sorry, Mei. I didn't . . ."

"It's cool," Mei-Lin said, shaking her head.

Changing the subject, Nessa looked at Kim and said, "So, what plans do you girls have tonight?"

Mei-Lin gave Nessa an exasperated look while Kim smiled. In a singsongy voice, she replied, "We're going to get some dinner at Applebee's; then we're going to a movie. The movie is at the multiplex and it starts at nine fifteen. It should be over by eleven thirty. I have to drop the other girls off first, but we'll be here by midnight and I'm spending the night. And yes, Ms. Chandler, my mother will be calling at midnight, so I hope you're awake."

"Cheeky girl," Nessa murmured. She looked at Mei-Lin. "You have your phone?"

A few minutes later, Nessa shut the door behind them. Alone in the house, she rested her head back against the door and sighed. Alone . . . and it was too quiet.

When silence came, the voice was louder.

The voice . . . Morgan's voice. Yes, she had Morgan's body, and she also had Morgan's . . . ghost, for lack of a better word.

"This is just too cute for words, you old hag. Look at you, playing house."

It was a taunting, angry jibe, but Nessa pretended to ignore it. Once she had noise, once she had something to occupy her hands, the voice of the dead woman would fade.

For a time.

How much longer, she wondered. How much longer would Morgan linger?

Even now, months, years later, the girl haunted her.

Morgan. Damn her. She'd ruined everything she touched. She brought death and destruction, blood and chaos. Even in death, she'd managed to ruin things. If the woman's body had just *died*, then Nessa could have died as well.

"Is this the reason you stole my body, so you could play Holly Homemaker?"

Nessa shoved away from the door and reached out. With the slightest flex of her magic, she turned on some music. *Loud.* But Morgan wasn't going to go quiet *that* easily.

"This is a fucking waste. Why did you take my body if this is all you're going to do? Shit, can't you even go out, find a guy, get drunk, get fucked? Something—anything— would be better than watching you play mama witch to that little idiot."

Nessa smirked. "Not while I've got a dead witch whining in the back of my head."

"I don't see why not. It's my body."

"Actually, no, it's not. If it was *your* body, you'd be able to take it back. But you can't." She knew what the girl was about—Morgan wanted to make Nessa feel guilty, wanted to exploit any and every little weakness.

"It damn well is my body," Morgan snarled, her mental voice an angry, ugly growl. *"Your body died. That old bag of bones is gone. Hypocritical bitch. How in the hell can you condemn me for taking blood when you took my damn body?"*

Narrowing her eyes, Nessa turned to the mirror and stared at her reflection. She saw her face—the face that had once belonged to Morgan. "You didn't just take *blood*, child. You took *lives*. You ended *lives*. When I came upon you, you stank of death. How many have you killed? Can you even remember?"

"The strong kill the weak. It's the way of the world."

"We could write your death off that way if you like."
Malicious cow—she knew just what words to use, when to
use them. Guilt tried to settle inside Nessa but she cast it
off. "And here's another way of the world. You can call it
karma. I prefer 'you shall reap what you sow.' You killed.
Blindly, indiscriminately, and you enjoyed it. You would
have sucked my body dry of magic, sucked me dry of life,
and then moved on to your next victim and your next. But
you couldn't beat me. I didn't *take* your body. Trust me,
precious, I didn't *want* your body. I didn't want this *life*. I
didn't take it—it was pushed on me. You don't like it and I
understand that. I don't like it, either. But we're both stuck
with it."

"I'll find a way to get my body back."

"No." Nessa shook her head. "You won't. You're just
a ghost, Morgan, clinging to life. You need to let go and
move on. It's not like there's much of anything keeping you
here now, is there?"

"There's plenty keeping me here. My body, for one."

Nessa stared at her reflection, knowing the ghost in the
back of her mind would see the insolent smile on her face.
That was where Morgan existed now—that was the *only*
place Morgan existed—within Nessa's mind.

"It's not *your* body. You went and got greedy, precious.
Tried to take things that didn't belong to you. This is
rather karmic, don't you think? You took power, you took
blood . . . and your body was taken from you. It's mine
now."

"Because you stole it."

Nessa sighed. "No, I didn't steal it."

After all, *stealing* another's body would imply that
Nessa wanted to live. She'd wanted anything but. She'd
gone into that battle with her eyes wide open, *knowing*
that after more than five hundred years, she could finally
rest. She would die, and on the other side, she'd find Elias.
Finally.

But fate hadn't worked out that way.

Nobody else knew. Nessa had told no one about Morgan.

Morgan was her burden, her problem. And she'd learned how to deal with the problem relatively well.

Smiling at her reflection, she leaned in and kissed the mirror. "I must get to work now. Toddle off now, precious. We living witches have things to do."

In the back of her mind, she heard Morgan shriek . . . just before she blocked her off.

Her workroom was tucked away down in the basement, and she might as well spend some time working on Mei-Lin's next lesson.

Focusing on the work, she lost track of time. It wasn't until she felt a brush against her senses that she looked up with a glance at the clock. Nearly ten. Time enough.

"You might as well come in, Mal. I'm alone for now."

The vampire appeared in front of her, materializing out of thin air. He cast a look around the small, dimly lit room and grimaced. "Fuck me, love. You could do far better than this, you know."

"*This* will do me fine, thank you." She made a few more notes in the margin of the paper and tossed her pencil down. Rising from the chair, she moved around the desk and rose on her toes to kiss Malachi's cool cheek.

The vampire was her oldest friend—in more ways than one. He was so old, he'd forgotten just how old he was. Nessa knew he'd been a Roman slave at some point during his human life.

She had met him shortly after she'd returned to Excelsior after Elias had died. Five hundred years of friendship.

She knew his moods. Though that pale, poetically handsome face showed no expression, something was bothering him.

He was worried.

"Where is Kelsey?"

"At the school." He brushed an absent hand down her hair and turned away. Restless, he roamed around the small room for a few moments before coming to a stop in front of the shelf of books.

Many of the books were old. Not a few decades or even

a couple of hundred years. They'd belonged to Nessa for several centuries. He studied them and then turned around, looking at Nessa with an unreadable expression.

Nessa sighed. "What it is, Mal?"

"I don't know." Dark, deep red hair fell to hide his face as he lowered his gaze to the floor. He stood in silence for a long, long moment.

Her skin started to buzz and adrenaline started to course through her. She didn't feel anything. But something had Malachi on edge. The bastard had walked this earth for even longer than Nessa—whatever bothered him, it wasn't going to be some mild little annoyance.

Finally, he lifted his head and pinned her with midnight blue eyes. "Kelsey wanted me here, pet. I don't know why. She doesn't know why. But she wanted me here."

"That doesn't sound good." Nessa rubbed and then lowered her head, mentally extending her senses. She felt nothing.

Absolutely nothing.

No nasty, hideous supernatural monster creeping close—*that* she would feel, just as she'd sensed Malachi's presence. The small town of Browning, Idaho, had a nearly nonexistent paranormal population. It was why Nessa had chosen to live here after she'd made the decision to take care of Mei-Lin. She didn't need to worry about any vampires or werewolves. The nearest wolf pack was close to a hundred miles away and the nearest vamp was even farther away. There were one or two lesser witches, a family of cat shifters and the odd random psychic.

If anything *new* had moved in, Nessa would have felt it.

"I don't feel anything," she said, although she knew it was unnecessary. Malachi might be a vampire and she a witch, but they were both Hunters, which meant they were tuned in to the monsters—the nonmortals that hunted and preyed on the innocent.

"Neither do I." A muscle twitched in his jaw.

Nessa felt the bottom of her stomach drop out. The look in his eyes, it nearly froze her to the bone. She closed her eyes and reached out, extending her mind until it brushed up against Mei-Lin's. She sensed the younger witch, sensed her surprise as Mei-Lin felt Nessa's presence.

She gave the nonverbal equivalent of *Shhh . . . it's okay. Just wanted to check on you.* And that she did—the girl was most definitely in the theater, as were her friends.

Feeling a bit reassured, she opened her eyes and focused on Malachi's face. "Mei-Lin will be here shortly. It's her birthday and she's gone to the pictures." She paused and took a deep breath. "She was to have a friend spend the night, but I guess I should reschedule that."

Malachi just watched her.

"She'll be cross with me," Nessa said, forcing a smile.

"She's a good lass. She'll understand."

"Hmmm. Perhaps. Although if I knew what the trouble was, it might make it easier to explain, wouldn't you agree?"

* * *

They left Nessa's small house to drive to the theater. Malachi wouldn't go for remaining at the house. Truthfully, Nessa was glad he came along, and not just because it was amusing to watch as the vampire forced his big body into the front seat of her Ford Fusion.

"I'd have more room in a tin can, love."

"Oh, nonsense. Besides, you can't drive a tin can." She started the car and backed up, zipping along the roads with careless speed.

"You can't crash a tin can, either," Malachi muttered, maintaining a white-knuckled grip on the door frame.

Plastic cracked and she shot him a disapproving glance. "If you make a mess of my car, vampire, I'll have your arse."

She could almost *see* how much it took for him to ease up. "How did you get any sort of license, driving like this?" He gave her a sour look. "You didn't magic some fool into it, did you?"

"Of course not." Nessa smiled serenely. "I don't have a license."

She checked the opposite lane of the narrow two-lane highway and darted around a semi, grinning as the driver laid on the horn when she squeezed in front of him.

"Fuck me," Malachi mumbled. He closed his eyes and rested his head against the back of the passenger seat. "Damn good thing I'm not mortal—you'd give me a heart attack."

As they neared the interstate, she reached over and patted the white-knuckled fist he had resting on his knee. "You worry too much, old friend. Turning into a boring old fusspot."

He shot her a narrow glance. "Very few people would dare call me a fusspot."

She opened her mouth but the words locked in her throat.

Blood roared in her ears. She barely had the presence of mind to pull the car onto the narrow shoulder before she wrecked it. Her hands shook, cold and clammy on the steering wheel.

"Mal . . ."

It came as a cold wind.

Death. Uncaring, unstoppable.

Malachi felt it as well—she could tell by the tight expression on his face, the blue light glowing in his eyes.

She shot him a dazed look. For a few short moments, she could hardly breathe.

The sound of her mobile phone buzzing hit like a fist, stealing the breath from her lungs. She grabbed it, recognizing Mei-Lin's picture on the display.

"Nessa, hey, you didn't answer the home phone."

"Mei-Lin, what's wrong?"

"Oh, nothing." Then she paused.

In the background, Nessa could hear the girls talking and their voices lacked the excited, happy tone from earlier. Then Mei-Lin sighed and said, "Kim ran into this guy she was dating at the theater. He started being a real jerk and I told him to back off. He started yelling at me and some guy in the row in front of us told him to back off and then . . ." Her voice trailed off. She was quiet for a minute and then said, "Kim just wanted to leave. So we left. I wanted to let you know we'd be there soon and—"

There was a scream.

A crash.

And Nessa felt it as death came in and claimed yet more lives.

***

She cried.

His pretty little witch was crying.

Standing in a field of stone, surrounded by people, yet utterly alone.

Day bled into night and the people drifted from her side and still she cried. She was alone now, save for one woman and one man.

Anger bit into him as the man—the *vampire*—dared to lift a hand to touch the witch. Dared to wrap a big arm around her slender shoulders and draw her close.

Tears choked him.

Her pain racked him.

He wanted to reach out to her. *He* wanted to be the one to comfort her, to hold her against him as she wept.

But when he whispered her name, she didn't hear him.

***

Dominic came awake with her name on his lips and a tearing pain in his heart.

Snarling, he fought free of the covers and dashed a hand over his damp face. Crying. Damn it. Again. Dreams of some woman he'd never met and he wakes up crying. He stared at the pink smears on his fingertips and stormed into the bathroom to wash away the blood-tinged tears.

With water dripping from his face, he looked at the mirror. A muscle worked in his jaw and he gripped the edge of the marble counter.

"This is fucking ridiculous," he muttered.

He was obsessed. Obsessed, dreaming about the same woman, night after night, year after year. And now he was even crying like some fucking pansy in his dreams.

"What in the hell is this?" Shoving away from the counter, he strode to the enclosed shower and turned on the water with an angry flick on his wrist. He needed a damn hot shower, he needed a good hard run, maybe even a down and dirty fight—if he could get all three of those, it might lighten his dark mood.

But somehow he doubted it.

The dreams were getting worse, and he had a bad feeling he knew why.

Dominic Ralston was going crazy.

Five minutes later, he climbed out of the shower and stood naked in front of the mirror as he towel-dried off. Although legend might say otherwise, vampires did have reflections, and Dominic's looked the same now as it had the night his human life had ended. Five foot ten, one hundred seventy pounds of lean, ropy muscle stretched over a frame that probably needed another twenty pounds on it. He'd been in medical school when the Change had been pushed onto him.

Now he'd forever look like that medical student, running on caffeine, nerves and not enough food or sleep. It was a fact he'd come to accept and he was grateful he'd been on the skinnier side since this was the body he'd live with until somebody put a knife through his heart or relieved him of the burden of his head.

There was no telling how long that could be, though. It could be tonight or it could be in a couple hundred years. Hunters lived erratic, somewhat dangerous lives. And very often, they were lonely lives.

Damned lonely. Damned empty.

Oh, he could have found a lover. He could maybe even have found one who understood his life, who would share those nights and days with him.

But unless it was the *right* someone, he wasn't interested.

And lately, it seemed the right someone only existed in his dreams.

Dreams about a sad, blue-eyed witch, dreams that left him crying in his sleep.

Yeah. He was pretty sure he was going crazy.